CHILDREN
OF THE
FIFTH SUN
RUBICON

T0288087

OTHER BOOKS BY GARETH WORTHINGTON

The Children of the Fifth Sun Trilogy

Children of the Fifth Sun (Book 1)
Children of the Fifth Sun: Echelon (Book 2)

OTHER BOOKS BY GARETH WORTHINGTON AND STU JONES

It Takes Death to Reach a Star Duology

It Takes Death to Reach a Star (Book 1)
In the Shadow of a Valiant Moon (Book 2)

FORTHCOMING BY GARETH WORTHINGTON

A Time for Monsters (2021)

AWARDS

It Takes Death to Reach a Star

2019 IPPY Bronze Award Science Fiction
2019 Feathered Quill Gold Award Winner Science Fiction
2018 Cygnus Award First Place Ribbon Dystopian Science Fiction
2018 Dragon Award Nominee Best Science Fiction Novel
2018 New York Book Festival Winner Science Fiction
2018 Readers' Favorite Honorable Mention Science Fiction

Children of the Fifth Sun

2019 Eric Hoffer Award Honorable Mention Science Fiction
2019 Eric Hoffer Award Grand Prize Shortlist
2019 Eric Hoffer Award First Horizon Finalist
2018 London Book Fesitval Winner Science Fiction
2018 Killer Nashville Silver Falchion Finalist Science Fiction

Children of the Fifth Sun: Echelon

2018 Hollywood Book Festival Winner Science Fiction

CHILDREN OF THE
FIFTH SUN
RUBICON

AWARD-WINNING AUTHOR
GARETH WORTHINGTON

Children of the Fifth Sun: Rubicon

This is a work of fiction. Names, characters, places, and incidents either are the product of the author's imagination or are used fictitiously. Any resemblance to actual persons, living or dead, events or locales is entirely coincidental.

Paperback ISBN: 978-1-64548-002-0

VESUVIAN BOOKS

Published by Vesuvian Books
www.vesuvianbooks.com

Printed in the United States of America

10 9 8 7 6 5 4 3 2 1

For mum.
You never know how strong you can be,
until you must be.

Author's note.

The seed of this story began when I was 14 years old. At the time of writing this I am 39. While the three books weave together the ancient world and science fiction, at the heart of this story is a lifetime of personal experiences, good and bad. Much like my twenty-odd years of writing Children of the Fifth Sun, the story itself spans a similar timeline, reflecting my own growth – from manic depressive and suicidal to a man whose entire life and priorities were changed by the birth of his children.

Beyond the action and the intrigue in Children of the Fifth Sun, if there was one thing I would want the reader to take away from this series it is this: if you think you do not matter, you're wrong. Your life touches many others and what you made people feel will long extend beyond your death. I once believed I would march through life, and if I died it wouldn't matter. I was wrong. No-one is an island. And I do mean no-one.
So, choose how you want to live and thus how you will be remembered. In the end, it's all we have.
Well, that and perhaps a book or two we wrote.

KEY PEOPLE IN THE SERIES

Prof. Alexander (deceased). Mastermind behind the original Huahuqui cloning project. Conspired with *General Benjamin Lloyd* to release all information on the Huahuqui to the public in an attempt to save humanity through their bond. Died in a Chinese airstrike.

The Doyen. Leader of Nine Veils. Little is known of him, other than he wishes to bring humans as far into the 'divine light' as possible and believes the Huahuqui are the key. He will stop at nothing to realize his vision.

Chris D'Souza (deceased). Best friend of *Kelly Graham*, brother to *Izel Graham* and son of *Alejandro D'Souza*. Died in a cross fire while the *Green and Red Society* attacked Area 51.

Alejandro D'Souza (deceased). Archeologist and linguistics expert. Father to *Izel and Chris D'Souza*. Died of cancer.

Tony Franco. Ex-NSA field agent turned private gun for hire and long-time friend of *Jonathan Teller*.

Carmen Graham (deceased). Daughter of *Kelly Graham* and *Izel Graham*. Died at the age of three in a tragic accident.

Izel Graham (deceased). Wife of *Kelly Graham*, sister of *Chris D'Souza* and daughter of *Alejandro D'Souza*. Committed suicide when her daughter *Carmen* died having fallen down the stairs.

Kelly Graham (deceased). Nature photographer and freediving champion recruited by *Freya Teller* for a secret mission. Became telepathically bonded to *K'in* and fathered a son, *KJ*, with Freya. Died trying to save *Victoria McKenzie* from her destructive bond with the Huahuqui known as *Wak*.

Kelly Graham Junior (aka KJ). Son of *Kelly Graham* and *Freya Teller*. First child to be born of a human who was bonded to a Huahuqui, KJ has special telepathic and wound-healing powers. Bonded to the Huahuqui known as *K'awin*.

Matthew Lauder. Commanding officer of a US military station in Africa. Long-time friend of *Kelly Graham*, and new friend of *Freya Teller*.

General Benjamin Lloyd (deceased). General in the US Army and godfather to *Freya Teller*. Tasked with leading the original Huahuqui cloning program. Disenfranchised, he sought to hide *K'in* from the world. Died saving Freya from an attack by *Aum Shinrikyo*.

Victoria McKenzie. Former naturalist for the BBC and long-time friend of *Kelly Graham*. Killed by an attack by Chinese military controlled by the Green and Red Society; then resurrected by the US government using the Huahuqui's regenerative DNA. Bonded to a weaponized Huahuqui, *Wak*, and driven mad, Victoria was responsible for the death of *Kelly Graham*. Now possibly affiliated with the *Nine Veils*.

Svetlana. Nenets tribe member bonded to the Huahuqui called *Ribka*. Childhood friend of *Kelly Graham Junior*. Abducted by the Nine Veils from Antarctica.

Masamune Sagane (aka the Shan Chu [deceased]). Japanese leader of a rogue faction within the *Green and Red Society*. Responsible for various attacks on the USA and trying to still *K'in*. Believed to be controlled by the Nine Veils. Killed by *Jonathan Teller* and *Sasha Vetrov* in Mexico.

Freya Teller (nee Nilsson). Former officer of a clandestine organization tasked with studying and weaponizing a cloned Huahuqui (see K'in). Mother to *Kelly Graham Junior* and wife to *Jonathan Teller*, Freya is now retired and suffering the last stages of Huntington's disease.

Jonathan Teller. Former naval officer and now an agent of the NSA. Husband to *Freya Teller*. A specialist in the Huahuqui, he and Freya set up Alpha Base to protect the Huahuqui and their bonded children.

Lucy Taylor. Now President of the united states, Lucy many times jeopardized her political career to *Freya and Jonathan Teller's* mission to protect the Huahuqui.

Nikolaj Teller (formerly Yermalov). Son of *Minya Yermalova*. After his mother's death he was adopted by *Freya and Jonathan Teller*. He is bonded to the Huahuqui called *Chernoukh*.

Sasha Vetrov (deceased). Russian intelligence officer who worked with the NSA to find and bring down the Shan Chu. Dies at sea protecting the Huahuqui and Nenets children from an attack by *Aum Shinrikyo*.

Minya Yermalova (deceased). Historian and linguistics expert who helped decipher an ancient artefact for *Freya Teller*. Mother of *Nikolaj*, she died when her boat was attacked by Japanese terrorist group *Aum Shinrikyo*.

KEY HUAHUQUI IN THE SERIES

K'in. Original clone of the corpse found frozen in Siberia. Became the focal point of a covert war between world governments and clandestine organizations. Bonded to *Kelly Graham* and died saving *Freya Teller* during a Mexican stand-off between the Chinese and American forces.

K'awin. A female Huahuqui found in Siberia, who immediately bonded to Kelly Junior when he was a young boy.

Ribka. A male Huahuqui, with a distinctive blue stripe running down his back, found in Siberia who bonded to the Nenets girl *Svetlana*.

Chernoukh. A male Huahuqui, with black gills, found in Siberia who bonded to *Nikolaj Teller*.

Wak (deceased). A US black-boxed experiment that resulted from bonding human and Huahuqui DNA. Became bonded to *Victoria McKenzie*, causing her to devolve. Wak was killed by *Freya Teller* in Teotihuacan.

Freckles (deceased). A female Huahuqui found in Siberia who never bonded with a human. Died saving *Freya Teller* in an Antarctic storm at sea.

KEY PLACES AND ORGANIZATIONS IN THE SERIES

Alpha Base. Base of operations for the Huahuqui and their bonded humans (collectively the Stratum). Scientists live here trying to understand the bond. Some military personnel also live here to ensure the safety of the Phalanx.

Aum Shinrikyo. Japanese cult whose mission was to bring about the end of days. Under the control of the Nine Veils.

Green and Red Society. A secret Chinese Society with close ties to the Yakuza and the Triads. Membership varies from opium dealers to college professors. The guiding principles of the Green and Red Society seem to be split. Rogue members under control of the Shan Chu tried to destroy the USA and take control of the Huahuqui *K'in.* Believed to be under the control of the Nine Veils.

The Nine Veils. Ancient cult responsible for manipulating most of the world's historic events all to favor their ambition: restore the Huahuqui to a place of power. No-one has been able to find the base of operations.

Teotihuacan. Mesoamerican archeological site believed to originally be a place where humans and Huahuqui lived in harmony.

PROLOGUE

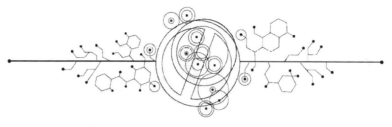

Location: Washington DC, USA

For the second time that morning Kelly Graham Junior's skin prickled. An electric tingle washed over him from the base of his skull to the tips of his toes. It could have been the crisp November breeze blowing through the steps of the Abraham Lincoln Memorial. It could even have been the buzz of adrenaline from finally reaching the moment for which he and his brothers and sisters had worked so hard. But, it wasn't either of those things. Something was off; though, what he just couldn't place.

KJ glanced down at K'awin, his Huahuqui symbiote, who sat as always at his side. Apparently feeling him stare, she looked up with big glassy blue eyes and blinked slowly, slapping her tiny lips together. Her large cerulean gills ruffled and billowed.

"I know girl, I feel it too," KJ whispered, rubbing her short snout.

Another squeal of feedback from the microphone drew KJ's attention to the ceremony. Two paces in front the President of the United States, Lucy Taylor, addressed a throng of citizens and press who shuffled to keep warm at the base of the steps.

"It is with no apology that I quote one of our greatest leaders in recent history, Barack Obama—albeit embellished with my own

1

flare," the president said.

KJ could only see the back of Lucy's blond-hair-covered head, but he knew she was flashing her enigmatic smile.

"President Obama said *we are a nation of Christians and Muslims, Jews and Hindus—and nonbelievers.* Well today we officially add The Stratum to our fold," Lucy continued. "He also reminded us that *we are shaped by every language and culture, drawn from every end of this Earth; and because we have tasted the bitter swill of civil war and segregation, and emerged from that dark chapter stronger and more united, we cannot help but believe that the old hatreds shall someday pass; that the lines of tribe shall soon dissolve; that as the world grows smaller, our common humanity shall reveal itself.*"

The tingle pulsed across KJ's skin again. This time it was strong, almost painful. He shot a glance at K'awin, who padded nervously on the spot. A quick check of the secret servicemen revealed nothing—they appeared unaware of any danger. KJ's head swiveled back and forth as he scanned for something, anything. The enormous statue of Abraham looked down upon him and seemed to press the urgency of this hidden danger.

"Today, not only America but our friends in Europe, China, and Russia have joined with us in this new vision of peace," Lucy said, waving at the live feed from around the world displayed on huge screens that hung from the fluted Doric columns.

A flash of pain pierced KJ's brain; another consciousness interfering with his. "There's someone else here," he whispered.

K'awin gave a low warble.

Lucy turned slowly to KJ to quieten him, then back to the crowd again, without breaking her flow. "Many thousands of years ago, the Huahuqui helped us climb to the pinnacle of who we could be at that time. Then, for a while, we had to go on without them. But now, now we have a second chance and the wisdom of hindsight—"

KJ had stopped listening. He was fixated on the small monitors, either side of the teleprompter, which displayed the simultaneous ceremonies in Paris, Moscow, and Shanghai. There was a scream from the crowd below, followed by pointing and shouting. Played out on the muted monitors, KJ watched the world leaders tumble off their podiums in a spray of blood. On the big screens, it would have been in horrific high definition.

Without thinking, KJ crashed into Lucy and dragged her to the ground. K'awin followed, protecting her symbiote. Behind them, Abraham's knee exploded in a cloud of powdered Georgia white marble. The crowd scattered like ants and the secret service surrounded the President before pulling KJ off and lifting America's leader from the ground. Shielding her with their bodies, they shuffled quickly away to the armored car waiting on the circle roadway.

"No, you need to protect KJ and K'awin!" Lucy shouted, clawing at the men's strong arms.

"You're priority one, Madam President," one of the operatives said as he pushed her head down and ushered her into the car.

It didn't matter, KJ wasn't going anywhere. He needed to find the shooter. He climbed to his feet and scanned the scene, taking in as many faces as possible. The people ran and screamed and fell over one another. Placards with images of the Huahuqui were trampled underfoot while cameras on tripods and white vans with satellite apparatus were abandoned. Only one woman stood fast, her camera man pointing his equipment at her while she gave a blow by blow account.

3

"Catherine!" KJ shouted. "Cat, did you see anything? Did you see the shooter?" He tore down the stone steps toward her, K'awin bounding along behind.

"KJ!" Catherine O'Reilly called back, having ended her broadcast. "You're okay? Oh, shit you've been hit?"

KJ glanced at his arm, and for the first time noticed a clean glistening wound through the tear in his leather jacket. The gash was already beginning to seal. "I'm fine, did you see the shooter?"

"No, where the hell is there to hide?" she replied.

KJ scanned the tree line along the reflecting pool. There was no way the secret service wouldn't have had that manned. His gaze followed the length of the sapphire-blue water, past the triumphal arches, bronze eagles and bas-relief panels of the World War II memorial, until reaching the Washington Monument pointing to the sky.

He squinted and, using his enhanced vision, focused on a shadow near the apex that was now moving down the great stone shaft in short bursts like a lizard descending the wall of a Mexican villa. At that distance, even KJ could not discern what it was.

"What the fuck?" he whispered to himself. KJ grabbed the camera from the shoulder of Catherine's man and pointed it at the monument. After swinging the heavy gear about he finally found his quarry. A quick focus adjustment and there it was: a Huahuqui climbing downward with a human rider dressed in gear color-matched to the stone of the pillar. "They took the shot from *there*?"

"What the hell is that?" Catherine asked.

KJ shoved the camera back into the arms of the crewman and tore off toward the reflecting pool. "K'awin, come!" he yelled.

K'awin raced after her companion and then overtook him. Still running, KJ ditched his jacket, mounted K'awin's back and held on to her upper-most gill stalks, one in each hand. The creature dove into the reflecting pool and disappeared underwater. KJ held his breath, water rushing over him, until moments later they popped from the surface. He managed to take a lungful of air before K'awin plunged in again. Porpoising along at high speed, they quickly cleared the length of the reflecting pool. With a cough, KJ dismounted and launched into a sprint, splashing through the shallow pool of the memorial, through the arch and across the grass directly for the monument.

"Hey!" KJ shouted.

The mystery Huahuqui—a bluish color with a distinctive darker stripe from the tip of its nose down its back—froze head downward, clinging to the stone pillar some twenty feet from the base. The rider's face was concealed in a snood, leaving only the eyes exposed. The would-be assassin and KJ locked gazes for what felt like an eternity, and his skin prickled with electricity. The killer's eyes were cobalt blue, hidden behind shapely epicanthic folds and long lashes.

This douchebag is a woman? KJ thought.

The Huahuqui on the pillar darted down again, breaking the stalemate, and leapt to the floor. As they crashed into the grass, the long rifle slung across the rider's shoulder slid off and *clunked* into the greenery. The pair sped off.

KJ launched after them, K'awin in tow. "They're heading for the river, if she makes it in we'll lose them!" he yelled over his shoulder.

K'awin acknowledged the danger, letting out a long trill battle cry.

The mystery Huahuqui stumbled, nearly throwing its rider, but managed to keep its stride.

"Good try, girl!" KJ yelled. If only he had a gun. Why would they never give him a gun?

KJ grunted with determination and pushed harder. His muscles burned, and his brain felt alive, as if every neuron was firing at once. K'awin's aura was within him, pushing him, powering him beyond human limits. Together they were stronger than alone, a unified being that was more than the sum of its parts. Yet, today the usual clarity brought by the bond was dulled. There was another consciousness mingling with his.

Who are you?

The shooter dashed across the Maine Highway, narrowly avoiding being mowed down by a Lexus, and sped toward the Floral Library. KJ and K'awin kept pace, ploughing through the traffic to the sound of angry horns and shouting, then tore through the tulip beds of the colorful garden. Petals and grass floated in the wake of the pursuit.

"She's headed for the basin!" KJ called to K'awin over the rush of air. "Go girl!"

K'awin pushed harder, closing the gap—but not enough. The shooter and her Huahuqui dived into the water and made a bee-line for the Jefferson Memorial.

"Fuck, we aren't gonna catch her this way!" KJ yelled. He quickly surveyed the nearby road and found what he wanted. "K'awin, don't let her out of your sight. You'll be faster without me."

K'awin warbled in understanding.

KJ sprinted toward his target: a motorcyclist dismounting his Italian sports bike.

"Sorry buddy," KJ said, flashing his empty wallet at the man. "Secret service."

The man stepped back, waving KJ to take his ride.

KJ jumped on the bike and turned the key still in the ignition. The electric display came to life, with simply the word "go" flashing in the middle. KJ grinned. *Let's see her get away now*, he thought, opening the throttle. The whine of the electric motor was piercing as the full 168 ft-lb of torque kicked in. In seconds he accelerated to 200 miles per hour along the small footpath, his chin-length wavy hair flapping in the wind.

Civilians threw themselves to the ground in every direction as KJ rounded the bend and followed the footpath across the river and southwest along the basin shoreline headed straight for the Jefferson Memorial. A quick glance to his right showed K'awin, closing the gap with the shooter.

The would-be assassin and her Huahuqui exploded from the water, followed by K'awin, landing at the base of the memorial steps. Unable to outrun their pursuers any longer, the woman turned her Huahuqui to face K'awin and dismounted.

A moment that felt stretched over eternity passed as KJ watched from his stolen bike. He opened the throttle as wide as possible. As KJ screamed ahead, the engine whine nearly splitting his eardrums, he held out one arm like a hook, and before the enemy knew what had happened, he had slammed into her at full speed—taking her and the bike crashing straight into the Tidal Basin.

KJ coughed and spluttered and swam for the surface; the electric bike plummeting to the basin floor below. He crawled out and onto the shore, t-shirt clinging to his skin, and shielded his eyes from the bright sun.

A shadow passed over KJ's face and he instinctively crossed his forearms, blocking the first strike. He rolled to the side and sprang to his feet, parrying and blocking a flurry of palm heel strikes, knees, and round house kicks.

"Hey, I make it a policy not to hit a lady," KJ said defending yet another knock-out blow to his jaw.

The attacker didn't understand or didn't care and pulled a serrated blade from its sheath on her belt.

"Hey, lookit, hot stuff. You can't go around stabbing people. It ain't polite," KJ said.

The woman stared at him from behind her snood, her cobalt-blue eyes like fire—full of anger and hatred.

K'awin twitched, waiting to intervene, but KJ held out a palm to ward her off.

The assassin seemed to gauge the situation, then gave her Huahuqui a nod. It launched itself at K'awin and the two creatures tumbled into the dirt.

"You bitch," KJ hissed through clenched teeth. "Now you've done it."

KJ came at the woman with his own combination of fist, knee, elbow strikes all the while avoiding being sliced open by the large blade in her hand. The two parried back and forth, neither one landing a clean hit. The woman threw a clumsy, long-arced slice which KJ ducked and used as an opportunity to spin to her back.

As she turned to face him, KJ managed to grab the back of the snood and it slid from her head. Long black flowing hair spilled out from underneath, covering most of her face. She huffed it away and crouched lower into yet another attacking position.

KJ stared at her, his mind awash with memories long buried. The woman was beautiful. So familiar. Her eyes, blue like the Stratum. The broad cheek bones and full lips. KJ wracked his brain. Could it be? Was it possible? He opened his mind further, reaching out to her.

The young woman hesitated, but only momentarily.

Lightning fast she pounced, knocked KJ to the ground, and pinned his arms with both her knees. Her blade rested on his throat. KJ glanced over to his companion who had also been defeated and forced down. The enemy Huahuqui pressed its large hand onto K'awin's head, squashing her into the concrete.

"Ribka …" KJ managed. "Don't."

The Huahuqui cocked its head and darted its gaze between the woman and KJ.

The shooter drew close to KJ's face, studying him with those blue eyes from behind a mass of thick dark hair.

KJ stopped struggling. "Svetlana, I know it's you. It's me … don't you remember?"

The assassin studied him, searching his eyes, her own squinted in concentration.

"Siberia, Africa, Antarctica… you were with me. And my mom, Freya. And K'awin." KJ flicked his glance in the direction of his symbiont, then back to his captor. "It's us, your friends."

The young woman seemed to relax; the blade at his neck no longer shaking with adrenaline.

The wail of police sirens screaming down Ohio Drive shattered the moment. The woman's face tightened again. She raised the knife quickly up and then down, striking KJ in the temple with the handle. The last thing KJ saw, through blurred vision, was the assassin mount her Huahuqui and disappear into the Tidal Basin with a splash. Then, everything went black.

CHAPTER ONE

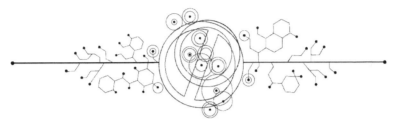

Location: Connecticut, USA

A dozen unanswered calls to KJ. Seven to Lucy, five to her contact in the NSA and countless more to anyone she could think of in Washington. No one had picked up. Freya's influence within both the government and the military had waned with her declining health. Though several breakthroughs had managed to slow her Huntington's significantly, there had been no cure. And not even long-time friend Lucy Taylor could ignore Freya's shaking hands, jerking limbs, and of course memory loss that would eventually lead to an Alzheimer's-like state. It was a miracle Freya had made it this long. Long enough to possibly witness the death of her only son on national television.

Jonathan stormed into the room.

"Have you heard anything?" Freya asked.

He shook his head. "I just spoke with Catherine. She said she saw KJ, but he went running after the attacker alone. No-one's seen him since. He's got too much of his father in him. Rash and hot headed."

"Please, Jonathan. Don't start. Right now, I just need to know KJ is alright."

Jonathan sighed. "Sure babe, I'll make some more calls." He

left again, punching yet another number into his phone.

Freya watched her husband leave. Jonathan Teller was a good man. For seventeen years he'd kept his promise. He married her and stuck by her side as the disease took hold. Even taken a sabbatical in the last year to care for her. And then, of course, there was KJ and Nikolaj. Jonathan had done his best to be a father to them both—especially as her condition meant he would never have any of his own. Nikolaj wasn't even Freya's, let alone Jonathan's, son. She'd adopted him. Of course, she had, what else was there to do? Freya felt never-ending guilt for his mother's death—Minya's, death. That day, that storm, had played over and over in Freya's mind for nearly two decades. How she held on to both Minya and KJ as they dangled over the side of a sinking boat in the freezing Southern Indian Ocean. How she only had the strength to save one. How she'd let go of Minya, to save KJ.

Over the years, Nikolaj had worked hard to be part of her clan, overachieving and ever attentive. He never questioned his mother's death, and rarely spoke of her. It was somewhat of a relief. Freya wasn't sure if her heart could take any more guilt. Nikolaj seemed to understand that. Such a sensitive and understanding young man.

KJ, on the other hand, was another story altogether. As he grew, the sweet little boy slipped away and a confident, even cocky, young man appeared. A carbon-copy of his father: Kelly Graham. Though incredibly intelligent, he did not apply himself. His wit and charm seemed to grease his way, letting him slip in and out of situations with annoying ease. When things didn't go his way, the rashness came bubbling forth. Jonathan had little tolerance for KJ's hot-headedness. In response, KJ had rejected Freya's married name, Teller, and taken his father's. The whole thing was exhausting. Luckily, K'awin kept Freya's son somewhat grounded. Perhaps the

11

Huahuqui would be able to help him to mature… if he hadn't already gotten himself killed.

Freya's phone burst to life. She fumbled with it, hands shaking with adrenaline and her sickness.

"Mom?"

"KJ! Where the hell have you been?"

"Relax, mom. I'm good. I had K'awin with me. She's always got my back, you know that."

"Jonathan said you ran after the shooter?"

There was a lasting silence on the end of the line. *"If I didn't do it, we would've lost them. I had to do something,"* KJ said finally.

"And did you catch them?" Freya asked, though knew the answer.

More silence.

"No, you didn't. Because you're not trained for it," Freya snapped. "You're not with the secret service, or the NSA or the FBI. You're barely out of your teens, all balls and no brains."

"Thanks, mom. Good pep talk."

Freya sighed. "I'm sorry, honey, really I am. You're an intelligent young man, more than intelligent, but you let your emotions get the better of you. The whole of the Stratum looks up to you. You're important."

"To who? You or America?"

"Me, America, the Stratum, our planet. KJ, I know it's not fair, but these responsibilities are yours—and mine. You have to step up."

KJ groaned. *"Oh, that ol' chestnut. Can I get a round of* you're not your father, *while we're at it?"*

The problem was, no matter how much she tried to convince KJ, or herself, he *was* his father. Through and through. The way he walked, talked, smiled. It was as if Kelly Graham had risen from the dead. KJ approached life with the same reckless abandon. Freya had always put Kelly's need to be in the line of fire down to the death of his first family. If KJ was anything to go by, it would seem being an adrenaline junkie was in the Graham blood.

"Just come home, okay? It's not safe there," Freya pleaded, her tone softer now.

"*Yeah, no can do. I'm gonna stick around. There's something bigger going on here. I think I saw—*"

"*Found the rifle, KJ. Exactly where you said it would be,*" a female voice in the background said.

"Wait, saw what?" Freya practically yelled. "Who is that? Catherine? Catherine, are you there?"

"*I gotta go, mom. I'm okay, I'll call in a while. Once I have this figured.*"

"Put Catherine on phone. KJ? I said, put—"

Click.

"Dammit!" Freya threw her cell phone at the leather couch.

"Hey, hey, what's going on?" Jonathan said, re-entering the room, his brow furrowed in worry. By his side, a small pinkish Huahuqui waddled along. "Was that KJ?"

Freya nodded. "You were right, he went after the shooter."

"Did he catch the guy?"

"What the hell kind of question is that?" Freya asked the same of KJ to prove a point. She was sure Jonathan asked because he genuinely considered the notion KJ might succeed.

"He's pretty resourceful. And sometimes being bull-headed pays off." Jonathan crouched down to Freya and rested one hand on an arm of her wheelchair, the other on the head of the Huahuqui. "*That* he didn't get from his father."

Freya met her husband's gaze and narrowed her eyes in disapproval. Though, she couldn't disagree. "It's Catherine. He looks up to her. Would follow her to the ends of the damn Earth," she said, changing the subject.

"You can't blame Catherine. She's just doing her job," Jonathan said.

"She's an adventure junkie just like him."

"And just like you, and his father," Jonathan replied, his tenor warm and wise. "Don't let that wheelchair cloud your memory. Or do you forget how *we* met?"

Freya's gaze dropped to her engagement ring, given to her in Antarctica. The piece of meteorite, now set into a platinum ring, twiddled between Freya's jittery fingers. "That was different," she whispered.

"Was it?" Jonathan said, raising Freya's face with a finger under chin.

What was he implying? Surely not? Freya thought. "You think he *likes* her, likes her? She's got twenty odd years on him."

Jonathan grinned. "You're talking to a guy who's into green women, remember? What's a few years?"

A torrent of retorts caught in Freya's throat, but none came forth. Instead, her limbs jerked several times. It was always worse when she was frustrated.

"You haven't spent time with Dacey today, have you?" Jonathan asked.

Freya glanced at the Huahuqui. The creature stared back. As always it had a comically happy expression plastered all over its tiny face. KJ had brought Dacey into Freya's home some five years ago. He insisted the Huahuqui had volunteered, though Freya had no way of discerning if that were true. She felt like a blind person with a seeing eye dog. And that didn't sit well. The Huahuqui were equals, not nurse maids. Still, it was hard to ignore that proximity to Dacey tempered Freya's symptoms. She rubbed Dacey's head, then cursed herself for the demeaning gesture.

"Babe, there's something else," Jonathan said, derailing Freya's train of thought. "Head office just called. They're pulling me back in. I don't have to go—"

"Yes, you do," Freya interrupted, her eyes wide and glassy. "They're back, Jonathan. I know they are. The Nine Veils. They're coming for my son."

Location: Wilkes Land, Antarctica

Koa Brown's teeth chattered. *Jesus H. Christ, it's cold,* he thought.

His family had thought him crazy. Having grown up in the Northern territory of Australia as part of a proud Aboriginal family, his choice of career—polar archeologist—was about as foreign a concept as could be. Right about now Koa was willing to concede, call up his dad and tell him the whole bloody idea was insane. There were literally no words that could describe just how soul-destroying-ly cold it was. It didn't help that the sun was almost permanently low in the sky at this time of year. Six months of darkness. He knew it was the middle of the night, but time had so little meaning that he worked when he felt like it. Of course, he also had to drag his colleague, Allison, along. She was less enthusiastic, using melatonin and sunlamps to maintain a normal circadian rhythm.

Can't stop now, Koa thought. *Too close. We're too damn close.*

Koa's PhD thesis had been on perfecting a type of ground-penetrating radar specifically for large ice masses. Just like the one on which he was standing. Of course, the arrival of the Stratum had scuppered his original application to explore Antarctica. The icy continent had been designated a no-go zone for anything other than research dedicated to understanding the Huahuqui.

Until a year ago.

After what felt like a lifetime of petitioning, groveling, throwing tantrums, and even shamelessly leveraging his minority status as a means to gain attention, he was finally granted access, though he would be working out of, and reporting to, Alpha Base. Still, for an archeologist of his ilk, it was like being given access to the Holy Grail. In 2006 a team of researchers had used NASA's GRACE satellites and gravity measurements to identify a 190-mile-wide mass concentration, centered within a larger ring-like structure in Wilkes Land, Antarctica. It was visible in radar images of the land surface beneath the ice cap. The scientists had suggested it may mark the site of a 300-mile-wide impact crater buried beneath the ice. If this were true, it would be more than two and a half times larger than the Chicxulub crater—believed to be the impact site for the asteroid that wiped out the dinosaurs.

"We're good to go, Koa. Dielectric is calibrated. You wanna do the honors?" Allison asked.

Koa give one of his huge child-like grins. "I'm so excited I think I might piss me grundies."

"Charming. You going to push this button or not?" Allison said, a thick-gloved finger hovering over the execute key.

"Don't you bloody dare!" Koa laughed and trudged over to his expedition partner.

The wind battered him and seemed to pierce any chink in his fur-lined armor. The small exposed spaces of skin on his face were burned and blistered. But it was worth it. It would all be worth it in the end. The Wilkes Land Crater would be renamed the Koa Brown Crater. Maybe, the *Koab Crater*. That had a nice ring to it.

Koa put his back to the frigid wind, threw one last glance at his colleague, then pressed the key.

On the embedded monitor, within a skeletonized image of a large cube, patterns began to form. The red, green and blue mottled mess, much like a thermal map, flashed up on the screen and slowly but surely worked its way from top to bottom within the cube. As the radar penetrated further, the computer interpreted the results and, on another monitor, produced a rough, luminous blue image of anything that wasn't ice.

Minutes passed as the GPR worked its magic.

A frown began to form in Koa's brow. He glanced at Allison. She had her head cocked to one side, her nose scrunched up in confusion. Koa turned his attention back to the image. "Uh, Allison, that look like an impact crater to you?"

"Nope," she replied.

"You're making fun of me, right? You set this up," Koa asked, a nervous chuckle in his throat.

"The hell I did," Allison fired back. "Are you seeing this, too?" She ran her finger along screen, tracking a perfectly straight line.

Koa turned to his friend, mind racing. "Run it again. And a third time. I have to radio this in."

Location: Potomac River, Washington, USA

Svetlana stormed down the white-walled corridor adorned with oil paintings from some forgotten era toward the command center. Ribka was already resting in one of the nine bathrooms of this enormous secluded New Age mansion, sat on the Potomac river—

only nine kilometers from the kill zone—hiding in plain sight. Her mind raced, rifling through twelve months of recon. She had inspected every inch of the Lincoln memorial, discovered every way in which a breeze could blow through the trees and the concrete. Accounted for humidity and temperature.

Still, she had missed. Because of *him*. Who was he?

It wasn't that he was Stratum. Going up against others bonded to Huahuqui was part of the mission. Executing any one of them wouldn't have been a problem. It couldn't have been his chiseled good looks and rugged chin-length hair, either. Such things had no effect on her hormones. Individuals did not matter, only the Phalanx. Her family. One mind. One mission. Yet, it was undeniable. When she'd seen him in her scope, standing next to the President of the United States, something in her stirred. Like a distant memory, buried long ago but forged in steel so strong it would not break. The consequences would be severe. Something was wrong with Svetlana. She was broken. And in the Phalanx, broken things were fixed. Mother would see to it.

Svetlana pushed through the large wooden double doors into the ballroom. The space was alive with her Phalanx cell running to and fro, tearing the room to pieces. Computers, monitors, interactive boards, satellite equipment— everything was being dismantled and destroyed beyond recognition.

"What the hell was that?" The burning blue-eyed stare of her Phalanx brother bored holes into Svetlana.

"Back off, Nyalku," she fired back. "You weren't there."

"You're damn right. Because if I had, she'd be dead." Nyalku raged up to Svetlana, stopping inches from her—using his full six-foot two height to tower over her mere five and half feet.

A swift knee to his balls doubled him over. Svetlana followed it with a sharp elbow strike to his temple that sent him sprawling to the cold floor. She drew back to kick him square in the stomach but was grabbed by several of her Phalanx brothers and sisters.

Svetlana shook herself free. "Get off me."

"We don't have time for this, 'Lana," Natascha said through clenched teeth. "We need to clear out and make it to the backup location as soon as possible. You two can beat each other to death later."

"He'll be the dead one," Svetlana snapped back.

"Whatever, look, Mother wants to talk to you. We haven't dismantled the Confessional yet. You got ten minutes. Make it fast."

The Confessional. The nickname her splinter had given the small converted cloakroom just off the ballroom. Shielded from interference and surveillance, there was only one secure communication channel in. And the only time it was ever used was when their Mother called. And if Mother called, someone was in line for punishment. More often than not, that someone was Svetlana.

She stepped inside and closed the door with a *thunk click*. The fluorescent lights flickered on revealing orange walls lined with material that resembled giant egg cartons, designed to absorb sound waves, and a single monitor with an embedded microphone.

The screen winked to life. On it was the cold face of Mother, hard and angular, framed by a severe greying blond bob. About her neck hung the inverted cross she always wore. Victoria McKenzie was not a woman with whom to trifle. Still, Svetlana couldn't show weakness.

"What happened, daughter?" Victoria asked.

"I missed," Svetlana replied without missing a beat.

"Evidently," Victoria replied, her tone sharp. "The question is, why?"

"I don't know, Mother. There was someone there. A man with a Huahuqui. He… um… I …"

"A man?" Victoria raised an eyebrow. "What man could make you miss a shot? You do not miss, Svetlana. You never miss."

Svetlana shook her head in shame. "I know. I don't understand it myself. I felt his aura. I felt him inside my head. He must be a strong one. His face was not on the list. They must have dropped him in last minute."

Victoria stared out from the monitor, as if contemplating the idea they'd missed something in the recon. "You need to come home."

"I'm fine. I can take a second shot. I won't miss."

"You're not fine. The jet is already waiting. You come home. Now. The assassination window has passed."

"But …"

"Not another word," Victoria shook with the words, her eyes afire.

"Yes, Mother."

The monitor clicked off and Svetlana was left bathing in the harsh fluorescent light. Why hadn't she told Mother that she thought she recognized him? Or that *he* seemed to recognize *her*? That was probably a mistake she would pay for later.

CHAPTER TWO

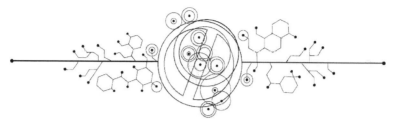

Location: The White House, Washington D.C., USA

Lucy made another lap of the Resolute desk in the Oval office. She stared at the scuffed carpet laid less than a year ago. If she wasn't careful, it would be worn out by tomorrow. She took a seat, rested her elbows on the desk, and pulled at her face.

Today had been a disaster.

Nearly two decades ago, she'd managed to set up Alpha Base allowing the Huahuqui and the children to live in relative peace. For nearly ten of those years she'd put her own political ambitions on hold—her desire for the Presidency—to focus entirely on the Antarctic Accords. This multi-national agreement provided protection for Huahuqui, but more importantly gave the best minds in the world time to find irrefutable proof that the Huahuqui were sentient and that their bond to the children was a mutually beneficial symbiosis.

It had drawn every valid scientist and contrasting nut job from the cracks of the known world. Alpha Base, governed by a body sanctioned by the United Nations, had received countless proposals for research on the Huahuqui – everything from behavioral observation to requests to euthanize some of the creatures to understand their biology.

And then, of course, there were the non-scientists.

A large faction of people of faith did not take well to the idea of the Huahuqui, or what they represented. Protests from hardline Christian and Islamic groups still popped up like violent brush fires, spreading quickly, and often required to be extinguished through use of military intervention. A decision taken by her predecessor—one she had put off revising despite her own moral struggle with it. At the other end of the scale, there were those who had abandoned their original faith, if they had one at all, in favor of deifying the Huahuqui. The largest group was headed by a rich and quite eccentric internet mogul by the name of Heston. He had used his wealth to create physical places of worship all over the world, and pseudo-science to stitch ancient texts into a single bible. The groups called themselves the Sixth Sun. Ironic given their reference to Mayan mythology would suggest the Fifth Sun had ended. It hadn't, and it wouldn't. Not on Lucy's watch.

Perhaps most painful was the constant stream of families attempting to make it to Antarctica in hopes of a cure for a loved one. News of the Huahuqui's extraordinary healing powers had spread quickly. For a mother whose child had incurable cancer, braving the icy seas was worth it. With tourist trips to the frozen continent now banned, families tried illegal journeys. Most died. Those who made it were simply deported back to their home country. It was so commonplace now, it barely made news.

Today's incident however, *was* news.

Instead of a day of celebration finally recognizing that humans must share this planet with an equal but different species, a bloodbath was broadcast live for the world to see. Leaders of three major powers cut down on television. Only Lucy had survived. Thanks to Kelly Graham Junior. She needed to thank him in person, at least at some point. The young man was smart and brave; the living embodiment of his father. And just as rash. Word was, he'd gone after the shooter alone.

The shooter.

Who the hell had the resources for an operation like that? It would be easy to chase down leads on the religious zealots, or perhaps extreme members of Tunbridge's cult who believed the Huahuqui deserved to be above humans. But, of course, Lucy knew the answer. She'd been waiting for them to show themselves. The Nine Veils.

"Madam President?"

Lucy looked through her fingers to see her Secretary of State hovering in the doorway. "Joshua, please come in."

He hesitated before slipping into the room and closed the door behind. "I have messages from Russia, China, France, the UK... not to mention the NSA, CIA, Alpha Base, Freya Teller, Jonathan Teller ..."

Lucy sighed and leaned back into her chair. "I get the picture."

"You need to start talking. Have a formal response. I'll send in Amanda."

"No," Lucy snapped. "No speech writers, no prepared press fluff today. The public will feel it. World leaders will feel it. It has to come from me."

Joshua tightened his lips. "Amanda won't like that."

"When has Amanda ever liked what I say?"

"She *is* the Press Secretary," Joshua replied. "With the country's best interests at heart, I might add."

"I know. It's why I hired her. She's a sounding board and a good one. But, her stance and my stance on how to approach the

Stratum issue differ." Lucy shook her head. "No, I'll deal with this."

Joshua nodded, but didn't leave.

"Is there something else?"

"At each site, well except ours, there was something left behind. A puzzle box."

Instantly, Lucy was transported back 17 years. Watching on the monitor as the American and Japanese strike teams stormed what they believed to be the Nine Veils nerve center. Instead they found her friend Steve Chang twisted beyond recognition and nailed to a tree. And in the tree, a Japanese puzzle box.

It took a long time for that box to be investigated, studied, and eventually opened for fear of what might happen if it were forced—perhaps releasing a toxin, another virus, or some unknown kind of bomb. It was none of those things. It was simply a scroll with Aymaran text: *the future is behind us.* Simply put, the world's governments were arrogant enough to think they knew what the future would hold. The Nine Veils disagreed. Now, there were new puzzle boxes. God only knew what they contained and how long it would take to find out—and what new nugget of terrifying wisdom they may bestow.

Location: Andrews Airforce Base, Washington DC, USA

KJ sat in the modified G800; an aircraft designed solely for trips between Alpha Base in Antarctica and key cities around the globe. There were several of these craft, outfitted for increased humidity—for the Huahuqui—and could transport a dozen pairs of symbiotes. There had been many protestors to the expense of these jets at the taxpayers cost, but traveling with everyday Joes just wasn't feasible. At least for now.

The jets engines roared, thrusting the sleek vessel down the runway and into the air, but KJ paid no attention; his mind was awash with the events of the morning. Had that really been Svetlana after all this time? What had the Nine Veils done to her? Was she a super assassin now? He was sure he saw the nine tattoo on her neck, and he knew what that meant. She'd go *ka-boom* any time her bosses chose. Just like the night Minya died on the Marion Dufresne II. Dropped into the freezing ocean by his mother—to save *him*. Minya… KJ hadn't thought of her in a long time but the memory immediately led to her son, Nikolaj. *He* would oppose KJ's plan for sure.

Following the death of Minya, the two boys had grown up under the same roof as brothers. Nikolaj and his Huahuqui, Chernoukh, were the golden duo. Always studious and helpful, trying to impress KJ's mom and Jonathan. Those two were every Alpha Base scientist's pet pair, helping to understand the biology behind the bond. Jonathan seemed to take special delight in their achievements.

KJ on the other hand didn't give a shit about any of that. It wasn't about science or numbers or theories—KJ could do all that in his sleep—it was about *feeling*. His own bond with K'awin was the strongest of any of the Stratum, and he did it without sticking his nose deep in some scientist's ass crack. It just was. And because of that, KJ had still inched Nikolaj out of the Washington ceremony at the last minute. Nikolaj had jibed that the only reason KJ got the spot was because of his father, Kelly; that Lucy felt some sort of responsibility to honor the memory of the man. KJ had punched him for that remark. Kelly Graham was a hero. A real man who thought on his feet, said what he meant, and followed through

25

on his promises—no matter what anyone else believed.

KJ shook his head. "Whatever," he said, under his breath. It didn't matter. With or without Nikolaj, he would gather his closest friends in the Stratum, find Svetlana, save her, and defeat the Nine Veils in the process. Because that was the right thing to do. Because it's what his father would have done.

"KJ, you okay?"

KJ looked up to the concerned gaze of Catherine, her orange locks tousled around her perfect face. Even though she was in her early forties, her porcelain skin still seemed flawless.

"Yeah, just thinking," KJ replied.

"Uh huh. So, you got a plan when we arrive in Antarctica?"

"Of course. I'll gather up any Stratum who'll follow me and find that shooter."

"You know there's entire government agencies looking now, right?" Catherine gave a knowing smile.

"C'mon, Cat. You know me better than that. And since when do you turn down an adventure?"

"Hey," she replied, raising her hands. "I'm all for a story. And if what you tell me is true, about who this could be, then if anyone can find her it's you. Have you told your mother you think it's Svetlana?"

KJ hadn't told anyone, not the president, not his mother. Not even his fellow Stratum, yet; he didn't want to risk telepathic conversation with this. After feeling Svetlana in his mind, it was now damn worrying that the Nine Veils could have been listening to him and his brethren conversing all these years. Proximity seemed to be key, but that wasn't a given. Something still itched at his brain, even at this distance.

"Not yet. Not 'til I'm sure," KJ said.

"She's gonna have an aneurism."

KJ laughed. "What else is new?"

"She'll blame me, you know."

He shook his head. "I won't let her."

"I'm not sure that's your choice."

"You'd be surprised," he said with a wink and patted K'awin who lay asleep at his side.

"Don't you dare do the mind thing, KJ. Last time, I ended up with no shirt."

KJ broke out into a belly laugh. "Yeah, sorry about that. I was just proving a point."

Catherine narrowed her eyes and pursed her lips. "You're not bloody sorry."

KJ loved that Irish accent. "No." He laughed. "I'm not."

Location: unknown

From the pinnacle of his stone temple, the Doyen admired the richly green, shallow-sloped, rice terraces decorated with pink peach and white pear blossom. A few quaint, abandoned, mushroom-shaped houses dotted the walkways. Hundreds of pools reflected the sea of colors and clouds in the sky. Originally farmed by locals, they were as beautiful as they were useful to his army of Huahuqui who now bathed in them.

In contrast to the warm view, a cold wind bit at his face. He gently placed a hand on the head of the Huahuqui at his side. The Doyen had claimed this large female specimen, with a mauve diamond patch on her forehead, as his own and named her Neith after the Egyptian goddess of war and of hunting—one of the most ancient deities and associated with the great flood. It seemed fitting.

He sucked in a sharp breath. The air was crisp and clean, not a single sound to be heard. But, this would not last. Soon, there would be chaos. Noise and bloodshed. The spilling of blood had never made him comfortable. It was a necessity. And as often as possible he had ensured someone else's hands had been stained, be it Aum Shinrikyo, the Green and Red Society, or some other pawn in this grand game of chess. However, in recent times, Victoria had advised direct war using the army of Russian orphans he had acquired, most notably to seize the children and Huahuqui in Antarctica nearly twenty years ago. He had to admit, it was effective. Yet, his forbears would likely turn in their grave.

For more than six thousand years his cult had orchestrated every major shift in the path of humanity. Operating in the shadows, whispering in the ears of the advisors to the advisors of the most powerful men on Earth. In antiquity, royal bloodlines ruled the world, and royal bloodlines were produced from the inbreeding of cretins. None more so than the Pharaohs of Egypt. Marrying their siblings to produce mindless offspring who were given the throne as mere children. They did not really rule, but were manipulated by even more moronic priests who worshipped the sun god Ra. These *spiritual* men had forgotten the teachings of the Knowledge Bringers—the Huahuqui—who were murdered eons earlier. But *his* predecessors had not forgotten. They desired to continue to shape the future of mankind in the ways of science. And so, the cult of Apep was born.

Mistakenly, the Pharaohs' priests believed the creature worshipped by the cult of Apep to be a serpent, not a Knowledge Bringer. And so Apep was personified and named a snake, Lord of Chaos, and enemy of Ra. So afraid of Apep were they, the priests even hijacked the stories of the orb of knowledge, allowing communication with Huahuqui, and transformed them into the book of Thoth. A poor attempt to wipe away the teachings of the Knowledge Bringers.

Direct conflict with the Pharaohs and their armies would have been futile. So instead, the cult of Apep infiltrated and slipped between the cracks to whisper in the ears of those who advised the kings of old. Pushing and pulling on the strings of fate. Over time, as the world changed, so did they. Their name too, ultimately becoming the Nine Veils. They had spread all over the globe and shaped history beyond the comprehension of any living person. Until the Huahuqui returned nearly twenty years ago. That had changed everything. They tried to work behind a curtain of misdirection, terrorist groups and zealots. But it had been only a partial success. Now, just as Victoria had advised, they had to take control themselves.

The Doyen turned from the setting sun, its warm orange hues glinting from the surface of the rice pools, and headed inside—Neith at his side. A long march through torchlit stone corridors and he reached the command center. Inside, Victoria surveyed a host of monitors.

"You made contact?" he asked, plainly.

Victoria turned to face him, her ice-cold eyes searching his face. "I did."

"And?"

"She doesn't know why. She says there was a man. A member of the Stratum who interfered with her concentration."

"Excellent."

"What?" Victoria spat.

The Doyen pursed his lips and exhaled frustration through his nose. "Do we have a close up of the male in question?"

Victoria nodded to one of the control operatives who duly punched a few keys. Every monitor flashed up the same image: a video frame of the podium at the Lincoln Memorial. In it, frozen mid speech, was the president of the United States. Just behind her was a young man in his early twenties with blue eyes and chin length wavy hair. At his side sat a bluish-skinned Huahuqui.

"Yes, just as I thought. Kelly Graham Junior. The first child of the Stratum," the Doyen said.

"I'll have him killed," Victoria hissed.

"You'll do no such thing," the Doyen interjected.

"But—"

The Doyen raised his hand to silence her. "He is the first to be born with the bond built into his DNA."

"But—"

"Your own DNA spliced with that of the Huahuqui, Wak, is not quite the same my dear," he interrupted again, predicting her objection.

Victoria bore a hateful stare into the image of the young man.

"No, let him go. He will be vital in the aftermath."

Victoria gave a slight bow, then stormed from the room.

The Doyen's gaze followed Victoria's explosive exit and came to rest on the large wooden doors which she near tore from their hinges. She was becoming a problem. Her temper grew inversely proportional to his wisdom. As his understanding of the Nine Veils grew, hers seemed to diminish. Victoria's anger had become a central tenet to her motivation. But, he was too close now to lose focus, and needed her to assist in the final stages.

His stare drifted back to the image on the screen. While the Doyen's own power was great, and his ability to convey the will of the universe to the Huahuqui under his wing through the last known orb in existence was strong, this American boy had the potential to lead humans and the Huahuqui into the next stage in evolution. He was the first. The strongest. His very being tied to the Knowledge Bringers from birth. The pieces of the grand puzzle were falling into place. *Everything in its time*, the Doyen thought. *The Great Syzygy is finally at hand.*

CHAPTER THREE

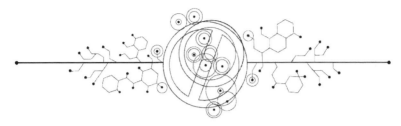

Location: Wilkes Land, Antarctica

"I don't like this, Koa."

Koa looked to Allison, his breath fogging the air. "What's not to like? At least we're not out in that bloody wind."

"Yeah and instead we're tottering our way down a narrow tunnel we found leading to a… well who knows what."

Koa shrugged. "Hey, we don't become world famous archeologists by following the rules. Alpha Base said they'd send people, but who knows how long that will take. They had their pants in a bunch about something."

"Still, this gives me the goddamn creeps." Allison shook her head and slowed her pace as they continued down the ever-darkening icy shaft just tall enough for a person. "This was drilled out, a beeline all the way to the structure. Someone's been here before us."

Koa clicked on his hand-held flashlight and scanned the icy, wet tunnel walls and ceiling. "Looking at the spiral on this, and the water samples we took, I'm guessing no more than a hundred years, dug out by a big bore. Slowly."

"Uh huh," Allison replied, switching on her own light.

The two friends meandered farther into the dark. While still freezing, relief from the battering wind meant Koa could drop his

32

hood. Allison followed suit. Their flashlights offered only meager circles of enlightenment to their surroundings. Ice glistened in the beams of yellow light. But so far, that's all it was. Ice. A never-ending tunnel that disappeared under the ice shelf at an almost perfect thirty-degree angle.

Koa checked his watch. They'd been marching for nearly an hour. A best guess at their pace was four kilometers, which from where they came in should put them right in the center of the gravitational mass. He glanced back to the freckle of light from the tunnel entrance. No going back now. Without turning properly, he took a stride forward only to be grabbed across the chest by Allison. Koa stumbled, his foot dangling in the darkness. Vast nothingness stretched out before him.

"Holy shit, I could've fallen," Koa exclaimed, his heart slamming against his rib cage.

"You're welcome," Allison replied through a clenched jaw.

In front, the tunnel ended abruptly and opened out into a pitch-black cavern. This was the Wilkes Land Crater. Koa held out the flashlight, but the dark swallowed its tiny stream of light revealing only that they stood on a precipice.

"That'll be a kilometer down," Allison said.

"Don't remind me. Any idea how we're getting down?" Koa asked.

"Not yet."

"There's gotta be a way," he pressed. "No one digs a tunnel down this far for the hell of it."

"Who dug this anyway?" Allison asked, searching the lip of the precipice.

"Could have been the Americans," Koa said without looking up.

"You think *everything* is the Americans."

"Everything *is* the Americans," Koa snapped back. "1946. Operation High Jump."

"Yeah, yeah, yeah. We've all heard it. The KGB released files that they knew the Americans sent a massive operation into Antarctica looking for aliens." Allison stopped and looked up at Koa. "You're not looking for *aliens,* are you?"

"Don't be daft," Koa scoffed. "But, if what we saw on the readout was at all real, then there is *something* down here. And maybe the Americans knew it back in '46. Timeline on that tunnel fits—"

"Hey, check this out!"

Koa trudged as fast as he could over to Allison, huffing hot breath and patting his arms to regain some feeling. "Whatcha got?"

"Stairs…" she replied, looking up at him. "I've got big-assed stairs."

Koa frowned and crouched down to his companion, guiding his flashlight over the edge. Sure enough, there were stairs—colossal, rock stairs laid down by someone in antiquity. He stood quickly, pulled a flare from his pocket and popped it. It fizzed bright red in his gloved hand for a second before he hurled it into the black chasm.

The crimson light penetrated somewhat more than their flashlights. As it sailed through the air, it revealed a fleeting glimpse of massive square structures. Some of the arrangements as big as houses, others smaller, and some seemed to form wide pool-like areas. The flare plummeted quickly down and clattered about a stone floor.

"If this was an asteroid crater, it isn't anymore," Allison said.

"I guess not," Koa replied without looking at her. "It's more

34

like a self-contained city. But arranged like an inverted pyramid. Did you see? There were four distinct sides on which the buildings sat—and the sides got narrower toward the bottom."

"Koa, I don't like this, we gotta go back up. Get a bigger team and more light and equipment."

"And we will," Koa replied already shuffling backward on his stomach, legs dangling over the edge. "But, I wanna see."

Allison grunted. "You're a pain in my ass, Brown."

Slowly, Koa lowered himself down. Each block dug into his ribs as he edged over and dropped to the next one. These bricks were easily six feet tall and rough as all hell, which made it even more difficult given his five-foot ten-inch stature. It was a never-ending joke for Allison who was an Amazonian six feet tall. Yet right now, he felt like a giant—an archeological giant. He'd just found a city beneath Antarctica. A goddamn city. Who built it? How old was it? He'd find out and he'd be famous. Hell, forget Koab Crater, he could name an ancient city after himself: Koatlan—Place of Koa, in Nahuatl. It was perfect.

After what felt like hours of grunting, scraping, shuffling and climbing, there were no more stone blocks. Koa's boots thumped on the bottom of the inverted pyramid city. He turned, holding the flashlight out to survey the surroundings. He was standing in an enormous concourse, though there was no telling how wide it was—the flashlight beam never penetrating far enough. That said, he surmised this must be the blunted tip of the inverted pyramid, so it was likely square.

Allison dropped down beside him with a thud, panting.

"You good?" Koa asked.

"Yeah," Allison said, brushing the dust and debris from her thick coat. "But you can push my ass back up there." She looked

35

up to the lip of the precipice.

Koa shone his flashlight beam to the path of her gaze. "Ah, yeah, hadn't thought of that."

"Shocker," Allison said with a huff and marched off into the dark of the courtyard. "Let's get this over with."

"Hey, wait up," Koa called, jogging to catch up.

They tread carefully into what Koa assumed was the center of the square, swinging their flashlights left and right. Tiny crystals embedded in the huge bricks glinted when struck with the yellow rays of light.

"Well at least we know what's causing the gravity well," Koa said, eyes squinting in the dark.

"We do?"

"Calaverite," he replied.

"You think?" Allison asked.

"Yeah. Did you get a good look at the rocks as we were climbing down? That greeny-yellow metallic sheen? These bricks weren't cut out of the rock, they were cast—mixed with a bunch of minerals, and a shit load of calaverite. It's dense as hell. Like a specific gravity of 9.5."

Allison stopped in her tracks to throw him an annoyed stare that penetrated the dark. She pointed the flashlight directly in his face. "You think I don't know what calaverite is?"

Koa shielded his eyes. "Hey, shit. Sorry, sure."

Allison grunted and continued on.

"All I was saying was, the density could account for the gravity well. But, why calaverite? Tellerium-gold compounds aren't the best building material in terms of longevity. Too damn brittle."

"But it's an awesome semiconductor used extensively in high-energy, low-heat environments—right?" Allison said.

Koa nodded. "Yeah, that's true. That would make this whole damn thing a massive semi-conductor?"

"Or a series of linked semi-conductors?"

"Like a computer ..." Koa said under his breath.

"Yep," Allison replied. "And every computer needs a core." She stopped dead and nodded ahead.

In the center of the courtyard stood a massive crucible atop a stem easily twenty feet tall and ornately carved. Koa ran up to it, pulled off his glove and ran his fingers along the cold surface. It was full of markings, many of which looked cuneiform, and images of what could only be described as beasts—human-sized animals with enormous frills about their heads and large eyes.

"Fuck me," Koa said aloud. "We've found a Knowledge Bringer site." He continued to circumnavigate the stone stem, fixated on the bas-reliefs and ancient script, until his foot caught on something and he crashed into the hard stone.

"Koa! Koa! Are you okay?" Allison yelled, running up to the stem.

"Yeah," he called out from the dark, his voice shaky. "I tripped over a... body."

"A body? Oh shit!" Allison found Koa and cast her flashlight onto him, then the withered frame at his feet. "Double shit ..." she said, her gaze roving over the tattered clothing of the carcass.

Koa looked up to Allison, his eyes wide. "I don't think it was the Americans."

Location: Washington DC, USA

The door to the presidential Cadillac swung open, revealing one of her regular stalwart Secret Service agents, dressed in a customary black suit and wearing dark sunglasses. Hunter was his name if she remembered well. The fact that only he and the other secret service agents even knew *how* to open the car door still amused Lucy. For all her effort to create a world of trust and edge ever closer to utopia, her beloved United States was still as paranoid as ever. Even the car she rode in, a far cry from the open top motorcade of Kennedy, screamed paranoia: bulletproof glass, hermetically sealed interior, rocket-propelled grenades, night vision optics, a tear gas cannon, onboard oxygen tanks, pump-action shotguns, and even two pints of blood of her exact type. The smirk slipped from her lips. The truth was, it wasn't paranoia. She and the other world leaders were under attack. They even knew *who* was attacking them yet were unable to find out *where* they were hiding.

Lucy stepped out into the midday sun and shielded her eyes. As her retinas became accustomed to the white light of day she could make out the Headquarters Building of the National Security Agency; a diffident nine-story structure with an air of the 1960s about it, tucked behind a lower, even older, mall-shaped building and a pair of much more modern blue-black boxes—Operations 2A and 2B. All four buildings were surrounded by a moat of cars belonging to the employees.

Flanked by her security contingent, Lucy made her way to the NSA building and passed through the various checkpoints and security measures until reaching a large meeting room with a single, long white table surrounded by ten or so chairs. The familiar face of Jonathan Teller greeted her. The last twenty years had taken its toll on Teller's boyish looks, replacing his dark hair with a salt and peppered crew cut. But more than that, his vigor had been diminished. Lucy could only imagine the strain of caring for someone with a disease like Huntington's while taking on two boys who weren't his own.

"Jonathan," Lucy said, giving him a brief hug.

"Madam President," Jonathan said, "sorry to drag you here on short notice."

Lucy nodded as Joshua, her Secretary of State, and Admiral Jim Waltham, NSA Director, entered the room. Each shook her hand, then the door was closed and everyone took a seat.

"Tell me," Lucy said. There was no need to specify, she needed to know *everything* they did.

"We're still chasing down all leads," replied Admiral Waltham. His deep grey eyes and greyer hair told of a man who had seen much, and refused to be fazed by even the most terrifying of circumstances. "Thanks to Kelly Graham Junior, we have the rifle used during the attempt on your life. There are no prints and so far not a single cell left on there to do any meaningful DNA analysis, but we're still looking. We're also monitoring as much data traffic as possible. If a four-year-old with a walkie talkie so much as whispers about something connected to this, we'll know about it."

"But I assume that makes the search harder, since everyone, everywhere is talking about this right now?" Lucy asked.

The Director gave a conceding nod.

"And the puzzle boxes?" Lucy asked.

"So far, they are of no threat. Initial analysis suggests no explosive, chemical, or biological intent. The boys in the lab are working on opening it now."

"It'll probably be another dead end, just like the one left by them the last time they reared their ugly head," Jonathan spat.

The President turned her attention to her Secretary of State. "Have any of our allies had any luck?"

"Nope. Nothing so far. Moscow thought they were close. I'm

waiting on an update," Joshua replied.

"Then why are we here?" Lucy asked, frustrated.

"I need authorization," came a voice from behind.

Lucy turned to see General Joseph Spratford, Chairman of the Joint Chiefs of Staff and Janette Stirling, Administrator of FEMA entering the room. Lucy stood, a frown creased into her forehead, and pushed a lock of greying blond hair behind her ear.

Both shook her hand, apologizing for their tardiness.

"Joe," Lucy began. "I'd like to say this is a pleasant surprise, but somehow I doubt it."

General Spratford took a seat, clasped his strong fingers together, and took a deep breath. "I'd like to put operation *Swiss Mountain* into effect. We both would," he said nodding to Janette.

This didn't make any sense. Operation Swiss Mountain had been conceived after the Green and Red Society had tried to fashion an atomic bomb to be exploded in the upper atmosphere, creating a hole in the ozone that would melt ice caps and flood coastal cities. A safety protocol was deemed necessary should such a global threat arise again. The Swiss already had such a contingency, building vast cave systems in the mountains to house nearly their entire population of 8 million people. Of course, there were 300 million in the USA and huge capital was needed. Capital the US didn't have to spare. But, when the Nine Veils had revealed themselves as the puppet masters of the Green and Red Society, and very much operational, the USA had shared the plan with Russia, Europe and China in hopes of obtaining help. A joint fund had been established and a unified project started. It had taken nearly twenty years, but they were almost finished. Still, evacuating more than fifty percent of the population was a task so vast and complicated it should only be triggered if absolutely necessary.

CHILDREN OF THE FIFTH SUN: RUBICON

"I was just informed that we don't know anything," Lucy began. "You can't ask me to sanction something like that without good cause. Half the people wouldn't even bother to leave their homes without an existential threat."

"We don't have to start moving people yet, but we can at least get the bunkers and biomes fired up. Prep the environmental systems and do a full check. Run some operational drills," the Admiral replied.

"Janette, you agree with this?" Lucy pressed.

The head of FEMA nodded. "I want to get ahead of anything that may come our way. As you said, evacuating fifty percent of our people is no easy task. It must run smoothly—or at least as smoothly as something like this can ever run. It's been twenty years, Madam President, and they've come out of hiding now. We don't know why. But the last time this organization decided to move, we were caught with our pants down."

Lucy looked to Jonathan and Joshua. They both nodded solemnly.

"I don't know," Lucy said, hesitation pulling at her conscience. "Even prepping these things could cause mass panic. The bunkers we could do, but the biomes... they're in the open. Too much activity and the public will notice. I'm not sure—"

A knock at the door.

An agent stepped in and whispered to Waltham, who nodded and excused the man.

"A call from Moscow," Waltham said. "They say it's urgent. May I?"

Lucy gestured to the phone on the table.

Jim punched the connect key and picked up the receiver. Initially his gaze was fixed on the table as he bobbed his head in understanding, but after a few moments his brow knitted and his stare moved to the President. "And you're sure it's related?" he asked the caller. "Okay, thank you." He stood but kept the receiver in his hand and immediately began dialing.

"Jim?" Lucy asked, her heart in her throat.

"That was Moscow. They unlocked their puzzle box," he replied, waiting with the phone to his ear. "As soon as they opened it—yes hello? Put me through to the lab. Tell them to stop whatever they're doing, now! Yes, I'm coming down." He slammed down the phone and made for the door.

"Jim!" Lucy demanded.

He turned to Lucy. "As soon as they opened it, they lost control of every nuclear power station in Russia. Complete lock out of every system. It must have released a virus or Trojan horse or something onto the internet, their systems—something." The Director's words were swallowed by the empty corridor as he sped out.

Lucy leapt to her feet and followed him, everyone else in tow. How was that possible? Something leaked through the Wi-Fi? Didn't Russia have firewalls? Could it breach the NSA system? A million possibilities rattled through the President's brain as they rifled through corridors and stairwells to the lab housing the puzzle box.

Inside the lab was another room built from reinforced glass, with a single door in and out. While the possibility of chemical or biological threat had been eliminated the team of two men inside still wore protective suits. One of them wandered up to the transparent wall and pressed the intercom.

"Sir?" said the man, his voice distorted.

"Do *not* open the box," the Director replied flatly.

"We haven't sir. Still figuring this one out… it's a doozy."

"Good. Let it be for now, until I tell you otherwise—"

"Frank?" came the voice of the second hazmat-suited man in the sealed lab. "It's clicking."

"What?" Frank left the intercom on and padded over to his colleague.

Everyone pushed up to the glass, but the Secret Service agents formed a shield between it and the President forcing her to peer over their shoulders.

The square, wooden puzzle about the size of a shoebox and covered in blue and yellow geometric patterns sat alone on a large plastic table. Through the intercom, faint humming and clicking like a motorized music box could be heard. Then, segments of the box's surface began to slide back and forth, snapping into place. Although Lucy could not determine a pattern, it seemed purposeful and logical.

"Can you stop it?" the director barked.

"*Stop* it?" replied Frank, his eyes wide behind the protective plastic of his suit. "I don't even know what *it's* doing."

The box stopped clicking, and a single side panel popped open.

The two men inside the lab jumped back.

No one dared draw breath.

Finally, a faint "fuck it" could be heard over the intercom and Frank stepped forward. He lowered down to see inside the box, pulling back the side panel which was hinged at one end. His shoulders seemed to relax, and he slipped in a gloved hand. A moment later, he pulled out a small piece of paper no bigger than a matchbox.

43

Frank stared at it and frowned.

"Well?" asked the Director.

Frank walked up to the glass and slapped the paper against the surface, holding it there with his palm so everyone could read. Scrawled in ink that had spread out on the rough, hand-made paper was a single word: *Pachakutiq*.

"What the hell is that supposed to mean?" the Director balked.

A moment of silence then Jonathan spoke up. "It's Aymara," he said quietly. "The kids, I mean the Stratum, speak it to each other sometimes. I figured I should learn some, you know because of my boys."

"What does it mean, Jonathan?" Lucy pressed.

"Pachacuti Inca Yupanqui, was a 15th Century Sapa Inca in the Kingdom of Cuzco. His name meant *He who remakes the world*. Pachakutiq on its own, just means… cataclysm."

The phone in the corner of the room began to ring. The Director stormed over and grabbed it up. "Yes? What? God dammit!" he slammed it down again and turned to the President. "We just lost our plants. We're locked out. If someone else has control, they could set every one of them to explode."

Fear streaked its way through Lucy's spine and into her stomach, stabbing at her over and over. There were more than sixty nuclear plants in the US alone. Four hundred more spread around the world. If they were rigged to detonate simultaneously… the ensuing radioactive fallout… the cloud… the rain…

"Madam President?" Janette said.

"Start Project Swiss Mountain, now," Lucy ordered, regaining her composure. "Joshua get me the Press Secretary. And find a way to get control on those damn reactors!"

Everyone darted from the room, sprinting off to their

respective duties. Everyone except Jonathan. He was standing in the corner, a cell phone pressed to one ear, a finger in the other. Lucy studied him, the pulse of her own heart throbbing in her hands and feet.

"Who the hell is Koa Brown?" Jonathan barked into the phone. "He found what?"

Location: Alpha Base, Vostok Lake, Antarctica

Biome One was abuzz. The usually serene, almost sterile and utopian, atmosphere was filled with anxiety. News of the assassinations had rippled all the way to Antarctica. Scientists ran through the corridors from lab to lab, instead of walking—as if fearing they'd be picked off by some concealed sniper—while the number of armed military personnel seemed to have multiplied tenfold. KJ was sure that was against the Antarctic Accords. Curiously, not a single member of the Stratum was around.

"Hey!" KJ called after a dark-haired woman in a white lab coat as she barreled past. "Uh …"

"Hui Yin," Catherine whispered.

"Yeah, Hui Yin, right?" KJ asked.

The woman span on her heel, eyes filled with worry. "Yes, yes that's me… who's… oh, Mr. Graham."

"KJ, yeah. You okay? What the hell's going on?"

"You didn't hear? Every nuclear powerplant on the planet just locked out. Someone else has access now. With the attack earlier, everyone is on high alert, in case something happens here at Alpha Base."

That was not good. It was surely the Nine Veils behind this, which made it more important to find Svetlana. KJ strolled up to

Hui Yin, K'awin at his side, and placed a hand on the woman's shoulder. Her body relaxed, muscles no longer taut like a bow string. "Chill, everything's gonna be fine, okay?"

Hui Yin gazed into KJ's bright blue eyes. "Sure, fine," she repeated.

"Tell me, Hui Yin, where can I find the other Stratum?"

"They're all down at the lake."

"Great, thanks. You be safe now, ya hear?" He gave her a half smirk.

"Sure, safe." She ambled off in the direction in which she had been running originally.

KJ shook his head. "Humans. C'mon, girl."

"You better not be talking about me, mister," Catherine said, eyes narrowed.

K'awin warbled quietly and followed her symbiote toward the entrance elevator that would take them down to the lake. KJ stepped inside followed by K'awin and Catherine. The glass doors slid closed and KJ watched the surface world disappear—an almost immediate transition, as they quickly passed through the ice and rock, and then into a vast expanse that was the underground lake.

On the surface, Alpha base was protected under a series of gigantic glass domes. Beneath them and below the ice, some four thousand meters, was Lake Vostok. KJ had been fascinated with it as a kid because it was like having another planet right here on Earth. Originally it was an oligotrophic extreme environment, supersaturated with nitrogen and oxygen. More than 160 miles long and 30 miles wide at its widest point, the lake covered nearly five thousand square miles. KJ had longed to be one of the scientists, suited up like astronauts, who helped terraform it for the Huahuqui. Of course, that dream had been the beginning of the feud with Nikolaj.

The terraforming had nearly finished completion; so there would be little opportunity to don a spacesuit and explore the vast icy world that was so fascinating. He may only be nine, but KJ knew the only thing to do was borrow a suit. Actually, build himself a suit. Which is exactly what he had done, spending three months rigging it to his size. Cutting and sewing, stealing components that were necessary to ensure a tight seal. Creating a frame to support the heavy helmet on his skinny neck had been the hardest part. Still, he'd been determined. Today was the payoff.

KJ dodged his mother and Jonathan, slipped out of the apartment and sneaked past the guards to the elevator, using his powers to coerce them, and made it all the way to the lake entrance, locked behind a seemingly impenetrable steel door. Standing in front of the colossal gate, his finger hovered over the keypad. He repeated the code back to himself. The one he'd gleaned from the mind of the scientist, Malcom, who sat in the lunch hall every day and ate the same cheese sandwich. KJ couldn't take the whole code in one go, Malcom would have noticed. But bit by bit, over several coincidental crossings, KJ had gathered the whole thing. It was fifteen characters long. Punching in the wrong character would likely set off the alarm.

"What are you doing, KJ?" came a voice.

Nikolaj.

KJ spun, and nearly fell over sideways with the weight of the helmet.

"I just wanna see, Nikolaj! It's like being on another planet.

You can go after me? We'll take turns."

"It's not safe, KJ! You can't go in there. You're just a kid."

"I'm not a kid! How'd you know I was here? Did you follow me?" KJ asked.

"I knew what you were up to for months. I just wanted to see if you were stupid enough to try."

"I'm not stupid. Look! I made it myself." KJ opened up his arms so that Nikolaj could see the suit in all its glory.

"You may be brain smart, but you're not street smart."

"I am too street smart," KJ said, tears welling up. "Kelly Graham was my dad, and mom says he was the most street-smart guy she ever knew!"

"No, she didn't. Mom said, he could handle himself. But he also got himself in trouble. You don't know everything KJ."

KJ sniffed back tears that threatened to tumble down his cheeks. "I know he's dead, and I wish he wasn't."

"Well Mom says wishing doesn't make things so."

"Stop calling her mom. She's not your mom. Your mom is dead just like my dad, remember?"

Nikolaj's eyes glassed over, and he swallowed, but he said nothing.

KJ knew that had been a step too far. A wound that never healed, and he had just slashed it open again.

"I'm sorry," KJ began. "She's my mom and—"

"I'm a mom to both of you," came Freya's voice from the tunnel as she stepped up behind Nikolaj. Her angry face appeared even harsher in the shadows. "And you are in deep trouble, mister."

"You told her?" KJ sobbed.

"For your own good," Nikolaj replied, wiping his face of a tear that must have escaped.

"Come on KJ, time to go," his mom said.

Defeated, KJ dragged his feet and moved as slowly as he could behind her. "Mom?" he said.

She turned and pressed the call button for the elevator and turned to him. "Yes?"

"Do you at least like my suit? I made it myself."

She sighed heavily and dropped down to his level. "I do indeed."

"Dad would have liked it too, huh? He was good at adventures, like me."

His mom didn't say anything but smiled softly and hugged him tight.

"Guys and gals, been a while," KJ announced loudly as he entered the underground lake, K'awin and Catherine at his side.

Carved through nearly four thousand meters of meteoric and accretion ice above him, the manufactured cave allowed access to the shallow end of Lake Vostok. Huge girders rose from the shoreline to the icy ceiling above and supported a network of lattices—all preventing millions of tons of frozen water suddenly crushing everyone below. Still, to KJ the metal work was somehow graceful and together with the rigged lighting and shimmering ice, it felt as if he were inside a giant Fabergé egg.

Though many scientists had protested the creation of this cave, given their desire to study the microbial life living in what was previously an extreme environment, politics had won out and a haven from attacks on Alpha Base above was needed. A complex purification system had been installed to sterilize the lake water and the constant stream of meltwater. At the far end of the cave, where the lake deepened and disappeared under the ice toward a hydrothermal vent, a barrier was installed to prevent anyone from venturing too far, becoming trapped and drowning.

The shore was lined with his Stratum family, hundreds of humans and Huahuqui. A few looked up, waved, and smiled. KJ's mind was awash with a warm sense of kin and friendship.

"KJ!" The unified voice of twins Merry and Lex called out. They ran up to greet him, their Huahuqui in tow.

The twins threw their arms around him.

"Where the hell," Merry began.

"Have you been?" Lex finished, giving a mock pout.

The twins' bond was so strong they almost never completed a sentence alone. It made much more sense when communicating telepathically, like they were one person. Clumsy, vocalized language only made them seem like teenage best friends.

The twins' Huahuqui companions rubbed snouts with K'awin, gills ruffling.

KJ laughed and did a little twirl. "Hey no bullet holes, see? I'm all good."

"Word was," Merry said.

"You went after the shooter," Lex interjected.

"By yourself," they finished in unison.

"Someone had to. And it's a good job I did. You're not gonna believe this—"

Believe what? Echoed a voice in KJ's head.

Nikolaj. Too lazy to open that superior mouth of yours? KJ projected from his mind.

Use it or lose it. You do not practice it enough.

Well, I leave Alpha Base occasionally and interact with other humans more, so— "I like to use my tongue." KJ threw the girls a smirk.

The twins giggled.

Nikolaj shook his head. "There's something big going down. The attacks, and now the nuclear power stations. So, if you know something, Kelly Junior, you should tell me."

KJ shrugged. "I gave them the gun I found. It's not my fault if they can't do anything with it."

"But that's not the whole story," Nikolaj pressed. *Tell me,* he projected.

"I don't have to tell you shit. You'll only go running to mom."

"We're not kids anymore, Junior. Time to grow up." Nikolaj's eyes held that look of contempt KJ knew all too well.

"Oh, fuck you, you pompous prick. And stop calling me *Junior*, Jesus." KJ turned, stormed past Catherine and through the doors of the underground lake toward the elevator to the surface. K'awin trotted after him.

Merry and Lex caught up, their Huahuqui alongside.

The doors to the elevator closed and they began to ascend.

KJ studied the young women. About his age, they had straight dark hair and the bright blue eyes associated with the Stratum. Both were Nenets from Siberia and part of the group of children rescued by his mother so long ago. Merry and Lex weren't their given names, but the twins had chosen them to distinguish themselves from the others. Siberian names were hard for many to pronounce. They might seem giggly and immature, yet they were both sharp as tacks, holding multiple degrees in important things that frankly sounded made up to KJ. And then of course there was their little parlor trick—something even KJ had never managed to achieve. It would come in handy.

Catherine ambled up, calm and collected. She said nothing, but KJ knew she didn't need to. She was already versed in his plan.

KJ beckoned them all closer. "It's the Nine Veils. I saw the tattoo. They're back."

You're sure? Merry and Lex asked in unison, telepathically.

I'm sure, KJ projected.

We need, Merry started.

To tell someone, Lex finished.

Not yet. There's something else. I think... I think the shooter was Svetlana. Our Svetlana. If Lucy and NATO, or whoever, find her before us, they'll kill her and all our brothers and sisters. Not because they want to, but it'll be all out war and you know it.

"Hey, you guys, wanna use your lips here?" Catherine interrupted. "You've been doing your thing …"

"Sorry. Nothing you don't already know. Be grateful we aren't using Aymara." KJ winked at Cat.

"So, what's the plan, KJ?" Lex asked.

"What do you have in mind?" Merry added.

"I can still feel her in my head. She's in here, like we're connected," KJ replied tapping on his temple. "Like her consciousness left a splinter lodged in my brain."

"Over this kind."

"Of distance?"

"Yes." KJ nodded. "And I think, if we put our heads together we can track her. We can *find* her. And bring her back, maybe bring them *all* back."

"Us."

"Three?"

"I'm along for the ride," Catherine offered.

"Right, and Kiska and Kroshka," KJ added pointing to the

Huahuqui at the girls' sides. "And K'awin."

"KJ, we love you but," Merry began.

"We're going to need more," Lex said.

"If you got Nikolaj."

"On board."

"It would."

"Be easier."

KJ shook his head. "Don't ask golden boy. Anyone else? Who can we trust?"

"Leo and Igor," the girls replied in unison.

Leo and Igor. Both were huge guys who to KJ's mind had grown beards as children. That was until they left for Songshan in Dengfeng. Unlike most of the Stratum, they had not pursued academia but instead had asked ever so politely to be trained at the Shaolin Temple. There, for fifteen years, they learned about the peaceful ways of Budhism, and of course also Shaolin Kung Fu.

KJ had become a student under Leo, but never had the patience for martial arts. After two years of trying to find his inner peace, KJ had only found his inner sarcastic asshole. But then again, the rumor was the boys' real secret was not in their fists, but in their ability to wage psychological war. If that were even half true, they could be of help.

KJ nodded to Merry and Lex. "Good idea. Meet me in the mess hall at midnight. Bring the boys."

Location: unknown

Victoria crouched at the edge of a pool empty of any Phalanx and stared into the glassy surface. Her reflection stared back, soaked in warm orange hues of sunset—yet her defiant eyes remained a cold, icy blue. The water rippled in a light breeze distorting her image until, when the waves subsided, another face peered back. Kelly Graham Junior's face, which quickly morphed into that of his father. Nausea crawled its way from deep within her, spreading from the pit of her stomach into her limbs. Kelly Graham. She had not thought of him in many years. Her one-time friend who she'd admired and studied, enjoying his knowledge of photography, sarcasm and wit, and even his back-handed compliments.

She closed her eyes and heard his coarse laughter, smelled his sweaty skin—and felt his ribs crack under her feet. She'd murdered him. Not for the want of killing, but through fear. Raw panic coursing through her as she was stalked and hunted from New Mexico to Teotihuacan. It was an accident. A stone grew in her throat and a warm salty tear slipped into the corner of her mouth. Victoria licked it away and exhaled loudly. *No, not an accident. Necessary,* she thought. Kelly Graham was the reason she was here now. Dragged by him into government conspiracies and battling cults.

She pulled a handkerchief from her pocket and wiped her mouth. The taste of raw fish and metallic scent of the blood was ever present. Tainting everything she ate and drank. She should have died in the Nevada Desert, when the truck was attacked. Back then, her soul was innocent. She should have ascended to heaven. But instead, her mangled corpse was reanimated using ill-gotten science and the genetic information of a mutated Huahuqui called Wak. Her humanity had been stripped away leaving only the most basic of animal instincts.

It was no wonder God had forsaken her.

Though Wak had been killed, releasing her from it's terrifying grip, Victoria's soul felt dirty. Marked. Unfit to be embraced by

God. In the years that followed, Victoria had tried to find Him. Church after Church, Catholic, Orthodox, Evangelical. From New Hampshire to New Mexico. She'd even travelled to Palestine and Israel in hopes of connecting with the very heart of Christianity. It didn't matter which denomination it was, as long as she once again could feel something. Yet, each place of worship felt empty and soulless. Brick and mortar, devoid of hope and life.

Finally, Victoria had ended up at Saint Hill in the rolling countryside of Sussex, England. With sandstone columns and a Union Jack flag fluttering in the wind, Saint Hill Manor looked like a quintessential English country house. But it was more than that; it was a central hub for the Church of Scientology. This is where the Doyen had found her.

Aboard a tour bus to the Manor, half listening to the spiel of the guide touting the benefits of paying for educational courses that would lead to enlightenment, *his* soft voice had come over her shoulder. Startled she'd turned to come face to face with the man who she would come to know as the Doyen. His eyes were wise and his face calming and soft, like a father she never knew.

He'd accompanied her on her walk around Saint Hill, more of a museum than active religious site, and just listened. He nodded in all the right places and never really said anything. In fact, he'd never actually given his real name. So comfortable was she, that within a matter of hours she had spilled the story of the Huahuqui, the cloning program, and her ordeal with Wak. He hadn't flinched. When she'd finished, the oil-painting stillness of his face had broken into a wide smile. It was then he revealed that he was the head of a group of like-minded individuals who were very aware of what the government had done and moreover whose mission it was to find those special people who would possess the ability to transcend nine barriers of knowledge, ultimately reaching God and understanding the universe.

The Doyen frequented scientology churches seeking out new members for his own cult, since many of the ideologies seemed to coincide. At least until the part where scientologists believed that an alien overlord named Xenu brought billions of his people, the Teegeeack, to Earth some 75 million years ago, then killed them all ensuring their souls could adhere to humans and cause spiritual harm. No, in this respect the Nine Veils, as the Doyen called his organization, differed.

Over a coffee in a small town in England, the Doyen had calmly explained that upon passing through the sixth barrier, or veil, we learn that beings like 'dragons' control the forces behind secret societies that controlled most of the major events on Earth. Once upon a time such a notion would have seemed ludicrous, but here with the knowledge of the Huahuqui, it seemed all too plausible. He believed the Huahuqui were those beings. But more than that, his ideology was not in opposition to God but in synchrony with Him. According to the teachings of the Nine Veils, God had bestowed the Huahuqui upon humanity. Finally, there was reconciliation.

For a time that had been enough. But, the darkness never left her.

Victoria swirled the water with a finger. Just as beneath the surface was a mottled mess of old rice, bacteria, and all manner of disgusting creatures, beneath her ageing beauty bubbled a putrid darkness. Wak had seeded within her something terrible, and over the course of twenty years it had germinated and grown into a black, creeping vine, penetrating her heart and mind. And now, her vision of the world was dark. Humanity had failed their God. He had sent his son, and we'd killed him. He had sent the Huahuqui, and we'd killed them too.

The Doyen had been her last hope, his vision for a synergy between humans and Huahuqui working together in the name of God. But his resolve seemed to wane. The leader of the Nine Veils had grown soft, rambling. He interfered more and more as the time of their ultimate goal grew nearer. His own arrogance ballooned with every brick of his fortress laid. Now that it was finished, his evolution into demi-God seemed complete; his previous business-driven nature now replaced with a priest-like demeanor—constantly spouting nonsensical proverbs.

She had to plan for his failure. It was her destiny to serve God, even if He had left her behind. Everything she had lived through had prepared her for this. Only one who had been cast aside could complete what needed to be done. Lucifer himself, also cast aside, had failed. She would not. And the spawn of Kelly Graham would not stand in her way now.

The first child of the Stratum needed to die.

Victoria turned from the pool and glanced at the orange sky for a lingering moment, then headed up the stone pathway toward her temple.

CHAPTER FOUR

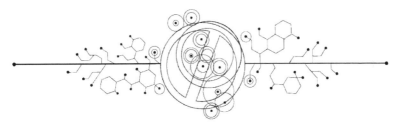

Location: Washington DC, USA

Jonathan rocked back and forth in the large leather chair, scanning the length of mahogany table sat in the middle of the White House's John F. Kennedy conference room. Lucy was at the head while her cabinet lined either side. All were staring expectantly at two large monitors. The first showed a very nervous-looking Koa Brown, while the second was a conference call collage displaying all the members of the Alpha Base UN Committee.

"Just tell the President what you told me, Dr. Brown," Jonathan said.

Koa cleared his throat. "It's a temple or something like one."

Lucy frowned. "A temple? What kind of temple?"

"Well, from what we can discern," Koa said, playing with his tie. "It was supposed to be a crater from a meteor, but my system showed that it was a temple. I mean, it may have been a crater once, and they built into it. Anyway, the temple, it looks kinda Mayan or perhaps Egyptian, though could be neither. You know, it could be a predecessor or maybe it came after though I doubt it, I mean—"

"Why do we *care*, Doctor Brown?" asked Schmidt, the German committee member. A rotund man with beady eyes. "We have other very pressing matters, if you hadn't heard."

"Well to start with, it's a huge archeological find. To be buried under that much ice, do you know when it must have been built? It'll throw off our thinking completely—"

Jonathan sighed. "Out with it man, get to the point."

"Right, yeah, well," Koa began. "Um where to start?"

Was this guy for real? Jonathan pulled at his face. "How about you start with the orb?"

Lucy shot a worried glance at Jonathan. He just nodded to the screen, urging her to be patient.

"Right, yeah the orb," continued Koa. "Bit of backstory, sorry but it's important. So, do you remember like twenty years ago, explorers discovered the remnants of a secret Nazi base hidden deep in the Arctic? It was like just 600 miles from the North Pole. The Russians found it."

Everyone stared blankly.

Koa coughed. "Okay, well they did. They were searching for stuff, on orders from Hitler. Weird stuff. Alien stuff. The theory goes that the Nazis also went south, claimed an area of Antarctica as German territory and sent an expedition there. Supposedly, they mapped the area and discovered a network of rivers and caves, one of which led to a large geothermal lake. We figured it might have been Vostok, but as Alpha base is there now, and we found nothing, that got ruled out."

Jonathan rolled his hand in a 'get on with it' motion.

"Anyhoo, the conspiracy nuts said a city-sized base was built somewhere in Antarctica, called *Base 22* or *New Berlin*. If you're really into this, then you'll know it was meant to be home to not only Nazis but also the Illuminati. There was even talk of the Germans discovering abandoned alien technology." Koa paused. "I think we found it."

"A Nazi base for aliens?" The skinny French committee member, Gaustav, laughed pretentiously.

"No," Koa replied. "I told you before it looks Mayan or Egyptian, like an inverted pyramid. The Nazi's didn't build it. We found the site, and what it really is."

"Which is?" pressed Lucy.

Koa wet his lips. "It's a site like Teotihuacan, a place built for humans and the Huahuqui to exist, but from what I can tell it might be the first site and the others were just copies. There's drawings all over the walls of the Huahuqui with people and a cuneiform script and hieroglyphs."

"You've been down there already? How is that possible? You can't have drilled that deep so quickly," Chinese member, Xi, said.

Koa nodded. "You're quite right. I said the Nazis didn't build it, they found it. They drilled a man-sized hole all the way through the ice. The entrance got covered, but the tunnel remained intact. We found weapons, empty supply containers and other junk. *Nazi* junk. That part the conspiracy nuts got right."

"They really went there?" Lucy asked, her brow creased.

"We found corpses in full regalia," Koa replied. "Hitler's special forces. Looks like something crushed them and they were just left."

"You said something about an orb, Doctor Brown," Lucy urged.

"Right, right an orb. So, this whole complex is like a super semi-conductor, made with calaverite. In the center is a massive crucible and from what I can determine, it held an orb. Like the ones that were destroyed years ago, the ones that can connect Huahuqui and humans. At least that's what I discerned from the writings on the walls. But, if I'm reading them correctly, this temple turns an orb into like a *super* orb. So perhaps this place was like a broadcasting station, you know? To the whole world."

"And you think the Nazis took it?" Gaustav interjected. "The orb?"

Koa nodded. "It's possible. I mean it's also possible there was nothing there. But the scratches on the crucible indicate something was dug out of it."

The German member squirmed uncomfortably. "Anything from that *period* has been handed over, put in a museum or destroyed."

"You and I both know that isn't true," Jonathan interjected.

"Excuse me?" Schmidt replied, his face red with anger.

"Members of the fourth Reich fled to Argentina after the war. A shit load of Nazi-era contraband was found in the back of a collector's house in Buenos Aires not so many years ago. The AFI confiscated it all."

Schmidt practically choked in disgust. "That was all proven to be fake. Carnival trinkets, no more."

"Yeah, that's what the official report said," Jonathan replied. "But, I heard things differently here. And as I understand it, AFI still has it all under lock and key. Why keep trinkets?"

"You think they have an orb?" Lucy asked.

Jonathan gave a shrug. "I don't know. I bet *they* don't even know. But if they do have one, and we can get at it—"

"Having an orb may mean we can do something about any potential Huahuqui army the Nine Veils has amassed," Lucy finished.

"Exactly. It's a long shot, but ..."

"I'll take anything, Mr. Teller."

Jonathan nodded.

"Good work, Doctor Brown. Keep studying. We will likely need you in the future."

The conference ended, and the cabinet shuffled out of the secure room, leaving Jonathan and Lucy alone. The President pushed her chair away and stood to leave.

"Madam President," Teller started. "Before I head to Argentina—"

"Lucy is fine Jonathan, we're alone. And we've known each other long enough." She gave a tired smile that also said they'd been *through* enough too.

"Whatever's going on, I don't think we're seeing the bigger picture. This feels like the beginning. It's been nearly twenty years. Why now? Why the assassination attempts? Why the power stations? I don't like it."

Lucy nodded solemnly. "I know, Jonathan. I know."

Location: Alpha Base, Antarctica

The mess hall was deathly still. No clicking of cutlery on plates, no chinking of glasses. No belly laughs or heated discussions between scientists and Stratum. KJ sat with K'awin in the dim lighting provided by a few low-level halogens embedded in the ceiling. They cast jagged shadows on the many white tables that littered the vast dining area.

He had no plan. Not one that made sense, anyway. Chasing after the Nine Veils with a handful of his Stratum brethren was infinitely stupid. KJ knew that. But, deep in his heart it felt right. And wasn't that the reason for doing anything? Because it was right? His father had taken on the task from the government because something inside him told him to. KJ's mother had never

CHILDREN OF THE FIFTH SUN: RUBICON

been able to explain it, only saying that his father had initially said no and then just as quickly changed his mind. After that, he had no reason to continue, to become part of the great conspiracy and covert war with China. To try and save everyone. But he did. He'd died saving everyone. In more than twenty years, KJ had heard only heroic stories of Kelly Graham. Well, except for Jonathan.

Sarah had lost her Huahuqui. The little creature had somehow slipped security and was wandering outside of Biome One. The young girl had run to KJ, crying, telling him that she was scared her Huahuqui would freeze to death.

KJ was only eleven, and knew full well he'd get into trouble, but he hadn't even given it a second thought. Someone needed his help, and he wouldn't let them down. K'awin wanted to come, but KJ refused and ordered her back to the apartment to lay on his bed. Then, donning his thickest coat, he marched up to the outer lock of Biome One, told the guard that he needed to leave and walked out as if he did it every day. It wouldn't be long before the guard realized that he'd been manipulated. KJ had to hurry.

Out in the frozen wasteland outside KJ called to the little lost Huahuqui. The howling wind stole his voice and numbed his lips, so KJ reached out with his mind. She was nowhere to be found. KJ checked his watch. He'd been outside for an hour. and shivering so hard he felt his bones may shatter, he'd been found—by Jonathan.

"What the hell were you thinking KJ?" Jonathan asked as KJ sat shivering next to a heater, clasping a mug of hot chocolate. "You could have died out there."

"So... so... could the Hua... Huahuqui," KJ stuttered

through chattering teeth.

"You should have come and got one of us," Jonathan nearly yelled, pacing back and forth like a caged tiger.

"No… no time. Had to save her …" KJ's eyes welled up, but he refused to cry.

"What on God's green Earth would possess you to do it alone? You're eleven," Jonathan said, dropping to his haunches.

KJ couldn't look him in the eye. "I was being brave… like my dad."

Jonathan sighed heavily. "KJ. Listen to me. Kelly, your dad, was a brave man. No-one doubts that. But bravery and intelligence are two different things. He was brave, and totally reckless and—"

KJ didn't want to hear another word, and so leapt up and ran to his room crying.

"He's here," came a whisper from the shadows breaking KJ's train of thought.

Lex and Merry slinked into the beam of a nearby halogen. By their side were their Huahuqui. Kiska was so named for his likeness to a cat; his blunted nose and feline almond-shaped eyes. He was forever swishing his tail and pouncing on insects or small animals that had stowed away on the G800s as they made their journey to and from the outside world. Kroshka, literally *little crumb*, was a tiny Huahuqui—much smaller than any of the others. For a long time, there was concern she wouldn't survive the cold of Antarctica, but Merry had stuck with her. Kroshka was resilient.

"Did you bring the boys?" KJ asked.

"Actually, *I* did," came Catherine's voice from the dark. She

64

stepped into the light with Igor, Leo and their symbiotes, Xu and Jin. "It was easier for me than the girls. Didn't want to arouse suspicion."

KJ nodded in approval and eyed the Shaolin monks. Their bald heads, which seemed to nearly touch the ceiling, shone in the spotlights. Leo and Igor were the only humans of African decent in the Stratum. The first children were comprised solely of Nenets, save for KJ and Nikolaj. In the early days, Alpha Base had allowed several groups of orphans to pair up with those Huahuqui who were without a human. There was some stigma attached to being a *secondo*, but at six foot five and built like brick shithouses, no one was going to ask Igor and Leo about it.

"Evening, boys," KJ said with a dip of his brow.

The men touched their palms together, and gave a shallow bow. In unison, their Huahuqui lowered their heads briefly.

"I'll cut to the chase. I found Svetlana. Our Svetlana. Or at least, I ran into her. She was the assassin in Washington who tried to shoot the President."

Catherine nodded in confirmation.

"Are you, sure, KJ?" Lex asked.

"Is it true?" Merry chimed in.

"Yep. Positive. And before you ask, no she didn't tell me, *Nikolaj*. You can come out of the shadows," KJ said, looking over Igor's shoulder.

"You think you can sneak away without me knowing, Junior? You should have learned as a kid, I always know." Nikolaj emerged from the darkness, his narrowed eyes glowing with condemnation.

KJ snorted. "And you should have figured out, I always know when you're following me. Your annoying, curious ass wouldn't be able to stay away from a secret meeting."

The Shaolin Monks glanced at each other but said nothing. They weren't known for their conversation skills; communicating with each other telepathically. Some thought they'd taken a vow of silence. KJ just understood most people's conversations weren't worth engaging.

"So, you think you found Svetlana, huh?" Nikolaj said, folding his arms across his large chest.

"I don't think, I know," KJ retorted.

"And now what do you propose to do about it?" Nikolaj fired back.

"I propose we go find her, and others who were taken, and bring them back."

Nikolaj rolled his eyes. "Why would we do that alone? Why wouldn't we talk with Alpha Base and the UN and all the people much more qualified than us to go get them?"

KJ rose to his feet, anger boiling up. "Because you know as well as I do, by the time this has made it through months of negotiation and planning, they'll send in the military. Our friends will all be killed. No one has a better chance of reaching them, but you can bet your perfect-grade-A-ass they won't send *us* in. We're too *important*. Besides, now they have their panties in a twist about the nuclear threat. It's gonna be red tape spaghetti."

"They haven't been our friends in nearly twenty years, Junior," Nikolaj said. "If the shooter was Svetlana, like you think, then they've done something to her. She's gone."

KJ banged a fist on the table and clenched his jaw. "Listen to me, you self-righteous prick. Twenty years ago, they didn't *have* any friends before your mom and my mom decided to try and save them. *Your* mom died trying to save them. How about we owe it to everyone on that mission to try?"

Nikolaj's expression softened. "I don't need to be reminded she died, asshole."

KJ exhaled out his anger. "Look man, the Nine Veils are planning something big. They waited seventeen years, then suddenly bust out of the closet like a repressed guy at Mardi Gras. That's not a coincidence and you know it. Whatever's up their sleeve, it's happening *now*. So, you go tell on me to mom if you like, but I'm going after Svetlana."

KJ felt Nikolaj's consciousness searching his, probably for some ulterior motive—for some selfish reason. The sensation waned as Nikolaj's gaze roved over each and every one of his fellow Stratum round the table.

"You all want to do this, don't you?" Nikolaj asked, though his tone suggested he knew the answer.

"We do," answered the girls. "We trust KJ."

Catherine nodded.

Nikolaj flicked his head, a silent question, to Leo and Igor.

They nodded once.

"Better this than all-out war?" Nikolaj said as if he'd read the monks' minds. He sighed heavily and took a seat opposite KJ. "Fine. We go look. But, if I get a whiff this is going south, I'm calling the cavalry, got it?"

KJ smirked and sat. "You got it, golden balls."

Nikolaj rubbed his crew-cut blond hair. "So, what's the move? How do we even locate her?"

"When we had our little tumble at the memorial, I felt her connect to me. Hell, I felt it all morning, at one hell of a distance. I think if we utilize our hive mind, we can zero in on her. Maybe even make contact."

"Wouldn't you have been able to do that before? Like in the

last twenty years?" Catherine asked.

"Not necessarily," Nikolaj said.

"If they'd shielded their minds somehow. But now they've come out, they're exposed," KJ finished.

"Careful, Junior, someone might remember there's a brain in there," Nikolaj said, a smug smirk once again plastered across his broad face.

"So, how," began Merry.

"Shall we do this?" Lex finished.

KJ pursed his lips. Use of the hive mind was rare these days. As children they would often move as one organism around Alpha base, communicating only telepathically or occasionally in Aymara—because it was fun to feel special and hide from the adults—but in their teens and early twenties diverging paths, careers, and responsibilities had meant they did this less and less. Still, the bond was always strong and while in Alpha Base every member of the Stratum could feel the telepathic tether to each and every one who resided there. It was comforting, and they certainly drew strength from their number.

"We do it old school," KJ said finally. "We hold hands and concentrate, like we used to."

The others looked nervously at each other, then shrugged and grabbed a seat. Their Huahuqui took a place by their side, then sat on the floor with their front legs placed on the table in readiness. KJ, Igor, Leo, Lex, Merry and Nikolaj each took one hand of the Huahuqui on either side, forming a complete circle. Everyone closed their eyes.

Click.

KJ opened one eye to see Catherine hovering over them, taking pictures.

"You mind?" he whispered. "We kinda got a thing going on here."

"Posterity," Catherine whispered.

"Noted. Just be aware, I'll be taking pictures of your posterity later."

Catherine smirked, but said nothing.

"Can we do this?" Nikolaj asked without opening his eyes.

"Sure," KJ said and settled back into concentration.

Though out of practice, connecting a small hive mind like this came back to him as if he did it every day. KJ's mind fluttered and crackled with firing neurons as everyone linked with him. Their consciousness tugged and pushed on his; but, much like daisy-chaining multiple CPUs, he could feel his processing power grow, the ability to entertain hundreds if not thousands of ideas simultaneously. He concentrated on his ordeal with Svetlana, on the lingering moment their eyes met. Next to him, K'awin warbled and padded on the spot though never broke the circle.

Svetlana's face, initially just a blur, came into sharp relief. The remnant of her invading KJs mind was shared between the friends as if it were a chunk of viral data to be replicated. Her shapely eyes, the long dark hair, and square jaw all seemed to morph back and forth with that of a child—*her* as a child—standing in a frigid squall on the Yamal Peninsula all that time ago.

There was no mistaking it was her, yet her mind was unlike any other KJ or his kin had encountered—two personalities, one lying atop the other masking the weaker one, controlling it. The group gathered their collective consciousness and pushed deeper into her psyche, pressing on the upper most personality and willing it to break.

The small child returned to the vision. *You can't be here,* the young girl said. *It's not safe.*

Svetlana, it's us. Your friends. KJ and Nikolaj. Do you not remember us? KJ projected.

The girl shook her head. *You shouldn't be here. It's not safe. She'll hear you.*

Who? Who Svetlana? KJ pressed.

The girls face suddenly contorted becoming that of the adult woman KJ had encountered, and then in a blinding flash of white and strange imagery her face was for an instant someone else entirely; a woman of sharp angles, cold eyes and blondish-grey hair. A shrill scream and the connection was severed.

Everyone jolted in their seat, breaking the circle and clasping their own heads.

"Jesus, fuck, what was that?" KJ said, his eyes scrunched together.

"I don't know," Nikolaj said through pressed teeth. "But it hurt."

"What did you see?" Catherine asked.

"Svetlana, it was Svetlana," KJ replied.

"You don't know that," Nikolaj said, rubbing his temples.

"How the fuck can you say that. You saw it. We all saw it," KJ protested, already rising from his seat.

"No, we saw *something*. You know the connection of minds is a tricky thing, Junior. Navigating the psyche, the imaginary from reality can be difficult. What we saw could have been cooked up in that brain of yours."

KJ clenched his jaw. "I ain't making shit up. That was Svetlana. I know it. You know it. Guys? Back me up here."

Merry and Lex looked to each other, and then gave an apologetic shrug.

"Sorry KJ," Merry said.

"It's difficult to tell," Lex finished.

"China."

KJ stared at Igor. The monks rarely spoke, and when they did, it was usually the absolute minimal amount of words possible.

"What?" KJ fired.

"China. She's in China," Igor replied as calm as a meadow stream, casting a sage gaze at each one of them.

"How the hell do you know that?" Nikolaj began.

"He's right," KJ interrupted. "When the connection broke, there was like, like a static. Residual memories randomly igniting. Images. Pools of water, but high up. Near the clouds. Green. And flowers. And farmers, Asian farmers in those funny hats. Igor— you're sure? China?"

Igor nodded.

Leo dipped his head in agreement.

"Yes!" KJ nearly shouted. That's what I'm fucking talking about. China. We go to China."

"We go to *China*," Nikolaj repeated. "Do you know how stupid you sound? China is massive, Junior. You're just going to drop into China and ask for directions? You're an idiot."

"Look, boy genius. If we can connect from here, then if I can get closer maybe the bond will be stronger. Ergo, I go to China. You can keep your boring ass here if you like. I don't need you. I have these guys. Right?" KJ looked expectantly at the other Stratum.

No one replied.

"Guys. C'mon, don't leave me hanging."

"I'll go," Catherine piped up from the corner.

KJ rolled his eyes. "You can't come."

"The hell I can't," she snapped back, the northern Irish accent becoming stronger with her irritation. "I'm the official journalist for the Stratum. Where you go, I go."

KJ pursed his lips, which then turned into a one-sided grin. "Fine, but I'm not paying for an extra hotel room—you have to bunk with me."

Catherine opened her mouth to retaliate but was interrupted by Lex.

"We'll go along," she said with a soft smile.

"For the ride," Merry completed.

KJ gave a triumphant bang on the table with his fist.

The monks looked to each other and held a silent gaze. KJ assumed they were communicating telepathically, since they had the ability to block others out. Another neat trick learned at the monastery. Eventually, they turned their attention to KJ and gave an imperceptible affirmation.

"Fine," Nikolaj conceded. "But, I'm going to keep your dumb ass out of trouble."

Location: somewhere in China

Svetlana's heart beat fiercely; so hard she could feel the pulse in her jugular. *What the hell had just happened?* she thought. She lay there on the damp mud, seemingly unable to move. Voices buzzed around above, and someone tugged at her arms, lifting her back to her feet. She swiveled her head around to make sense of her surroundings. The heat of anger subsided and was replaced with a longing pain in her chest.

The noise of her own thoughts faded and melded with the relentless whirr of the chopper rotors. Svetlana's attention snapped into sharp relief. She was home. The helicopter had landed, and she'd been climbing out when the mental-attack hit. Too far from the compound to be protected by the psychic barrier—the only thing that had kept the Phalanx hidden for so long.

In the heat haze, a tall slender woman stormed toward Svetlana. While her features were masked in the shimmer, Svetlana knew who it was: Victoria, the Phalanx Mother.

"What the hell is wrong with her?" Victoria yelled at the chopper pilot as she approached.

"We don't know Mother," he replied. "She just collapsed."

Victoria clasped a bony hand around Svetlana's arm, her claw like nails digging through the fabric. Heat rose in Svetlana's chest and her limbs tingled with adrenaline. The desire to rip the woman's head off was overwhelming. But, as every time these thoughts filled her mind, they were pressed away. What would Victoria do to her, or worse her Phalanx? Svetlana swallowed away her pride.

"Move your incompetent self," Victoria snarled.

Svetlana was tugged hard and pulled like a disobedient child toward the great temple. And much like a child, she ensured the progress was slow, dragging her feet and walking purposefully slowly along the main path, referred to by the Doyen as *Miccaotli*. The man's penchant for old Nahuatl permeated everything. Miccaotli meant 'Avenue of the Dead'; a famous path at Teotihuacan. In fact, he'd designed the whole compound as a tribute to the ancient Mesoamerican site. Covering more than twenty square kilometres, his complex—built on the Chinese mountainside—contained nearly 2,000 single-story apartment compounds, and a multitude of pyramids, plazas, and temples all interspersed with reflecting pools connected by channels for the

Huahuqui. The Doyen called his palace *Tocayōtla*, literally: namesake.

At the northern end of the Miccaotli was the Pyramid of the Moon. The second largest building, at more than forty meters high and 150 meters wide, played home to Victoria. It was the shrew-like woman's very own shrine. And as such it remained empty of any other person and Huahuqui. The cold bitch kept herself isolated. Refusing to be bonded to a Huahuqui, she remained outside of the Phalanx hive mind. It made Svetlana trust the woman even less. Yet despite such inner hatred she was unable to disobey Victoria's command.

They trudged along the wide stone path that cut its way through the sloped rice terraces and many reflecting pools of various sizes, toward the largest temple which sat just south of the Pyramid of the Moon. The colossal truncated step pyramid stood more than sixty meters high, 230 meters wide, and was adorned with numerous stone heads. At the site of Teotihuacan these heads were of Quetzalcoatl the feathered serpent, but here, in deference to the Nine Veils and their Phalanx, the carvings looked more like the Huahuqui.

As she began to climb the hundreds of steps to the top, Svetlana fixed her gaze on one of the stone heads. Its glossy, obsidian, eyes cast her convex reflection back. It seemed fitting: a distorted image that she knew was her, but somehow felt foreign. She'd stared at these inky black marbles many times as a child. They had been a fixing point when Mother publicly reprimanded her on the stairs of the Temple of Quetzalcoatl.

Their Phalanx Mother had tried all kinds of methods to establish control of the children and the Huahuqui, while still maintaining some lucidity so they were useful. LSD and other chemicals, hypnosis, sensory deprivation, isolation, verbal and even sexual abuse. Most of these techniques left the victims in a catatonic state at best. Svetlana couldn't pinpoint when the torture had stopped, but one day it just did. Svetlana later learned that the Doyen had stepped in and decreed that the Phalanx's devotion would come from understanding their place in the world and his ultimate vision. Their Mother had disagreed but was forced to find other means of control.

In the end, the trick to controlling the Phalanx had been a simple one. Something the Chinese and Koreans had perfected ages ago and put to great use on the American POWs of the Korean War: criticism and self-criticism. Constant put downs of the individual and friends by superiors, and then told to publicly announce one's own faults and the faults of one's comrades. The human psyche was evolutionarily built to crave approval of peers, of those seen as providers. The psychic connection between the Phalanx only served to strengthen the desire for acceptance among the group. Never being alone; always a collective, single minded belief—all amplified the technique a thousand-fold. And while every one of them knew they were being manipulated, nothing could be done to stop it. Fear of punishment, fear of punishment of their friends. Of course, the ultimate penalty being death.

Svetlana rubbed at the tattooed number nine on her neck, a chemical compound that could be activated by highly focused radio waves, forcing an exothermic reaction. In short: *boom*. The victim's head exploded.

As Svetlana reached the top of the stair case of the Quetzalcoatl's replica pyramid, Victoria violently spun her about face. From the summit, Svetlana could survey the whole southern half of the complex. The sun glinting off the pools' surfaces, the flower blossoms gently ruffling in the breeze. And hundreds of pairs of eyes—human and Huahuqui—stared back at her. She could feel the fear in them, the apprehension. Would she be flayed today? Would someone else? Would she be made to pick one of the Phalanx for further humiliation.

As it turned out, Victoria was fixated on Svetlana.

"Tell them," Victoria bellowed. "Tell them of your failure, Svetlana. Tell them of your shame. Your one task. The only thing asked of you, for the good of your Phalanx. For the good of your *nocnehuan*!"

Svetlana froze as hundreds of minds loosed their individual fears at her. The Phalanx were afraid of what was to come. She could not be the one to hurt them. "My *nocnehuan*—" she began.

"What is the meaning of this?" a deep, calm, and commanding voice came from behind.

Svetlana did not need to turn around. She knew it to be the Doyen. A serene man, with a narrow waist, broad shoulders, deep brown eyes, and thick black beard. His demeanor was careful, each word and movement planned and articulated in a way that made you believe him to be wiser than the God with whom he claimed to converse. It was said he was the only living human to have pierced all nine veils of enlightenment. For reasons beyond Svetlana's understanding, he had taken to her and favored her above all others. A fact Mother hated.

"I was punishing our daughter for her failure," Victoria replied, her tone sharp.

"Is that so?" replied the Doyen.

Svetlana felt a large paw of a hand slide over her shoulder and squeeze gently. Still she did not turn around.

"Do you believe that this is still necessary? Our Phalanx are true and loyal. Svetlana's task in Washington played out as it should have, according to the divine plan."

Victoria cut a scathing stare at Svetlana.

"You have yet to perfect your understanding of the Eighth Veil, Victoria," continued the Doyen. "If you ever wish to pierce the Ninth," he paused, as Svetlana knew he always did, to allow his words to sink in, "perfecting the pure energy known as love and thus become truly one with the Creator's formulations. By achieving this pure energy, one then fully understands charity and therein gains full comprehension of the universal plan of sacrifice, death, and redemption."

The hand on her shoulder squeezed again.

"Of course, Doyen," Mother said, though her words were bitten off in anger. She then gave a shallow bow, turned and stomped down the colossal staircase.

Svetlana turned to the Doyen, who stood in his usual white robes, Neith at his side. He said nothing, instead opening his arms. She stepped forward into his embrace, but it was neither warm nor comforting. He projected a fatherly, even spiritual, demeanor yet she only sensed a cold and calculating core. Perhaps this was as close as he got to love. She closed her eyes and tried to focus on the connections of her watching Phalanx. If she had them, everything would be fine.

Location: Connecticut, USA

Freya sat in her wheelchair, alone in her apartment. Dacey was curled up in a ball at her side. Only the light from the television illuminated the little Huahuqui's form which rose and fell with contented breathing. Freya stared at the flickering images with the sound off. It was another of those infomercials from Heston Tunbridge and his religious nutbags, the Sixth Sun. Once again, the crazy old man was touting for the weak minded to join him and his sheep at one of their numerous retreats in the mountains. Word was he'd managed to fund sites in Europe and Asia now. It was amazing to Freya that people would donate their hard-earned cash. Cults seemed to be a staple throughout history. But God forbid anyone give money to an orphanage or relief aid in a middle eastern war zone.

She clicked off the television and sat in the dark for a few moments, limbs shaking.

This was excruciating. Waiting. Alone. Helpless. No idea where her sons were. Her husband off on a mission and therefore not looking for her children. Even Nikolaj had not returned her calls or messages. The Nine Veils were back in the picture, now in control of the world's nuclear power stations. It was all going to hell in a hand basket and for the first time in Freya's life, she wasn't in the thick of it. Hell, she wasn't in the *thin* of it. Her Huntington's had sidelined her. Her only job now to wait for updates when people felt she should know.

"Fuck this," Freya said to herself, waking Dacey. "C'mon Freya. Think. Everyone else is working on the nuclear problem and finding where the Nine Veils are. What can you do?"

The room didn't answer. Dacey snuggled back down to sleep and once again Freya swam in the sea of her own thoughts; a feeling of self-loathing creeping over her.

The cell phone hummed in her pocket. Freya fished it out and stared at the screen, which simply said: withheld. She slid her finger across the unlock key. "Jonathan?"

"Hey babe, yeah, it's me. Can't talk long. Wanted to check in on

you. You okay?"

"No, I'm not okay. Have you heard from KJ or Nikolaj?"

There was a long silence on the other end.

"He took a jet," Jonathan said, finally.

"To Antarctica, yes I know."

"No," Jonathan interrupted. *"Another jet. On its way to Shanghai."*

"What? You have to go get him, Jonathan."

"Go get him? He's a grown man, Freya. And I'm on a mission. I can't just drop it to go looking for him." Jonathan paused, seemingly weighing his words. *"We have bigger problems."*

"Don't you dare give me a needs of the many speech, Spock. Or I swear to God I will run you down in my wheelchair."

"Look," Jonathan said. *"He'll get picked up by the Chinese when he lands. From what we can tell, he's got Nikolaj with him and a few of the Stratum. He'll be okay. When I'm done here, I'll go get him, okay?"*

"No, not okay. What the hell is he doing? What's he searching for?"

Jonathan sighed. *"Hell if I know."*

"I want to go to Shanghai."

"That won't help. The Chinese will turn him around once he's there. He's got no clearance."

"Then I want to go to Alpha Base. Maybe I can figure out from there what he was looking for. Or at least be there to kick his ass when he gets back."

"Fine. I'll arrange it. The transport will come to get you and put you on the jet in a few hours. Can you keep out of trouble 'til then?"

Freya snorted. "Of course."

"Good. I'll call again when I can. Lov—"

Freya cut the call.

Jonathan was on a mission, and the mission came first. It always came first. If Kelly was still here, he'd have car jacked someone and be on his way to the far East now, hot on the trail of his son. The slight smile on Freya's lips slipped away. Kelly wasn't here. He was dead. For being reckless. Just like his son was being now. Sadness melted into guilt for thinking of Kelly. Jonathan was a good man. Her husband. And right. The man was always right. "Stop it Freya," she said aloud. "KJ's fine. The Chinese will turn him around. Just get to Antarctica so you can be there when KJ gets back, then murder him yourself."

Location: On the G800, somewhere over Asia

"We're gonna what?" Nikolaj yelled.

"Jump," KJ repeated. "You think we were just going to land in Shanghai? We'd get picked up immediately. The whole friggin' world is on high alert. You know that. The AI will bring the jet in after we're gone."

"This is insane, Junior! If I'd known this is what you were planning, I would never have agreed." Panic danced on the surface of Nikolaj's eyes. Chernoukh's black gills ruffled as the Huahuqui felt his symbiote's fear.

KJ grinned while slipping into the straps of his parachute. "He's afraid of heights," he said to Catherine.

"He's not the only one, you arse," Catherine fired back, tying her orange locks back. "If we don't die doing this, I'm going to kill you."

From under the seat, KJ pulled another 'chute, this one specifically designed for the Huahuqui. He slipped it over K'awin's back and clipped it securely around her fore- and hindlegs. "There," he said with grunt, ensuring the fit was tight. "That'll do it."

"This won't work. We're too high. The AI flies a specific course," Nikolaj said, shaking his head.

KJ simply raised one eyebrow and gave his most smug grin.

Nikolaj sighed. "You messed with the AI."

"Of course I did," KJ said, then winked at Merry and Lex.

The girls tried to hide their smiles.

"Junior, if you would apply half of that damn brain of yours—" Nikolaj started.

"Yeah, well be glad I don't, otherwise I would have figured out a way to give you a sense of humor."

"Listen here, ass—" Nikolaj started.

KJ held up his finger and looked at his watch. "Five, four, three, two, hold on to your pantyhose."

The jet dropped making everyone flail for support.

"Express elevator to hell, going down!" KJ yelled.

"You and your damn 80s movies, KJ," Catherine moaned, her voice strained as she struggled to hang on to the nearest seat.

"Okay boys and girls, time to go," KJ said, pulling on the emergency exit and popping the door out of the frame.

Cold air blasted into the cabin. Everyone pulled goggles over their eyes, and then clipped their Huahuqui to their own gear.

"This is bullshit Junior. I told you if things got out of hand I'd call in the cavalry." Nikolaj held up his satellite-linked phone.

KJ snatched it from Nikolaj's hand, threw it out the door, watched it fall away toward the ground and then looked back to Nikolaj with a mock look of sorrow.

"You asshat."

"No time to cry, big brother," KJ said, then grabbed hold of K'awin and jumped through the doorway into the atmosphere.

As he plummeted backward through the sky toward the dense green below, KJ watched the tiny specs that were his friends leap out after him. He counted them off guessing the first two were Igor and Leo, clutching their Huahuqui. Then was probably Merry and Lex, with their symbiotes. Next must have been Catherine. And then nothing. No Nikolaj. The air rushed past, deafening him. KJ clamped K'awin to his chest and stared at the plane as it rapidly shrank away.

C'mon, don't let me down, KJ thought.

The alarm on KJs watch sounded. He had to pull the 'chute.

He flipped onto his front, held K'awin with one arm and pulled on the cord. The line snatch halted his fall as the canopy left its packing container and began to expand, and then almost immediately the inflation force lifted him as the 'chute pressurized. The deafening rush of air subsided. As he floated down, admiring the lush greenery of the forest, he felt decidedly peaceful. Even K'awin seemed to be enjoying herself, giving a little warble of delight at being pushed around by the breeze.

Beside KJ, a few hundred feet away, Merry, Lex, Igor, and Leo floated toward the forest. But, there was no sign of Nikolaj… or Catherine. Where was she? KJ frantically scanned in all directions. His heart cramped. A hundred feet below, Catherine was freefalling, her parachute unopened.

"Fuck!" KJ yelled. "It didn't open." *Guys, Catherine's chute didn't open, it didn't open!* KJ projected out to the others.

Didn't her emergency chute work? Merry replied.

You have to do something, Lex finished.

Mother fucker. "Okay girl, we gotta go after her, okay?"

K'awin trilled in agreement.

KJ pulled on another cord that released his primary chute. Immediately he plummeted, the alarm on his watch screaming that he was now past the safe zone. He tilted forward and streamlined his body, aiming himself at the flailing Catherine. Beyond her, the forest canopy hurtled toward him.

He stretched out his arms, his fingers straining.

The ground seemed to rush faster at them the closer they came.

K'awin, being slightly closer reached out a forelimb and managed to grasp one of Catherine's shoulder straps. The Huahuqui yanked on it, pulling the Irish woman to her and KJ, who immediately swung his legs around and clamped on.

The reporter screamed something, but it was lost to the roar of rushing air. He pulled on Catherine's main shoot handle. Nothing. Then on the emergency shoot cord. Again, nothing. KJ cursed, struggling to hold on to Catherine as they tumbled through the sky. Doing the only thing he could think of, KJ clipped his own gear to Catherine's, held on to K'awin and pulled on his Huahuqui's chute.

They jerked twice as the canopy opened. KJ and Catherine flipped into an inverted position, hanging from K'awins's gear. Even with the chute open, their descent was too fast. With arms covering their heads, KJ and Catherine crashed into the trees—branches snapping and catching on their skin and clothes.

The parachute snagged in the upper canopy, jerking them to a hard stop. The clip broke and both KJ and Catherine tumbled through yet more tree arms and branches before landing in a heap on the forest floor.

KJ lay there in a patch of broken bamboo, panting, staring up through the foliage. Sunlight cut through the gaps, making the wet atmosphere sparkle. Above, K'awin dangled from the caught 'chute.

Catherine leaned over him, blocking out the sun.

KJ propped himself up on his elbows. "You're ok—"

A punch landed square in his mouth, knocking the back of his head into the earth.

"Mother fucker, what was that for?" he asked, rubbing his face.

"For making me jump out of a plane and almost die, asshole," Catherine snapped then slumped back to the leafy ground.

KJ continued to stare upward at his Huahuqui fruitlessly struggling to escape her gear. "Feel better?" he asked without turning to Catherine.

"A bit," Catherine wheezed.

The snap of branches made KJ sit bolt upright.

"KJ, you're alive!" Merry said, walking toward him, a huge smile on her face.

"And so is Catherine," Lex finished.

"But, your leg!" They both exclaimed in unison.

"Huh?" KJ looked down and for the first time saw that the right leg of his cargo pants was torn open and a good six inches of thick bamboo was protruding from his thigh, blood running freely from the hollow. "Well would you look at that?" Suddenly dizzy, KJ flopped to his back, head fuzzy.

K'awin sidled up to him and nuzzled his leg.

"Hey," KJ slurred. "How did you get down?"

"I let her down," came a voice from across the clearing.

KJ focused on the source. Nikolaj came stomping over in heavy boots.

"So, you *did* jump, you chicken shit—"

KJ's head jolted backward as yet another punch landed across his jaw.

"Hey, what the fuck? Will people quit punching me?"

"That was for almost getting Catherine killed, idiot," Nikolaj snapped back.

"She's alive ain't she? Anyway, it's me suffering here." KJ rubbed his aching jaw and pointed at the large bamboo straw exiting his leg, leaking blood onto his pants.

"Right, well let's get that thing out and your leg closed up so you can do your super healing thing," Nikolaj said.

"You're just jealous you can't do it," KJ fired back, wheezing.

"I'm not jealous right now, Kelly Junior," Nikolaj replied, then tugged the bamboo free.

KJ yelped and clamped onto his thigh, holding the wound closed. "Fucking asshole," he seethed between his teeth.

A large, bear-like hand clamped down over KJ's hand and pressed with an inhuman strength, keeping pressure on the wound. KJ looked up to see Leo peering down at him. The monk said nothing, but KJ felt the weight of Leo's consciousness in his mind: they were to set up here for the night.

"So, uh, we should probably regroup and stay the night, before we move on," KJ said.

"Here?" Nikolaj spat. "And just where is *here*?"

"Laos," KJ replied calmly, his hand now losing circulation as Leo kept pressure.

"Laos?" Merry and Lex said in unison.

"What the hell are we doing in Laos?" Nikolaj nearly yelled.

KJ shook his head. "For being the clever one, you're dumb sometimes. You think we could parachute into China? The jet will land in Shanghai, more than two thousand kilometers away. Needed to put a lot of distance between us, it, and anyone who comes looking for us. I want as much time as possible." He glanced down at his numb hand, then up at Leo. "I think you can let go now, pal."

Leo complied.

KJ quickly shook the blood back into his fingers sucking air through his teeth. Just as he had predicted, the leg wound was already starting to heal. Still, he had lost quite a lot of blood. Trekking through the jungle now would not be a good idea.

"And where are we meant to stay?" Nikolaj's frustration was growing. "Any equipment we may have had was on the damn plane."

"C'mon man, give me some credit." KJ raised an arm for Leo to hold and was yanked to his feet. "We're not too far from a WCS trail. Just up ahead should be some bamboo sleeping nests suspended in the trees. You think I'd land us in the middle of nowhere?"

Catherine stormed off ahead. "You think of *everything*," she called over her shoulder.

"I try!" KJ called, and began limping after her, K'awin in tow.

The others followed behind.

CHAPTER FIVE

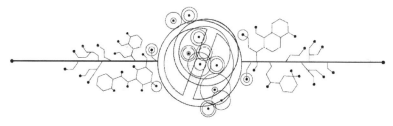

Location: Tocayōtla, somewhere in China

Victoria paced inside her sleeping quarters, buried underneath her vast temple. A simple room with a metal bed, a doorless wardrobe, and an uncomfortable-looking chair. She stormed into the sparse en-suite bathroom, her angry reflection in the cabinet mirror growing larger with her approach. She placed both hands on the cold, white sink and stared into her own icy eyes. She had aged slower than most, thanks to her spliced DNA. But her inner youth had been sapped—no stolen—by men like Kelly Graham, by the US government, by the Doyen.

The mirror shattered as Victoria slammed her forehead into it. In the remains of the silvered glass, she watched tributaries of blood meander down her face. A thousand small gashes leaked her life away. Of course, within a few minutes they already began to heal.

Victoria focused on the wounds as they sewed themselves closed. If it weren't for her ability to heal, she might die from such injuries. No one cared about her. After years of loyal service, the Doyen still favored that defiant little bitch Svetlana over Victoria. Long ago, he listened. The explosive tattoos had been her idea. The army created from Russian orphans had been created on her advice—an army needed to both capture the Huahuqui and form the Phalanx. Yet he grew weak. His love for the Huahuqui and the children blinding him to their purpose as tools in the greater plan. Victoria had wanted absolute control. A decade ago, she'd achieved it, only to have the Doyen dismiss her work as out of alignment with the Nine Veils philosophy.

The monitor flickered, the image temporarily freezing and sliding across the glass, before resuming the live feed from inside the makeshift laboratory. A young boy sat on a steel chair in the middle of the dusty room comprised of sand-colored stone and lit by a single unshaded bulb hanging from the ceiling. A simple, dirty and tattered garment was draped about his skinny frame, leaving his bony arms and legs bare. Lank black hair obscured his face. In a wire cage by his side lay the gaunt form of a Huahuqui. Even in the grainy image, it was clear the animal's skin and gills were desiccated and brittle.

Victoria glanced at the Doyen, who stood next to her, arms folded, and brow furrowed. "Watch. Just watch," she said.

The Doyen didn't reply, fixated on the jittery monitor feed.

"Unlike our army comprised of Russian orphans," Victoria continued, "the Nenets' bond to the Huahuqui and exposure to the Americans means they are not so easily manipulated. Even the use of the explosive tattoo does not seem to curb their defiance. Their own death means little to them."

The Doyen met her cold gaze; but expressed no emotion. No look of eager anticipation as she had hoped. "What kind of control are you talking about, Victoria?" he asked.

"I began with the basics, retreading the steps of Project

MKUltra; a covert operation carried out by the CIA in the 1950s that lasted nearly 20 years," Victoria said. "LCD, barbiturates, amphetamines, hypnosis, sound therapy, electroconvulsive therapy."

The leader of the Nine Veils shuffled uncomfortably. "We should not need such methods. The Huahuqui are divine. They will understand the great plan, and thus so will the children."

Victoria snorted. "And yet they are yet to perform as our Russian army does." She ran a handkerchief across her lips. "Just as the CIA, I had little success. Subjects died when exposed to the mind-altering drugs and other torturous techniques. Sent mad, the Huahuqui drove their heads into the walls until their skulls cracked, their bonded children suffering from phantom injuries to the brain which could only be attributed to their telepathic connection. It was an abject failure. Until now."

Victoria slipped a hand-held radio from her belt and keyed it up. "Send it in."

On the screen a door opened, and another figure entered—a young man wearing riot armor and brandishing a two-meter-long staff with syringes attached to both ends. He inched forward, slid the first syringe through the bars of the cage and jabbed the needle into the flesh of the Huahuqui. The liquid inside drained into the animal. He yanked it out, twirled the staff 180 degrees and quickly jabbed the young man in the thigh. Again, the syringe emptied.

Victoria held her breath, though not so visibly as to show her keenness.

The concoction in the syringes contained *The Devil's Breath*, a drug popular among organ thieves in South America, derived from the seeds of the *Borrachero* tree. The active ingredient, *scopolamine,* had the ability to rob people of their free will, making them susceptible to suggestion. The problem had been dosing correctly—just enough for a lasting effect without killing them, little enough to allow them to still be useful. One gram of The Devil's Breath could kill up to fifteen people. Throwing in a little hallucinogenic provided the visions everyone believed they'd see once penetrating the last veil. Today, she'd had an epiphany and added one more ingredient. She called her creation: *The Eye of God.*

The Huahuqui in the cage began to convulse, its thrashes jolting the cage left and right. The youth's bound limbs jerked against the restraints, his fight becoming more vigorous until he finally threw his head back and let out a terrible scream through a gnarled mouth. The room became silent and still.

The armored soldier looked up to the camera, waiting for instruction.

Victoria studied the monitor then simply said into the radio, "proceed."

The guard gingerly stepped up to the cage and unlocked it, then pulled a revolver from his belt and placed it into the limp hand of the boy. He curled the young man's fingers around the weapon to ensure a weak grip, then backed off a few paces.

Slowly, the Huahuqui crawled from its cage, dragging its belly across the dusty floor. With each step of its alligator-like gait, the animal seemed to grow a little stronger, a little more lucid. In the chair, the prisoner's head lolled but steadily his neck gained strength and his back straightened until he was upright, chest rising and falling with quick breaths.

The Doyen turned to Victoria, his eyes wide.

Victoria pressed a key on the makeshift dash in front of her that read *lock*, then pulled on a microphone stalk so that the foam tip aligned with her lips. "Zoika, my little symbiotic friend," she began.

The Huahuqui cocked its head at hearing the voice over the intercom.

"The guard, tear his armor off," Victoria finished.

Without hesitation, the creature pounced, landing on the guard's chest with all four limbs. Together, they crashed into the stony ground, a cloud of dust puffing up around them. The Huahuqui began clawing at the man's chest and arms, ripping the ballistic gear from him as he fruitlessly struggled underneath the animal's weight and strength.

"Enough," Victoria commanded.

Zoika climbed off and paced back and forth like a trapped tiger—its stare never leaving the guard, who had scrambled to the exit and was banging his fists on a door that would not open.

Victoria pulled on the microphone again, licked her lips and said: "Nyalku. Shoot him."

The frail boy rose from his chair and leveled the revolver at the guard who had no time to beg for his life. Nyalku pulled the trigger and instantly the man's chest peeled open. He slumped into a bloody heap against the doorframe.

The Doyen stared at the screen, still agog.

"Good," Victoria said. "Now shoot Zoika."

Nyalku turned to the animal, pointed the barrel at her head and blasted a whole through her eye. Zoika flopped to the floor and leaked blood from her open face into the dirt.

"No!" the Doyen screamed.

"And now you," Victoria said. "Put the gun to you head and pull the trigger."

Nyalku lifted the gun to his temple.

The Doyen had grabbed the microphone. "No, Nyalku stand

down! Throw the weapon away!"

"What are you doing?" Victoria spat.

"This is an abomination. The Huahuqui are sacred. This must end now. Get him out of there. Find another way." The Doyen stormed from her laboratory, believing his word was final.

It wasn't.

Victoria wiped the blood from her face and watched the last of the wounds zip closed. She *had* found another way, but not abandoned her greatest work. Even all those years ago, she had known her creation would be needed. And now, at the penultimate stage she was right. There could be no resistance to her vision. From the Doyen, Svetlana, or anyone else.

Location: Buenos Aires, Argentina

Jonathan stared out of the Chevrolet Suburban window, lost in thought. Freya was so angry he hadn't chased after KJ. But, how could he? The greatest terrorist threat ever known had suddenly emerged from nearly two decades of silence and somehow taken over every nuclear power station on the planet. More than four hundred reactors exploding simultaneously would throw a radioactive cloud into the atmosphere that would likely kill anything on the Earth's surface—slowly and painfully. The CIA were looking for the Nine Veils, and his NSA colleagues were tasked with regaining control of the stations. His mission, though a long shot, was to find a way to *beat* the Nine Veils. As much as Freya—and he—hated it, KJ would have to wait.

Early morning traffic outside the Federal Government Office on Avenue Rivadavia had slowed his progress to a crawl. Across the narrow street sat on an intersection was the main building of the AFI. It was an unassuming, brown stone building with rows and rows of square windows and arches on the ground floor—just like every other structure on the adjoining Avenue 25 de Mayo. Where US Federal agency buildings were heavily fortified, here one could be forgiven for passing by it never knowing who, or what, was inside.

To Jonathan, the lack of security seemed a little arrogant given that the rebel group, *Resistencia Ancestral Mapuche*, had increased its attack frequency in the seventeen years following the revelation of the Huahuqui's existence. RAM believed the Huahuqui to be *Ngen-ko*—water spirits in their religion—and thus a sign that their mission to make Chile and Argentina a Mapuche nation was divine. Frankly, he'd rather be anywhere but here, but duty called and as always Jonathan answered.

He took a deep breath and held it for a moment, then opened the door of the SUV. Before his security contingent could argue, Jonathan jumped down to the road and worked his way through stationary yellow and black cabs and beat up Toyotas, dodging the menagerie of motorcycles that jostled through the gaps. Teller glanced back to see two of his newly assigned team, Higgs and Hicks, hop down and chase after him.

After announcing himself at the reception desk, and confirming his meeting with the Director General of the AFI, Jonathan and his men were escorted through security—being made to hand over their weapons for inspection and pass through the mandatory metal detectors. As Jonathan stood there, arms wide for the pat down, he surveyed the inside: museum-like, with potted plants and paintings of confident-looking Argentinian leaders adorning the walls.

Jonathan knew better.

The AFI had a long history of shady deals and its fair share of corruption allegations. Initially it was formed to arrange the post-war transport of Nazi war criminals to Argentina—the whole reason Jonathan was here. Since the 1940s it had changed remit and even name several times. In the last few decades alone it had been known as SIDE, SI and now the AFI, been involved in domestic spying on a scale that rivalled the level seen in Eastern Europe before the fall of the Berlin wall and was implicated in collusion with Iranian-led terrorist attacks.

"Mr. Teller," came a heavily Argentinian-Spanish-accented voice, breaking Jonathan's train of thought. "To what do I owe the pleasure of the NSA's most highly regarded officer? A key member of Alpha Base as well!"

Jonathan received and holstered his Glock, then turned to the balding man who approached with two security contingent—one with a thick beard, the other thinner with a moustache. The Director General of the AFI, Juan Peron, was short and with a square head and dark narrow eyes. Known to be a charismatic man who laughed a lot, he was still shrewd and made few public appearances. Leaving his office to meet Jonathan was already suspicious.

"Director Peron," Jonathan started, and offered a hand. "Nice of you to meet us at the front door."

Peron shook Jonathan's hand vigorously. "It is not every day we have a celebrity in the building. At least you are a celebrity in the spy world, Mr. Teller." The Director winked and gave a sly smile.

"Indeed."

"Shall we walk?" Peron asked.

"Sure," Jonathan said.

The two men started a slow walk to the staircase.

"I like to take the stairs," Peron said. "Keep these old legs working."

"Be my guest," Jonathan replied, then said, "Security seems a little light."

The Director shrugged. "If you are referring to RAM, their *attacks* tend to be nothing more than roadblocks and demonstrations. They don't have the *cajones* to man an actual offensive strike."

"That's not the way I hear it," Teller said. "Didn't they hit the Palace of Justice not two weeks ago? Took a judge hostage, no?"

"For six hours, Mr. Teller. It was always in our control."

"Uh huh," Teller replied.

"Would you like to tell me why you are here?"

"I need to have a poke around your vault, or wherever you keep your Nazi hoard," Jonathan said as the two men ascended the stairs, security in tow.

Peron stopped mid stride, half way up the staircase, a quizzical expression etched into his leathery face. "*Que?*" he said. "Nazi hoard?"

"Yeah. You know, the big ol' archive of crap you guys keep in storage from after the war. You know you have it. We know you have it. So, let's cut the bullshit and get to the bit where you give me access."

The Director continued to climb the stairwell, talking without looking at Teller. "If we had such an archive, which we don't Mr. Teller, might I know what NSA would be looking for? What possible use could you have for trinkets more than 80 years old?"

"I can't tell you that," Jonathan said. "But what I can tell you, is that it may help to fight the bastards who just took control of all the nuclear power stations. You have three, if I'm not mistaken."

"Four," Peron replied, opening the door to his office. "One came online last month. Our people are working on the problem. We will have control again soon."

Both sets of security waited outside.

The office felt regal. Dark-wood shelving filled with red and green leather-bound books, Chesterfield couches worn but cared for, gold gilding on anything that could be gilded, and of course an oversized oil painting of Peron himself hanging behind his desk.

"And whatever it is you seek, you believe it can help in this situation?" the Director asked.

"It might."

"A little trust would go a long way, Mr. Teller," Peron said, sarcasm dripping from his words, as he sat behind his large timber desk.

"The AFI aren't known for being… trustworthy, Director," Jonathan replied, leaning back into his chair.

"And the NSA aren't supposed to have field agents, Mr. Teller. But you seem to have enjoyed many a military flight."

"Touché." Jonathan considered his approach. There was no way the Director was going to just give him access, and if he told Peron what he was looking for then he'd *not* get access and the Argentinians would have it. Right now, he just needed to know *where* it might be. "How about this. You let me look, and if I find it, I'll tell you."

"You say what you are looking for may be able to stop those who are now in control of the reactors, yes? But, it seems to me this may have more to do with our fishy friends, no?"

Teller narrowed his eyes. He was now convinced the orb was here, or at least in Buenos Aires.

"Come, Mr. Teller. We are all friendly spies here. We know what you know."

"Then you already know what I'm looking for," Teller replied.

Peron's grin grew into a gap-toothed smile. "*Touché.*"

"Look we can play this horseshit spy game all day. Or you can just give me what I came for. The US government would be willing to pay."

"Let's say I know what you're looking for. I couldn't give it to you, anyway."

"Fuck sake–"

The building shook, vibrations reaching from deep within the foundations and pulsing up the walls. Both Teller's and Peron's security contingent burst into the room.

"Must be a breech," one of the American's said. "We need to leave."

The only door in or out was closed and locked, the four security men pointing their hand guns at it. Gun fire rattled from somewhere on a lower floor. Peron and Teller crouched down.

"Do we know who it is?" Teller said, pulling the slide on his Glock.

"*Resistencia Ancestral Mapuche,*" replied one of Peron's men.

Teller turned to the Director. "No *cajones*, eh?"

"If they've bothered to do this, then they are here for you, Mr. Teller. An Alpha Base operative with direct access to the Huahuqui. To their *Ngen-ko.*"

Teller paused. Peron was an asshole, but he wasn't wrong. The likelihood was they *were* here for *him*. "Shit. We need to get the hell out of here." Teller grabbed a handheld radio from his belt and keyed it up. "Delta Six we have a hostile gorilla in the play pen. Do you have eyes on? Copy."

"Delta Six. We Don't have eyes on. Permission to enter playpen. Copy."

Jonathan turned to Peron's men. "Any idea how many we're dealing with?"

"No," said the bearded one. "I saw maybe ten or twelve. Could be more."

"We're penned in," Teller said.

"There's an escape tunnel. Behind the bookcase," Peron interjected. "We can leave through that."

Teller nodded then keyed up the radio again. "Negative, Delta Six. Gorilla could be huge. We have an out. Copy."

"Copy team leader. Confirm extraction point."

"Peron where does the exit—"

Peron was already standing and shifting toward the rear of the room.

"No, get down!" Teller yelled.

The tinkling of broken glass and the thud of the bullet hitting Peron in the chest was separated by microseconds. He crumpled to the floor, blood spreading through his white shirt and pooling around his shoulder.

"Fuck!" Teller yelled, crawling toward the Director. He pressed a hand over the wound, which made Peron yell out in pain. With his free hand, Jonathan activated the radio. "Delta Six we have a sniper, South side. Confirm shoot to kill. Take that fucker out!"

The voice over the radio confirmed the order, but Teller wasn't listening. He inched closer to Peron's face, whilst maintaining pressure on the wound. "Tell me. Tell me where you keep the stash. I know you have it."

Peron coughed and gurgled blood as he tried to answer. "I told you, I can't help you."

"Seriously? Even now? You're gonna die, Peron. Just tell me."

The Director shook his head in short uncomfortable jerks. "No," he coughed. "You don't understand. We don't ha—have it. We sol—sold it. For oil."

Jonathan's stomach knotted. "Sold what?"

"Everything we had accumulated after the w—war." Peron hacked again, forcing more blood through his nose and the gaping wound in his chest. "They came to u—us, asking."

"Sir we have to move," Hicks said.

"Sold it for *oil*? To who?" Jonathan pressed.

"Th—the Ir—anians. After Alpha Base was... set up. They t-took it all." Peron wheezed a final exhale then lay still, staring off into space.

"Fuck, fuck, fuck!" Teller yelled.

The gun fire grew louder. Jonathan surmised the guerrillas must have made it to the upper floors.

"Sir?" pressed Higgs.

"Team leader, sniper is down. Repeat sniper is down. Copy."

"Ok we go. Stay away from the windows. Keep down."

The secret escape route was exactly where Peron said it would be. Dragging the book case away from the wall revealed a metal door and a keypad. The moustached guard punched in a number and the door popped open. Teller and his men were ushered inside.

"Go," said the moustached man. "Take the stairs down into the tunnel. It will lead out to Plaza de Mayo. There is no code to exit."

"Delta Six. Extraction point Plaza de Mayo. Copy," Teller said into the radio.

"Copy good, team leader. On our way."

Before Teller could ask any more questions, the door was slammed in his face. Standing in the dimly lit stairwell, Jonathan regained his composure, took the vanguard—Glock in hand—and made his way down.

The tunnel wasn't long and soon Teller and his men were confronted by another stairwell. He stared up, following its length to a simple metallic ladder, bolted to the damp wall, that led up to a large panel in the ceiling. If the panel led directly out into the open, they would likely get their head taken off by a sniper.

Teller brought the radio up. "Delta Six, we are at the extraction point. Seems to be a plate in the floor. Location within Plaza de Mayo unknown. Do you have eyes on?"

Only static.

"Shit. Must be too much metal between us and them." Teller stared at the panel again. "Guess we go up."

"Let me sir," said Hicks.

Teller nodded and held his breath hoping his teammate wouldn't take a bullet to the eye the minute he cracked the exit plate.

Hicks climbed the stairs, followed by Teller and finally Higgs. Together they ascended the ladder until Hicks reached the panel in the ceiling. It was locked with a thick steel bar attached to a wheel. Hicks holstered his weapon and grabbed the wheel. A quick jerk and it squealed loose. With a full 180 degree turn of the wheel, the bar slid away. Hicks pulled his Glock, pressed his shoulder into the heavy metal panel and shoved it until the gap was big enough for him to peer out.

"What do you see?" whispered Teller.

"Crosses," Hicks called down. "White crosses. It's brought us up in the middle of a damn cemetery."

"Classy," Teller said. "Is it clear?"

"A few civilians but looks clear."

Teller sucked in a breath and let it go slowly. "Let's go."

Hicks shoved the plate hard with his shoulder until it flipped back onto the grass. Quickly, he scrambled out and took a defensive position, scanning the perimeter. Teller and Higgs followed. The sun was bright, temporarily blinding Jonathan. He imagined that in those few seconds he'd be gunned down. But as the world came back into focus, he was relieved to be without bullet holes.

Out in the open, they were met by the gasps and horrified faces of a smattering of civilians. Teller took stock of their surroundings and realized they had emerged from an actual grave, complete with its own white cross. To the onlookers the dead had risen—with Glocks.

"Sorry folks," he said. "State business." He then keyed up his radio. "Delta Six, confirm the cemetery as extraction point. Get us the hell out of here."

"Copy good, team leader. Two minutes out."

"Now what?" Higgs said.

Teller sighed. "Now I need to talk to the President. Someone needs to have a chat with the Iranians."

CHAPTER SIX

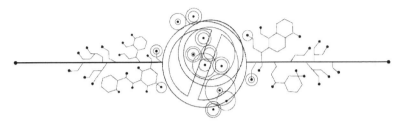

Location: Vietnamese border, Laos.

KJ and his crew marched through Laos' forest of thick bamboo and lush ferns. The group made their journey in silence, eagerly watching for the next wonderful animal to emerge from the greenery; Stump-tailed Macaques, Asian Antelope, Silver Pheasants, or perhaps Lao leaf monkeys. A gathering of marigold butterflies fluttered past. Though he had never been in Laos before, KJ felt at home. Much like his father had in such places, at least according to his mother.

KJ munched on another helping of *kao tom*—purple rice and peanuts wrapped in banana palm – a snack Igor and Leo had obtained from a village a few kilometers back. Though more than eighty languages were spoken in Laos, a variation of mandarin was spoken by descendants who migrated to Laos from Sichuan and Guangdong provinces. The monk brothers' time in the Buddhist monastery had been useful for more than skills in martial arts; they were able to barter for food.

Leo and Igor paused again at a post, laid a little pile of rice and moved on. Even their Huahuqui gave a slight bow of respect before following their human companions.

Catherine and KJ lagged at the back, K'awin waddling

between them.

"What are they doing?" Catherine asked.

Not wanting to question whether Catherine had forgiven him for the parachute incident, he duly answered: "It's a spirit post. They're leaving an offering to ensure we have a safe journey."

"You really are a boy genius, aren't you?" Catherine said. "It's a shame you're so damn pig headed."

"Hey, that's not—"

"Check it out!" Nikolaj called back. "Anyone feeling hot?"

Catherine and KJ caught up and pushed through a particularly dense patch of gnarled liana knots, adorned with white and orange orchids, to reveal a cascading spring water that had collected into pools. Nikolaj, Merry, and Lex were already stripping down and splashing into the cool water, their four-legged symbiotes chirruping in delight at relief from the heat.

"You coming in?" Catherine asked, slipping the pack from her shoulders.

"I don't think so," KJ replied, his brow knitted.

Catherine laughed. "Since when is Kelly Graham Junior shy? What's up? You put on a few pounds?"

"Fuck off," KJ snapped back. "It's not that. It's just …"

K'awin looked up at KJ and gave her saddest, wide-eyed expression, padding on the spot.

KJ peered down at her desperate face. "I'm not trying to be awkward, I'm just, it's just—"

A massive splash threw so much water out it nearly drowned KJ where he stood. Irritated and drenched, he turned to see Igor and Leo standing shirtless and waist deep in the pool with enormous childish grins on their faces. KJ sighed and flicked his head at the water. "Go on then."

K'awin didn't need to be told twice. She bounded in and crashed beneath the surface. KJ's heart warmed as he felt her joy. In fact, for a moment, he felt all of them happy. He smiled to himself and decided he might as well join them, given he was drenched anyway. He dropped his pack and wriggled free of his shirt and boots—hopping around on one foot as one simply wouldn't come off. Finally standing only in his shorts, KJ prepared to dive in.

Something whipped past his ear and twanged as it struck a bamboo stalk.

KJ hit the earth with a thud, covering his head. "What the fuck?"

The Huahuqui disappeared under the pool's surface.

"Don't move," whispered Catherine. "We've got company."

KJ slowly raised his head enough to see.

Standing among the ferns and banana fronds were the weathered faces of presumably Laotian locals. A few held long bows, arrows notched, but most clasped old, heavy-looking machine guns. Their modern clothing, sportswear, and beaten up sneakers were juxtaposed to the raw nature of the forest.

"I think we were dipping our giblets in their drinking water," KJ whispered through still lips, like a ventriloquist.

Why are you whispering, idiot? Just project. Nikolaj's voice penetrated KJ's mind.

Oh yeah, forgot.

What do, Merry started.

We do? Lex finished.

We treat them with respect, and try to communicate, Nikolaj offered.

We don't have time for this shit, KJ interjected. *K'awin!*

KJ's Huahuqui exploded from the pool and landed on all fours. A blue miasma formed around her and KJ, their eyes becoming iridescent topaz.

The Laotians reeled and fired their weapons in all directions.

KJ hit the ground, again, bracing for the white-hot pain of lead ripping through his body. But nothing came. He slowly opened his eyes to see Merry, Lex, Kroshka, and Kiska standing on the bank of the spring. Munitions arced off an invisible barrier in front of the women—a transparent dome of telekinetic energy. Their parlor trick usually reserved for beating him at dodgeball. He'd hoped it would work on bullets too.

"Thank fuck for that." KJ huffed, climbing to his feet.

"How are they doing that?" Catherine shouted, while scrambling to her camera gear, apparently unafraid of the onslaught of firepower and completely unaware she was wearing only her very wet and near-transparent undergarments.

"I wish I knew," KJ said. "Never been able to figure out how they do that. But I know how I do this." He clenched his fists, connected his mind to K'awin, and forced his way into the men's psyche, compelling them to halt their onslaught.

The Laotians continued to jabber among themselves but were unable to fire their weapons.

"Put the guns down," KJ commanded.

"I don't think they speak English, Junior," Nikolaj said.

"You gonna make annoying comments or help us, ass face?" KJ fired back without breaking his concentration.

Igor and Leo emerged from the pool, water streaming over their dark-skinned muscles. The monk brothers silently called their Huahuqui, who appeared from the pool, and took a place by the side of their fellow Stratum. The blue miasma intensified, engulfing them all—except Nikolaj.

The Laotians' guns clacked and clattered to the earth.

"Okay boys, you're up," KJ said. His command wasn't directed at anyone, but Igor and Leo acknowledged it was for them and stepped forward.

Igor was the first to speak. His baritone voice demanded respect, yet the calmness with which he spoke provided a strange comfort. Leo's timber was equally deep and wise. The two monks spoke together with fluidity, sharing pieces of whatever story they were spinning. KJ had absolutely no idea what they were saying.

One of the Laotian men replied. His impressive demeanor suggested a leadership role. He fired words at the monks, and they replied calmly back. All the while, KJ concentrated on not letting the potential attackers pick up their arsenal.

Click. Click. Click. Catherine shuffled from one spot to the next, taking picture after picture.

"Hey you mind? I'm concentrating here," KJ said, his gaze fixed on the Laotians.

"You're here to rescue Svetlana. I'm here to document it," Catherine said, clicking another four shots in a row.

A few of the Laotian men kept mumbling the same words over and over in the background, their eyes wide and gazes fixed on the Huahuqui.

"What the hell are they saying?" KJ asked.

Igor suddenly turned to KJ. "Phaya Naga. You may stop," he said. "They shall not harm us."

KJ glanced at the men, then his Stratum. Reluctantly he lessened his control, the blue radiance fading until it eventually disappeared. Merry and Lex fell to the ground, exhausted from the concentration. KJ ran and dropped to his knees beside them.

"You okay?" KJ asked.

Merry and Lex, out of breath, nodded.

"Not quite the same," Lex said.

"As dodgeball," Merry finished.

KJ gave a weak smile, then turned back to the monk brothers. The Laotians took a few paces forward, staring at the Huahuqui and whispering among themselves.

"What's Phaya Naga?" Catherine asked as she knelt closer to the Laotians to take a better shot.

"River dragon," Leo replied, then took a step back. The glow in his eyes subsided and his body relaxed.

"In China, but also bleeding into Vietnam, Laos, Thailand, and Cambodia there is a common theme: dragons who are wise and knowing and connected to the creation of things," KJ offered. "In this area, it's Phaya Naga. Divine demi-creatures, which possess supernatural powers."

"These people must be Lao Theung. Maabris," Nikolaj said. "The oldest of the peoples in Laos. They still very much believe in spirits and the netherworld. The Huahuqui must seem like living proof of their beliefs."

"Bravo, fuckstick. You just repeated what I said. You're officially useless." KJ rolled his eyes and strolled over to Merry and Lex to ensure they were okay. "So, what now?" he asked, looking up at Igor.

"They take us to their village, and we may eat and drink before continuing our journey," Igor replied.

"Great," Catherine said. "This is gonna make an amazing story."

KJ grinned at her.

"What's your problem?" Catherine snapped.

107

"You might wanna put on some clothes there, Jungle Jane." KJ laughed. "And, Hello Kitty? Really?"

Catherine blushed and twisted to see the Japanese cartoon cat on the seat of her underwear. "I didn't think I'd be showing them to anyone—"

"Hey, I'm not judging." KJ smirked and sauntered off in the direction the Laotians were walking.

Location: CIA Headquarters, Langley, Washington, USA

Teller sat in a familiar clean room inside Langley, waiting for his meeting with the Karachi Station Chief who was in town for a few days. Jonathan hoped the CIA would allow him to speak with their asset in Tehran who might know something about what was bought from the Argentinians.

While NSA and the CIA were meant to be on the same side, there was a chasm of mistrust between them. In his opinion, the NSA were much more concerned with protection of US citizens than meddling in the political affairs of other countries for financial gain. The CIA on the other hand was a different story. No other agency in the history of the world had interfered with the affairs of other countries—with disastrous results. The death of Teller's grandfather, a former spook, was testament to that. Jonathan found himself musing on George Teller more and more in the past few days; perhaps brought on by the pending end of the world. But in his gut, Teller knew his fear was more about dying while on the job, away from his family—just another KIA, a body never to be found. Never able to say goodbye. Teller shook off the cold crawling its way across his skin. *Concentrate on the task at hand,* he thought.

Mike Weinberg bowled into the office. A tall man with shrewd grey eyes and a broad chest, he was known as *the Drone*. Cold and emotionless like the pilotless death dealers he controlled, the Karachi Station Chief had conducted more strikes and killed more enemies in the region than any CIA operative on record. Collateral damage was a calculated factor, and he was infamous for using a specific equation to determine if the percentage of civilian causalities was acceptable—though only he knew the details of the computation.

"Mike," Teller said, offering a hand.

"Mr. Teller," Weinberg said, shaking Jonathan's hand. "Shall we?"

Teller sat back down in the uncomfortable plastic chair. "I know you're only here for a few days, so I'm gonna get down to brass tacks. I need to speak with your asset in Tehran."

Mike's expression didn't move. "As I told you on the phone, I need to know more. Iran is not exactly a place I want to be opening up for no good reason. As you can appreciate, they're pretty unfriendly."

Teller almost laughed. "Iran is still pissed about the CIA ousting their democratically appointed leader in 1953. All over a spat with the British about control of oil production."

Weinberg sniffed once and ran his tongue over his teeth, indicating his indifference.

"I'm here on the President's orders," Teller said. "I need info out of Iran, urgently. They may have something we need."

Weinberg remained stony.

Jonathan eyed the man. "You're aware of the orbs, the ones that seemed to allow a greater connection with the Huahuqui and humans, right?"

"They were destroyed."

"Right," Teller confirmed. "To cut a long story short, we have intel that suggests one may still be in existence. If we get it, it might allow connection or control of a large population of Huahuqui."

Weinberg rubbed his smooth jaw. "You want to control the Nine Veils army."

Teller bobbed his head. "Exactly. So, we think the Nazis found it during World War II, but had no idea what it was. We tracked it to Argentina only to find out they probably sold it to the Iranians not long after Alpha Base was started. Apparently, they went to the AFI *asking* to buy their Nazi hoard."

The Station Chief frowned. "You sure an orb is among the Nazi stuff?"

"I'm working off a hunch."

"A hunch? That's one hell of a hunch, Teller."

"Everyone else is busy with the stations or trying to find these bastards. I'm working a lead to find anything that can help us beat them."

There was a long silence. The Station Chief seemed to be regarding Teller with a certain amount of disdain for this foolhardy endeavor. Teller couldn't blame him. Here he was, traipsing around the world looking for something that may not exist. Meanwhile, KJ and Nikolaj were jetting off to China for God knows what reason, Freya was seething that he wasn't hot on their trail, and the Earth may soon be plummeted into nuclear winter. If he had been on the receiving end of this story he'd also think the narrator was a damn idiot.

Eventually Weinberg pulled an older-looking cell phone from his pocket and placed it on the table between them."It's a burner," Mike said, nodding to the phone. "Tensions are high right now.

The Iranian's think this power station threat has been orchestrated by the USA to impede their nuclear program."

"Has it?" Teller asked.

Weinberg's eyes narrowed, but he ignored the jibe. "Five minutes, that's it. Keep to the point."

"Sure," Teller said.

The phone hummed a few times before a man answered with a simple, *"yes?"*

"Jester, this is Louis the Fourth," the Station Chief said.

"Louis the fourth was an idiot," came the reply. *"He fell from his horse."*

"That he did. Jester, we have a friend here from the NSA."

Teller launched into his questions. "We have intel that 16 or 17 years ago, the Iranian government obtained the whole Argentine stash of Nazi items gained from World War II in exchange for oil. Does that sound right?"

There was a pause, then: *"I believe this to be true. Sanctioned by the Head of the Intelligence agency. But it yielded no results."*

"Dammit!" Teller exclaimed. "Do you know what they were looking for?"

"Something important, related to the Jinn.*"*

Jinn. The word for Huahuqui across the Middle East. While initially the religious world had exploded at the revelation of the Huahuqui, Islam had been able to reconcile the notion of these sentient creatures with their faith. The teachings of the Quran already referred to such beings on Earth before and alongside humans—beings that were faster and stronger; the Jinn. While strictly invisible deities according to their holy book, the ability of the Muslim world to accept these creatures, as not only created by God but also equal to humans, had far exceeded that of the Judeo-

Christian community.

Jonathan turned to the Station Chief. "At least we were on the right track."

Mike nodded, apparently in thought.

"What about the U-boat?" said the voice on the phone.

"U-boat?" Jonathan asked.

"Iranian Intelligence has started using back channels to gain permits under false enterprises to salvage a sunken German U-boat, just off the coast of Denmark."

"A type XXI to be precise," Weinberg said. "The most advanced U-boat of its time, but a relic by our standards. Sank with all 58 crewmembers the day after the end of the war. Their mission is unknown, but rumors were rife that it had Nazi gold on board or that high-ranking Nazi officers, including Hitler himself, were on it. All fairy tales."

"So far, no permits have been provided, but it is possible the Danish government may concede if the right offer was made. This is all I know."

The call cut off. Weinberg slipped the burner phone into his pocket.

"They're still looking …" Teller said. "They didn't find it in the Argentine stash but went looking for a U-boat."

Weinberg rose to his feet and buttoned his suit jacket. "As I said, fairy tales."

"I've made a career chasing fairy tales, Mike. More often than not there's been some truth in them." Jonathan stood and pushed his chair back, its feet screeching on the floor.

"Going somewhere?"

Teller smirked. "Denmark, Mike. I'm going to Denmark."

CHAPTER SEVEN

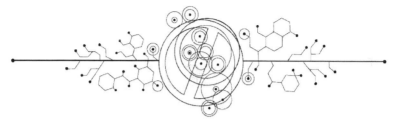

Location: Tocayōtla, somewhere in China

Svetlana knelt in her communal dorm, eyes closed, Ribka curled up at her side. Meditation had become harder and harder. Even with her Phalanx family surrounding her, each providing a link in the collective consciousness, she felt alone. Whatever that man, KJ, had done to her, it seemed to be permanent. No amount of shadow boxing, sparring, or introspection seemed to help. His consciousness was now a splinter in her mind, digging its way deeper and causing an infection.

As much as she hated Mother, Svetlana may well need her now. There had been rumors that the woman had perfected a new form of control, derived from her research years earlier. A serum that would render the Phalanx completely susceptible to her command. Svetlana doubted the Doyen had sanctioned it and would never let it be used. He seemed to be enamored with the idea the Phalanx truly believed in his plan.

But, what *was* his plan? Svetlana and the Phalanx had not been explicitly told. Only that soon the end of the Fifth Sun would come and the righteous, those loyal to the Huahuqui, would survive to set humanity on a new trajectory toward greatness. To ensure such a glorious path, the old ways of thinking— the dogma instilled by governments and institutions who had forgotten the Huahuqui—must be removed from power. She and the Phalanx would be key to this.

A hand slid over her shoulder and Svetlana opened her eyes.

"Nyalku, when did you arrive?" Svetlana said without turning.

"A day or so ago," he said.

Svetlana shrugged off his hand and rose to her feet. "This isn't your dorm."

"I just figured you may need company," he said, stepping away. "I heard Mother called you out in public again. You shouldn't be alone."

"*Kóoto'obe 'ku máano'ob tu juun, size'obe' múuch u máano'ob,*" Svetlana replied in Mayan.

"Yes, yes I've heard it before: the eagle flies alone, while we follow the herd."

"Then you know to get lost," Svetlana fired back. "You were the first to jump on my back after… what happened."

"Yeah," he said rubbing at his neck. "I was mad. But, it doesn't matter. The final plan is still on track."

"And what *is* that, Nyalku?" Svetlana's eyes flared.

Nyalku squirmed, his gaze falling away from hers. "To usher in the Sixth Sun," he said finally. "To rebalance the world, with the Huahuqui in their rightful place."

"Whatever that means," Svetlana said.

"You need to get your head straight. Mother is pissed, and it's at you—again. One of these days she'll do something bad to you. The Doyen won't be able to protect you forever."

Svetlana grabbed Nyalku by his military jacket and slammed him against the wall. Nyalku broke free and shoved her back several paces.

"You really wanna do this?" he fired at her.

"Just stay out of my face, Nyalku, got it?" Svetlana snapped back.

Nyalku's eyes were glassy, his fear palpable. "It's not just about you, 'lana."

Svetlana stormed past, shoulder barging him as she went.

As much as Nyalku irritated her, he wasn't wrong. Her head wasn't straight. It *had* been. For years. She had believed in the Doyen's words, in his teaching. But now something felt different, the pit of her stomach constantly nagging at her.

Being outside of the place they called home high in the rice terraces had impacted her psyche far more than she could have anticipated. Watching other humans go about their lives, oblivious to the danger around them. Laughing, smiling, loving and fighting without a care in the world. And then, the chance connection in Washington with the man named KJ and his Huahuqui, K'awin. Everything had become... confused... like looking through a prism. The once clean, single truth now fractured into multiple realities and possibilities.

The pressure inside her head was unbearable.

Svetlana peered down the Avenue of the Dead toward the Pyramid of the Moon—Victoria's abode. It stood alone, just like Mother, tall and proud and strong. Svetlana needed something more, something to take the growing migraine, the doubt, away. Perhaps Mother would take pity on her, offer the drug she'd been working on. Then Svetlana could rest, could rejoin her Phalanx without fear or hesitation. Powering forward, mind made up, Svetlana headed for the Pyramid of the Moon.

Three steps into her stride, Ribka blocked her path. The little Huahuqui stared up at Svetlana, gills billowing and tiny lips smacking together.

"What?" Svetlana snapped, then instantly regretted her outburst.

Ribka nuzzled Svetlana's boot.

"Don't worry, you won't lose me." Svetlana knelt and rubbed her symbiote's head. "I'll still be me, just clearer. I promise."

Ribka seemed unconvinced, wrapping herself around Svetlana's legs, preventing her from walking any further

"Daughter, are you well?"

Svetlana froze and rose to her feet, coming face to face with the Doyen.

"Yes, I mean no, I mean …"

"You are confused, child. I can feel it," the Doyen said.

Neith, his Huahuqui, warbled and touched snouts with Ribka.

"I have headaches. I just want them to go away, I need clarity. Purpose. I am failing my Phalanx."

"Is that so? And what clarity do you seek? Perhaps how to pierce the Eighth veil? You have stalled at the seventh for some time."

Svetlana's heart beat faster. That wasn't what she meant. "I want to understand my purpose, *our* purpose. How killing heads of state will bring about the Sixth Sun and allow the Huahuqui to take their rightful place." She swallowed, expecting to be reprimanded.

"They are one and the same child," the Doyen said, breaking into a wise smile. "You have perfected the understanding of mathematics and all the universe has to offer in the form of logic. Now you must understand its—God's—will. Come." He waved a robed arm toward the Pyramid of the Sun, *his* personal sanctuary.

Svetlana walked behind him along the Avenue of the Dead,

studying his calm gait and flowing robes. The Doyen had changed over the years. Once a harsh man with hard features who demanded absolute fealty, now seemed softer with older age—wiser and more satisfied in his existence and that his plan would come to fruition. Perhaps he really had pierced the Ninth Veil and knew God's greater design.

The Doyen nodded to the two guards posted at the large entrance which was carved directly into the stone steps in front of them. Svetlana had only been inside once before. The image of his large wooden desk, replete with a leather chair and sculpture of a gnarled tree, peered out from the recesses of her mind.

They sauntered through the pass-code-locked door and into the main foyer. Svetlana's eye's widened. Here in this massive empty expanse inside the structure was a nursery of sorts. At least a hundred pairs of plastic cribs. Each was filled with soft white linens and a fleshy, pink human or murky water and a tiny, translucent Huahuqui. Two women, presumably nurses, flitted from crib to crib, tending to the infants.

The Doyen stopped by a crib, lifted a baby out, and held it to his chest. "Not everyone in the Phalanx are soldiers," he said softly. "We are rebuilding the world. New life must be born. Life that knows only of the bond with the knowledge bringers. A life untainted by the society we have created. We will create this world for them."

He handed Svetlana the child. She took it into her arms and studied its wrinkled skin and tiny fingers that grasped at the air, feeling for a connection to something—someone. A lump formed in her throat. She had never seen a newborn before. The idea of babies being born here at the Temple had never crossed her mind.

"Who's are they?" she asked.

117

"Members of your brethren. Your Phalanx whose bond was so strong they felt compelled to procreate."

"Of their own free will?" she pressed.

The Doyen laughed out loud and took the baby from Svetlana. "Of course, child."

"How did I not feel them, in the hive?"

"They're shielded in here," he said, placing the infant back into the crib. "The children and the parents. It would not do to distract everyone."

Even in here, we hide things from each other, she thought. "Then why tell me?" The question blurted out before Svetlana could contain it.

The Doyen turned and began walking the length of the room toward the secure elevator. "You felt a bond with the boy, Kelly Graham Junior, yes?" he said over his shoulder.

Svetlana's skin prickled.

"This is divine providence. He is first to be born of a person bonded to a knowledge bringer. The infants you see downstairs are like him. They are… special. With powers beyond even you and the Phalanx. He will be the key to leading them, understanding them. His bond to you will be to our advantage. You will be able to show him our way. Show him what we will achieve and the righteousness of it. This is your destiny."

Svetlana stopped in her tracks. "You knew. You knew I would meet him."

The Doyen turned to her. "I did. Your bond as children was always strong. You have been one of my most treasured, Svetlana, full of spirit and understanding. One day I will need you to lead with Kelly Graham Junior at your side. It is God's will. Shall we?" He motioned to the elevator.

Svetlana cautiously stepped inside, Ribka in tow.

A short ride to the pinnacle of the pyramid, and they had reached the Doyen's private quarters. Through the sliding doors, Svetlana followed him into the darkened office which formed the entrance to his living space. It was whispered he never slept, but she spied a bed through a half-closed door off to the right and another room off to the left.

The Doyen slipped a hand over her shoulder, making her skin prickle, then he slowly walked behind his desk and took a seat in the large black leather chair. Behind him, just as she remembered, was a sculpture of a gnarled tree.

"You wish to understand how we shall create a world for you and the children."

Svetlana nodded, Ribka padding nervously at her side.

"Watch," he said, his deep voice filling the room with such reverence it seemed the walls had been designed to amplify his every word.

The room lights, already low, dimmed further. Then, in a burst of color, the very universe itself was projected from a light in the floor onto the ceiling and every wall. Purple, red, and yellow clouds of dust and white stars slid across the room's surfaces—some even seemed to pass in front of her very eyes. The imagery slowly swirled and zoomed out.

"This is the greater plan. This is what we have been building toward. It is not my plan. I am simply putting us back on track for what was always inevitable."

Svetlana surveyed the churning gassy masses and the tiny blue marble that was the Earth. Slowly the holographic imagery shifted and swirled, and an ancient story silently unfolded. Finally, she understood. Finally, it made sense. She looked to the Doyen, who simply smiled back.

"Now, for phase two," he said.

Location: Lackland Airforce Base, San Antonio, Texas, USA

Lucy's gaze ambled over the various monitors and rows of elevated control stations, flashing lights, and keyboards, to the massive wall some fifty feet across and twenty feet high comprised entirely of flexible organic light-emitting diodes. One giant screen that simultaneously displayed surveillance from city cameras all over the world, complex mathematical operations streaming like waterfalls, news station broadcasts, satellite feeds and a plethora of other information. All of it filtered into the NSA's most secretive cyber warfare unit—the Office of Tailored Access Operations.

TAO's area of operations, as explained to her by Jim Waltham, ranged from counterterrorism to cyber-attacks to good old-fashioned traditional espionage. A unit born of the internet, TAO was touted as being able to 'get the ungettable' by acquiring pervasive, persistent access to the entire global network of all known CPUs. Like many such programs before it, including ECHELON that had been hijacked by the Nine Veils seventeen years ago, there was concern over breach of civil liberty. Lucy herself had several times asked for more information on TAO and its ability to infiltrate and even control the lives of ordinary citizens. Now it would seem, this clandestine organization might be their only hope to regain control of the power stations.

The go to plan had been to manually shut down the power plants using a SCRAM—insertion of a large amount of negative reactivity mass into the midst of the fissile material. The majority of stations in the western world had these—neutron-absorbing control rods or a neutron poison—connected to some emergency system which responded to a break in the electrical power. The problem was, the hackers had put in a failsafe. It seemed as soon as SCRAM use was attempted the stations would blow.

Lucy pulled at her face and paced some more. Back and forth, eyeing the highly trained personnel as they diligently worked in near silence on their small portion of the problem. Impatience growing, Lucy approached a woman at one of the terminals. Her name was Caroline, if memory served. This woman was responsible for attempting to ascertain if there was a timer built into the hack— would the stations explode automatically or would they be manually triggered?

"Anything?" Lucy asked.

"No, Ma'am," came the patient reply in a sweet southern accent.

Lucy checked her watch. Of course, she'd asked the same question fifteen minutes earlier.

"Any sign of a timer at all?"

The woman shook her head but didn't look up from her monitor. "No, Ma'am. Not so far. But this hack is… complicated. I've not seen anything like it before. None of us have."

A flurry of activity on the far side of the room drew Lucy's attention. She near ran in her stilettos across the uncarpeted floor, the heels rapidly clacking. "What is it?" she asked the agent, furiously tapping away at his keyboard.

"I… I mean… we've been locked out," he stammered.

"Locked out, locked out of what?" Lucy demanded.

"Project Swiss Mountain. The biomes, the bunkers …" he stopped typing, hands hovering in mid-air as if one more keystroke might end them all. "They've locked down. And we've lost control."

"What?" Lucy barked again.

Waltham stormed into the command center. "What's going on?"

Lucy spun, her eyes wide. "We've just lost Swiss Mountain. What the hell, Jim?"

He shook his head, leaning over his agent, staring at the screen. He tapped a few more keys which cleared the giant wall monitor of all information save a map of the world punctuated with bright lights where the other biomes and bunkers were located. Next to each was a no entry icon. "We only achieved two percent capacity before we lost control," he said.

Lucy's mind reeled as her stare darted from Paris, to Shanghai to Perth. Two percent. That was no coincidence. Two percent of the total population to be ushered into these safe-houses was to be made up of the intellectual elite. They were given this privilege on the understanding it was their responsibility to rebuild if the worst happened. They were also the first on the list to be moved. The Nine Veils had effectively just taken them all hostage.

"What the hell is going on, Jim?" Lucy said, her voice wavering as she fought back tears.

"I don't know Madam President. But, I'll find out. We'll crack this and find those bastards."

His words were not comforting. She just watched the USA's best cyber team lose even more control. They needed a miracle. They needed an orb to find the Nine Veils. Lucy wiped her face and pushed a lock of unruly blondish hair behind her ear in defiance. "Get me an outside line to Jonathan Teller. I need to speak with Teller."

CHAPTER EIGHT

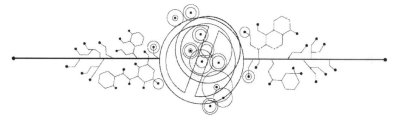

Location: Ten nautical miles north of Skagen, Denmark.

Teller sat in the diving chamber aboard the *Vina*, a massive research vessel owned by the Danish Thyborøn War Museum. It felt like a lifetime since Teller had been near the ocean and submarine—a time before the NSA, a time before Freya.

Ten miles north of Skagen, the sea was choppy even for the seventy-meter monstrosity on which he and his crew were traveling. Here, the Skagerrak and Kattegat seas clashed as if nature itself was battling for which body of water would emerge victorious. This marine skirmish was the reason the German U-boat for which Teller was about to dive had been missing for so long—the current had dragged the submarine's carcass far away from where it was believed to have sunk.

He surveyed his new crew: another team whom he did not know, assembled from a few Navy Seals—who happened to be stationed at Thule Deepwater Port in Greenland—and some of the museum's scientists to ensure the wreck was treated with some respect. His gaze roved to the most important members of this rag tag team: the Stratum. It took a little convincing of the Alpha Base leadership, but four Huahuqui and their symbiotes had been dispatched to Skagen. Three female Huahuqui and one male, whose names he could neither remember, let alone pronounce. Their human counterparts were four women in their late teens.

Teller eyed the young women. Despite abilities such as accelerated healing and a stronger bond with animals, they would not be allowed to dive—none had the training or experience. Not like KJ or Nikolaj. Teller had taught them to dive at a young age, even in the frigid Antarctic waters. Nikolaj was competent, but cautious. A conscientious diver who refused to push boundaries and always followed protocol. KJ had taken to diving as if he had been a dolphin in another life. Much like his father, the boy was comfortable in the ocean, and the water and its inhabitants seemed comfortable with him—schools of fish and pods of cetaceans following KJ and K'awin wherever they went. If Teller was honest, the boy was probably one of the best divers he'd ever worked with. Of course, Teller would never tell him that. KJ was well aware of his talent; over enthusiastic and wholly arrogant. A dangerous mix when diving. Teller sighed. On a mission like this, in the turbulent waters, he would really have no one else than KJ at his side. Now, instead, he would have to rely on these Huahuqui. They would be the most skilled underwater, and most likely to find an orb should it be down there.

"Teller?" one of the Navy Seals, a broad, clean shaven man, said.

"Uh, Phelps, right?"

"Yeah. You have a satellite call. The president."

Jonathan swallowed, his throat suddenly dry, and took the phone. "Madam President?"

"Jonathan, where are we on the orb?"

"I am just about to dive now. There is no guarantee, but if it's down there I'll find it."

There was a lasting silence on the phone.

"*I understand,*" she said finally.

"Is there something else?" Jonathan pressed, impatient to begin his mission.

"*Project Swiss Mountain,*" she began. "*We... lost control.*"

The words were dense, pushing their way slowly into his brain. He blinked slowly, unable to focus on anything. Did she just say they'd lost control of Swiss Mountain? What did that even mean?

"*Jonathan?*"

Teller gripped the dive knife in his free hand, squeezing the handle as hard as he could. "Sorry, yes. Lost control? Lost control how?"

"*They've been locked down. No one in or out.*"

"Are there people inside?"

The president seemed to hold her breath for a moment. "Yes. The protocol was to move those at the top of the list first. Scientists, artists, musicians, mathematicians... It's a few thousand people, globally."

"Shit." The word just slipped out. "Sorry. I just don't understand why... unless... unless they were planning to blow the stations and save a few of us?" He shook his head, disagreeing with his own theory. "But irradiating the whole planet would render it uninhabitable for decades. Would the bunkers even last that long?"

"*I don't know the answer. But the importance of finding the orb is greater than ever. If we can link to them, maybe we can find out.*"

"I know, I know. If it exists, I'll find it." He began to lift the phone from his ear. "Thank you, Mad—"

"*One more thing, Jonathan.*"

"Yes?"

"Your sons. They never landed in Shanghai. Somehow they

rigged the computer's AI and parachuted out long before it landed."

Jonathan's chest inflated with anger, disappointment, even guilt, swirling and colliding inside him until none made sense. In the middle of all of this, KJ and Nikolaj were galivanting off to who knew where, doing who knew what. He squeezed his eyes shut and clenched his jaw, breathing through his nose. *Think Jonathan. Think. Trust them.* KJ was rash, but not stupid. Nikolaj was contentious. They must have had a reason. "I'll go find them," he said. "When I'm done here."

"You need to concentrate on the orb."

"And I will. I'll take it to the scientists at Alpha Base. Freya is there, she can act as a liaison for you. I won't be any help if—when I find it. I'm better off finding the boys and preventing an international incident with China."

The president audibly murmured but then conceded.

"Thank you, Madam President."

"Good luck, Jonathan."

The call clicked off and Teller handed the phone back to the seal.

"Fuck sake," Teller said through gnashed teeth and sheathed his dive knife.

"Problem," Doctor Skarsgaard, Head of the Museum, said as he adjusted the hoses on his dry suit.

"Kids," Teller replied without looking up. "I'll deal with it later."

"Ah, I know the problem," the skinny wire-haired man replied. "Mine are all grown up, but always come back to the nest."

"I kinda have the opposite problem."

Skarsgaard nodded. "Often, the apple doesn't fall far from the tree. I'm sure you were just the same when you were young."

Jonathan didn't reply. KJ was not his son, and Freya had refused to have more children for fear of them suffering her disease.

"Come," Skarsgaard said, clearly recognizing Jonathan's pained expression. "We should go while the weather is good, this wreck is quite the find. We'd always wanted to raise it, but never found the funding. It will be a pleasure to investigate."

Jonathan nodded in agreement. "So, what are we looking at here? What's the situation down there?"

Skarsgaard led Jonathan into the briefing room, followed by the Navy Seals and the four pairs of Stratum. A monitor on the wall showed a three-dimensional multi-beam generated image of the submarine, or at least part of it.

"The bow of the 250-foot-long submarine," Skarsgaard began, "is stabbed into the seafloor some 400 feet below the surface, slanting upward with the boat's stern floating 65 feet above the bottom of the sea. We will be able to search the stern, but it is very unlikely that it will be possible to enter anywhere else."

Teller nodded then looked to the four young women. "Did our aquatic friends understand?"

The women murmured their acknowledgment. The Huahuqui were good to go.

Even in a dry suit, the water was freezing—the cold penetrating through his thick Alpaca socks and two layers of shirt and pants. Teller had forgotten how much he hated dry-suit diving. Everything felt sluggish, clumsy, primarily due to the fact he had to control buoyancy by adding or releasing air into the suit.

Nevertheless, without these cumbersome suits he and his rag tag crew would die of hypothermia damn quickly.

The sea was dark and uninviting, light attenuating quickly until they had to rely on their lights and comms. Teller had buddied up with Phelps, while the other Navy Seals had taken the scientists. The Huahuqui had been fitted with flashing strobes attached to harnesses, making it easier to track them, though they swam so quickly it was difficult to keep up.

Releasing air from his suit, and pointing his weighted feet downward, Teller allowed himself to sink slowly toward the position of the submarine. Even more than dry suit diving, Teller hated night dives. The pitch-black water and absence of sound was claustrophobic. Only frequent checks to his right, keeping Phelps in view, helped calm the panicked feeling growing in his chest. He peered down to ensure the faint strobing from the Huahuqui could still be seen.

Here in the inky darkness, cut off from almost every sense, thoughts and emotions repressed over the longest time seemed to take the quiet opportunity to emerge and invade Teller's mind. The frustration of not being able to move, see, hear, or feel as he would want was now a stark reminder of how Freya, the love of his life, felt every day. This level of frustration filled her emotional cup to the brim so that she was quick to snap or attack at the slightest provocation. It was easy to become irritated with her demeanor. Yet, his own dissatisfaction was not with her deteriorating condition—that was at least an enemy he could combat with medicine and therapists—but with her pushing him down the priority list of her life. KJ was at the top. He always had been. It wasn't that Teller was jealous of KJ, or wished the kid away, but he often wondered whether the devotion was as much to do with motherhood as it was to do with her son's growing similarity to his late father.

A sadness grew inside Jonathan, a sorrow at not being recognized for the sacrifices *he* had made—to raise two children who were not his own, to care for Freya as her health faded, to agree to never have his own children, and finally to step away from his own career aspirations so he could do all these things. Perhaps most frustrating was that, while in his heart he hoped Freya saw his efforts, KJ seemingly did not. Teller was the enemy and Kelly Graham was a hero who could not be dethroned. *Heroes come in many guises,* thought Teller. *They don't all wear capes.* Still, it was undeniable: as KJ grew so did the legend Kelly Graham. The memory of the man seemed to inflate and become more fantastical every year; the brave hero who gave his life to save the world. The legend. Except he didn't. Yes, he'd trotted the globe and played his part in saving the world, but he'd died trying to save one woman— Victoria McKenzie—from her ungodly bond with Wak. And in her devolved state she'd killed him.

Jonathan sucked in a deep breath and exhaled slowly—the bubbles crashing about the glass of his mask. Victoria. He hadn't thought of her in a long time, and no one knew what happened to her. The CIA had tracked her for a while, but after several years it seemed she was simply on a pilgrimage. Teller's feet hit something hard and metallic and he jolted to a stop. Suddenly aware that he'd drifted off into thought, his heartbeat quickened. "Phelps you there?"

The comms inside Teller's full-face mask buzzed with static.

"Here," Phelps replied then waved his flashlight, so Teller could see him not more than twenty feet away.

"You think we'll see any corpses down here?" Phelps said,

swimming closer.

"*No,*" came Skarsgaard's voice over the comms. "*The fish would have picked the bones by now. You may see some uniforms and skeletons.*"

"Peachy," Teller said. "To boldly go and all that."

"*A Star Trek reference?*" Skarsgaard asked.

Teller had forgotten no-one here knew his little quirks. "Forget it."

"*I have the pulse induction detector and my assistant, Erika, has the very low frequency detector. We'll make a sweep of the seabed around the submarine,*" the professor said.

"Understood," Teller replied. "I'll follow the Huahuqui, see if they can sniff something out." Jonathan opened the strap on his flashlight and fixed it to the top of his mask, freeing both his hands, then adjusted the buoyancy of his dry suit to allow him to swim along the exposed keel of the submarine.

The huge tube poked from the sand like a giant metallic mollusc. Time had transformed the vessel into a reef, teeming with animals, sponges, and plant life. Rather than the colorful bouquet of reds and oranges seen in the tropics, here herring and mackerel gave everything a silver, mirrored, effect as if the ocean were alive with shards of glass that reflected the divers' lights in the dark. Teller couldn't help but wonder if Hans Christian Andersson's Little Mermaid might swim by. He wanted to make a joke about green women, but realized that, again, there was no-one here who would appreciate the humor.

As Jonathan and Phelps skimmed the rusted and crusty surface of the U-boat, following its angle down toward the seabed, Jonathan noted that all four of the Huahuqui had gathered at a single spot, a few feet from where the metal tube disappeared into the seabed. Fighting the current, and pushing through another school of silver fish, he descended until he reached the bottom. Here the hull of the ship seemed to have split, perhaps under its own weight or through the stresses of the current on the aft portion. The tear was considerable.

"Hey Skarsgaard, you nearby? I think we may have something here," Teller said into the microphone.

"Where are you?" came the reply.

"Starboard side. Seabed, maybe ten feet from the vessel's entry point."

"Okay, I'll be there in a few minutes."

Skarsgaard was true to his word. Moments later he appeared over the hull of the U-boat, his Navy Seal buddy in tow, and drifted down to where Teller was—careful not to blind anyone with his flashlight. The Huahuqui were swirling around and around, their gills floating and flitting with the motion of the water. The strobes on their backs flashed incessantly.

"Here?" Skarsgaard said, pointing at the seabed.

"Inside, I think," Teller replied.

The professor looked to the rip in the hull of the submarine, swam over and waved his pulse inductor detector, a handheld device that looked much like a metal detector beachgoers may use, over the gap. *"There's definitely something in there,"* he said. *"Not clear what. It's not a precious metal, but whatever it is, there's a strange signal. It's not sea trash."*

Teller swallowed hard. "I guess we go in."

The gash in the metal appeared larger than it actually was. It took a little maneuvering, particularly with their tanks, to squeeze through without tearing their dry suits or accidentally slicing a hose on a jagged edge.

Inside the submarine, it was even darker. Their flashlights provided little in the way of illumination. Instead Teller had to use his cone of light to follow the professor, who himself seemed to be guided more by the pinging of his instrument than sight. From what Teller could see the sediment had been swept inside the sub, probably through the opening, filling the cavity. It wasn't quite full to the seabed level outside, but it was damn close.

The professor homed in on a given area of sand and pointed. *"Somewhere here."*

Phelps began digging with a short metallic shovel. Silt and sand billowed up obscuring what little light they had. Occasionally he'd grab a metallic box, inspect it, and throw it to the side, letting it float away. After several minutes of furious gouging, he stopped. *"I've hit something,"* he said. *"Hard. Really hard."*

"Okay, let's pry it out," Skarsgaard suggested.

Phelps delved back into his ditch, shoving his gloved hands into the sand and pulled.

"You okay there Phelps?" Teller asked.

Phelps grunted with effort then backed off. *"Okay whatever that thing is it's buried good, I can't pull it out."*

"The detector says it's just a couple of feet below the surface. And it's maybe five feet across. Box shaped. It can't be that hard."

Teller's flashlight gave enough light to see the irritated look on Phelps' face.

"Be my guest, prof," Phelps said.

The professor handed his detector to the Navy Seal by his side and began digging around the object, which Teller could now see was a box. Skarsgaard had wedged his hands underneath in an effort to lift it. He tugged several times, but the thing didn't budge.

"Problem?" Phelps jibed.

"It must be incredibly dense," Skarsgaard said.

"Maybe it's the box?" Teller offered. "Looks like a mineral or something. Maybe it's just real heavy."

"Possibly," the professor said.

"So, we open it," Phelps offered. *"If it's a box, it'll have a hinge or a seal or something right?"*

Teller checked his oxygen gauge. Twenty minutes left. "Okay, let's crack this sucker open. We don't have much time."

Without a reply, Phelps unsheathed his serrated dive knife and sank down to the seabed to investigate. Teller watched as the Navy Seal searched the box, running the knife along its surface to detect a groove.

"Got it," Phelps said with satisfaction.

Teller held his breath.

The soldier crammed the edge of his blade into a furrow that seemed to run the length of the heavy container. *"If this thing is heavy, it's going to take a few of us to pry it off."*

Teller didn't need to be prompted, his own blade now forced into the same slight gap. Skarsgaard shoved his knife inside and waited for the signal. The three men pressed down on their blades, trying to force the lid off. It raised slightly, perhaps an inch.

Phelps grunted. *"Dammit."*

"What if the Huahuqui help?" Teller suggested. "They're stronger than us, and more capable in the water. They can pull on it while we lever it."

"How are we going to explain that to them? Their symbiotes are at the surface?" Phelps asked.

Teller checked his gauge again. Thirteen minutes. "They'll get it," he said then swam over to the nearest Huahuqui who stopped swirling and faced him. *Here goes nothing,* he thought, then began pointing and miming his desire for help to open the box.

The Huahuqui, Taika Teller recalled, cocked its broad head and stared at him for a moment. Then, in what could only be described as an 'ah-ha' moment, Taika dove down toward to the sea floor followed closely by her three companions. Teller adjusted his buoyancy and trailed them down.

Now ready, everyone tried again. Teller, Phelps and Skarsgaard levered the lid with their knives and the Huahuqui slipped their fingers into the gap and pulled on the lid. It popped off in a puff of silt and debris, floated less than two feet away, and quickly sank back to the sand.

The cloud of silt dissipated, and Teller breathed a sigh of relief. There in the black mineral box was a glowing blue gelatinous orb about the size of a grapefruit. Preserved in seawater, it had not desiccated. In fact, it seemed in near-perfect condition. The Huahuqui spun and circled in excitement, a curtain of bubbles forming around the group.

Skarsgaard looked up to Teller. *"Is this what you were looking for?"*

Teller nodded, heart still hammering at the prospect of having the upper hand against the Nine Veils. But, perhaps more than that, he couldn't wait to tell Freya that his jaunt had been worth it. That not going after KJ had been the right choice. "That it is, Professor. That it is."

Location: Tocayōtla, China

Under a purple night sky, the Doyen stood at the foot of the Temple of the Moon. Victoria's temple. He'd granted her this place—built it for her—as thanks for her devotion to the Nine

Veils and her assistance in understanding the Huahuqui. When he'd chanced upon her all those years ago, the only adult human alive who had experienced the bond with a knowledge bringer, the opportunity could not pass him by. He believed her invaluable to the universe's great plan. In fact, he had believed it divine providence that their paths had crossed at all.

At first, his belief in her had seemed founded. She was lost, both mentally and spiritually, and so had readily accepted the teachings of the Nine Veils. With a voracious appetite to understand her own existence and that of the world, she'd crashed through five of the veils within a year. And with each elevation in her understanding, the Doyen had allowed her deeper into the sanctum of Nine Veils, revealing their place in history and of course the future.

Until, eventually, it came to light that he and his cult had been the force controlling the Green and Red Society—who more than twenty years ago had attacked the USA to steal K'in. An attack that resulted in her temporary death and subsequent resurrection owed to the mixing of her DNA with the creature Wak.

The Doyen could not be sure if it was that moment Victoria's persona had begun to twist, but it *was* the moment that her eagerness to raise the Nine Veils to a position of power exploded. Frustrated with playing the shadows, utilising existing terrorist factions, she had suggested that they begin to build their own army—a division of highly trained assassins to infiltrate and execute key figures in government structures. This way, they would accelerate the Nine Veils ascension and bring back a global belief in God and his plan. And in those days, he was a younger and more ambitious man. Her strategy had seemed reasonable. As a first step, he used his influence to hack ECHELON to listen to the world's conversations and choose where to strike. First priority was money for the facilities and resources for their army. A manipulated stock market had provided.

Millions of dollars were accumulated and added to the Nine Veils already sizeable stockpile. In the modern capitalist world, there really wasn't anything he couldn't purchase. Aircraft, man power, weapons, land. And so, the process of creating a loyal army, grown from young men and women—orphans taken from abject poverty in Russia—began. Being young, they were impressionable and easily coerced. Fealty given freely. Yet, paranoid as she was, Victoria insisted on a safety protocol should one ever be captured: death by remotely triggered explosive ink. Crude, but necessary. His older self would now not agree.

While his discomfort with how the children were managed by Victoria grew, he could not deny their critical role when once again the hand of fate intervened: a sink hole in Siberia opened and provided not one but a nest of Huahuqui for the taking. Just as Victoria had predicted, using out-dated terrorist cells had failed in obtaining the creatures. He had not counted on Freya Nilsson or the USA government interceding. In the end, it was her orphan army that was, at least partially, successful.

Half of the known Huahuqui and their bonded children were stolen from Antarctica.

As with all stolen beings, the Huahuqui and children did not give away their loyalty. In fact, they fought Victoria's rule with all they had. None more so than Svetlana. This infuriated Victoria beyond all measure.

Neith sat at the Doyen's heel, and he subconsciously rubbed at her raised snout. The touch of her smooth skin drove the Doyen's train of thought to Victoria's continued refusal to bond with a Huahuqui. He'd tried to convince her that perhaps that would be a way to reach the children and the other Huahuqui. But she refused. Or maybe the Huahuqui rejected her. It was never clear.

What *was* clear, was Victoria would stop at nothing to achieve absolute control.

He stared at the Temple even harder, as if the extra effort might make the very stone walls transparent for him to see inside. It was in this place she'd experimented on the children. For a time, he'd let it continue. Turned a blind eye. Until ... Nyalku. That day the experiments stopped. He sucked in a cold crisp breath of night air.

"Looking for me?" Victoria sidled next to him, her stare also fixed on her lonely abode.

Without turning the Doyen said, "in a manner of speaking, yes." He paused, calculating his next words. "Two decades is a long time."

A long silence filled the distance between them. Another cold breeze whipped at the brickwork and his robes.

"Phase two is complete," she continued, ignoring his olive branch. "We have control of Swiss Mountain."

"Then everything is on track," the Doyen replied.

More silence.

"The Americans," Victoria said, her tone flat and emotionless. "They have an orb."

"I know."

"And if they find a way to use it against us?" she asked.

"We are safe here. The shield has protected us all this time." The Doyen nodded to a metallic protrusion sat like a crown on the very pinnacle of his own temple. "Besides, the orb will not stay in their possession for long."

That grabbed Victoria's attention. She stepped in front of him, her ice-cold eyes searching his. "One of your spies?"

The Doyen simply smiled.

"Your arrogance will be the failure of our plan," Victoria said, wagging a finger at him.

"Not *our* plan. The universe's plan. God's plan."

"That's what I am talking about," she said, her tone growing harder. "You cannot rely on a misplaced faith in fate."

The Doyen's eyebrows raised. "Do you not believe in God's greater plan?"

"I believe He gave us free will for a reason," she replied through a now clenched jaw.

"Perhaps free will is but an illusion," he said, satisfied with his own wise words. "Perhaps our actions are but patterns we cannot see for the vastness of time over which they are enacted in the universe. Each human's step incremental in the journey of everything."

Victoria's calm expression contorted. "What happened to you? You have become lost in your own self-importance. You think you see all, but you don't."

"What don't I see, Victoria?"

His protégé didn't answer. Her cold eyes seemed to burn with icy fire. Then, without another word she stormed toward her temple. He watched her silhouette grow smaller until it disappeared through the security doors. The Doyen considered what it was she might do in there all alone. But of course, nothing of significance happened within Tocayōtla of which he didn't know. Not after her experiments. Victoria's anger had grown beyond control. But soon it would not matter. Soon the Great Syzygy would come to pass,

CHILDREN OF THE FIFTH SUN: RUBICON

and the universe's will would be known. Everything was already in motion. There was no stopping fate.

Location: Alpha Base, Antarctica

It had been a while since Freya had been to Alpha Base. With her condition deteriorating Jonathan had insisted she be as comfortable as possible. To be fair, the cold didn't help the already strange numb feeling of limbs that were less and less under her control.

Freya sat in the massive mess hall in Biome One, surrounded by the familiar hustle and bustle of scientists and Stratum passing through, though it felt different than before. The last time she was here the place felt utopian: the most educated men and women on the planet working together with the children and the Huahuqui to unlock secrets of a better humanity—secrets we had unraveled in antiquity. If Atlantis had ever existed, Biome One—how it was—is how she imagined it.

Now there was an air of fear.

The biologists and chemists wore grey expressions, heavy with worry. The Stratum were not lively yet seemed to rush from place to place. With what they were so busy was unclear. The Nine Veils had injected dread into the minds and hearts of these good people—a cancer that was spreading throughout Alpha Base. To Freya, the little Huahuqui looked lost and alone. And in her mind, it was because they didn't have a leader—*their* leader: KJ. They may be a hive, but even hives had queen bees.

As much as KJ hated to hear it, he *was* their leader. Young, testosterone-fueled and rash, but a leader nonetheless. The Stratum looked to him for his strength, his confidence, in the face of all obstacles. Never one to be beaten or admit defeat, KJ drove through. Just like he had the night Alpha Base lost all power, nearly turning everyone into a popsicles. He huddled everyone together in the very canteen in which she sat. He organized a rotation system, like penguins, to ensure everyone had some heat for some of the time. He told knock-knock jokes for four hours straight to make them all laugh.

Freya sighed. He was also the one who stole a jet, pretended to fly to China, and apparently parachuted out beforehand. According to the flight computer onboard, the plane dropped to a reasonable parachuting height in Northern Laos. *Why the hell would he go to Laos*, Freya thought. *What the hell is he looking for?*

"Mind if I sit?"

Freya looked up from her note pad. "Sorry?"

"Can I sit? Seems everyone's running around like headless chickens."

"Sure, uh …"

"Koa, Brown," the man said and took a seat.

"Freya Teller," she replied.

"Oh? You any relation to Jonathan Teller?" Koa said, sipping on his hot coffee.

"He's my husband."

"Gotcha," Koa said. "Geez, everyone around here's gone batshit. I tried for years to get into this place. Not quite what I imagined."

"Well we're kinda facing total nuclear destruction, or don't you watch the news?" Freya pointed to a muted TV hanging on the opposite wall, a newsreader outside a nuclear power station giving a silent spiel. Her arm jerked and she quickly withdrew it into her lap.

Koa didn't seem to notice. "Yeah, hard to miss really. Typical,

I make the discovery of a lifetime and the world descends into nuclear winter." He shook his head and took another long slurp of his hot drink. "Koatlan was so close."

Freya screwed up her nose in irritation. "I'm sorry who are you? What is it you do here?"

"He's the famous Koa Brown, didn't you know?" a woman said, her tone dripping with sarcasm. She clunked a dinner try on the table and took a seat.

"Piss off, Allison," Koa said, disappearing behind his mug.

Freya tightened her lips and then buried herself back in her notes. She didn't have time for this shit, she was trying to find a clue to the Nine Veils and what they were up to. How the hell they had managed to infiltrate Project Swiss Mountain. More to the point, *why* had they infiltrated it? What was the damn point? How were the power stations and the bunkers connected?

"Ugh this guy," Allison said.

Freya huffed and looked up.

"He's friggin everywhere y'know? I mean how much money does the guy have to have to be able to put on commercials like all the time, across multiple continents?" Allison waved at the TV as if it would magically make it change channel.

"Well, you might wanna think about joining the cult of the Sixth Sun," Koa said. "If the world goes all radioactive his temples might be the only places viable."

Something in Freya's chest stirred. "What did you say?" she asked, now staring at the screen. The image of Heston Tunbridge, a broad man with a square jaw and greying beard stared back.

"Just our luck, it'll be his crazy cult creeps who inherit the Earth," Allison said.

Freya grabbed both wheels of her chair and stared into space, her mind crackling with the realization. "Heston Tunbridge. The Nine Veils. Building temples," she said aloud. "Of course."

"Huh?" Koa said.

"I'm sorry," Freya said, wheeling her chair away from the table. "I really need to speak with my husband, he'll be here shortly."

"Sure." Koa nodded. "Let him know I'll be going back out to the site and will meet him there."

Freya stopped and wheeled back to Koa. "Meet you at *what* site? What did you say you do again?"

Koa wiped his hand on his coat and offered it for Freya to shake. "Doctor Koa Brown, archeologist. I, uh we," he glanced at Allison, "found a temple buried in the ice not too far from Alpha Base. A Huahuqui temple. We think it's a broadcasting station, to all the Huahuqui of the world. Your husband went to find an orb to power it."

Freya's heart stopped. "All the orbs were destroyed."

"Apparently not," Allison interjected. "He found one and is on his way here."

CHAPTER NINE

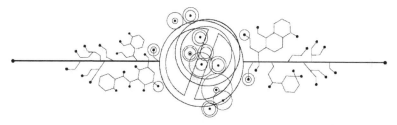

Location: Theung Village, Laos

The small village comprised of well-constructed houses of woven bamboo, sawn lumber and grass thatch, all sat on bamboo piles six feet above the ground. Inside the chief's house, near the far end by the rice barn, it was surprisingly cozy; an open hearth warming the interior. The group of Stratum humans and Catherine sat cross legged in a circle with the chief, his wife, and several of their children, hungrily munching down more purple rice in banana leaves. The Huahuqui curled up next to their symbiotes, sleeping soundly.

The chief, a short slender man of some fifty years, talked at length—pausing at regular intervals to allow Igor and Leo to translate. As suspected, KJ's hosts were Laos Theung, a semi-sedentary people who derived their living from the forest, fishing, small local craftsmanship, and cultivating rice, fruit, and vegetables. Their people did not write, instead passing knowledge via spoken stories—stories steeped in witchcraft, spirits, the after-life and Hell. It seemed that many of the stories revolved around the Phi and the Phaya Naga, whom the locals believed the Huahuqui to be. It was for this reason KJ and his friends were being hosted at all.

KJ rubbed the top of K'awin's head gently, musing on the next steps. This was a good place to stop, but they couldn't stay for long. Svetlana still had to be found and he still had to lead them across the border into China.

"So, I think we need to try again," KJ said, feeling a prolonged gap in the conversation.

"Try again?" Merry and Lex repeated.

"Yeah, to connect with Svetlana," KJ pressed. "We're much closer now. That was the idea, right?"

The group looked to each other, then nodded and shrugged in agreement.

"I guess so," Nikolaj said.

Everyone shuffled in closer to one another, stirring their Huahuqui awake.

The chief frowned, asking something of Igor, who quickly replied.

"What did he say?" Catherine asked, pulling her camera from its bag.

"He wanted to know what we are doing," Igor replied. "I told him we must complete a special prayer for a friend."

KJ took K'awin's forelimb with his left hand, Merry's hand with his right. The circle complete, the friends closed their eyes and concentrated. Unlike being in the Antarctic, cold and barren, here in the forest of Laos a connection to the living world around them filled their minds and hearts. As KJ sank deeper into the trance he could feel the breathing of his brethren in the room but also the trees outside, intertwining with each of them through their network of roots. His own pulse slowed to match the steady drum-like heartbeat of a nearby tiger stalking a macaque through the dense ferns. It was as if had spent his whole life viewing the world in monochrome and suddenly he was now exposed to a rainbow in all its glory. This was what the Earth was supposed to feel like, not empty and bleak or even filled with obnoxious humans in sprawling metropoles.

KJ concentrated harder, pushing through the leaves and branches and mammalian limbs and lizard tongues, all sensing their environment to reach out to her—to Svetlana. The room grew warmer with their power, sweat beads forming on KJ's brow. Yet no matter how hard he pressed, Svetlana could not be found. Her consciousness was not to be reached, as if it had disappeared from the world entirely.

"It's not working KJ," Nikolaj said.

"Just a little longer," KJ urged. "I know she's out there."

"We can't." Merry said, her voice strained.

"Hold on," Lex finished.

The break in their mental chain hit KJ like a hammer to the back of the head. He yelped, let go of his companions' hands and slammed his fists on the floor. "Mother fucker!" KJ unscrewed is eyes. Merry and Lex were comforting each other, while Igor and Leo had taken to sitting in a praying position in silence. Catherine, her face full of concern, sat by Nikolaj who kept blinking as if trying to focus on the room. "What the hell *was* that?"

"You pushed it too long," Nikolaj said with a grunt and rose to his feet. "We need to come out of a connection that deep properly, controlled. If we're in too long and become exhausted, someone drops out and we crash. It's like yanking a server from a mainframe. You screw the whole system."

"Did you at least find her?" Catherine asked. "Svetlana?"

KJ shook his head.

"This whole thing's a damn waste of time," Nikolaj spat, then pushed through the door and stood alone on the wooden porch.

"What are you going to do, KJ?" Catherine asked, packing her camera back into the bag.

"I don't know. She must be shielded again, somehow. Like before. We'd need to catch her unprotected again."

Merry sighed. "KJ, we couldn't hold that for 10 minutes."

"Let alone 10 hours or days to catch her at the right moment," Lex finished.

KJ's shoulders slumped in defeat. "I know, I know. I'm thinking."

"Maybe you should go talk to Nikolaj?" Catherine offered, touching KJ's shoulder.

"Why? So, he can give one of his famous lectures?"

"Because he's your brother," Catherine replied softly.

KJ rolled his eyes, then pushed out onto the porch anyway.

Nikolaj was leaning on his elbows over the bamboo railing, staring off into the night. This high up in the mountains, the air was cool and crisp, making KJ's skin prickle. He rubbed his arms and stared at his adopted brother but said nothing. What was he supposed to say? That he was wrong? That they were in the middle of Laos eating purple rice without a damn clue where they were supposed to go? He didn't need to state the obvious. And he sure as hell didn't need a lecture. KJ turned to leave Nikolaj to his brooding.

"You remember the time I told a teacher to fuck off?" Nikolaj said without turning around.

KJ stopped. "Yeah, some kid had mowed me down in the play zone and you'd run over to see what happened." He laughed. "The teacher, Mrs. Gray, she came over to see what the fuss was about."

"She tried to pick you up while you were crying."

KJ sauntered over to the railing and leaned over, peering off into the dark. "Technically you told her to *put me down and fuck off.*"

"I was worried. Thought you may have really been injured. Moving you without checking was stupid, and I knew it."

"You didn't have to make her slap herself in the face," KJ said, turning to his brother.

Nikolaj's stern face broke into a smile. "That was just for fun. I got in so much trouble that day."

"Yeah, Mom was pissed."

The brothers laughed.

"Your ass is always getting me in trouble," Nikolaj said.

KJ sighed. "Yeah, I know, bro."

"Why is this so important to you?"

KJ looked to Nikolaj. "You know how messed up for us it is sometimes? Being controlled. Groomed. Watched. Studied. Groomed some more? I mean I feel like a fucking dog at Crufts man. Poke your butt out. Sit up. Bark. Good boy."

Nikolaj held up a hand. "I get it, what's your point?"

"Now imagine what it's like for Svetlana and all the other kids that were taken by the Nine Veils. We had the good version. I saw it in her eyes, man. I felt it in her mind. They did something bad to her and the others. That could have been us. If it wasn't for your mom, and mine."

"And you think it is our responsibility to do something about it?"

"It was *always* ours. The world is changing, whether the old world wants to see it or not. The way governments will function, how decisions will be made with us in key positions. Only we know the truth of it. What it is to be Stratum. To calculate a thousand outcomes at once and know the best course of action."

Nikolaj laughed. "And you think *this* is it?"

"I think the other ways are worse."

KJ felt a nudge at his knee and peered down to see a little girl, paper in hand. She waved it at him. KJ smiled and took it. She'd scrawled an image of a Huahuqui, big blue gills, pale blue body, bright blue eyes and stripe running the length of its back.

"Wow," Nikolaj said. "We're already famous."

KJ laughed and was about to hand the drawing back but stopped. He stared at the crude image.

"Something up?" Nikolaj asked.

"Any of our Huahuqui have a stripe, right down their back?" KJ replied, running his finger along the drawing for Nikolaj to see.

"No, don't think so. Creative licence?"

KJ shook his head. "I don't think so."

"TV?"

"You see a TV since we've been here?"

"True …"

KJ pushed his way back into the house, nearly taking the door off its twine hinges. Nikolaj hurried in after. Inside, the conversation immediately stopped, everyone staring. Even the Huahuqui sat bolt upright, their eyes wide. KJ held the paper up to the chief but directed his words at Igor and Leo. "Ask him if he's seen the Huahuqui before. Not on TV, in real life."

The monk brothers looked to each other, frowning, then back to KJ.

"Please, ask him," KJ pressed.

Igor cleared his throat and spoke calmly and slowly to the chief. The Theung elder nodded, replying with fervour.

"Yes," Igor said. "He says they have seen them many times over the years, moving through the forest at night. He thought we were with them."

KJ tried to control his excitement. "Have they seen this *specific* Huahuqui, with a dark stripe down its back?"

While KJ didn't understand the brief exchange, the nodding of heads was all he needed. They'd seen Ribka, and probably Svetlana.

"What's with the stripe?" Catherine asked.

"Svetlana's Huahuqui, Ribka, has a distinctive stripe running down his back. I'd bet my ass this pic is him. We're on the right path."

"China was a good guess, Junior," Nikolaj said with a smirk. "Laos was pretty close."

"They're not in Laos," Leo interrupted. "The elder says they move in and out of Laos, but the village hunters tracked them all the way to some rice terraces just over the border, in China."

KJ couldn't help a smug grin from spreading across his face.

Nikolaj rolled his eyes. "Oh, fuck off."

Everyone laughed.

"Yes," Leo said.

"Yes, what?" KJ asked.

"Yes, before you ask, they will take us at least part of the way."

"We're going to walk," Merry started.

"To China?" Lex finished.

That made both Igor and Leo laugh—big, deep, belly laughs. KJ wasn't sure he'd seen that before.

"They have trucks," Igor said, composing himself.

"Oh, that's better," Merry and Lex said in unison.

KJ nodded. "Yeah, it's damn good."

Location: Alpha Base, Antarctica

Freya hugged Jonathan tighter than she had in a long time. She'd been a bitch and she knew it. Once again, her husband had shown strength and honor and put the needs of the world before his own. He'd found an orb. One that, according to that crazy Ozzy scientist, could communicate with Huahuqui all over the world— even those controlled by the Nine Veils. Following his mission meant he could probably save KJ and the rest of the world.

"Hey, hey, you okay?" Jonathan said, his chin on her shoulder.

Freya squeezed him tighter for a second then let go. "Just glad you're here."

"I found an orb!" he blurted out.

The excitement in her husband's eyes made her hold her tongue. She knew what he had found, but why take the moment from him? "I thought they were all destroyed?" she asked.

Jonathan sat on the floor of their quarters and patted her Huahuqui, who as always doted at Freya's side, on the head. "Nope. We got a lead. I had to go to Argentina, got hit by a crazed-out death squad, managed to escape then went to Denmark and dived a U-boat wreck from World War II. But, we found it."

Freya smiled. The excitement on his face. The life he was born to live but had increasingly sacrificed to care for her, KJ, and Nikolaj. In a strange way, he even reminded her of Kelly a little. That burning energy for adventure. Just a thousand times more mature.

"We might have the upper hand now, we might be able to control the Nine Veils' Huahuqui. Or maybe talk to them, convince them to turn to our side."

"That's amazing. You're amazing, really."

Jonathan smiled, but it quickly faded. "I'm sorry I didn't go after KJ and Nikolaj."

"I know," Freya soothed and took his hand in her shaking fingers. "You made the right call."

Jonathan heaved himself to his knees. "But, I'm going find them now. The president made it a priority. Seems our boys are part of an international incident. China will be pissed."

Freya couldn't help but laugh. "Of course they are."

Her husband sighed. "So, I'll work out roughly where we think the boys exited along the flight path and go get him."

"Laos," Freya said. "The flight computer said they dropped to an exit height in northern Laos."

"What the hell are they doing in Laos?"

"Maybe avoiding parachuting into China and being shot out of the sky?"

"He always was a smart kid."

"He gets it from his mom," Freya said with a smirk.

"You know something… don't you?" Teller asked, studying her eyes.

"Hand me that laptop," Freya said and pointed at the desk.

Teller climbed to his feet with a groan, grabbed the laptop and handed it to her, standing behind her so he could see.

Freya opened it up and pulled up the internet search engine with numerous tabs already open.

"So, I was watching one of those damn infomercials with Heston Tunbridge and his Sixth Sun loonies. He's been building temples for like twenty odd years, right?"

"Don't even go there. We investigated Tunbridge. For years. Trust me when I tell you a billionaire has a lot of lawyer power. Kept tying us up in knots, but we never found anything. He's clean."

Freya scoffed and waved a hand. "Of course, I know that. But it got me thinking. We've been building the bunkers and domes for years too. If you wanted control of something like Project Swiss

Mountain, which should have completely unhackable code—built bespoke with the world's top minds—how would you do it?"

Her husband scratched his jaw. "I'd… be the one to build it and bake in a back door." His eyes widened in realization.

"Hacking nuclear power stations is one thing. Hacking something built by multiple governments across the globe, with the sole purpose of protecting the people from the Nine Veils? That's another."

"So, who built the biomes?" Jonathan asked.

"The Takamatsu Construction Group," Freya said opening another tab. "A Japanese company based out of Osaka with twenty-one subsidiaries. They're into high-rise buildings, health and welfare facilities, shrines & temples, and public civil engineering projects such as airports."

"Okay, well we know the Nine Veils has a penchant for Japan," Jonathan said, nodding.

"Not just Japan. Ancient Japan," Freya said, clicking more links. "There would have been security checks done on any construction company contracted for Project Swiss Mountain. But what the checks might have missed is the acquisition of a tiny little company of less than one hundred employees back in 2006."

"Okay so what's the company?"

"Kongō Gumi," Freya replied pulling up the penultimate tab. "The oldest operating construction company on the planet. They trace their roots back to 578 AD."

"Holy shit," Jonathan exclaimed.

"Holy shit is right. You know who worked for KG? Tatsuro Sagane."

"Sagane? You have to be fucking kidding me," Jonathan said and dropped to his knees to rest his forehead on the arm of Freya's chair.

"Any record of the original cloning program, including the incursion into China in the 40s and later when I went in there, the showdown with Masamune Sagane—the Shan Chu—in Teotihuacan, everything, was destroyed. Lucy saw to that. Long before we found the Huahuqui nest in Siberia. No one would have been looking for his name. And no one asked us to check the screen."

Jonathan lifted his head. "Son of a bitch. What is he, the Shan Chu's son or something?"

"It's a bit convoluted, but from what I can see, the Shan Chu cultivated Japanese orphans to become Yakuza and infiltrate the Triads. He gave some of them, the worthiest, his family name. When he died the program died with him. But the kids didn't."

"So, we have a construction company most likely with ties to the Nine Veils just through damn history who, at a minimum, had one employee directly related to the Shan Chu who tried to end the world once already."

Freya nodded. That did about sum it up. She rested a hand on Jonathan's and craned her neck to look in his eyes. "If we find Sagane, we might find the Nine Veils. *You*, might find them."

Jonathan shook his. "No."

"What?"

"I promised you that I'd go after KJ and Nikolaj now. I meant it."

Freya opened her mouth to protest.

"Stop right there. This isn't a debate."

It was difficult to describe the pain in her chest at that moment. The conflict between the burning need for her husband to go after her boys, and knowing he was probably key to saving the world. "That doesn't make sense and you know it. The needs of the many—"

Teller squeezed her hand. "They are not the few, they are my kids. I did my job. I found the orb. Doctor Brown can figure out how to use it. The NSA and CIA are working on finding the Nine Veils. We can give them your insight to help." He paused looking into her eyes. "Now, I go find our sons."

The stone in Freya's throat threatened to choke off her words. "Okay," was all she could manage.

"Besides, something tells me KJ and Nikolaj are smarter than our government agencies. For whatever reason they are in Laos, I bet it's a good one."

"You always have faith in them, don't you?" Guilt filled Freya for doubting her boys, especially KJ.

"They've always been smart kids. Now they're smart men. They'll lead the world, babe. Gotta let them try."

Freya gave a weak smile. "If there is anything left to lead. Jonathan, the only logical reason to take the bunkers is because they plan on blowing up the power stations. They're taking those people they think will be valuable and killing everyone else."

Jonathan mused on the thought. "It's possible," he said. "But, then they'd irradiate so much of the Earth for such a long time. Far longer than there are resources in the bunkers to feed everyone. We're talking decades if not hundreds of years."

Freya's limbs shook, and her mind felt fuzzy again. "Then, I don't know. I don't get it. Hostages maybe, they're going to demand something?"

"Now that sounds more plausible," Jonathan said. "But I'll leave that to the agencies to figure out. I'm going to Laos, apparently." He offered a weak smile.

"So, what shall I do, sat in *this* thing?" she said, patting her wheelchair.

Her husband laughed. "Like that thing has ever stopped you giving orders. We'll talk to the president first, and we'll ask for you to be assigned to Dr Brown. All these scientists may have the degrees, but you have experience and worked with the Huahuqui longer than anyone. We need that orb up and running."

Freya tightened her lips in determination. Her husband was right. Damn the chair and damn the disease. Her brain still worked. She reached out her shaking arms to hold both of Jonathan's hands. "Come home safe. I want all three of my boys right here with me."

Her husband squeezed her fingers. "I promise."

CHAPTER TEN

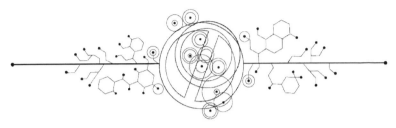

Location: South East Rice Terraces, China

The pick-up truck hurtled along the dirt road through a dense forest of bamboo and fern. Despite blankets and cushion's lining the flatbed, the jolts and bumps jarred KJ's spine. It hurt like hell. The drone of the old engine and the grinding of the mismatched tires on the hard earth made it difficult to talk to his brethren—verbally or telepathically. He could barely hear his own thoughts. KJ rubbed his hands together, friction warming them. The sun was quickly slipping away and this high up, even in the tropical forests, the cold would seep deep into his bones by nightfall.

The long trip gave KJ too much time to think. Normally his quick actions had rapid consequences. Problems were solved in the moment. But it had been days now since they left to find Svetlana, and the time alone in his own head only served to allow doubt to creep in. If KJ was honest, this mission was a really stupid idea. He could just imagine the berating he would receive from his mom and Jonathan—if he made it back alive. Even if he found Svetlana he, and his friends, could very well be killed on sight. His crew were smart and loyal and willing, but they weren't military. In fact, it dawned on him that they didn't even have any weapons at all.

"Uh, Nikolaj?" KJ called over the din.

What?" Nikolaj replied in KJ's head.

"So, you think these farm boys will give up some of their guns?"

"Guns?"

"Yeah you know, in case."

"In case there's a damn army waiting for us?"

"Yeah."

Nikolaj scowled. *"I thought this was going to be covert. Go in, get Svetlana, get out?"*

"Sure. But, you never know."

Igor nudged Leo, nodding to KJ and Nikolaj. *"Something up?"* he asked them both.

"Kelly Junior wants guns."

"Of course," Igor said. *"The Thueng agreed to lend us some firearms. It seemed prudent. I would not wish to use them, merely as a deterrent."*

KJ grinned at Nikolaj.

"Don't even," Nikolaj projected.

The truck slowed and then skidded to an awkward stop. The engines were cut and the Thueng drivers stepped out.

Another break already? KJ thought.

Igor and Leo leapt down to the ground and sauntered over to the villagers. There was a brief exchange, with the drivers pointing off into the distance. KJ's gaze followed their arms into deepening forest but as he continued the path beyond, and above the canopy, his breath caught in his chest. Set against the orange sky and red sun were thousands of glass-like pools that seemed to float on perfectly cut steps in the mountainside. They glistened and sparkled in the light, making the nearby flowers pale in comparison.

K'awin and the Huahuqui warbled.

KJ's gaze climbed the terraces until there, high up near the flattened summit, he saw it: a collection of man-made temples. The stepped pyramids and smaller ancillary buildings were stark black shadows against the sky. KJ instantly recognized their South American design. Even from this distance their arrangement was clear—this site was a replica of Teotihuacan.

"That's it," KJ said. "That's where she is."

"Can you," Lex started.

"Feel her?" Merry finished.

KJ shook his head. "No, but I know it. That's where she is. Shielded perhaps. But there."

"So, what's the plan?" Catherine asked, one eye wedged into the viewfinder of her camera. Rapid clicks signalled her snapping the strange clash of Asian countryside and South American architecture.

"We leave the truck here. That's probably five clicks out, and god knows how high up. We have to walk it."

"We scan it, Kelly Junior," Nikolaj said. It sounded like an instruction, not a suggestion. "Stick to the perimeter. Once out of the forest it is pretty exposed, we would have no place to hide."

KJ thought about arguing, but Nikolaj was right. "That's fair. We get the scope of the situation. It'll be dark soon, then we can get a little closer and see what's what."

"And when we find her?" Merry and Lex said in unison.

"That's when our companions here help us out," KJ said, motioning to the Huahuqui. "If we can catch her alone, it'll be all of our minds against hers."

Nikolaj shook his head. "Your plans are always hinged on a bunch of *ifs, buts, and maybes*, you know that?"

"Our whole existence is coincidence. Every single one of us is here because just one of our ancestors didn't die. Wasn't killed in a war, taken by a plague, or stepped on by a mastodon," KJ said, though his tone seemed without inflection, detached from him somehow. "The series of events that had to occur to ensure every sperm met every egg in every coupling that led to you or me is statistically mindboggling. If you think on it too long, it'll fry your brain. In the end, you have to believe there is some order. Some reasoning. A pattern. Everything led to here. We'll find her."

"Jesus, KJ, that was profound," Catherine said, he camera limp in her grasp.

KJ looked up and realized that everyone was staring. He shook off the claustrophobic feeling crawling over him. "Hey, I have my moments." Though he wasn't sure it was *his* moment. He rubbed K'awin's head and stared back up at the temples.

"Let's set up a base here. If we get Svetlana out, the truck is our getaway," Nikolaj suggested.

Everyone nodded and set about preparing a camp. Everyone except KJ, who wandered up to the nearest tree and leaned against it. K'awin waddled up next to him and plopped herself down.

KJ felt a nudge at his arm. He turned to see Catherine. For once she didn't have a camera in her hand. Her mismatched eyes sparkled. He felt his stomach knot just a little. K'awin head-butted his knee and gave him a knowing look.

"How you doing?" she asked in that soft Irish lilt.

"Yeah, great. Almost there. What did I tell ya?"

Catherine smiled. "You wanna tell me the real reason we're doing this?"

KJ wrinkled up his nose. "It's our responsibility—"

"You know, your mom makes that same expression when she's

159

mad—or lying."

KJ exhaled and turned back to a sky now dotted with the first winking stars.

Catherine placed a hand on his shoulder.

"I fucked up," KJ said, finally.

"Fucked up?" Catherine repeated. "How?"

KJ shrugged. "She misses my dad so much, you know? Mom. A guy I never met. Never knew. But, I knew *about* him. I'd watch the light dance on her eyes every time his name was mentioned, and then I'd watch that happiness fade. Knowing he was dead."

"I'm not sure what that has to do with you. I'm sure she does miss him, but she loves Jonathan too."

"Oh, I know," KJ said and kicked at a stone. "But she needed both. Every time I did something that reminded her of him, that little spark would come back. I could see it. I could do all the academic stuff. It was embarrassingly easy. But they had golden balls back there for that." He motioned to Nikolaj. "He could tick that box. Besides, he needed it. He wasn't blood. After what happened to his mom, he needed something to tie him to us."

"So, you gave Nikolaj ... a break?"

KJ shrugged again.

"And then you tried to fill your dad's shoes?" Catherine said.

"I guess," KJ said. "I loved seeing her happy. She'd always tell me off for pulling a stunt, but in her eyes... they told another story. And to be fair, I loved the idea that my old man would be proud if I was like him, too. Ya know? Brave. But, now we're here. And it's real and people could get hurt. I fucked up. Should've come alone."

Catherine's tone hardened. "Now that *would* have been a fuck up. Coming here alone? We're your friends. They followed you here because they believe in you."

160

KJ scoffed.

"They do. *I* do. You got us this far. Let's get Svetlana. If we can bring her back, hell, she may be able to help us end these assholes for good."

KJ looked to Catherine, and their gazes locked. He wanted to grab her and kiss her so badly he thought he may explode. But she wasn't a Stratum groupie, or a naive young girl he could manipulate with his powers. He *could* manipulate her, but he refused. She was a real woman and deserved respect. He opened his mouth, but no words came. Instead, K'awin leaped up between them like a jealous dog, slapping her tiny lips together.

"Yeah you're right girl," KJ said, already turning to the camp. "We should eat."

Once the sun had disappeared behind the rice terraces, darkness fell upon the forest. A full blue-grey moon hung high in the sky, its metallic glow reflected in the many pools. Just enough light to maneuver without flashlights, but not so bright as to be seen easily. While the west side of the terraces had a conveniently carved path that cut in a winding fashion up the mountain and right to the front door, KJ and his crew agreed that approaching from the south was better. Though more of a climb, it provided a little cover and perhaps even a covert way into the compound.

The Thueng had given everyone moving up the mountain a weapon and stayed with the truck. KJ took the vanguard with K'awin, clawing at the soft water-logged mud as he climbed. His fatigues quickly became caked in muck, weighing him down. The exertion at this altitude was more exhausting than he had anticipated, but with labored breaths, he kept low to the ground and pressed on. Merry, Lex, Kiska and Kroshka, and Igor, Leo and their Huahuqui held the center. Catherine was sandwiched between them. Nikolaj and Chernoukh brought up the rear.

They reached the lip of a shelf two lower than the summit on which the compound sat. KJ crouched down, K'awin by his side, and caught his breath—which was now beginning to fog the air as the warmth of the day dissipated. He scanned the grassy ledge punctuated with great pools. Up close they were just as beautiful, the details of the starry heavens mirrored in exquisite accuracy—amplified even, so the amethyst wash of the Milky Way seemed to swirl through the very land on which they sat.

"You feel that?" KJ whispered.

Nikolaj sidled up with Chernoukh whose black gills were billowing with each deep breath. "Yeah… they're here. Lots of them, it's hard to say how many. At least as many as we have at Alpha Base. Maybe more?"

KJ closed his eyes, allowing the warm completeness to fill his chest.

"KJ," Catherine said. "If you can feel *them*, they can feel *you*, right?"

Merry and Lex nodded, glancing between KJ, Nikolaj, and Catherine.

"We're kinda like white noise. There are so many here… but we can shut ourselves off from them somewhat." KJ laughed to himself. "So many… but, they're not looking for us, so won't probe the collective consciousness for us."

"You know that for a fact?" Nikolaj asked, though his head was cocked in a way that KJ knew the question was rhetorical. "Because you said Svetlana is still in that fat head of yours."

"It's an educated guess," KJ said, winking at Merry and Lex.

"So how do we find her?" Nikolaj asked.

"I guess we look. Climb up to the uppermost platform and see what we can see."

"I really don't like this, Junior," Nikolaj said through clenched teeth.

"We're here now. In for a penny—" KJ didn't bother to finish his proverb, already climbing again. Behind he could hear Nikolaj muttering.

The last few natural shelves in the mountain were the hardest. More pools meant less solid earth on which to hold and the ground that was available was like clay, sucking at their boots. Catherine complained with seemingly every inch, while Igor and Leo grunted and pushed forward, somehow moving stealthily despite their sizeable bulk. The Huahuqui had the easiest time, their slightly webbed feet and powerful limbs allowed them to push against the slush and spring from one grassy outcropping to the next. Eventually, they neared the summit.

KJ had never been to Teotihuacan, but now, peering over the edge of the grassy shelf, it was as if he was in South America, not China. Every stone, every small wall, building and temple, seemed to be in the exact place he had seen in every photo. The only difference was that here the reflecting pools were full and connected by narrow channels.

The compound was deathly still.

A light breeze blew across KJ's neck and his skin prickled. "I don't like it," he said.

"It looks deserted," Catherine said.

KJ shook his head. "No, they're here. It's just—" his voice trailed off.

"What," Catherine said inching forward.

KJ held his arm out to stay the reporter.

"What's up?" Catherine asked.

"She's here," KJ hissed.

"Who, Svetlana?" Nikolaj pressed.

KJ nodded. "She knows I'm here."

"What? How's tha—" Catherine started.

One after the other, massive floodlights clapped to life drowning KJ and his companions in blinding yellow light. The moon paled against the false illumination which revealed row upon row of shadows, both human and Huahuqui.

"Fuck!" KJ shouted. "Run!"

They scattered, clambering over the mud, struggling to flee. The *whizz pop* of gun fire and snap of bullets striking the ground and water around them was deafening. It lasted only seconds but was long enough to make KJ and his friends freeze on the spot.

"I wouldn't bother," came a female voice.

KJ looked up to see Svetlana slink from the shadows into a cone of light, Ribka at her side. She wore a military style jumpsuit and carried a katana on her back. Her Huahuqui seemed to eye K'awin and then the others in KJ's group, sizing up the competition.

"Svetlana," KJ said, his voice trailing off as his focus was drawn to the figure who walked with a malevolent gait up to the side of his long-lost friend.

"Young Kelly Graham," the woman said. She had bobbed greying hair that was once likely blond and cold blue eyes. Her accent was British, harsh, each syllable enunciated in such a way that every word felt as if it were designed to cut to the bone.

"Do I know you, lady?" KJ fired back.

"In a way. I knew your father, very well."

KJ's heart stopped. Who the hell was this woman? "So?" KJ retorted. "He's pretty famous. I'm sure you're just another fan."

Nikolaj glared at KJ. *"Really?"* he projected. *"Provoking the crazy woman?"*

The woman laughed, a contemptuous shrill sound. "It seems having a big mouth runs in the family. As does sticking your nose in where it doesn't belong."

"Feeling butt hurt he didn't respond to an Instagram message or something? Or was it a fax in your day?" KJ slowly began to pull the revolver from the back of his pants as he spoke. "I forget how it works with old people."

The woman's face fell into a cruel, knowing snarl. "His idiocy got him killed. I should know. I'm the one who killed him."

KJ's skin prickled hot. He yanked the pistol out, pointed at the woman, and pulled the trigger. The muzzle flashed, and the British witch went down.

The air set ablaze with gunfire, ammunition raining down on KJ and his friends like hell fire itself. KJ dove on top of Catherine, shielding her with his body. But no bullets tore through him. None of his friends screamed. He lifted his head, squinting to see. Standing in the vanguard, behind a dome of telekinetic energy that flashed bright with gunfire were Merry and Lex. They screamed long and loud in defiance matching the roar of exploding shells.

And above their war cry, KJ could make out another voice. Svetlana's voice yelling for it to end.

"Stop!" another voice commanded above the din. The British woman slowly rose from the ground, seemingly unfazed. She brushed down her clothes and stepped once again into the harsh yellow of the floodlights. A thick gash cut through the meat of her right cheek, apparently where KJ's bullet had passed through. Yet, as KJ stared at the bloodied wound, he watched in awe as it slowly began to seal on its own—just as his wounds did.

KJ glanced at Nikolaj, whose face was slack, and then back to the woman.

"Who the fuck *are* you, lady?" KJ shouted.

The woman wiped the blood away from the nearly healed wound and leveled a desert eagle at KJ's head.

KJ held her stare, his stomach knotting. He tried to control her mind, but it was unlike any other he'd encountered. Dark, lifeless. A void.

"Wait!" Svetlana yelled. "The Doyen wants him alive."

Victoria took another step forward, re-aiming her weapon.

"Svetlana is correct, Victoria. I do." The army parted in two as if they were the Red Sea and the large man in flowing robes who glided through their ranks was Moses himself. "We will have much to discuss, he and I. Once the Great Syzygy has come to pass."

CHAPTER ELEVEN

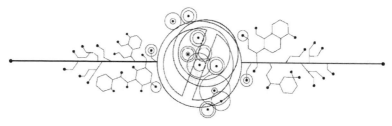

Location: TAO headquarters, Texas, USA

Lucy paced inside the TAO situation room. Keyboards clicked and clacked with furious effort. People with clipboards ran from station to station. The monitors flicked from image to image so quickly that she could barely recognize what was being shown. And at the front of the room, like a silent conductor, Jim Waltham conducted everything.

"Sir, we have a communication coming in for the President," said one of the operatives at a station.

The room quietened.

"Demands for the hostages?" Lucy asked, her heart in her throat.

"It's Alpha Base. Jonathan Teller?"

Lucy heaved a sigh of exasperation. She was sure Jonathan would be calling for good reason, but every minute that passed without demands for the hostages added yet more weight to her emotional baggage.

"Put him on the screen," the admiral ordered.

The OLED wall screen faded to black, clearing all previous feeds, then illuminated with the faces of both Jonathan and Freya Teller.

"Madam President," Jonathan said.

"Hello Jonathan. I hope you are calling because you've made it to Alpha Base with the orb, and connected with Doctor Brown?"

"I did. But it will take time to see if we can do anything with it. I'll get to that in a moment, if you don't mind," Jonathan said.

"Okay, you have me intrigued. What's on your mind, Jonathan?" Lucy asked.

"Ma'am, you need to find a man named Tatsuro Sagane."

"Who?" Waltham asked.

Lucy's head swam. Sagane? Another Sagane?

"It's a long story," Jonathan continued. *"I'll send over a report and research. The short version is he's affiliated with the Shan Chu, from the incident in Mexico. He was an employee of the company that built the biomes and bunkers for Project Swiss Mountain. We think he may have put in a back door to the project. Find him and you might be able to get the bunkers back. You might even find how they hacked the power stations."*

Lucy sighed heavily, some of her burden escaping through her lips. They finally had a lead. "Thank you, Jonathan. Great work."

Jonathan shook his head. "Not me, Madam President. This was all Freya."

The president turned her gaze to her long-time associate who now looked thin and frail in her wheelchair. Lucy knew Freya Nilsson may appear beaten, but she would be a force to be reckoned with right to the end. "Thank you, Freya."

Freya simply nodded.

"And the orb, Jonathan?" Lucy pressed, hoping to ride the wave of good news.

"It arrived safely with us. Dr Brown is about to take it to the site. But… I'd like to ask permission for Freya to go with him. She's got the most experience with these things than anyone—"

Lucy gave a curt nod. "Granted. A security detail from Alpha Basc goes with them."

"Agreed," Jonathan said.

"And you?"

"I'm going to find KJ and Nikolaj," Teller replied resolutely. *"As instructed. Every other base is covered. I'm no extra help here. And something tells me KJ has sniffed something out."*

Lucy looked to the Admiral.

"I concur, Teller," the admiral said.

"Thank you, sir," Jonathan replied.

"Jonathan …" the words stuck in Lucy's throat. "Good luck."

"Thank you, ma'am."

The video call clicked off.

Lucy turned to Waltham. "We need to find Sagane. Now. He may be our best lead."

Jim nodded. "We'll root this bastard out."

"Good. Oh and, Jim, once you have him find out if he knows of any other hack. Something tells me it's not just the stations and the bunkers."

Jim dipped his head in acknowledgment and left Lucy to her thoughts.

Lucy eyed the room for the thousandth time. Despite all the technology and expertise filling that one chamber, she felt horribly ill-equipped to deal with the situation. The world had been slow to understand the value of the Huahuqui—squabbling more over who should work with them, or how could their existence be monetized. By comparison the Nine Veils had decided a long time ago the creatures' worth and now were executing a plan so long in the making it was terrifying to think on how it would all end.

Location: Alpha Base, Antarctica

Jonathan stuffed his backpack with the final few items he may need and then secured it with the fasteners. The table in the prep room was littered with an assortment of weapons. He picked up the surprisingly light HK416 fully automatic rifle with an EOTech optic, a sound/flash suppressor, and an AN/PEQ-2. All purpose, night and day. He checked the action and the magazine, then placed it back on the table. The Glock 19 with M-6 laser light and a Duane Dieter's Master of Defense CQD knife slipped into the holsters strapped to his thighs. Finally, a multiband Inter/Intra Team Radio for communication between him and his team in the field—his team. This time, Teller knew with whom he was working, because he'd called in the cavalry.

Tony Franco had arrived a few hours earlier. Franco had left Teller's squad after the incident in Antarctica to head up his own private security team, often used by the CIA in Syria. He and Teller had remained firm friends, and he was one of the few people with whom Jonathan could talk about everything. When he wasn't chauffeuring important people around the war-torn country, Tony would visit and have dinner with Freya and the family. More importantly, he was like an uncle to KJ and Nikolaj. Teller trusted him with their lives.

Then of course, there was Matthew Lauder. Not one of Teller's original team, but the soldier who had rescued Freya in Somalia and helped get them to Madagascar, and eventually La Reunion. Without him she would have died at the hands of local militants, organized by the Nine Veils. Whether it was fate or Lauder's own request was never clear, but he ended up doing several tours of duty at Alpha Base. He felt an allegiance to Freya and the boys, and that worked for Teller. It just so happened, he was now stationed in South East Asia. He would meet Teller at the rendezvous point in Laos.

"You okay?" Freya wheeled into the room, Dacey at her side.

"Yeah, I'm good. All packed. We head out in an hour."

Freya inhaled deeply. "You have any idea where the boys were going?"

"No, but they are smart kids. If they had a direction, then we'll be able to figure it out. Tony's one of the best trackers I know. He'll pick up their trail." It wasn't a total lie. Tony was a great tracker, but the trail was probably long since cold. "And we'll have a couple Huahuqui with us, that'll help. Anyway, are you all set to head out with Dr Brown?"

Freya rolled her eyes. "Yeah, the transport is ready. They are rigging some gear to get me to the base of this site. Apparently, it's not wheelchair friendly."

They both laughed nervously.

"Hey, if the world goes… you know …" Teller started.

Freya grabbed his hand. "I know," she said and kissed his fingers. "You're a good man, Jonathan Teller."

Teller tightened his lips and swallowed the stone in his throat.

"Boss?" came a voice from the doorway.

"Tony!" Freya said and wheeled over.

Franco hugged her.

"We ready to go?" Teller asked.

Tony nodded. "Yeah, the boys are loaded up. Though I'm not crazy about taking such a large civilian contingent."

Teller slapped his friend's shoulder. "The Huahuqui are going to be our best chance of finding the boys and their companions. They stay with us, in our protection. Just a couple."

"A couple? You sure about that?"

"What do you mean?" Freya interrupted.

"Have you been to Biome One?" Franco asked, already turning to the door.

Freya wheeled after him. Teller rubbed Dacey's nose, slung his pack, and brought up the rear. The friends headed to the elevator that would take them up to Biome One and the main exit.

The doors to the elevator slid open. The noise in the foyer was deafening. Hundreds of Stratum filling the entire space talking among themselves. Pink and blue gills of the Huahuqui bobbed and quivered as they padded and pranced about. The young men and women, none older than thirty, packed the chairs, benches, and sofas. At least half were carrying gear—backpacks and equipment—as if they were about to embark on an adventure holiday. The room quickly grew silent at Teller's entrance.

"What's going on?" Teller asked to no one in particular.

"The time is coming, and we must make a stand," came a voice from within the crowd.

"The time for what?" Freya asked.

"The setting of the Fifth Sun," said another.

Teller couldn't tell from whom the voices were coming. "You think the end time is coming?"

"It has already started," came a third voice.

Teller dropped his pack and rubbed his face in exasperation.

"Okay, I don't know what is going on, but can someone take the lead here. Kinda weird talking to no-one."

A faint blue haze grew around the Stratum.

"We are one," said a chorus of voices in Teller's head.

Freya shot a look at him and then Franco.

"Yeah, I heard it," Teller said.

"Without Kelly Junior, they're relying on their hive mind," Freya said.

Teller redirected his attention to the Stratum. "What do you want?"

"To help. To bring an end to the Fifth Sun and usher in the Sixth with as little bloodshed as possible. It is our fate, our destiny and our responsibility." Their metallic voices in unison were choir-like, musical.

"I can't let you come with me," Teller said. "I can't risk you all."

"We are already at risk. All life on this planet is at risk."

"Sorry, guys," Teller said picking up his pack again and walking toward the loading bay. "Another time."

Teller's legs stopped working and he froze in place. He turned to the Stratum whose blue haze had now become an intense cerulean glow encompassing all of them.

"We could make you, Jonathan Teller. But we would rather have co-operation."

Teller's eyes widened, his stare moving to Freya who sat, taut and frustrated.

"Half of us will go with you to find Kelly Junior and our companions. They were looking for our lost brethren. They need our help now."

"They were looking for your lost brethren," Freya said. "They got a lead on the Nine Veils? On the other Huahuqui!"

"Half will go with you, Jonathan Teller. Half will remain here with Freya Teller and Doctor Brown."

"The orb," Teller said in realization. "They know about the orb."

"Jonathan," Freya said, gliding to him. "You have to let them. This is bigger than all of us. They are the future. They always were."

Teller relaxed and doing so seemed to be given back control of his limbs. He turned to his wife. "I don't have a choice in this, do I?"

Freya glanced at Dacey, then the Stratum and back to Teller. "No, I don't think you do."

Teller stood and looked to Tony. "We're gonna need a bigger plane."

Location: Tocayōtla, Southwest Rice Terraces, China

Svetlana paced the subterranean chamber liked a caged jaguar. She often came down here, into the galleries beneath the Temple of the Feathered Serpent, to think. Away from the prying eyes of her Phalanx, the Doyen, and especially Mother. While she could feel her brethren, the stillness of the galleries calmed her nerves.

She sat on the dirty ground, back to a wall and Ribka at her side, fingering one of the hundreds of metallized spheres strewn about. She had no idea what these little balls were for. Neither did the Doyen, but he was insistent on everything being recreated just as it was in Mexico. In fact, he'd imported the actual artifacts at great cost: from spiral seashells, cat bones, wooden masks covered with inlaid rock jade and quartz, elaborate necklaces, rings, and even greenstone crocodile teeth. Perhaps the most impressive was the miniature mountainous landscape, sat in the middle of the room, complete with tiny pools of liquid mercury representing lakes.

Svetlana examined the walls and ceiling, impregnated with mineral powder comprising magnetite, pyrite and hematite. They shimmered and glittered as if she were outside, sitting under the stars. But she wasn't. She was in here again, doubting everything; herself and her purpose. The Doyen had shown her. Made her understand the divine plan. One that was not even of his making; instead he simply accepted it and worked tirelessly to ensure it manifested as it was supposed to. Yet, the moment she saw *him*—Kelly Junior Graham, according to Mother—her mind and will seemed, once again, not to be hers.

The prisoners now languished in a building at the end of the Avenue of the Dead. Why were they here? Had they tracked her all the way to China because she'd attempted to assassinate the president? If they'd tracked her, then why hadn't the full force of the US military come with them? There were too many questions, and too few answers. And to make it worse, now they were inside the interference field, they were constantly in her mind. Especially Kelly Junior. His chi was a relentless nag in the back of her consciousness, an infected splinter that refused to be dug out. *Why him? Why this man?* she thought.

Svetlana clambered to her feet and tossed the ball back to the dirt, a renewed energy coursing through her at the thought of obtaining resolution. With Ribka in tow, she stormed the long corridor, climbed the makeshift ladder, and nearly exploded from the entrance out into the night air. Under a starry sky unpolluted by city lights, Svetlana stomped with purpose toward the prisoner compound, nearly bowling Nyalku over. She ignored his complaints and continued toward the prison.

A quick conversation with the guards, and Svetlana slipped into the building.

Behind narrowly spaced steel bars, strangely anachronistic with the ancient Mexican replica structure, sat the prisoners. Much like her own Phalanx, each human had a Huahuqui with them, huddled in a ball or curled around a leg. All except the woman who'd been carrying the camera equipment. She seemed to be alone.

"Svetlana," came a voice from the cage. It was Kelly Junior.

She eyed him carefully, probing his mind, but he seemed able to block her attempt at extracting detailed thoughts. "How do you know me, Kelly Graham Junior?"

The young man stood and took a few paces toward her, his fingers slipping around the bars. "That's a long story," he said with a half-smile plastered over his face.

He looked smug. Svetlana already didn't like him. "Tell me," she said through gnashed teeth.

Ribka warbled in agreement.

"You can probe my head all you want, I'm not giving up anything for free." He sauntered to the back of the cage and plonked himself next to a Huahuqui.

"I could make you. You are not strong enough against our Phalanx," Svetlana said.

"Phalanx? Phalanx?" KJ said, feigning a search of his brain for the word. "Nikolaj, isn't that the thing that dangles at the back of your throat?"

"You," Svetlana said, pointing at Nikolaj. "Tell me how you know me."

"I can't believe I'm saying this, but I agree with Junior,"

Nikolaj said. "We'll tell you anything you wish to know, but you have to tell us things too."

Svetlana considered the proposal for a moment. Revealing the greater plan was not an issue, since it was the universe's plan. Whether or not they knew of it, it could not be stopped. And besides, Mother would soon have control of them. They may have been too old to be trained as she was, but Mother's serum, the one she'd been working on, that would make them see the truth of the Nine Veils. "Fine," she said, finally.

Kelly leapt to his feet. "Who's the British witch you're hanging with?" he blurted out.

"I actually had bigger questions, Junior," Nikolaj interjected.

"Her name is Victoria McKenzie," Svetlana replied. "She's the Doyen's right hand. One of the first humans to encounter the Huahuqui. One of the first to be blended with the Huahuqui. She carries their DNA."

"Holy shit," Catherine said. "I heard about her. The original science team spliced in genes. Helped her regrow limbs. She went a little bat shit."

"And killed my dad, it would seem," Kelly Junior said, though quietly.

"I would not know such things," Svetlana answered. "Now, how do you know me? Why are you in my head?"

"We were friends once," Nikolaj said, approaching the bars, his black-gilled Huahuqui accompanying him. "This is Chernoukh. Do you really not remember?"

Svetlana stared at the blond man and his oddly colored companion, struggling to draw some ancient memory from the depths of her mind. But nothing would come. "I don't know you."

"Yes, you do," Kelly said, rising again. "You are Nenets, a

wanderer, born in Siberia. A sink hole opened nearly twenty years ago near your village. Inside were hundreds of Huahuqui. One of them found you. Ribka, little fish." He pointed to her Huahuqui. "All the children of your village were bonded to a Huahuqui. The Nine Veils tried to kidnap you all. My mom, and his mom," he nodded to Nikolaj, "they saved you, at least for a while. Don't you remember? We had to fly to Africa, and then to Madagascar and we took a boat—but it was attacked. It went down."

Pain stabbed Svetlana in the front of her brain. A flash of white blinded her momentarily. She stumbled a little, her legs weak. "I… I… don't …"

"My mom died that night," Nikolaj pressed, his eyes full with sadness. "But Kelly Junior's mom, with the help of others got us all to Antarctica."

Another stab, worse than last time, knocked her to her ass. She clasped at her head. There were no memories, only flashes of white and sharp, hot pain in her brain tissue.

"But *they* came for us," Kelly Junior pressed. "The Nine Veils. My mom couldn't stop them all. They took you and Ribka and half the children and their Huahuqui."

"I … don't remember that… I don't remember anything… there is only the Phalanx," she moaned, grasping at her black hair.

"No, there is *us*," KJ said. "We came for you, Svetlana. We came for all of you. Not NATO, or Alpha Base, *us*. Because no-one knows what it is to be Stratum *but* us."

"But we are not Stratum," came a male voice. "We are Phalanx."

Svetlana looked up to see Nyalku standing over her. He stretched out a hand. She grabbed his wrist and allowed herself to be pulled up.

"What are the Nine Veils planning?" Nikolaj called after her. "Why the shootings, why the power stations? What are you doing?" His voice faded as Nyalku took her by the arm and escorted her away.

"Why did you go to them?" Nyalku asked. "This was not a good idea. If Mother finds out—"

Svetlana wasn't listening. Her mind was swamped with another voice. Kelly Junior's voice.

"We were friends, Svetlana, you and I. You must remember. I'm coming for you. I promise."

CHAPTER TWELVE

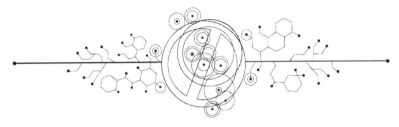

Location: Alpha Base, Antarctica

Koa scratched his head. Of course, he'd read about the orbs, but that information was squeezed from the minds of those who had come into contact with one some twenty years ago. According to released files by the NSA, the original research from the 1960s had been destroyed following the fallout of the Huahuqui cloning program.

He stared at it again, floating in its glass box, pulsating with blue-green light. Alive. Probably full of knowledge he could never unlock. Normally, there would be time to investigate. To study and learn. But *now* was anything but normal. They were out of time.

"Finished staring at it?" came a voice over his shoulder.

Koa jumped back. "Oh hey, Melissa. Um , yeah, I'm good. Just looking."

"Don't mind him. He always gets flustered around women he likes," Allison said, then pushed past and marched across the courtyard to the stone tower in the center.

Koa felt his face flush. Melissa was Alpha Base's assigned xenobiologist. She was young, pretty, and damn smart.

"So," Melissa said seemingly ignoring the jibe. "Do the inscriptions say anything about how we connect this puppy up?"

Koa tried not to stare into the big brown eyes for too long, before managing to say, "from what I've been able to decipher so far, the orb sits in the crucible. This whole place is constructed with calaverite in the stones, which is a great conductor. We think it may act like a transmission station."

"Wouldn't that require a power source?" Melissa said, brushing an extra curly lock of dark hair behind her ear.

"Well it all could be chemical power of some kind," Koa replied, helping her to lift the heavy container. "The structure here comprises calaverite for sure, but a lot of pyrite and other things we haven't identified yet. If perhaps there is something in that crucible that interacts with the orb, maybe it acts like a battery of some kind—self-perpetuating?"

Melissa glanced around the structure as they shuffled toward the heart of the concourse. "You know, with all this pyrite and calaverite, this place looks like it's made of gold. See how it shimmers in the spotlight? It's like the lost city of gold."

"El Dorado?" Koa laughed, then stopped and nearly tripped over his own feet. He shot a glance at Allison.

Allison looked back from the pillar with one eyebrow raised. "She could be on to something."

Koa began trundling again, adjusting his fingers to maintain a hold on the tank. "El Dorado was originally a story about a chieftain in what we now think of as Colombia. He covered himself in gold dust as part of a ritual. *El Hombre Dorado*. The story became blended with others until it developed into a tale about a city, not a man. It's possible the stories were based in truth, referring to this temple."

"No wonder the conquistadors couldn't find it. They were looking in the wrong places," Allison said, a big grin on her face.

Koa and Melissa lowered the tank with a *thunk*. The water sloshed around, the orb swirling within.

"So, what, we think we *plop* it in the crucible?" Koa asked.

"Well, there are no external limbs, flagellae, pili—anything that would indicate that it could attach to something," Melissa said. "It seems perfectly smooth. For now. Could be microscopic I suppose. Or become externalized by a trigger. But, without the time or equipment to examine it, it's a guessing game."

"So, we *plop*," Allison said, her tone flat.

"Sure, if you want it to desiccate damn quickly," came a voice from behind him.

Koa turned to see Freya Teller, clad in a massive down-filled jacket being lowered by two large soldiers into her wheelchair. His gaze moved between her and the armed men. "Miss Nilsson, glad you could make it. How did you …?"

"Ungracefully," Freya interrupted.

"Are your friends staying?" Koa asked, nodding to the soldiers.

"We don't know what activating the orb will do. Best to be prepared," she replied.

Koa noted her shaking limbs. "Are you sure you'll be okay? It is very cold down here."

Freya clamped her hands together until the knuckles were white. "As I was saying, if you leave that thing in the open too long, especially in an environment like this, it will dehydrate and shrivel up like a raisin."

"I would agree," Melissa said. "We'd need to find a way to keep it hydrated."

"We could run a line from outside," Koa said. "Pump water from …" He trailed off, thinking. "But if it's chemical power, what salts are in the water may be important. New Berlin was supposed to be built on a geothermal lake. There must be one around, maybe… maybe beneath us?"

The echoed padding of webbed feet filled the underground cavern as Dacey came bounding out from the dark and into the spotlights. The excited Huahuqui sniffed and waddled around the tank, her big blue gills ruffling. She made the occasional warble and nudged the Perspex with her nose. The orb seemed to pulsate and glow with greater intensity in the presence of the creature.

"Dacey, come back here please," Freya said.

The Huahuqui duly trotted back to Freya and plonked herself beside the wheelchair, seemingly unaffected by the cold stone floor.

"I don't know what New Berlin is. But the Huahuqui were always associated with water and the temples were considered to have pools or lakes or rivers near, or even *in*, them," Freya said. "If this site is truly made for them, it makes sense that there would be a body of water nearby."

"Maybe this is of interest," Allison said. "Koa did you see these?"

Koa meandered over to the stone pillar to investigate.

"Look," Allison said, running her fingers along very thin grooves in the rock. "They transverse the length from the top where the crucible is, right down to the bottom."

"Uh-huh," Koa said, then winked at Melissa.

Allison punched him in the arm. "Stop thinking with your dick and use your brain. The grooves don't stop at the bottom, they *disappear* beneath the surface—underneath where we are."

Koa rubbed his shoulder, thinking. "Capillary action? Water was drawn up from underneath. But now it's dry, or there's a blockage?"

"Right," Allison said, nodding. "Let's get our equipment down here and see if we can penetrate the structure and see what's below us.

"Sounds like a plan," Freya said.

Allison ran off toward two scientists at the edge of the plaza unpacking telemetry equipment and waved for them to follow her to the surface.

Koa turned back to the pillar. The problem was, even if a lake sat right beneath them how would they access it? Drilling through the rocks would take too long. And calaverite was quite brittle. Impacting the colossal stones on which they stood could bring the whole place down. He had to hope that there was a body of water below them, and that a frozen section was preventing any water from rising to the surface. If it was anything else, they had a much bigger problem on their hands.

Location: TAO headquarters, Texas, USA

Lucy sat nervously in a private room just off the control center. Never in her life had she felt so helpless. Frustrated at being the most powerful person in America yet waiting for a thousand other people to do their job so she had enough information to do hers. For now, all she could do was sit. She took another sip of cold coffee and managed to swallow, though it hit her knotted stomach like a brick.

"Madam President?"

"Yes!" Lucy practically leapt from her seat. "What news do we have?"

"I have an update on this Sagane character," Jim said.

"Oh?"

Jim took a seat. "We brought him in with the help of the

Japanese government. Turns out the little weasel really did have a back door built into the Swiss Mountain protocols."

"But you have him, so he can tell you how he did it and reverse it, right?"

"Maybe."

"Maybe?"

"Sagane isn't a programmer, but we did some digging and it seems he linked up with some pretty high-profile hackers across the globe. This wasn't a one-man operation." He slipped an open folder with photos from surveillance cameras across the table. "Constantine Popescu from Romania, Lala Grimshaw out of Alaska, Jonas Soul from the USA, and Liana Gärtner from Austria. None of them have met each other, they're rivals for clients, but they have all met with Sagane. Since they never met, and compete for business, individual countries had no reason to share info on who these guys were talking to. Throw the fact that Sagane wasn't on anyone's wanted list, facial recognition software wouldn't even make the connection."

"The dates on these photos span years," Lucy said, pawing through them.

Waltham nodded. "Another reason nothing was spotted. This was done over two decades. Methodically and slowly as to not rouse suspicion. And since nothing was activated until now, there was no threat. The fact it was done this way probably means each hacker was used for a different country, or maybe different power plant sites across countries."

"Does all this info on hackers help us?" Lucy asked, still glancing through the photos.

"Each one has their own methodology and if they are feeling brash, a calling card to let the world know it was them. Working with our allies we are determining which hack is likely to have penetrated which powerplant systems."

"I see." Lucy knew she should have been focusing on the answer, but one photo had caught her eye. Sagane meeting with a blonde woman. The image was grainy, but the angular features, her straight posture. It looked like—

"Yeah we don't know her," the admiral interrupted. "We're trying to work on enhancing the image, but it's very blurred and quite old. Besides there's a bigger problem."

"I know who it is," Lucy said without looking up. "That's Victoria McKenzie." Lucy's throat went dry. "She was part of the original Huahuqui programs. Well, when I say part, I mean she was caught in the cross fire. Some bad things happened to her. No one has seen her in years. We... lost track." Victoria was involved in this? Was it retribution for what had been done to her? Had the US government failed her so badly after Teotihuacan? *Need to tell Jonathan*, Lucy thought. Then suddenly, Jim's full answer dawned on Lucy. "What *bigger* problem?"

His face became pallid.

"What is it Jim?"

He swallowed hard before opening his mouth. "We ran a few algorithms based on the known techniques of these hackers, to see what other systems may be affected."

"Did you find something?"

Jim licked his lips. "Project Rubicon."

Lucy sat back in her chair, eyes screwed together. There were so many projects, so many code names. It was difficult to remember them all. Swiss Mountain had been such a mammoth task that it was permanently lodged in her brain. But Rubicon? What the hell was that? A vague something crawled its way to the front of her mind. "Isn't that a NASA thing?"

He nodded. "Yes."

The vague memory began to crystalize. It was something set up along with Sentry. Something to do with deflection strategies. "They've hacked a NASA asteroid deflection program?"

"Madam President, I'm not the best to explain. Lena Bowski, NASA Administrator, and Janette the Head of FEMA will be here shortly."

Lucy wrinkled up her nose in frustration. "You can friggin try, Jim. What the hell is going on?"

The admiral exhaled purposefully. "This wouldn't have hit your radar, it was before your time as President and considered dealt with."

"*What* was dealt with?" Lucy pressed, clamping her sweaty hands together.

"In 2004, a couple of astronomers identified an asteroid, on a possible impact course with Earth. At the time, it was suggested there was a 1 in 300 chance of hitting us in 2029. It was all over the news."

"I remember that I think," Lucy said. "There was a big hype, and then literally on the same day, NASA admitted they'd got it wrong and the threat was eliminated."

"That's half right," a woman said upon entering. "I'm Doctor Bowski."

There was a brief shake of hands before the doctor took a seat.

Lucy opened her mouth to ask her question again, when her entire cabinet entered the room.

"Madam President, what's going on?" Vice President Charles asked.

"I was about to find that out myself," Lucy said. "It seems

Doctor Bowski here has the answers."

Charles looked at Jim. "You look white as a sheet, is it the reactors?"

Jim shook his head. "Just listen to Doctor Bowski."

The doctor, a woman in her fifties with bobbed auburn hair and thick-framed glasses perched on the end of her nose, cleared her throat and slid a large tablet into the center of the table. She initiated the 3D holographic module which brought up a perfect rendering of the Earth that floated two feet above the screen.

"The American people were lied to," the doctor began. "An asteroid, colloquially named Apophis after a character on a damned TV show, was flagged by two astronomers and verified by Sentry in 2004." The hologram Earth shrank to allow the orbit of an asteroid to be shown, an orange-lined elliptic. "Initial calculations suggested that Apophis would pass through a gravitational keyhole that would mean its trajectory would be altered so it would impact with Earth in 2029. Within hours that calculation was reworked with new data, and a 2029 impact was ruled out."

Lucy nodded, but said nothing.

"Because the asteroid has an orbit, it keeps passing Earth over and over," the doctor continued, manipulating the tablet to show a luminous brick-shaped asteroid flying by the Earth. At that scale, it looked dangerously close. "In fact, in 2029 it actually passed Earth closer than some of our geosynchronous satellites."

"Okay, so it didn't hit us and we watched it go by. What's your point?" the Vice President asked.

"As I mentioned, Aphosis' orbit means it continually circles, and every large heavenly body it comes close to adjusts its orbit slightly. There were also predictions it would hit Earth in 2036, or 2069. Both were shown to be unlikely, but eventually it would happen even if far in the future."

"What does this have to do with what we're dealing with right now?" asked the Secretary of Homeland security, a burly man with a bald head and thick grey beard.

"We used the 2029 pass as an opportunity," Dr Bowski said in an even tone that belied the fear in her eyes. "Working with the Chinese, we attached a device to the asteroid, something that would help to push it far off course so that it would never hit us. That was Project Rubicon."

"So, they hacked our deflection program," Lucy stated.

"Yes," Doctor Bowski confirmed.

"To what end?" the Secretary of State asked.

"We don't know for sure. Now the hack has been exposed, we can't rely on the last seven years of telemetry. And since we were using project Rubicon to track, we haven't pointed any of our other telescopes at Apophis since. But if we were to guess …"

A deep murmur filled the room, side conversations being had beside and across the table.

"They hacked our system, pushed the asteroid into a different orbit and fed false info for seven years," the Secretary of Defense recapped aloud. "Presumably to put it on a collision path with Earth. So, in what year will it hit us now?"

The doctor rubbed nervously at her neck. "Unclear. We're currently searching the skies to find it again based on predictions of where it could be."

"Given that the Nine Veils have come out of hiding now, and an impact was predicted in 2036—this year—we can assume we don't have long," Lucy said.

More murmuring

"How big is the asteroid?" Lucy managed, after pulling her

mind from the fog.

Doctor Bowski cleared her throat again. "To the public we reported it to be around 450 meters, with an impact force of around 750 megatons. To give perspective, the 1883 Krakatoa eruption released around 200 megatons."

Gasps filled the room and seemed to hang in the air.

"I didn't ask for what you told the public," Lucy pressed.

Doctor Bowski was sweating, her skin pallid. "We lied," she said, her voice shaky. "2029 wasn't far away, and we didn't want a world-wide panic."

"How. Big?" Lucy demanded.

"It's much bigger. With an impact force of twenty-five teratons."

"Teratons?" the Secretary of Homeland Security said, nearly choking on a mouthful of vendor machine coffee. "What the hell does that mean?"

Doctor Bowski coughed into her hand, then pressed a button on the tablet. The brick-shaped orb struck the holographic Earth impacting in Bolivia. It threw a ring of debris up into the atmosphere and created a shockwave that pushed out from the impact site, crumpling the mainland and into the oceans, forcing a tidal wave to fan out in all directions, just as when a stone is dropped into a pond. The wave smashed into the coasts of the other continents, flooding hundreds if not thousands of miles inland.

"It's an extinction level event. The asteroid that wiped out the dinosaurs released 100 teratons of kinetic energy. Based on our calculations, we're looking at an immediate loss of 70 percent of life in the lowlands. If it strikes the ocean, it may be slightly less, and have fewer after effects in terms of dust in the atmosphere blocking the sun. Either way …" the doctor couldn't seem to finish her sentence.

The room fell silent.

Lucy's mind spun and spun. But not with thoughts of the Earth, it's inhabitants, or even the now dim future of humanity. Instead, she filled with memories of her brother and his goofy smile, a birthday party when she was five and had a unicorn cake, her first kiss with Robert Gough. Her last kiss with her ex-husband Jeremy. Every conceivable regret over the span of her life burst from the crevices in her heart, revealing themselves in all their painful glory. All at once they mattered and then didn't anymore. "Are there contingencies?" Charles asked.

"It all depends on how far away it is," Doctor Bowski replied. "Most ideas to throw an arsenal at an asteroid come with many other risks. Blasting it into smaller chunks that rain down on us for one. And that's assuming our telescopes can find it. Ultimately, the best chance we have is regaining control of Rubicon and praying to the Good Lord that it's far enough away we can still push it off course."

Lucy snapped back to the conversation. "Then you best get on that, Doctor Bowski. Use whatever resources you need. They tried pulling this stunt once before—resetting the world to one that would leave the Huahuqui, and presumably them, in control. By detonating a nuclear weapon in the upper atmosphere. Seems this time they have found a more efficient method."

The doctor tapped the tablet again, dissolving the image of the Earth and replacing it with strange symbols streaming in straight lines across the air. "Then we need to figure out what the hell this is. It's a code within a code, embedded in the hack and we have no idea what language this is."

Location: Tocayōtla, Southwest Rice Terraces, China

Victoria lingered in the shadows, her gaze fixed on the caged prisoners—specifically the son of Kelly Graham. The boy, twenty odd years old, was a carbon copy of his father. The long hair, the half-baked smirk, even the gait of his walk. She hadn't thought about Kelly until recently. Bile once again filled her throat, exacerbating the metallic taste in her mouth. She spat on the ground and wiped her lips. He was dead. Feeling guilty about it helped no one. It was his own fault. He'd chased her to Teotihuacan just as his son had chased Svetlana here. They had both chosen death, even if they didn't know it. Everyone everywhere had chosen death and didn't know it. At least not yet.

Victoria swallowed the stone in her throat and stormed toward the prison. Its occupants shuffled inside, squirming at her coming. The two guards, wearing the ballistic gear, stared outward stalwart and unmoving, their Huahuqui at their side.

"The famed First Child of the Stratum," Victoria said, running her fingers across the bars.

"First bitch of the Nine Veils," Kelly's son fired back.

Victoria stopped and turned to him, her eyes burning with indignation. "You have a sharp tongue, just like your father."

"Yeah you keep saying cryptic shit like that. You ever actually make sense?"

"Everything will make sense soon enough."

"You guys actually buy this?" KJ directed his question at the guards.

They didn't move.

"You have no influence here," Victoria balked. "They are loyal to me, their Mother."

A woman with curly orange hair and mismatched eyes,

standing at the back of the prison, snorted. "You're nobody's mother, that's for damn sure."

Victoria stared at her. "And you are? No Huahuqui. You had no weapons. Just a camera. A fangirl? The lengths sluts like you will go to get laid."

The woman leaped at the bars, forcing her pale arm through.

Victoria stepped back, a shrill laugh echoing into the cold air. "So easy. Manipulating humans, that is. Since the dawn of time the fate of the world has rested on the shoulders of a few. And it takes but a whisper in their ears to change the future."

"And that's what you're doing?" the male with a slight Russian accent and the Huahuqui with black gills said. A quick glance into his mind told her his name was Nikolaj.

"Absolutely. I am the only one who can."

"You're a fucking nutbag," Kelly Junior said. "Just here to gloat?"

Victoria shrugged. "I was curious."

"About?"

"What makes you so special, Kelly Graham Junior. But from what I can see, there is nothing. You are your father reincarnate. Hot headed, rash, impetuous. You know he had a family before you, right? A wife and a daughter. They died. Because he was off on an adventure. People were hurt, died, in the wake of his ignorance. He's the reason I am what I am. And I'm the reason he's dead. The Doyen is a fool to believe you would be well placed in our Phalanx. The chain is only as strong as its weakest link. And you, boy, are the weakest of all. Broken and deluded."

"What the fuck are you talking about?" Kelly Junior fired back, his brow knitted in concentration.

Victoria couldn't help another shrill laugh escaping her lips. "You cannot see in my head. I am immune. But do not think I cannot see into your mind, child. You're a lost little boy. Afraid of yourself, that for all your power you amount to nothing. Yearning to be as important as your idiotic father. Unable to save your dying mother. In love with… this one," she pointed at the curly haired Irish woman, "but not having the testicular fortitude to do anything about it."

There was no retort this time. No quip or slur. The man-child just stared back at her, eyes glassy.

"You are a fraud. A wannabe. Not man enough to be brave—if not stupid—like your father. Fit to lead no one. Not that it matters."

Kelly Graham's son slumped to the floor, his eyes wide. The two females that seemed permanently glued together dashed to his side. The Irish woman's gaze was fixed on the broken boy.

"Not that what matters?" Nikolaj asked.

"Well aren't you the sharp one?" Victoria said, feeling a wry grin spread across her face. "Now you could have been useful. Such a pity."

Victoria turned and began to walk away toward her private temple. Behind, she could hear the prisoners calling out and demanding answers to unimportant questions. There was only one answer worth knowing and it wasn't discovered by breaking the Ninth Veil or blindly following an ancient philosophy outdated in a modern, and very sick, world. No, only Victoria through her experience, through being broken down and reformed, could see it. And only she, neither human nor Huahuqui, had the selflessness to comprehend it.

From across the courtyard, crouched down behind a low stone wall, Svetlana watched her Mother leave. Her gaze followed the woman until she was but a speck in the distance, and then turned back to the prisoners. An empathetic knot in her gut tightened. She'd been on the other end of one of Mother's mind delves. Your worst fears and desires dragged from your psyche and displayed for all the world to see. Humiliating. Her calf muscles tingled with an unexpected urge to run to the bars and… and what? Comfort him? Why? Because they may have been friends when they wore diapers and shared a tent in a far-off land?

No. This wasn't right.

Svetlana slowly rose to her feet, Ribka swishing his tail at her side. She was Phalanx. She was part of something. To leave them would mean leaving a family. And the Doyen's prophesy, the will of the universe, would soon be upon them. Once Apophis had come, the deluge would follow and bring about the next step in the journey of humankind. Yet, even as Svetlana tried to convince herself, doubt gnawed at her. What had Victoria said? *Not that it matters.* Why wouldn't having a leader of the Phalanx matter? The Doyen wanted this man to lead. He had told her as much. Perhaps she had misunderstood his words? Mother would not contradict the Doyen's wisdom, would she? Only he had penetrated all nine veils. Svetlana's head swam with possibilities and conflicting loyalties. She needed to rest, to meditate. She spun and sprinted off toward her communal dwelling, Ribka bounding behind.

CHAPTER THIRTEEN

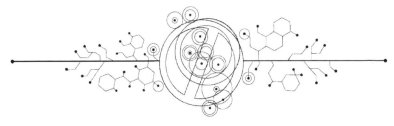

Location: Alpha Base, Antarctica

The subglacial temple was freezing and claustrophobic. With the only light coming from spotlights and battery powered-generators that had to be changed every few hours, Freya had the growing feeling this must be what it's like to die: slowly, cold, the world closing in on you. The Huntington's would get her eventually and she'd accepted that. Her own death didn't bother her any more. Jonathan would be okay. He was a strong man. A good man. Unlike Kelly who could not escape the death of his wife Izel, Jonathan would not wallow in the pain of losing Freya. She was sure he would be able to find love again—if not for a while. As for her boys, KJ and Nikolaj, they were grown and able to fend for themselves. But, she knew she was the anchor for their hodgepodge family unit. Without her, KJ would probably drift away from Jonathan and Nikolaj—who themselves were so stalwart and career driven that only public holidays would be reason enough to bring them together. This is what saddened her. The family she'd created would disintegrate upon her death.

Where the hell were the boys headed, anyway? she thought. She hoped KJ would not give Jonathan too much of a hard time when he finally caught up. It wasn't like Jonathan could spank KJ and march him home. Though, for a grown man, being thrown in the back of a jet or helicopter and escorted back was pretty much the same. KJ may never forgive Jonathan—or her. Was that her fault? The boys should have said what they were doing and where they were going. Of course, KJ was his father's son. And Nikolaj, despite his more mature nature, was still the son of Minya Yermalova. And neither would shy away from an adventure.

Freya's heart hurt at the thought of her friend. The nightmares of Minya slipping from Freya's grip and plummeting to her death in the icy ocean had subsided over the years. But the hole left behind seemed as deep and unforgiving as ever. Nikolaj had asked many times for stories about his mother, but when Freya searched for the answers it became clear that she knew very little detail, despite their closeness. Perhaps it was a friendship forged by their shared experience with the Huahuqui. Perhaps they were just two mothers with special sons. Either way, Freya had little to tell Nikolaj. In fact, what she did know—Minya's time in the Siberian gulags, her rape resulting in Nikolaj's conception—was just too painful to talk about. Nikolaj didn't need to know these things about his mother or ancestry. Minya was a brilliant historian, expert in the ancient languages, and devoted mother. Nothing else mattered.

Yes, a devoted mother. Nothing else matters, Freya thought.

"Nothing yet," Doctor Brown said.

Freya's attention was drawn to the screen. Dr Brown's ice penetrating radar had been modified to see through the brickwork underneath the crucible tower, and thus hopefully enlighten everyone as to whether there was a free and accessible water source. The image slowly appeared, line by line, as the scan penetrated the rock. From what she could tell, the masonry ran quite a few meters deep, then the Antarctic bedrock. A lot of it. As the image gained resolution, hope of a water source began to fade.

"Well shit," Freya said, slapping the arm of her wheelchair.

"Don't jump to conclusions yet, Mrs. Teller," Koa said, then turned to his colleague. "Allison, you seein' this?"

Allison ran her finger down the screen. "It looks like a hairline crack in the rock, but it's too uniform."

"A capillary maybe?" Koa said.

"Can we push deeper?" Allison asked.

"We can try," the doctor replied. "It may be a bit fuzzy, but if there is a large enough body of water, it won't matter."

More of the image built up, blurred as Koa said it might be. The solid coloring indicating brickwork suddenly opened out into a chasm. A hole that grew and grew, deeper and wider, then closed in on itself, like a bubble in the rock.

"Holy shit," Koa said. "It's a subterranean reservoir. It's huge. That's water. We have water!"

Freya exhaled a sigh of relief.

"That capillary should be bringing it to the surface. So, it must be blocked," Allison said.

"Blocked how?" Freya pressed. "Debris? Just frozen?"

"I can't really tell," Koa replied. I imagine, given how narrow this capillary is, that it's just frozen over."

"So, we what? Pour some hot water down the tube?" Freya asked.

Koa and Allison turned to Freya. The amusement at her suggestion was irritating.

"Well, how do we unblock it?" Freya asked.

"Well you weren't totally wrong. Yes, we need to melt it but pouring water down there is just going to freeze pretty damn quickly again. And if it's a blockage of some kind, will just do nothing."

"What about a heated drilling fluid?" Allison asked, scratching her head and staring at the screen. "We could modify the composition of the fluid we use when drilling for ice cores. Make it a little less viscous. It would melt the ice, and probably help break up and suspend any debris in there."

Koa nodded. "That just might work."

Allison ran off in to the dark and supposedly up to the surface to collect this drilling fluid. Freya figured it would take some time to retrieve. She sat in her chair, hands trembling, lost in thought. One of her arms shot out. Freya reeled it back in and clamped it down by the wrist into her lap.

"That isn't the cold is it?" Koa asked, nodding at her hands.

Freya looked up to the doctor. His question seemed earnest. "Huntington's," Freya replied plainly. "Had it a long time, but I think we're near the end game."

Koa gave a slight bob of his head in respectful understanding.

Dacey nuzzled up to Freya's legs.

"Dacey here, she's been kind enough to keep my symptoms at bay," Freya said, rubbing the Huahuqui's nose. "But there is only so much she can do."

"I'm sorry," Koa said.

"Me too," Freya replied.

The uncomfortable silence was worse than the cold.

"So," came Melissa's voice.

Freya jumped in her chair. She'd forgotten the xenobiologist was even there. "You might wanna wear a bell or something."

Koa laughed.

Melissa blushed. "Sorry, but I've been thinking."

"Uh huh?" Koa said.

"This orb. It doesn't have a consciousness of its own. It's a connector, a conduit, to bond and communicate with the Huahuqui more fully. At least as I understand it."

Freya nodded. That is how she'd seen it work. When the Shan Chu, Victoria, and Wak all tried to use it at the same time, during the battle under Teotihuacan, it seemed to drive everyone mad. It was damn intense.

"So," Melissa continued, "to use this place as a broadcasting station, someone has to have something to say. The Huahuqui don't tend to communicate on an individual basis per se. At least not with each other. They dumb it down for us, for humans, but with each other it's a hive mind. The only person who has ever had a lead role is Kelly Junior, and he's not here."

"What's your point?" Koa asked.

"If we can get the orb connected, and if this broadcasting station is still operational, how do we operate it? Drag the Huahuqui from Alpha Base to here? And hope they can correctly convey the message."

Freya checked her watch then turned back to the two scientists. "Actually, that's exactly what they asked to do."

"They?" Koa asked, an eyebrow raised.

"They," Freya repeated.

The courtyard of the subglacial temple rumbled and echoed with the sounds of booted feet and webbed paws. From within the dark, at least one hundred Huahuqui and their human companions appeared. The gloom was pushed back by an effervescent blue light that covered them all. In its tank, the orb began to glow and pulsate with greater intensity as if it sensed the presence of the Huahuqui. Dacey warbled loudly, bouncing in excited circles.

"Woah," Koa said. "I've never seen so many at once... it's ..."

"Magnificent," Melissa finished.

Freya just smiled. It was easy to forget that most humans hadn't seen a Huahuqui in real life, let alone half the hive of Alpha Base. She had to admit, even for her, it was impressive.

Koa and Melissa ran up to the Stratum, to say hello Freya imagined.

"Ma'am?" came a voice.

"Yes?" Freya spun her chair to face a young soldier.

"A message from the President." He handed Freya a tablet. A quick fingerprint ID scan and the memo appeared.

Koa came bounding over, full of childlike energy. "Wow, that's just wow! I mean, that feeling. In your chest? You know? It's like... I don't know what it's like. Can you des—"

"Look at this," Freya interrupted and handed him the tablet. "The president sent it over. Symbols of some kind. Being used as code to mask the hacks on the power stations. Any idea what it is?"

Koa took the pad and stared at it carefully, pawing at the screen to enlarge and rotate the images. He shook his head. "I can't say I do. They look kind of familiar, but I can't place it. Scrawling, really."

"Jiahu," Allison said, peering over Koa's shoulder.

"You know this?" Freya asked, hopefully.

Allison bobbed her head. "Yeah, they look like Jiahu symbols."

Koa snapped his fingers. "Yes, that's it. You have a mind like a steel trap, you know that?"

"That's because I keep mine out of my pants," Allison fired back, then took the tablet from Koa. "Jiahu symbols are literally just sixteen distinct markings on several prehistoric artifacts found in a Neolithic Peiligang culture site at Henan, China."

Koa shuffled around to Allison's side to study the screen again.

Without looking up he said, "Weren't Jiahu considered to not be writing itself, but more like sign-use which eventually led to a writing system?"

"True," Alison confirmed. "But didn't Mrs. Teller just say they are being used to mask a code? If whoever is using this has attributed the symbols to writing or a pictorial system, then it may be possible to form a kind of cypher."

Freya watched Koa's face flush as he stared at Allison.

"What?" Allison said.

"Nothing," Koa replied. "Nothing at all."

Allison handed Freya the tablet.

"Thanks," Freya said. "I'll fire this info off to the President. You were fetching some drilling fluid?"

Allison seemed to curse herself under her breath. "Yes, sure. Sorry. I'll go now." She ran off into the dark.

Freya watched the woman go, then focused on the mass of Huahuqui and their human companions who had gathered around the orb in the center of the courtyard. Broadcasting station or not, the localized power of the thing was clear. A bluish glow had encapsulated these Stratum who had grown not only silent but also formed much more structured concentric circles. The hive mind must have been much stronger with the orb in play. Freya could only hope they could utilize the temple to amplify this power and reach out to those Huahuqui controlled by the Nine Veils. The fate of everyone very well might depend on it.

Location: Tocayōtla, Southwest Rice Terraces, China

"You ready for this?" KJ asked, bouncing up and down like a fighter waiting to enter the ring.

Nikolaj stared his brother in the face. "Not really, this is possibly the dumbest idea you've had. Forget that witch, you have nothing to prove."

"You got a better idea? Besides, I bet secretly you've wanted to do this forever." KJ winked though it didn't feel genuine, even to him. This was going to hurt. He'd heal quickly, but that wasn't the point. It had to be bad enough to make the guards pay attention. He glanced at Catherine before fixing back on his brother.

"Can't you guys try manipulating the security again?" Catherine pleaded, pacing the cell.

"It's hard to manipulate others who are bonded. You have to convince them, and we're running out of time," KJ said.

K'awin padded around KJ, nudging his ankles with her snout, her little face tortured with worry.

KJ dropped to his haunches and held K'awin's pear shaped head in his hands, forcing her to make eye contact with him. "It'll be okay. I'll be fine. I trust Nikolaj. But you must block me out of your mind for now, right? I don't want you to feel this."

A pained warble escaped K'awin's tiny mouth.

KJ stood again. "That goes for the rest of you. Shut me out of your heads."

Merry and Lex huddled together, Kiska and Kroshka wrapped around them. Leo and Igor sat, cross legged, their eyes closed in mediation. Jin and Xue adopted similar poses.

"So, are we gonna do this or what?" KJ said, bouncing on the spot like a cage fighter waiting for the bell to ring.

"Wait!" Catherine yelped.

"What?" said KJ and Nikolaj together.

Catherine stepped to KJ and kissed him on the cheek. "Don't die."

For a moment, words evaded him. Her mismatched eyes were fixed on his, as if staring into his soul. She may not have been Stratum, but right then it felt like she knew him better than anyone. A feeling he wasn't sure with what to do. So, he just winked. "You're gonna owe me more than tha—ughhh!" KJ collapsed to the ground.

Sharpened flint protruded from his shirt, right where his liver would be. The shirt began to stain red. He clasped at the wound and curled into a ball in the dirt. "Mother fucker," he wheezed. "We were meant to argue first… make… make it look like a fight."

"Shit, sorry," Nikolaj said his hands trembling. "I just did it."

"Fuuuuuck," KJ moaned loudly, screwing his eyes shut. "Okay, we gotta pull it out now. It's gotta bleed …"

Nikolaj knelt next to KJ. "Sorry, Junior." He yanked the shiv from KJ's torso.

KJ yelped long and loud.

Then, the blood came. It flowed from the gaping wound, drenched his t-shirt and pooled in the dirt. KJ's normally tan complexion drained to chalk white and the iridescence in his eyes faded. K'awin trilled and collapsed next to her companion, clawing at her own midriff.

"No, no." KJ hacked, blood dribbling from his lips. "K'awin, you… you were supposed… to disconnect."

KJ felt hands on him—Catherine's hands. She pressed down, elbow locked, trying to stem the flow, but blood seeped between her fingers.

"It's too deep," she cried. "He won't heal before he bleeds out. Shit, shit, shit. C'mon."

"What the hell is going on?" came a young man's voice.

Through bleary eyes and much pain, KJ could make out the form of two guards at the cage gate.

"He's dying!" Catherine screamed. "You have to take him to… to… to whatever hospital you have!"

"We're not taking him anywhere!" one of the guards said.

"Then you're fucking idiots!" Catherine shouted back. "Do you know who this is? It's Kelly Junior Graham, first child of the Stratum. You think your boss is going to want him dead? If that were the case, he'd be fucking dead already! But you can bet your dumb ass, if you let him die here, you'll be lined up against a wall and shot in the head."

KJ couldn't quite make out what happened next. Through agony and fatigue he could only see shapes and shadows. There were *peeps*, perhaps a code being punched in, then a *clunk*. The gate maybe. Two shadows entered, carrying… guns, they were guns. One came closer to him, mumbling something. Then two much larger shadows that could only have belonged to the monk brothers loomed. There was a scuffle, scratching and kicking, followed by gurgling sounds and then nothing.

"C'mon, we gotta move," Nikolaj said.

"It's too deep," Catherine repeated. "He'll bleed out."

"We have to move," Lex said.

"It's our only chance," Merry finished.

"Let me tie him off first!" Catherine cried.

KJ was hoisted to a sitting position and he felt something wrap around his midriff at least once then suddenly tighten exactly where he'd been stabbed. A fresh spike of pain ripped through him, the world once again darkening.

"That'll have to hold," Nikolaj said. "He'll heal… he has to heal…"

Lifted from the ground, KJ's arms were slung over two sets of powerful shoulders. They must have belonged to Leo and Igor. KJ's stomach roiled with pain, his insides feeling as if they may split open and empty his gizzards over his boots. From the corner of his eye, he spied Nikolaj scoop up K'awin and push to the front.

Under a purple sky, he was dragged left and right. Merry and Lex took the vanguard, searching for a path. Slinking from shadow to shadow, hiding behind small dwellings and concealed from the moon's bright eye, KJ realized they were headed *out* of the compound.

"No …" KJ wheezed.

The troop halted.

"No what?" Nikolaj asked, still holding K'awin, searching for reinforcements.

"We have… to find… Svetlana." KJ managed.

"Not a chance," Nikolaj fired back, now very much focused on KJ. "There's no way we'll find her. You're in no condition and we're outnumbered. We have to leave before those guards wake up. Time to go."

"No, she… needs us," KJ slurred.

"You don't get to make the call this time," Nikolaj said. "We're leaving." He turned, checked for danger, and headed for the shadow of the next building.

KJ gave up providing what little help he was giving the monk brothers and dropped his weight completely. It was enough to take them by surprise and allow him to slip from their grip. He tumbled into the mud and laid there panting.

Svetlana clasped at her stomach. The pain was excruciating. Scrunched into a ball in her bunk, she cried out. White hot and sharp, it felt as if she'd been run through with a newly forged sabre. For a moment she lay there in the fetal position, gently rocking back and forth. The pain spread from her middle, creeping into her chest, neck, and finally her brain. Here it took hold, stabbing at her. Each invisible wound seemed to cut slices in the veil over her consciousness.

"KJ," Svetlana said aloud.

Ribka, curled up next to her, wailed.

Nyalku stepped to her bed. "Svetlana, are you okay?"

She didn't reply.

Nyalku touched her arm, and she instinctively recoiled.

"Woah, what the hell is going on?" Nyalku said.

"I... I don't know... KJ, he's hurt. Badly. He needs help."

"KJ? The prisoner? Are you insane?" Nyalku said and grabbed her by the shoulders.

"Get the fuck off me!" Svetlana wrenched free, climbed off the bed, and shoved him in the chest.

The other Phalanx bunkmates stirred in their cots, propping themselves up on elbows to watch the commotion.

"What the hell are you talking about?" Nyalku said, taking a defensive stance.

"I... I need to see the Doyen ..."

Nyalku snorted. "You see Mother first. You know that."

"I don't have to. The Doyen talks with me. Listens. I... I have to see him. I have to make sense ..."

"You need to go to Mother. She can help you. The Doyen won't be in charge much longer. His ways are too slow. Mother will lead us to glory!"

Svetlana pressed her teeth together. "Mother will lead us to glory? What does that even mean? She's going to overthrow him?"

"We must put our trust in her," Nyalku said reaching out for her.

She glanced at the welts on Nyalku's neck. Puncture wounds. "It's real, isn't it? Her cocktail. To control us."

"It doesn't control, it sets us free. I can see clearly the wisdom in her words. Her plan surpasses the Doyen's."

"Surpasses? Do you even know what the Doyen was trying to achieve?" Svetlana snorted. "This is all bullshit. I'm leaving."

"You're coming with me, to see Mother."

"Make me."

Nyalku's fist came at her jaw, but Svetlana rolled backward off her bunk and into a standing position on the other side. Her Phalanx brother attacked again, using the mattress as a spring board to launch a flying roundhouse kick. Again, Svetlana ducked the strike. He was predictable, his fight pattern always the same. Unable to shield his mind well, he thought too much about his moves—he might as well have telegraphed his strategy.

Svetlana parried and blocked, using as little energy as possible, all the while waiting for Nyalku to tire. It didn't take long. He paused for a breath. Svetlana took the advantage, signaling with her mind the intent to deliver a kick to his ribcage. Nyalku took the bait, dropping his arm to catch her ankle. At the last second Svetlana twisted her leg to deliver a powerful pressing kick to his face. Blood spurted from his mouth and nose as her foot made contact. His neck torqued back, and his feet left the ground. He hit the deck with a *thud*. Taking no chances Svetlana sprinted for the door, Ribka in tow. In the distance an alarm sounded.

"Jesus fucking Christ, you two knuckle draggers can't hold him up?" Catherine spat.

KJ didn't see the monk brothers react. Instead, they clasped KJ by the arms, hoisted him up, reaffirmed their grip, and began walking again. KJ wanted to stay, to fight, to find Svetlana. His plan had gone awry. He'd been so sure he'd heal quickly, but he'd lost so much blood. He was being dragged away and there was nothing he could do about it.

They stopped for a moment to take stock of the situation. KJ could make out Nikolaj up front, holding K'awin. Nikolaj nodded and the troop trotted out. The moon must have been covered by a cloud, making it seem darker—and safer—than it was, because as soon as they stepped from the shadow, a cone of bright white moonlight shone down on them.

"Hey!" came a shout from across the courtyard.

"Fuck," Catherine said. "Run!"

KJ was thrown over Leo's shoulder. He flopped and flailed like a rag doll as the monk bounded across the stonework. Unable to see, KJ could only make out shouting, and the occasional sound of knuckles or boots contacting flesh. He hoped his friends were winning.

More running. They must have made it through that encounter.

Suddenly the monk stopped, shoulders heaving with his labored breathing.

"Put him down," came a female voice.

KJ was released to the mud. He looked up to see three guards, a woman and two men, all in field armor and headgear, like the cell guards. There would be no mind manipulation here.

"Now on your knees," the female soldier said leveling a rifle at them.

His friends complied.

"Fuck it all to hell," Catherine said.

"He's hurt," Lex said.

"Badly," Merry finished.

No one seemed to care.

"We have escaped prisoners here," said a male guard, speaking into a hand-held radio. "All seem to be accounted for. One injury. May need medical assistance. Copy."

"*Copy that*", came the reply.

"I'm sorry, KJ," Nikolaj said.

KJ could only wheeze, a vignette of darkness obscuring his vision. He'd pass out soon for sure.

"I'll take them," came a new female voice.

KJ lifted his heavy head to see Svetlana march up to the soldiers, her face stern.

"You can't take them *all*, Svetlana," the first woman said.

"No, but I can take you, Alyona," Svetlana fired back.

Before Alyona could reply, Svetlana had struck her in the face. There was a blur of activity—a flurry of punches, elbows and kicks. Ribka bounded from the dark and into the fray. Several shots were fired off, but always seemed to miss their target. Both Igor and Leo joined the fracas, until eventually the three guards lay unconscious on the ground.

Catherine leaped forward. "What's this bullshit? What the fuck is going on?"

Svetlana took a step back. "Get out of my face, I'm here to help."

"Why should we believe you?" Catherine yelled.

KJ crawled forward and tried to clamber to his knees but failed miserably.

Svetlana stared at each one of KJ's friends. "You have to trust me. Read my mind, I'm not lying."

KJ used what little energy he had to probe Svetlana's consciousness. She wasn't lying. She remembered.

Nikolaj climbed to his feet. "What now? We've got to get out of here."

Svetlana shook her head. "Leaving won't help you. Follow me."

KJ was once again unceremoniously dragged from the ground. The troop scurried from shadow to shadow, through a small set of double doors that sat at the foot of one of the great temples, then down into a long corridor underground. One more uncomfortable drop down a makeshift ladder and KJ was eventually dumped, back against a wall, on a dusty floor littered with small metallic orbs.

"We'll be safe here for a minute. No one comes down here except me. But you all need to block your minds. No telepathy," Svetlana said.

"We need to help KJ," Merry said, her hand on his shoulder.

"He's still bleeding," Lex finished.

"I brought a med kit," Svetlana said, yanking a small bag from her utility belt. She emptied the contents onto KJ's lap.

He stared at the items. "A staple gun and a syringe? You shouldn't have …"

"Always the damn joker," Catherine said.

Svetlana grabbed up the staple gun, prepped it and held it near his wound. "Hold his shirt up," she said.

Merry and Lex grabbed either side of his top and lifted to reveal the large open wound in his stomach.

"This is gonna hurt," Svetlana said, then pinched the wound and fired the first staple.

KJ yelped in pain, then covered his mouth to muffle the

sound. It was like being stabbed all over again. "Fuck, how many of those?" KJ asked.

Svetlana eyed his wound. "Six."

"Jesus, fu—"

Another staple was stamped into the slash.

KJ screamed through his fingers.

"Why are we here?" Nikolaj demanded. "You said leaving wouldn't matter."

Svetlana put another staple in KJ and without looking up said: "You're safer here, everyone else is going to die."

"I'm sorry, you want to repeat that?" Catherine snapped, her Irish lilt becoming stronger with her stress level. "I couldn't quite make it out over his screaming."

Svetlana turned to the reporter. "Everyone else will die, only we and a few others will survive. Mostly those who are part of the Nine Veils. We are all in places like this, high in the mountains, self-sufficient. We're the only ones who'll survive it."

"Survive what?" Nikolaj asked. "The nuclear stations going critical?"

Svetlana pulled the trigger, delivering another painful staple. "No, the asteroid."

"Asteroid?" KJ said through gnashed teeth and screwed up eyes.

Svetlana sighed. "The stations, the assassinations were just meant to put the world on high alert, force the governments to initiate an 'end of days' protocol they'd designed. Something called Project Swiss Mountain. A proportion of the world's population could be saved inside. Certain scientists, doctors, lawyers, whatever, would be moved in first. He has control of the project too."

"I don't get it," Catherine said. "Why would the Nine Veils

want to save people?"

"The Doyen wanted to start again, with those loyal to the Huahuqui as leaders, and the world's top minds at his disposal. Everyone else is collateral damage. He said it was the universe's will."

"Hang on," Nikolaj interjected. "Who the hell is the Doyen? And NASA has detection systems for near Earth objects. They would have seen this."

Svetlana delivered the final two staples, causing KJ to cry out. "The Doyen is the leader of the Nine Veils. And you're right. Sentry did pick up the asteroid. The Doyen hijacked NASAs systems and made it say everything was okay. In fact, he turned NASAs own deflection program against them. He engineered the asteroid to *ensure* it hit us."

"Jesus fucking Christ," Catherine said, slumping to the ground. "When? How big is it?"

"It'll kill most life on earth," Svetlana said flatly.

KJ stopped pawing at his wound and looked up. "How long?"

Svetlana shook her head. "I don't know. Soon, I guess. We began ramping up operations in the last few weeks. He wouldn't wait all this time just to rush it now."

"Can they stop it?" Nikolaj said. "NASA, I mean."

"I have no idea," Svetlana replied, inspecting her handiwork. "I don't even think they know they've been compromised. That's why it's safer here."

"If it's safer here, why the rescue?" Catherine asked.

"Because the Doyen wants to save those bonded to the Huahuqui, but I think Mother wants to end us all."

"Victoria you mean," Catherine said.

Svetlana nodded. "However bad you think the Doyen is, she's

worse. He has… rules. A code handed down by the Nine Veils over millennia. She doesn't."

"We have to overthrow them both," Nikolaj said.

Svetlana raised her gaze to meet Nikolaj's. "We just need to get to the Doyen. He will explain everything to you. You will see that this is all the universe's plan. But Mother …"

"Are you insane?" Catherine snapped. "He sounds just as crazy as she does. We need to stop whatever they are both doing. Do you not see that? He stole you and the others here from their homes and made an army that would rule after he helps an asteroid destroy the world. That's the very fucking definition of insane."

Svetlana hesitated, the words seemingly unable to flow freely "The universe… it was already going to happen …"

"You don't know that!" Merry and Lex said in unison.

"They're right," Nikolaj added. "And even if it was going to happen—what? He gets to make sure it does? Why does he get to choose who lives?"

Svetlana screwed her eyes closed.

KJ groaned. The injury hurt like hell, but he could feel it starting to heal, sewing together one cell at a time. He shifted to a slightly more comfortable position, though the wall still dug into his back. "If the Doyen is as reasonable as you say he is, he'll stop this bullshit. But, we need to take the British witch out, and probably convince the Huahuqui loyal to the Doyen not to kill us, without weapons or an army." He looked to Nikolaj. "And you thought *I* came up with stupid ideas."

Svetlana shot KJ a scathing stare. "You are in no condition to do anything. You stay here and let me go find the Doyen. If I don't come back in an hour, then …"

"Then we're all dead anyway," Catherine offered.

214

Svetlana gave an almost imperceptible nod.

"Fine," Nikolaj said. "Go."

Before KJ could protest, Svetlana had disappeared back out into the tunnel.

"Nice going, asshole," KJ said, wheezing.

"We can't rely on her," Nikolaj replied, flatly. "We have to get a message to Alpha Base. You think the Doyen is going to stop what he's planning? You think *she* can convince him?"

KJ couldn't argue. He was certain they could save Svetlana, but the Doyen? Whatever plan had been cooked up in the last twenty years wasn't just going to be abandoned. "What do you suggest?" he said, pawing at the staples in his gash.

Nikolaj rubbed his jaw. "They must have a dampening field. Otherwise we would have detected this Phalanx before. A signal jammer. If we can find it, and knock it out …"

"Great," KJ said, groaning as he tried and failed to climb to his feet.

"Not you." Nikolaj knelt and pressed a hand against KJ's shoulder, forcing him gently back to the wall. He searched KJ's eyes. "Not you. She wasn't wrong about that. K'awin and Catherine can stay here with you. Everyone else comes with me."

For the second time in the space of just a few minutes, KJ watched friends dash into the dark tunnel. They were off to save the world. He'd dragged them all the way here, against their will, and yet now he was the one near death on the floor of a hidey hole, while they were out there finishing what he'd started. He tried to think of what his father would do now, but nothing came. Because he didn't know his father. He never did. Instead, his thoughts drifted to his mom and Jonathan. They'd told him, warned him: his father was brave, but reckless. It's what had gotten him killed.

And now here KJ was. History repeating itself. What would Jonathan or his mom do now? They'd take responsibility for their actions. That's what they'd do.

"I know that look, KJ," Catherine said.

KJ snapped from his trance and fixed his stare on Catherine. "It's my fault everyone's here. And now they're out there, risking their lives and I'm in here. I can't just sit here."

"I didn't think you would," Catherine said, eyebrows raised as if waiting for the rest of his idea to tumble out.

"Nikolaj went after the telepathy jamming device. Svetlana went after the Doyen. What's the one piece everyone's forgetting?"

Catherine searched his eyes He didn't project the answer but did will her to find it on her own.

"The other Nenets and their Huahuqui," Catherine said, finally.

"Bingo," KJ said. "No army, no war."

"You can't take on an entire army."

"I don't intend to. But, if I can get the Stratum to follow me, maybe I can get these guys to as well. Mom keeps telling me I'm special. That I must step up and lead. Well, now's my chance." KJ climbed to his knees and pushed out a hand which Catherine grabbed and hoisted him to his feet. "Time to do what I was born to do."

Location: Theung village, Northern Laos

Jonathan crouched in the dark at the edge of the small village. Dark heavy rain clouds ambled across the sky, slowly and evenly emptying their contents, obscuring the moon and stars. The boys' trail from the parachute site and their subsequent tracks in the jungle had ended abruptly at this small collection of huts. Their footprints never left the area, only tire marks did, suggesting they went in a vehicle or ... He swallowed hard. The mere thought the boys were dead made the stone in his stomach grow so large it felt as if its weight may anchor him to the spot. Freya would never forgive him for not coming sooner. He'd never forgive himself. *What the hell are they doing here?* he thought.

The light, rhythmic patter of rain had offered some semblance of comfort, but now it began to fall as if God himself had emptied His bathwater on the world hoping to wash them all away. Jonathan adjusted his jungle issue hat, adorned with a banana frond, and wiped his drenched, camouflage-paint-covered face. Waiting to engage the village was like hovering over Schrodinger's box; right now, his sons could be alive or dead. Going in would give him an answer either way.

Tony Franco's voice came over the radio. *"Boss, checked and double checked. Can't see your boys or their companions. Looks like locals only. No major fire arms, women and children. But, could be an ambush."*

Teller keyed up the walkie talkie. "Roger that. Lauder, you see anything?"

Matt's husky voice whispered from the speaker. *"Confirmed. So far just locals. It's been a half hour, are we going in or what?"*

Teller sighed. "Confirmed. Close in on target."

Shuffling close to the ground, Jonathan slinked from under the cover of a tree exposing himself to the full force of the downpour. The raindrops were huge, each one slapping the brim of his hat and the wet mud at his feet. He moved slowly, scanning his three and nine positions, gun held high, and clocked Lauder and Franco closing in on opposite sides of the village. Behind each lead, a handful of men brought up the rear.

In the bushes off to his right he spotted the square pink snout of one of the Huahuqui poking out, sniffing the air. A human's arms slipped from between the leaves and reigned the creature back in. Teller clenched his jaw. The Stratum had insisted on coming along, but they had to stay out of sight and out of trouble.

Teller switched to hand signals and directed everyone within visual range to breach the doors—all of them simultaneously. Two of Teller's crew flanked him and climbed the wooden stairs to the entrance of the nearest hut. Jonathan silently counted out to three, then kicked in the door shouting for the occupants to drop their weapons and lie on the floor.

Men shouted, women and children screamed. But no-one fired anything. Teller stared at the scared eyes of the inhabitants, shock etched into their sunbaked faces. They were not soldiers, assassins or even opportunists who could have robbed and killed KJ and Nikolaj.

The bawling subsided. Teller and his soldiers lowered their weapons.

"Anything at your end?" Teller called into the radio.

"That's a negative Boss. I have a couple of families here," Tony replied.

"Same here," Lauder agreed.

The radio crackled with more confirmations from the other dwellings.

"Fuck it," Teller said, pulling off his hat. "Get up, you can get up."

The villagers didn't move.

Teller waved them up.

The locals slowly climbed to their feet.

"Have some American's been through here?" Teller asked the nearest grey-haired Laotian.

The man just stared blankly.

"American?" Teller pressed. "Uh... my Cantonese is rusty. *Mei gwok jan?*"

More blank stares from the small throng.

Teller shook his head. *Right, this is Laos,* he thought.

The door to the abode creaked open. Teller swung his weapon around and pointed it at the intruder only to find the same square pink snout he'd seen before poking through the gap. A young Huahuqui, plump and playful, waddled into the room sniffing the air and slapping its tiny lips together. The creature toddled around Teller's legs and rubbed itself on his fatigues like a cat before noting the villagers and with outward warble of glee trotted over to them. Jonathan turned to the locals, convinced he would have to calm them a second time, but it wasn't necessary. The old grey-haired man with whom Teller had failed to converse was now on his haunches stroking the gills of the little creature, a huge smile creasing his leathery skin.

"Wow these critters sure do have a way with people," one of the soldiers said.

"This is more than that," Teller replied, more to himself. "They've seen the Huahuqui before. No not seen... been near. Interacted with."

"Phaya Naga," the old man said, nodding to the Huahuqui.

Teller offered a weak smile. "Phaya Naga," he repeated, then keyed up the radio. "Lauder, Franco, I think these guys have seen the Huahuqui before. I think they may have seen *our* Huahuqui before."

"So far we haven't been able to get two words out of them," Tony

said.

"Maybe we don't need words," Teller replied, then pulled his cell phone from his pocket. He tabbed the photo gallery app, which burst to life with floating images, the most frequently accessed hovering at the top of the screen. For a moment he just stared at them. The most accessed photos were easily ten years old, his sons and their mother all squashed together to take selfies on Jonathan's phone. They'd done it to surprise him, so when he opened his phone at work he'd see the images. It was so long ago, but they were still his favorite. The smile slipped from his lips. Did he even have a recent photo of the boys?

Teller skipped through the gallery until he came to a picture from Thanksgiving two years ago. The last time he'd really spoken to KJ face to face. While he knew the villagers wouldn't care that the image was so old, he swallowed away his guilt and turned the phone to them.

"Have you seen these men?" Teller asked, showing the image to each of the locals.

They all murmured until the old man rose back to his feet and walked to the window. He pointed out into the dark, nodding.

"They were here," Teller said, exhaling his worry. "They took a car?" he asked, making his voice louder as if it may help, then added a driving charade just in case.

The old man bobbed his head again.

"Hell yes." Teller pulled a map from his side pocket and dropped to the floor where he could spread it out. The door pushed open again. Another Huahuqui wandered in as if it owned the place. Then another, and another. Soon the room was near full of Huahuqui and their human companions. Teller was on all fours, literally nose to nose with one of the creatures. He grabbed the map and stood up. "Can you show me where they went?" he asked tapping the chart.

The old man gave him a quizzical stare.

"Goddammit, I wish someone could speak Laotian," Teller said.

A blue haze began to emanate from the Stratum, and a low hum rumbled through the wooden walls and floorboards. The glow enveloped everyone, soaking into their very being. Teller searched the eyes of those nearest him, and though he could not hear their thoughts, he felt one with them; he understood them, and they understood him. His gaze roved to the old Laotian man and without uttering a word he knew that not only did the elder know where KJ was, he'd even take Teller there. Jonathan just hoped he wasn't too far behind.

CHAPTER FOURTEEN

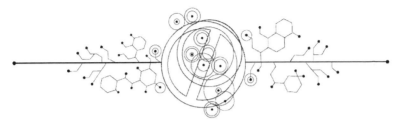

Location: Tocayōtla, Southwest Rice Terraces, China

"What do you mean, you don't know where they are?" The Doyen said, his tone even despite his annoyance.

Victoria shoved Nyalku in the back, making him take another step toward their leader, who sat in his large chair behind the even larger desk. The orb, in its container, glowed and pulsated in the dimly lit room.

"They escaped from the hold, but we can't find them on the perimeter, and aerial sweeps haven't picked them up on the rice terraces. They must still be hiding here," Nyalku said without lifting his gaze from the floor.

"How could they hide inside our own complex?" the Doyen replied, his eyes narrowed.

"Svetlana is helping them," Victoria interjected, practically spitting the words.

"*My* Svetlana?" the Doyen asked.

"Yes, *your* precious Svetlana. She's out of control."

The Doyen stroked the top of Neith's head, confident in his plans—the cosmos's plans. "You have learned nothing if you think I let things happen by chance, Victoria. You think I do not know my own daughter? It is her defiance and her buried bond to her past that brought young Kelly Junior to us. Do you not see? It could only be her. If we had chased him down, we would have failed."

"You used her? You knew she'd fumble the shot and that he'd come looking for her."

"All part of the great plan. All hoped-for things will come to you, who have the strength to watch and wait."

"Don't quote Fane at me," Victoria nearly choked on her words. "Your great scheme has backfired. She's betrayed you."

The Doyen shook his head. "She has lost her way, confused, as was to be expected. Soon it will all fall into place. The Great Syzygy will come to pass, and the Universe's will shall become known."

"Universe's will?" Victoria scoffed. "You really believe your own bullshit now, don't you? I told you we should have dealt with her my way."

Anger, an emotion the Doyen disliked feeling, rose in his chest. "Your mind control serum? Yes, I am aware you continue your research. Nothing happens in these walls without me knowing. You forget your place, Victoria. The Children of the Sixth Sun are to be revered, not poisoned with chemicals."

Neith, his Huahuqui, warbled in agreement.

Victoria's face twisted into a snarl. "You have grown weak, Doyen. If anyone here has been poisoned it's you! Drunk on your own superiority and belief in your damn veils. You may know everything within these walls, but not everything outside of them."

The Doyen rose from his chair, the thin curtain of serenity stripped away, the blood in his veins hot. Victoria's knowledge of the Huahuqui had been invaluable, and until recently her loyalty unfailing. But the bitterness inside her had grown and mutated. She was not pure, neither human nor Huahuqui. A bastard of the US government, grown in a tube. He had tried to bring her into the fold, but it was no use. No Huahuqui could bond with her. No human could stand to be near her. She was malignant and needed to be cut out. "You will remove yourself to your temple," the Doyen said. The orb on his desk began to glow while Neith padded on the spot.

Victoria laughed, long and shrill. "Your feeble hypnotic tricks won't work on me. Whatever was done to me, I am immune."

The Doyen banged his fist on the desk. "You think yourself better than us?"

The woman's laugh subsided, her features growing cold. "I am an abomination, despised by humans, the Huahuqui, and by God. But soon, it will not matter."

"What do you mean?" the Doyen asked.

Victoria's expression sank into a cruel leer.

"Victoria, what have you done?" the Doyen pressed, his heart beating faster at the thought of his life's work ruined.

"Your problem is that you believe yourself to be equal to God. You're not. Saving your own pitiful lives and the lives of those you deem worthy. Our creator needs a clean slate. No humans, no Huahuqui. Nothing."

"The coming of Apophis will reset the world, and bring in the age of the Sixth—"

"Oh, enough of your Sixth Sun," Victoria snapped. "Apophis is not enough. Humanity must be wiped from the planet."

"You believe that you are more powerful than Apophis? More powerful than the universe?"

"The human race thought itself more powerful. Now I will

demonstrate what happens when you combine man's ignorance with God's divinity. Imagine the destructive force of Apophis and the nuclear power stations exploding!"

The Doyen's eyes widened. The asteroid's impact would create a global shift in weather systems, spreading the devastating radioactivity. The chances of even his temple surviving were infinitesimal. Perhaps the only ones to survive would be those—

"Of course, I don't want to forget those locked away in the bunkers," Victoria sneered, apparently reading his thoughts. "How long does it take for one to starve?"

What had she done? He'd left too many things in her charge; the power stations, the biomes, leading the Phalanx. She'd lost her mind. The universe had a will, an unspoken plan. Apophis was always to strike the Earth, he had just ensured humans had not deflected it. But this… if she had really engineered the power stations to explode and the biomes to seal shut … There would be nothing left. No seed of humanity or the Huahuqui to germinate and flourish in a new world. Her vision was one of an irradiated and barren land, inhospitable to any life that had come before.

"You're insane," the Doyen said. "We did not plan for the power stations to explode."

"You may not have."

"You have failed God and the universe."

His words seemed to dent her resolve.

"I failed God by trusting those in power, including you. I believed in you. I waited and hoped against hope that you would emerge from whatever self-righteous buffoonery you had wrapped yourself in and come to your senses. You could have submitted to God and led my Phalanx into a new future."

"You're doing this because you feel wronged by me?"

Nyalku shuffled on the spot, fear growing in his eyes as the tension ballooned, threatening to pop at any moment.

"I am doing this because you have shown me that you are too weak!" Victoria near shouted. "If you are the best that can be made from God's great experiment, then He needs the opportunity to start over. Humanity and the Huahuqui were shaped and molded over and over, but to no avail. We had our chance. One can only rework a sword so many times before it becomes brittle. God must make something entirely new."

"Your soul is black, it's opaqueness obscuring your vision."

"I am the only one seeing clearly," Victoria retorted.

"Father!" Svetlana near crashed through the sliding doors to the private abode, Ribka following close behind.

The Doyen's heart slowed, his confident resolve returning. Svetlana had come, as he knew she would. His faith in her was well placed. She and the Phalanx would protect him. He waited another beat for the doors to once again slide open and for his children to pour through the gap to his aid. But the doors remained closed. No cavalry stormed them.

"Svetlana, you came… alone?" he said.

The young woman stepped in front of Victoria, her back very slightly turned to him, to form a human shield. Svetlana spoke without turning, her gaze presumably fixed on her Mother and Nyalku. "She means to overthrow you, to take over. She has something planned. I know it."

Ribka warbled, angrily.

Victoria just gave a horrible, sarcastic laugh. "Child, as always you are ten steps behind and only half right."

"Your Mother wants to kill us all," the Doyen said dryly. "A nuclear winter amplified beyond all measure by the coming of

Apophis. She wishes to bastardize God's great plan. But she forgets her place, and my understanding of the universe."

Svetlana wheeled, her shapely eyes afire. "You can't let her do this. You must stop Apophis and the power stations. Without it, she can't do anything. There must be another way to reset the world, a peaceful way."

Another way? There was no other way. He had spent decades forging this great plan. Timing it perfectly. He shook his head. "The Great Syzygy is at hand. We have helped tip the hand of God. The worthy will inherit the Earth… as long as we prevent *her* from making it uninhabitable for millennia."

"Me?" Victoria snarled. "God's hand? You are not worthy to even think of Him. It all ends, now."

His daughter's gaze snapped from him to Victoria and back again. "You're both going to ruin everything."

"The Phalanx will remain," the Doyen said.

Victoria laughed again; a smug, knowing snicker. "We are not bickering parents, girl. This is not a divorce. There is no happy ending. Even for the Phalanx."

The Doyen glanced at Nyalku, the boy's eyes glassy with fear. "You will kill your own children?"

That barb seemed to dig deep, Victoria's contemptuous expression breaking for just a moment. "I have no children," she hissed. "The government made sure of that. This… form… is incapable of bearing children. And these… ingrates?" she motioned to Svetlana and Nyalku. "They'll serve me to fulfill the destruction of the world. And when they're done, I'll destroy them, too."

Svetlana rubbed at the tattoo just behind her ear.

The Doyen's stomach knotted. She'd planned it, down to the minutest of details. He pressed his fists, knuckles down, on the table and cocked his head defiantly. "You may have branded my children, but I have no such tattoo."

"True," Victoria replied, then pulled a Glock from a holster on the back of her belt.

The hammer slammed down, and a resounding crack echoed around the room. Neith yelped and crashed into the floor, blood oozing from an open wound in her chest. The Huahuqui laid there, bleeding out, her breathing shallow.

Anguish surged into the Doyen's own chest, his link with Neith transferring the white-hot pain into his flesh as if he too had been gunned down. He collapsed to the floor, clutching at the phantom wound and clawed his way toward his fallen companion. "Neith …" the Doyen called.

Svetlana screamed and launched at Victoria. Following his symbiote's lead, Ribka slammed into Nyalku sending the young man sprawling.

The Doyen held on to Neith, hands clamped down on the gushing wound, and watched through tear-filled eyes as Svetlana pummeled Victoria. Punch after punch landed squarely across Victoria's face. A roundhouse kick to her ribs doubled the woman over and was followed by a spinning back elbow that connected with her temple. The Glock clattered to the floor and Victoria crashed into the wall, her arms raised to her face. Svetlana gave no quarter, grabbing Victoria behind the neck to gain purchase for a series of brutal knee strikes. The crunch of ribs breaking was horribly audible. Victoria was a mentally powerful woman, but physically was no match for Svetlana's youth, speed, or training. Deep in his heart, though he knew to be wrong and against his supposed enlightenment through the Nine Veils, the Doyen enjoyed Victoria's pounding. And, if he were really honest with himself, he hoped for everyone's sake that she died.

Another gunshot rang out.

The Doyen's attention snapped to Nyalku, the smoking Glock raised high in his hand. He slowly leveled it at Ribka who was now lying on the floor, breathing labored, blood trickling from his nose. Svetlana ceased her onslaught and was now fixated on her Phalanx brother. Nyalku shook. Whether it was fear or anger or frustration, the Doyen could not tell. But, there was surely madness behind those eyes. Whoever Nyalku had once been, he was no longer that person.

"Don't," was all that Svetlana could manage.

Victoria grunted defiantly and forced herself up, using the wall as a brace. "Kill it," she hissed through bloodied lips.

"Don't," Svetlana said again. "You don't want to do this, Nyalku."

"She's right child," the Doyen agreed, though his words were lost to wheezing. "She has gone mad. Only the coming of Apophis, as it was mea—"

"Oh, fuck your Apophis!" Svetlana screamed. "Nyalku, we are Phalanx. We are family. Maybe it's time we stopped listening to *them* and what they want for us. Maybe *we* need to call the shots. If we are the future, then don't we get a say in it?"

Nyalku didn't move, his gun arm quivering, sweat beading on his brow. "A say? I don't have anything to say. I just want my Phalanx. My family. That's all that matters."

"Right," Svetlana said, nodding gently and easing her way toward Nyalku. "Family. You don't want to kill Ribka or me."

"Damn it," Victoria snapped, "just do it, boy."

Nyalku turned his worried gaze to his Mother, who had now righted herself. The visible bruising already beginning to yellow and heal. "Can… can there be another way?"

"No," she replied without hesitation. "The time is now. Everyone dies."

"But," Nyalku stammered. "If we kill Svetlana now, control over the Phalanx will be lost. She's too important to them. With the other prisoners escaped, we'll need help. They'll try and stop you. You must complete the plan, personally. You know this."

"Maybe no-one has to die," Svetlana offered, gaining another few inches toward her Phalanx brother. "Maybe the coming of the Sixth Sun isn't a physical event. Maybe its's just another way of thinking. Maybe it's us… and the Stratum."

A small smile broke across the Doyen's lips. The coming of Apophis was necessary, but Svetlana's wisdom had come to fruition just as he had planned. The joining of the Phalanx and the Stratum to rule a new world. The moment of pride was brief, and his smile slipped away as Victoria's hand, holding a syringe, slipped around Svetlana's throat. He opened his mouth to warn her, but the needle had already pierced her skin and the liquid inside emptied into his daughter's jugular. He reached for her with feeble, blood-covered fingers.

Svetlana crumpled to the floor, clasping at the puncture wound. A short series of spasms, legs and arms awkwardly flailing, and then she became stiff and unmoving.

Victoria stepped over Svetlana's body and snatched the Glock from Nyalku. "Perhaps you are right. We may need her, for now. But we don't need him."

The Doyen stared up, focusing on the black hole bored into the Glock's barrel. Behind it, the unearthly light of the orb on his desk cast ghastly shadows across his former protégé's unfocused features. *This was not how it was supposed to be.* Surely, not what the universe had planned all along? His demise and the fall of the Nine Veils? A flash from the muzzle ended his train of thought, and his life.

Location: TAO Command Center, Texas, USA

Lucy sat, fidgeting, in TAO command center, waiting for Jim Waltham to return. While she had been advised to go to a safe location, Lucy had used her Presidential power to unilaterally overrule such suggestions. She was originally on the list to be saved by Project Swiss Mountain, but Lucy had overruled that too. In fact, she'd mandated that as few politicians as possible—who would only continue to fight age-old partisan lines—would be included in the primary list. Scientists, artists, creators, farmers, plumbers, technicians… those who could literally rebuild the world were the priority.

The door hissed open and Jim bowled in, a tablet in hand and a gaggle of his agents at his side.

For the first time, Jim looked his sixty years of age. Normally he was an organized and calm man, who had lived through more wars and crises than Lucy dared try to fathom and considered by his colleagues to be the smartest and most shrewd officer in the military. However, today Jim was a mess; his inability to control the situation had stripped away his confidence and the people's confidence in the government. From the assassinations to the power stations being taken over, to the biomes locking down and project Rubicon falling under the control of the Nine Veils, the NSA's credibility had crumbled. They had failed to detect what was clearly two decades of planning and subterfuge that had now culminated in the very real possibility that an asteroid would, at some unknown time in the near future, smash into Earth and wipe out the majority of life.

"How are we doing, Jim?" she asked.

Waltham sat down at the desk. His team also took chairs next to him, setting up their laptops. "The info you got from your contact at Alpha Base, on the Jiahu symbols, paid off. At least partially. They are being used as a cypher. But not the same one each time. Since they are not a true writing system, the symbols themselves can be attributed to almost anything to use as a key. From what we can figure out, they used different cyphers for the power stations, Project Swiss Mountain and project Rubicon… and …"

"And what?"

The Admiral looked up, his eyes wide. "We might be able to get the power stations back. Maybe. But …"

"But?"

"If the stations are to blow if and when the asteroid hits, then… then it's being done manually. From what we can see, there is no timer in the code. No count down."

"Manually? How would that even work?"

Waltham took a breath. "We lost something else."

Lucy's skin crawled, and a horrible electrical pulse worked its way up her spine. "What are you talking about, Jim?"

There was another plan in place, to defend against the Nine Veils should we ever need it. It was classified Ultra Top Secret. That branch of the military… only just owned up to losing it. They thought they could get it back."

"Jesus fucking Christ, Jim, get what back?" Lucy near screamed, causing the whole room to fall still save the hum of cooling fans.

"Zeus," he said almost meekly.

Lucy rubbed at her temples in frustration, the migraine in her head growing with every passing minute. "Zeus. What the hell is Zeus?"

The admiral cleared his throat. "NATO agreed to side step the Outer Space Treaty that prevented us from creating space to earth weapons. Zeus is a kinetic bombardment system—it launches inert projectiles that cause vast damage to targets purely through the speed and mass of the object. The fallout and collateral damage is normally minimal, since there is no warhead."

"Usually," Lucy repeated, her gaze fixed on his.

"If Zeus was used to target nuclear power stations ..."

"Fuck me," Lucy said, forgetting all presidential decorum.

"Zeus wouldn't be on a timer. It would be manually controlled. Someone has the trigger."

"But you have the hack code, right? You can get Zeus back?"

The admiral's already pale complexion drained into a sickly green. "It's not the same. At all."

Lucy slumped into her chair, stomach roiling and her mind awash. The Nine Veils had thought of everything. Planned it down to the last detail. They had to be found. The orb and temple in Antarctica may be the only way. Freya was perhaps their very last hope. At least for the threat of nuclear winter. But the asteroid...

"Apophis," Lucy said, without breaking her stare into space, then snapped her attention to Waltham. "Have you found Apophis? And with the code you do have, can you deflect it?"

Jim rubbed his face. "We have the European and Indian Space agencies helping on it. We're searching the skies, but we're using data well over seven years old on last known co-ordinates and we have to point the telescopes on the ground and in orbit at a given sector. It takes time, and patience."

"I have neither right now, Jim."

The old man sighed. "I know."

"Find it, Jim. Get Rubicon and Zeus back. I'll make calls to Freya and Jonathan. They need to hear this from me. *And* I'm telling you, when this is all over I'm shutting down every goddamn military operation I find."

"Yes, Ma'am," the admiral said.

Lucy rose from her seat and left the room—her heels clip clopping on the floor as she marched toward the elevator—her security in tow. Wordlessly she descended, exited the lift and passed through the various security checks until reaching her car. She slipped inside, her mind a fog, and barely noticed the *clunk* of the door closing behind her. A clumsy fumble in her handbag and Lucy pulled out her cell phone, brought up her contacts and pressed the image of the recipient. The dialing tone hummed a few times before the call connected.

"Hello?" came a man's voice. *"Lucy, you there? It's been a while. Lucy?"*

"Christian," Lucy began, wiping her nose and swallowing away the stone in her throat. "Sorry I haven't called, been a little busy."

"Sis, you've been busy for the last two years. But, you're the president. Though a dinner here or there wouldn't—"

"Christian, listen to me," Lucy interrupted. "I have to tell you something."

CHAPTER FIFTEEN

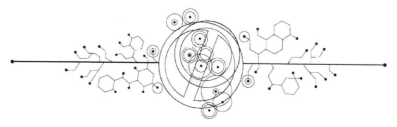

Location: Eldorado, Antarctica

Freya sat in her chair watching Koa Brown precariously perched at the top of a ladder, which rested against the pillar, totally mesmerized by the glowing gelatinous orb cradled in the pinnacle's bowl. He had been giddy as hell since the Huahuqui had arrived and seemed downright obsessed with their connection. The last few hours he hadn't left their side, strolling in between them and touching as many as he could.

By contrast, Freya had kept her distance. While she knew them to be peaceful and benevolent by nature, she'd also seen the darker side of the bonding with humans. Kelly became sick when separated from K'in, and Victoria—well she'd gone bat shit crazy when connected to Wak. That creature just operated on instinct and caused the death of too many people... including Kelly.

Dacey seemed to understand Freya's hesitance, and despite the creature's brethren forming a hive unit in concentric circles around the column, apparently enjoying the intensified bond that the orb brought, she remained at Freya's side. Ever attentive, ever vigilant. Freya wasn't sure she could name a human friend who would be so devoted. Freya placed a shaky hand on Dacey's head, feeling the warmth run through her fingertips up her arm and into her chest.

A knot of guilt cramped Freya's heart for enjoying this moment while her husband and sons were somewhere in Laos, probably in grave danger. This must have been how Kelly felt when he bonded to K'in; happy and guilty at the same time. All humans believed they had the right to pursuit of happiness, but in the end did they all feel guilty for actually finding it? Freya shook off the melancholic thought and focused on Melissa scurrying between monitors, keyboards and little arrays that were apparently sensory equipment—at least that's what the good doctor had said. She was observing their link and the relative output of the hive mind. To understand if the site was indeed a broadcasting station, they needed to know the potential range—hopefully it was truly global.

"How goes it?" Freya asked, wheeling over to the scientist.

Melissa looked up from her clipboard, breath fogging the air. "Good, I think. It's like nothing I've ever seen. I've studied the Huahuqui for years, and their bond. When they're a hive, individuals create a neuro-electrical field that allows communication of feelings and emotion, and other subconscious activity to those in immediate proximity. The fields harmonise allowing many individuals to literally be on the same wavelength."

"So, we think this thing is amplifying that field?" Freya asked.

Melissa bobbed her head. "In humans neural signals are sent via mechanisms such as synaptic transmission, gap junctions, and diffusion processes, but a very small percentage of brain waves are transmitted by a weak electrical field—somewhere in the region of 2–6 mV per millimeter. In the Huahuqui, the percentage of activity driven this way is much higher and much greater in power." She motioned to the orb up high on the column, then took more notes. "This place is pumping it out like a rock concert. And the power only gets stronger the longer they are bonded to it and each other.

Like it's warming up."

Freya's arms twitched and jerked with her growing feeling of hope, so she clamped her hands together. This was great news. They could reach out to the other Huahuqui, maybe even KJ and Nikolaj. "Can we ask them to send specific information?" she asked.

"I'm not sure. Generally, the Huahuqui's communication is more of an overall influence on the brain patterns such that they collectively arrive at the same conclusion. Expression of emotion and modulation in brain activity seems to unlock intellectual potential like logic gates in a computer—a yes or no type of decision making happening at an incredible speed." She chewed the end of her pen, her gaze drifting off into space as she thought. "They are able to converse telepathically, but short distances only as I understand it. But I guess that's what this building is for."

"Mrs. Teller?" came a man's voice.

Freya turned to the soldier holding a satellite phone. "Yes?"

"It's the President," the soldier replied holding out the device.

Melissa acknowledged the conversation was over and meandered off to the column again.

Freya took the phone and wheeled back just a couple of paces. "Madam President."

"Freya, I have... news."

"Good news?"

There was a lasting silence before the president spoke. *"Freya you have to know... since perhaps your work there may yield results before ours does. The Nine Veils they... they hijacked a NASA defense system designed to deflect near Earth objects that may collide with us and turned it against us. We believe that an asteroid called Apophis will impact Earth in the very near future."*

Freya's lungs faltered, and the room began to spin. She blinked away the nausea and tried to focus. "How… how bad?"

"If we don't stop it, we're looking at seventy percent of all life gone."

"Seventy percent?"

"Yes. But … there's more."

"More?"

"A second system has been compromised. A top-secret military operation designed to fight the Nine Veils. Project Zeus. We had considered that the nuclear power stations would explode at the same time as the asteroid hit, to maximize the devastation. We managed to regain control, but intelligence suggests that they'll use Zeus, a space to Earth weapon, to target the power stations. We've been chasing our tails."

Silence engulfed Freya, the darkness of the subglacial temple closing in. "And something like that, a weapon, would need to be triggered manually. Couldn't risk automation. So, the Nine Veils have the trigger?"

"We believe so."

"When? If they're maximizing destruction, when does the asteroid hit?"

"We're trying to track it and consider any contingency plans. But you might beat us to it. If you can contact the Nine Veils through the broadcasting station, perhaps they have the information. Perhaps, you can even make them stop."

Freya sat in her chair, silent and deflated, the phone held limp in her hand.

"Freya? Are you there?"

"I'm here. I understand," Freya said, her voice weak.

"You know if we don't manage to stop it, I'll have to keep the

biomes closed to save some of us… and hope they find a way out eventually."

Freya nodded, even though the president obviously couldn't see.

"Good luck, Freya. I'm sure you'll do your best. God save us all." The call ended.

For a moment, all sounds within the temple melded into white noise. Freya's mind spun with endless possibilities, but they all culminated in the same conclusion: she'd never see KJ, Nikolaj, or Jonathan again. Freya clenched her jaw and cleared her throat. "I have an announcement." Her voice echoed off the temple walls.

The hustle and bustle faded, workers maintaining the lighting system in the back halted, Melissa froze to the spot, Koa looked down from his ladder and Allison narrowed her eyes from across the courtyard. Even the Stratum seemed to break their bond to listen, the blue miasma fading, and their glassy blue eyes focused on her.

"That was the President of the United States," Freya said in the most commanding tone she could muster, though her hands still shook. "I have good news, and bad news. And given the nature of the information, I think you all deserve to know."

"What's up?" Koa called down from above.

"I'll start with the good news," she continued. "We've probably got the power stations back. They won't go critical. Allison, that's largely thanks to you. Good catch on the Jiahu symbols."

Allison gave a curt nod, but a blush belied her collected response.

"Is that so?" Koa said.

The Stratum murmured amongst themselves.

Freya could almost feel the relief wave throughout them. "But," she said, holding up her hands to quiet them. "The biomes are still locked down... and may need to stay that way."

"What do you mean?" Melissa asked.

Freya swallowed hard. "The Nine Veils, they hijacked a NASA system. It's a long story, but they have managed to manipulate a large asteroid to impact Earth."

"Jesus," said the soldier next to Freya.

"How bad and when?" Melissa's beauty seemed sucked away, her features drawn and worried in the harsh spotlights.

"It's bad. A global killer," Freya said, masking as much of the quiver in her voice as possible. "We don't know when, but soon. And... they have found a way to make the stations explode, whether we take them back or not. Asteroid plus nuclear winter equals one fucked up Earth." Freya couldn't help but think that's how Kelly would have summed it up. "So, our work just became unbelievably important. We may be the only hope. Connecting with the Huahuqui in the Nine Veils may be the last chance to stop all of this."

"Well shit," Koa said.

"I know," Freya replied.

"We can't have that can we?" Koa continued, then pulled a pistol from the back of his pants.

"What the hell are you doing?" Allison yelled.

The two soldiers in the room aimed their weapons at Koa, who pointed the weapon at the orb.

Freya waved the soldiers down. "If he destroys that we're fucked."

They relaxed their fix on him; but kept the weapons ready.

"You had to figure it out, didn't you Allison?" Koa said,

shaking his head. "Jiahu symbols? Really? You know how long it took us to find a writing system obscure enough to hide the code?"

"You're with *them*?" Freya exclaimed.

"You always were an egotistical asshole, now I know why," Allison said, shaking a fist at him. "And you always underestimated me."

Koa bobbed his head in agreement, a smug grin on his face. "You're right. Won't be making that mistake again." He leveled the pistol at Allison and pulled the trigger. The blast ripped through her shoulder, sending her sprawling to the stony floor.

Koa retrained the weapon on the orb.

"You sick bastard!" Melissa screamed, dashing to the fallen Allison.

Koa just laughed. "I'm not sick, I see clearly. I pierced most of the Veils before I was ten."

"I don't get it," Freya said. "You were the one who found this place and helped us get it up and running."

"For us! Once it's connected the Doyen and Victoria will have complete control of all Huahuqui all over the world!"

"Who?" Freya barked, her limbs jerking.

"The Doyen, the master of the Nine Veils and his right hand, Victoria," he replied while using his spare hand to type a message on a cellular device.

Freya's heart stopped beating. He couldn't mean Victoria McKenzie, could he? Had Victoria been recruited by the Nine Veils? Had she been twisted beyond belief? No one had heard from her after Teotihuacan. Guilt crept into Freya's chest. Was all this because they hadn't bothered to care for Victoria afterward?

"You won't get away with this," Melissa said, eyes glassy. "We'll stop you."

"How quaint," Koa replied with a cruel smile. He slipped the communication device into his pocket and slid his now free hand toward the orb. "You can't stop all of *them*." His stare fell on the Stratum below.

The soldiers edged forward, weapons locked on the crazed Australian. Again, Freya waved them down.

"I wouldn't do that if I were you," Freya called up to Koa. "I've seen what happens."

"Well, of course *you* wouldn't do it. You're a dying cripple. You don't have the mental power for it."

A shot rang out and pinged off the crucible, barely missing Koa's face.

The soldier beside her gasped at his mistake.

"No!" Freya yelled.

Koa snarled, then clamped his hand around the orb.

The Stratum squirmed and writhed in pain as an intellect not meant to be bonded to them surged into their collective consciousness. They warbled and squealed, dropping to the stony floor, clasping at their heads. Above, Koa arched his spine and pushed out his chest as the raw power of so many minds entered his. The veins in his necked bulged and the blue haze from the Stratum crept its way up the column to him.

The soldiers readied their rifles again, eyes wide and full of panic.

"Don't!" Melissa yelped. "If you kill him and break the link suddenly it could hurt them all."

The two men looked to Freya, who shook her head. "She's right."

Freya's heart beat so fast it felt as if it would explode through her ribcage. There was no telling what would happen. The Shan

Chu had been driven mad trying to take Wak from Victoria, clawing at his own face and head until Jonathan and Sasha could kill him. But, this was different. A whole hive of Huahuqui, and a natural amplifier.

A spotlight crashed into the floor as one of the Huahuqui blindly fell into its base.

"Yes!" Koa screamed. "I feel them all!"

"What do we do?" Melissa cried.

Freya looked from Koa to the writhing Stratum and to Dacey who stared back at her. *She's not connected*, Freya thought, and in that moment knew what to do. She placed a hand on Dacey's head and gazed into the little creature's cobalt eyes. "You gonna help me?"

Dacey blinked and ruffled her gills.

The connection to the hive mind swamped Freya's consciousness. Pain, agony, fear, anguish, all seemed to overwrite her own emotions, filling her body with dread. Never had she felt this through the Huahuqui—before, only serenity and calm prevailed. Freya clenched her teeth and screwed her eyes together, trying to push back against the darkness. Deep in the jumbled mess of sensations was another consciousness, a gangrenous splinter polluting everything. Koa. That was Koa. Freya held her breath, forcing her way through the thick soup of intellects to reach him, but it was no use. This is what a poisoned mind could do to a perfect well of empathy and love. The Stratum were afraid and chaotic. His hold on the orb exaggerating his presence in the hive. She needed to calm them, to give them focus. What would give them focus? What gave *her* focus?

Freya exhaled slowly and concentrated on the only thing that truly made her happy.

From the dark, KJ's tiny face as a child appeared. His half-cocked smile like his father, bright blue eyes staring out from locks of dark hair before he had bonded with K'awin and gone blond. His soft voice calling her "mommy". The image skipped forward, and he was now sat in her lap, drinking hot chocolate from his favorite Iron Man mug. And then he was blond, K'awin by his side, playing in the snow with whatever animal had passed by and stopped to pay him attention—to bond with him in a way she never could. All too soon he was a man. A leader. Strong willed and minded, gathering the Stratum behind him. He was grown. More than a man; he was the future of mankind. A lump formed in Freya's throat. She had to let him go to become what he was supposed to be.

The smoky darkness in her mind began to dissipate. The more she focused on thoughts of KJ, the more organized the hive consciousness became. The singular and unwavering love for her son an anchor in an angry sea of sensation. They clung to this one thought, gathering around it like a beacon. From within the dark, a blade of light appeared slicing through the smog, growing brighter and brighter.

Freya clamped her eyes closed as tightly as she could, one hand gripping the arm of her wheelchair the other firmly on Dacey's head. She could feel the creature beside her, separate from everyone else, but herding them toward her like an ethereal sheepdog. Until, with a snap, the blade of light exploded and scorched away the dark.

Freya's eyes snapped open just as Koa tumbled from the ladder and crashed into the stones below with a sickening crunch. A warm trickle of blood ran from Freya's nose and dripped from her lip into her lap. She wiped it away with her sleeve, hoping that nobody saw, then wheeled awkwardly over the uneven stones. She rounded the pillar to find Koa lay on his back. He coughed up a glob of blood.

Allison hobbled over, clutching her shoulder, Melissa supporting her. "You fucking idiot."

Koa's gaze shifted from a point in space to Allison. "You think they'll name this place after me now?"

"I'll make sure no-one ever says your name again," Allison replied through a clenched jaw.

Koa didn't respond, his eyes now lifeless.

"Shit," Freya said. "These bastards really are everywhere. We need to tell Jonathan. I need to reach him. If Victoria is with the Nine Veils, there is more at play here than world domination. It's personal. She'll be after my son."

"I'll get him on the sat phone," Tribz said.

Freya bent over and fished around in Koa's pocket for the communication device he'd used. He'd failed to lock it. She eagerly clicked through the various messaging apps until she chanced up the most recent, sent using an encrypted messaging service. It read: *power stations lost. But orb secured.* "Wrong about that, asshole," Freya said aloud. He had been premature in communicating his victory. Perhaps, for a moment, they had the upper hand.

CHAPTER SIXTEEN

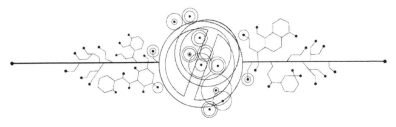

Location: Tocayōtla, Southwest Rice Terraces, China

The sun rising in the sky shone down, glaring a spotlight on them, providing no place for KJ and Catherine to hide. They slinked from small building to small building, concealed in what little shadow they could find. KJ's wound was much more healed now, though still hurt like hell and sharp movements made him wince, the tear pulling taut. He scanned the road once more, touched Catherine's elbow and scurried across the muddy path to the corner of the next shelter.

"Hmm," KJ mumbled.

"What?" Catherine asked.

"This doesn't bother you?" he said nodding out into the open.

Catherine glanced around, peering through a small slit-like window of the abode next to her, and searched the street once more. "There's no one here," she said finally.

"Exactly," KJ agreed. "Not a damn one. Where the hell is everyone?"

"Nutflies," Catherine offered.

KJ smirked. "You got that right."

"So, we wait?"

"No time," he said, shaking his head. We have to get to the

Phalanx."

"Where are they? Can't you feel them?"

KJ froze and stared down at K'awin. "You haven't been trying, have you girl?"

"Hey, don't blame her," Catherine scolded.

His sheepish gaze raised to meet Catherine's. "Yeah, okay. My bad."

"Geniuses. Zero common sense."

Without responding, KJ knelt next to K'awin, placed a hand on her broad forehead and closed his eyes. His consciousness intermingled with hers and together they reached out into the world around them. Through the rice pools, over the muddy flats teeming with insects until, eventually, a swarm of minds slipping and sliding over each other emerged from the fog. They were not focused, not coherent. Instead, they seemed to bump and shuffle into one another waiting for something, someone, to give them direction. Both human and Huahuqui were conscious but not awake, not aware. KJ could only consider them zombies. He pushed a little further, entering the mind of a young woman.

Through her confused eyes KJ could make out the stone courtyard, surrounded by short stacked buildings, and filled with what seemed to be the entirety of the Phalanx. Dominating the skyline was an enormous step pyramid—the Temple of the Sun. Atop the enormous structure was a podium and a sacrificial table. The Phalanx shuffled like sheep, all staring up at the pyramid's pinnacle. As the young woman's gaze floated from person to person and back to the pyramid, KJ could make out that each member of the Phalanx held something in their hand. A syringe.

High atop the pyramid of the Sun, four figures appeared. The first was clearly Victoria, her sharp angles and thin body made a distinctive silhouette against the blazing sun. Beside her a young man, stiff and awkward, waddled on the spot. KJ didn't recognize him. But the third and fourth he did: Svetlana and Ribka. He strained his mind to keep a hold over the human window into the unfolding scene. Svetlana looked different—she was blue. Actually, naked and *painted* blue, a pointed feather headdress her only attire. Ribka was similarly painted.

"Oh shit," Kelly said aloud. The link was lost, and he tumbled out of the young woman's mind and back to his own reality. He crashed to the ground. The lasting image of Victoria holding high a glowing orb burned into his brain.

Catherine slipped her hands under his armpits to steady him. "Are you okay? What did you see?"

KJ shook his head but the images remained. "The Phalanx, they're… they're in the courtyard of the sun Pyramid. All of them." He pointed down the Avenue of the Dead. "But, they aren't themselves. I mean, they feel zombified. Victoria has an orb… and… Svetlana…"

"What about her?"

"It's a ritual. I think that British witch is gonna kill her."

"Then we need to move," Catherine said.

"Maybe if I can get the orb," KJ said. "I can help them."

Catherine nodded.

KJ pushed off the ground only to be shoved back down again. "Hey what the fu—" He looked up to see a familiar shadow staring down at him, the white sun giving his brother a sort of halo. "Nikolaj?"

"What the hell are you doing up here?" Nikolaj hissed through gnashed teeth, then dropped to his haunches.

"Looking for the Phalanx," KJ snapped back. "I thought you

went for the shield transmitter?"

"We did a quick survey, it's up there I think. On top of the biggest temple." He nodded at the replica of the Temple of the Feathered Serpent.

"Great then you head for that. I gotta get to the pyramid of the sun."

"Why," Merry said

"There?" Lex finished.

The young women knelt down beside him, their Huahuqui equally attentive.

KJ scanned for the monk brothers. Sure enough, they were there too—both studying KJ and Catherine. "The Phalanx is there. All of them. Svetlana too," he said.

"I thought she'd gone to the Doyen?" Nikolaj interrupted.

"Guess that didn't work out so well for her."

"And you have to go there, why? You're still injured," Nikolaj pressed, motioning to KJ's stained shirt.

"Because I'm the only one who can, man." KJ exhaled out resolutely. "If I can get hold of the orb Victoria has, maybe I can reach them. Maybe I can save them all. If you guys listen to me, maybe they will too."

Nikolaj stared deep into KJ's eyes, his mind gently testing KJ's for the truth. "You're serious," Nikolaj said, finally. "Not playing hero. You really want to do this."

KJ just nodded.

"You'll need help," Nikolaj said. "Remember not all the Phalanx have Huahuqui. Some are made up of the Militia of Russian orphans. You might not be able to reach them."

"We'll go with him," Igor offered.

His brother bowed in agreement.

Nikolaj pursed his lips then gave a curt bob of his head. "Merry, Lex, and I will get the jamming signal down. We might at least get a message out to Alpha Base."

KJ clambered to his feet and turned to leave, when Nikolaj grabbed his shoulder.

He stared at KJ for a long while before offering out his hand to shake. "Good luck."

KJ frowned, then did something he knew he should have done a long time ago. He lunged into Nikolaj and hugged him tight. "We got this, man. Let's get it finished."

Nikolaj, apparently taken aback, patted KJ on the shoulders then released him and without a word took off toward the Pyramid of the Feathered Serpent, his crew in tow.

"We ready?" Catherine asked.

"Let's go," KJ said.

Sweat dripped from KJ's face as he and his band of friends made their way to the Pyramid of the Sun. Without the need to lurk and sneak from building to building, KJ simply kept in the shade as much as possible, jogging a steady pace to the courtyard. As they neared, the murmuring of the Phalanx could be heard, but above all was another voice. Svetlana's voice.

KJ ducked behind a wall. His crew followed suit, K'awin rubbing up against his leg. He peered around the corner. Rows upon rows of the Phalanx filled the area, human and Huahuqui alike. Intermingled with them were the orphan soldiers. He followed their gaze to the naked form of Svetlana high above.

Arms spread wide Svetlana near shouted her sermon to the

crowd below. "My brothers and sisters. Soon the Sixth Sun will be upon us, and a new time for our planet will have arrived. Apophis will free the world from tyranny!"

A murmur of agreement washed through the crowd.

"We must sacrifice ourselves for the greater good! For the will of God! I will show you what sacrifice means, and in my giving see yourselves and your place in history! You must find and stop the Stratum!"

The crowd grew louder.

Victoria stepped forward, holding the orb aloft. It glowed and pulsated in her bony fingers. "In your hand you hold the Eye of God, the final key to breaching the Ninth Veil," she shouted. "Take it and see Svetlana's soul leave her corporeal shell for a higher plane!"

KJ watched the Phalanx lift the syringes in their hands, a movement of such co-ordination, and then push the needles into their necks before pressing down on the plungers and draining the fluid inside. Each member began to shake and convulse on the spot, as if the holy spirit had entered them. High above, Svetlana lay on the curved stone, her chest forced outward, and allowed the young man to tie her arms and legs so that she was splayed—open and vulnerable.

"Jesus fucking Christ," KJ exclaimed. "It's a fucking sacrificial ritual. He's gonna cut out her fucking heart."

"What?" Catherine exclaimed.

The monk brothers peered out from behind the brickwork to snatch a glance.

"It's a Mayan sacrifice. They cut her open!" KJ pushed off to sprint to Svetlana's aid.

Catherine grabbed him by the shirt. "What are you doing?"

"I have to save her!"

"How? By fighting the whole Phalanx? Think, KJ. Think!"

KJ's breathing quickened. "How do we do this?"

"You need the orb to do it right? If they are under her influence they won't listen to you," Catherine confirmed.

KJ nodded.

"Then we distract her. And them. You sneak around the back, come up the other side of the temple, and take that skinny bitch by surprise," Catherine suggested, her eyes burning with hate for the woman.

KJ looked to the monk brothers and their Huahuqui, then back to Catherine. "I can't risk losing you."

"If we don't do this, we're all lost anyway."

She was right of course, and KJ knew it. He'd dragged them all this far. Now it was crunch time. "I have an idea," he said turning to the monks. "Boys, can you still do that thing you learned in the monastery? I know you took a vow."

"What thing?" Catherine asked, eyes narrowed.

KJ focused his attention back on the reporter. "They can temporarily sever the bond between Huahuqui and humans. It's pretty draining for them and devastating for the bonded pair. Used it once in a training session. The... sparring partners were hospitalized for a week. Imagine like a really painful feedback loop—static that squeals in your head, but covering your ears does nothing. Trust me, it's shitty. They vowed never to use it."

Catherine shuffled uneasily on the spot. "There's gotta be a hundred pairs out there, easily. More maybe. Can they interfere with that many minds at once?"

KJ stole another glance at the ritual playing out. Victoria was ranting about something. Svetlana was still alive. "Not all the minds. One. Hers. We can't get into her head, but maybe you can block the orb, the telepathic signal, she's putting out?"

Igor and Leo looked to each other, then their Huahuqui, before giving only a curt nod.

"Okay," KJ said resolutely. "We're running out of time. Let's go."

He turned to circumvent the crowd but was once again yanked back. "What now?"

Catherine searched his eyes, with handfuls of his shirt clutched tightly. She drew him close and pressed her soft lips against his. KJ's heart skipped. He'd wanted to feel that forever. But he knew he couldn't linger in the moment. He pulled away, held Catherine's gaze for another moment, and then darted away.

Catherine took a sharp breath and then stepped into the harsh sunlight.

"Stop!" she screamed.

The man high up on the temple halted his downstroke of the blade. The Phalanx around turned as one, every pair of eyes fixated on her.

A shrill laugh broke out from atop the pyramid.

Victoria.

"Stupid girl!" she said, clasping the orb in one hand while taking purposefully heavy strides down the stone staircase that ran the length of the temple. "Here I am rallying my Phalanx to find you, and you deliver yourself to me alone and unarmed?"

"Stupidity and bravery… it's a thin line," Catherine replied.

The monk brothers and their symbiotes stepped out from the

shadows, flanking Catherine. Their stance remaining one of serene calm. Meditative even. In a strange way, they gave her confidence too. Their years of mental training transferred to her. Perhaps it was emanating from them and their Huahuqui. Perhaps she just *really* wanted this woman dead.

Victoria laughed, again. "I see you brought Tweedle Dee and Tweedle Dumb. Where, pray tell, is your boy toy?"

Catherine ignored the question and focused on the Phalanx. Some were already wearing battle gear with machine guns slung across their chests and side arms strapped to their hips. Others seemed to be clothed in civilian attire, yet still wore an expression of war. "I don't know why you're doing this, but you don't have to. None of you have to," she called out.

"They do as they are commanded, because they understand I am their Mother," Victoria snapped. "Their reason for being. Without me, they would not exist."

"Yes, they would. They'd just be like the Stratum. Working toward a better future for everyone. Humans and Huahuqui," Catherine yelled back.

"You're a puppet for the powers that be. Everyone is just a puppet. Soon that will end."

"The asteroid? You don't think we'll stop you?"

Victoria paused, halfway down the stairs. "You really are just a fan girl. A good reporter would have found the signs. Dug for the evidence. Seen what is to come."

"Dug for what? Seen what?"

Victoria's eyes narrowed, her head swiveling on her shoulders, searching. "You're stalling."

"Whatever you're going to do, do it now," Catherine said under her breath, but loud enough for the monks to hear.

Victoria held the orb high and screamed into the air. "Kill them!"

Igor and Leo took another step forward while Jin and Xue stood fast like stalwart guard dogs. All four closed their eyes in concentration. A topaz haze formed around them, engulfing Catherine too.

The first row of Phalanx marched forward a few paces, weapons trained on her and the monks, but then slowed. Their gait became clumsy, their weapon-bearing arms weak and unable to hold a good aim. Deep in her core Catherine could feel a swelling of energy, something not of her making, but seeping into her from the blue miasma in which she was now immersed, obscuring her view.

The ball of light, as that is only how she could explain it, grew and as it did the silhouettes and shadows of the Phalanx beyond the blue cloud stumbled and collided with each other and the soldiers. In the distance, she could hear Victoria screaming orders to murder all five of them.

And then, as if the very limits of her physical being to contain the sphere of light had been reached, she convulsed. Catherine stretched out on tip toes, arms spread wide, as the energy exploded from her being and out into the courtyard. The monks roared long and loud, their Huahuqui warbling in unison. The Phalanx cried out, clutching at their heads, weapons clanging to the floor. The militia looked to each other in confusion.

Catherine fell to the ground, panting. Her limbs were weak and her mind fuzzy as if her very life force had been spent. On hands and knees, she looked up through the dissipating iridescent fog to high up on the temple where Svetlana laid spread-eagled. There was a scuffle, and Catherine could only hope KJ was winning.

The temple was a lot damn higher than KJ had anticipated. Especially when trying his best to be stealthy. Shielding his mind as best he could took energy. Energy that wasn't available to climb. Out of breath and tired from schlepping himself up countless stone stairs, KJ reached the summit. He peered carefully over the heavy, dusty, brickwork. Just a few feet in front was the young man wielding the blade, hovering it over Svetlana's naked chest. Ribka paced in a circle around the stone alter on which she lay. He peered a little further, over the top of the pyramid out toward the Temple of the Sun. There, climbing the outer wall was Nikolaj, Merry, Lex and their Huahuqui. Unknown to his friends, a patrol of guards walked the upper quadrant of the temple. They were about to be met with force and there was nothing KJ could do about it.

He cursed their damn plan, then refocused on the blade-wielding man ahead. KJ couldn't see Victoria, so had to assume she'd descended the other side and was making her way down to Catherine and the boys. That would mean he would have to get past knife-boy and down the other side. But, that was it. As far as he remembered, she had no guards with her on the temple. He just had to wait for the monk brothers to do their thing.

KJ closed his eyes, slowed his breathing, and tried the meditation technique Igor had attempted to teach him. In through the nose, out through the mouth. Control the heart rhythm. A dragonfly so large it's buzz nearly deafened him whizzed by his face. He swatted it away and readjusted himself, but K'awin nuzzled his arm which made KJ open his eyes again. He rubbed his symbiote's head softly. "It'll be alright girl, we got this," he whispered. "You take Ribka, and I'll get the machete-wielding maniac there. We untie Svetlana and then I go get the orb from her royal bitchiness."

K'awin ruffled her gills in response.

The corona of a blue haze lifted above the stonework. The monks were about to unleash their weapon. KJ grabbed K'awin. "Disconnect from me. Now! Just in case. They're messing with the orb, but just in case."

K'awin cocked her head and stared into his eyes, her expression and consciousness suggesting he'd just asked her to jump off a cliff. She'd never break the bond. She'd die first, and he knew it.

Screams echoed out from the courtyard on the other side of the temple. Svetlana shook and convulsed on the stone table; Ribka dropped to the floor writhing in pain. The man with the knife took a few steps back, seemingly confused. KJ launched from his position and tackled the man from behind, sending him sprawling into the stone and nearly off the top of the summit. The blade clattered away.

Without thinking KJ repeatedly punched Svetlana's would be killer in the face, bloodying his nose and mouth until he lay unconscious. KJ turned to check on K'awin who had pinned an incapacitated Ribka face down. KJ grabbed up the blade, the metallic scraping ringing out as it dragged from the floor and raced to free Svetlana. She struggled against the ropes, thrashing in pain. Sawing as quickly as he could, without accidentally cutting into her flesh, KJ cut through her bonds. She slipped from the alter to the ground and stopped moving.

KJ froze, his ears now pricked. The screaming had stopped. The boys had spent their energy. He placed a hand on Svetlana who lay, breathing labored on the floor. He removed his jacket and laid it over her painted skin, then stormed to the edge of the temple's summit ready to charge down the other side and take out Victoria. But as he reached the edge, her greying blonde bob and angular face crested the final step.

"Foolish boy," Victoria spat as she stomped up and into the platform. "You thought what? You could stop me? You have no idea the lengths I've gone to. There is no stopping it."

"Watch me," KJ fired back.

Victoria just gave a horrible knowing smile. "Kill him."

KJ's panicked stare flicked to where the blade-wielding man had laid. Still lay. His brow knitted in confusion, and only too late he realized Svetlana's foot speeding toward his face.

CHAPTER SEVENTEEN

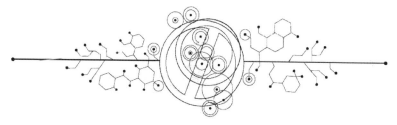

Location: Southwest Rice Terraces, China

Jonathan handed the satellite phone back to Tony.

"Something up boss? The little lady okay?"

"She's been better," Teller said, looking to his friend. He considered relaying everything he'd just learned: Koa Brown being a mole, Freya making progress with the orb; Victoria McKenzie probably now part of the Nine Veils; but, most importantly, about the killer asteroid and Project Zeus. In the end, Teller decided that the mission would be compromised if his team had such worries on their minds. They needed to focus. *He* needed to focus. So instead he said: "The power stations may be retrievable. And the team at Alpha Base may have a way of getting friendly Huahuqui to connect with the Nine Veils, make them see sense."

"That's great news, boss," Tony said, patting Teller on the shoulder.

Teller settled back into his chair and gazed out the passenger window. The sun was low in the sky, lazily creeping its way upward, dragging its yellow orange halo higher and higher to burn away the purple of night. High up on a peak in the distance were the silhouettes of several structures. Their distinctive shapes, step pyramids and square buildings—out of place and time—told Teller they had found what they were looking for. This is where the final battle would happen. Asteroid or not, he'd probably die here.

It was ironic, given his grandfather had died in Laos. Not something he talked about—mainly because he was ashamed—but Jonathan's grandfather had been in the CIA and fought a covert war in Laos the the late 1950s, codenamed: Erawan. President Kennedy had refused to send more American soldiers to fight in Southeast Asia and instead asked the CIA to use tribal forces in Laos to launch guerrilla operations in North Vietnam. It was the largest CIA paramilitary operation in history, spanning thirteen years. It also resulted in a civil war, with the CIA's recruited Laotian forces fighting communist Laotians. More than half a million bombing missions took place in Laos during that time. Countless innocents died; all to fight an idea: communism. Was Teller now any different than his grandfather? World powers wanted to wage a civil war between two Huahuqui factions to fight an idea that the Nine Veils had been attempting to elevate for an age: restart the world with the Huahuqui as supreme beings.

But, fighting for the greater good was not why Jonathan was here now.

Throughout his career, Teller had worked on the premise that the needs of the many outweighed the needs of the few. Freya had always mocked him for making a *Star Trek* reference a guiding principle in his life. For him, it had just made sense. Until now. Now, he was here risking his life and those of his brothers in arms and the Huahuqui to rescue his sons from whatever lay ahead. KJ and Nikolaj were all that mattered. A whole country could burn as long as he got to save them—long enough to tell them he loved them, before an asteroid wiped them all out anyway.

"We're coming up to it," Lauder said over the radio from the lead vehicle. *"Don't wanna get too close though."*

The vehicle ground to a halt and Teller jumped out, cautiously taking in his surroundings. Tony exited the passenger side, while Lauder stepped down from his wagon and instructed the Laotian driver to stay inside. The Stratum fidgeted in the rear flatbeds.

"What's the plan?" Lauder asked.

"Recon for now—"

"Boss!" Tony interrupted. "We got something here."

Teller drew his Glock and cautiously stepped over to the grassy ridge where Tony was standing. Lauder stayed with the trucks, his men fanning out to protect the perimeter. Just below the ridge were a couple more vehicles of a similar make to those they had arrived in. Two Laotian man laid in one of the flatbeds, smoking.

Teller pulled his radio, keyed it up, and whispered to Lauder: "We have possible friendlies here, but I want to be sure. Bring your driver to me."

"Copy that."

Lauder duly brought their driver to the ridge, flanking the man—weapon ready. The driver, some forty years old with greying hair and more than a few missing teeth, trotted over to Teller who pointed below them.

"These guys with you?" Teller said, hoping that more pointing might help the language barrier.

"*Saibaidee!*" yelled their driver.

Startled, the two men below looked up then waved with big grins.

"Jesus man, not so loud," Lauder said through gnashed teeth, his eagle eyes searching the surrounding forest.

Teller holstered his gun and with their driver, Tony, and a few of Tony's crew, worked his way over the ridge to the two Laotian men below.

261

Neither of the men appeared apprehensive. They sucked on their cigarettes and exhaled the smoke in big lazy clouds. The Laotian men spoke amongst themselves, chattering away, pointing back the way the caravan had come and off into the distance where the silhouettes were. Teller figured they had probably seen their fair share of war, soldiers, and even Huahuqui. But, the real question was: had they seen his sons?

Teller held up his phone again, with the picture of KJ and Nikolaj. He tapped on it, hopefully.

The Laotian men chattered again, nodding and pointing up to the structures at the top of the rice terrace.

"Great, they're up there. I just hope they are okay," Teller said rubbing the back of his neck.

"Let's just take a little looksee, shall we?" Tony said, slipping his rucksack off.

"Whatcha got there?" Teller asked.

"A little toy we use in Syria a lot," Tony replied and pulled several small mechanical insects from individual cases.

"Drones?" Teller inquired.

"Griffinfly Personal Reconnaissance Systems. Five-mile range at speeds of up to 20 mph and able to fly for up to an hour on a single charge." He held one up on the palm of his hand. The dragon-fly looking drone was around six inches long.

"Good, that's good." Teller said, fiddling with his wedding ring.

"Each one of these little suckers can take HD photos and provide live video feeds. Data is sent to this," Tony said, holding up a small remote control with a large screen, divided into six feeds. "Fully encrypted. Autopilot for the most part, but you can take control of individuals."

"Then what are you waiting for?" Teller said. "Fuck sake, send them out, Tony."

Franco looked up, his expression saying more than words ever could.

Teller took a deep breath and held it a few seconds before exhaling. "Sorry, Tony. I'm just worried. Just send them out."

"I know, boss. We'll find them."

Tony pressed a button on the drones. The flexible transparent wings slowly began to flap then kicked into high gear such that they were barely visible. All six hovered an inch or so from the ground and then zipped off into the air. Tony stared intently at the monitor, watching the tree tops whizz by in a blur of green.

"Let me know when you get a visual," Teller said, then patted his long-time friend on the shoulder.

"Ah, Jon boy? You may wanna get up here," Lauder said over the radio.

"What now?" Teller replied into the mic.

"We have a situation."

Teller turned to Tony. "You tell me as soon as you get something."

Tony nodded, fixated on the display from his drones.

A quick scramble up the rise and Teller crested the ridge, coming face to face with the entirety of the Stratum that had come with him, now having formed regimented lines like infantry soldiers. They stared out toward the silhouettes in the distance, an azure pall encapsulating them.

"Ah shit, they're doing their thing again," Teller said, wiping the sweat from his forehead.

"Yep," Lauder agreed, "but that's not what I called you up here for. Look behind them."

Teller peered past the growing blue glow, beyond the Stratum. There, gathering in greater numbers were more and more Theung men and women, melee weapons in hand.

"What the hell?" Jonathan said, trying to count just how many were pouring in. "Why are they here?"

"Damned if I know," Lauder replied. "But if their arsenal is anything to go by, we just acquired an army."

Teller's mind immediately went to project Erawan. A makeshift Laotian army about to fight on the side of the Americans. His gut knotted. "We don't even know if we need an army."

The radio in Teller's hand crackled to life.

"Boss, you will not believe what I'm seeing here. We need to get our ass in gear, shit's going down."

Teller's heart leaped into his throat. He was already over the ridge and sliding down to the trucks before Tony had finished his transmission. He grabbed the remote and glared at the screen. In feed four was Nikolaj and a few other Stratum, pinned down on the side of a huge temple—a rain of ammunition pummelling the stone. They seemed to be heading for the summit and some sort of equipment at the top.

"Where's KJ?" Teller asked.

"On top of another pyramid."

Teller took control of Griffinfly one and steered it down the streets, twisting and turning. The blurry images it sent back, though HD, moved almost too quickly to comprehend. The Griffinfly buzzed past a group of soldiers wearing combat gear, advancing down an alley. Each carried considerable firepower. The drone flitted and skipped from stone corner to stone corner, through a courtyard teeming with a legion of soldiers and Huahuqui. The sand-colored brick work zipped by in a blur as the metallic insect soared up the pyramid, until finally KJ appeared on screen. He was with K'awin at the summit, locked in battle with a young woman who was naked and painted blue. And then, Teller saw *her*. Victoria McKenzie—her face contorted in anger. The fly zipped past her head, but as Teller steered it away Victoria lashed out and disintegrated it with a single strike. Feed one crashed into static.

"Jesus," Jonathan said. "Victoria. The Huahuqui. It's the damn Nine Veils. We found the fuckers!"

"Seriously?" Tony said.

"Well, my sons found them. Son of a bitch. Tony, get on the horn to HQ. The president has to know."

"Of course, but, your boys. They're in two different locales," Tony said, giving Teller a knowing look. "Which means we need to be, too."

Jonathan's limbs began to tingle. He couldn't lead both teams. "Boss?"

Teller swallowed and looked at the remote screen again. In feed four, Nikolaj and his team hadn't moved from their trapped position. He keyed up the radio. "Lauder, we're on. I'm heading to the Northern temple to get KJ. You take the southern block. Nikolaj is pinned down. Tony will take the courtyard."

"What about the Stratum and locals here?" Lauder asked.

"Bring them," Teller said, checking the chamber to his Glock. "Bring them all."

Location: Eldorado, Antarctica

Koa's limp body was dragged away by one of the security contingent, leaving behind a streak of blood on the stonework.

Freya focused on his lifeless expression until the shadows swallowed his features and he was gone. Another traitor. Another mole inside the deepest circles of the governments and organizations sworn to serve and protect humanity. How was she so blind to such things? First Tom Radley, working with the Shan Chu to track them through South America, and now Koa Brown. Tom's betrayal cost Kelly's life. Koa's could have cost them everything.

"She needs to go to the surface too," Melissa said, nodding at Allison who still lay in her arms.

Her mind foggy, Freya turned to the xenobiologist. "I'm sorry?"

"Allison," Melissa said. "I've patched up the wound, but she'll need medical care back at Alpha Base."

"Sure, sure," Freya agreed.

Allison was hauled to her feet by the last remaining soldier who beckoned help from a nearby technician. Allison, her good arm around the soldier and held at the waist by the new guy, turned back to Freya and gave a curt nod. Freya offered a weak smile in return. Then the three figures disappeared from the harsh yellow spotlight and headed out.

A light touch on Freya's shaking limbs brought her gaze to Melissa.

"How'd you do it?" Melissa asked.

"Do what?" Freya replied, her nose wrinkled.

"Help the Huahuqui fight back against Koa?"

Freya wrung her hands together. "I don't know really. I just focused on something important, I guess. Why we're all doing this."

Dacey warbled and rubbed up against Freya's wheelchair.

Melissa nodded. "They're going to need you, you know."

266

"Who, the Stratum?" Freya balked. "They don't need me. Without Koa they'll be able to use the orb and reach out to the others in the Nine Veils."

Melissa shook her head. "You see, it doesn't quite work like that."

"Come again?"

"Look," Melissa said in her ever-calm tone. "The Stratum are strong, and usually as a group act like a hive mind. They can make complex decisions in a fraction of the time you or I could. And without the orb, they are somewhat protected in their bubble. But the orb is like a gateway for true communication. Think of it like a computer network, lots of brains connected by a node. What we just saw is what happens when a virus is introduced."

Freya glanced up at the orb in the crucible and then to the Stratum milling around the courtyard. "I still don't see why they need me. In my state? My brain is dying, I can barely remember what I ate for breakfast yesterday."

Melissa shook her head. "You just showed how strong you are. If the Stratum do make contact with the Nine Veils, they will be just as open to a viral attack on the other end. They're not trained to deal with something like that. But if the Nine Veils are …"

"Then the Stratum will need someone to help focus their hive mind," Freya finished.

"Right."

Freya sighed. "So, what am I supposed to do? It was hard enough to fight back Koa."

The biologist pointed up to the orb.

"No way. I've seen people go mad touching one of those things."

"Not everyone does …"

267

She didn't have to say it, Freya knew Melissa was referring to Kelly. He'd been bonded to K'in by an orb when he was captured by the Green and Red Society and held in a submarine. It hadn't driven him mad, it had strengthened his bond with K'in. But, Freya wasn't Kelly. Her bond with Dacey was weak at best, because Freya had kept it that way.

"You might be their only hope," Melissa pressed.

"If you haven't noticed, I can't climb ladders," Freya snapped.

Melissa's face hardened, and she lifted one pant leg to reveal a prosthetic leg. "Not such a good experience with a crocodile some years back. There's no such thing as can't. You just told us that we may all be wiped out by an asteroid unless we make contact with the Nine Veils and figure out how to stop it."

Freya stared at the usually demure woman. She had a fire in her eyes that Freya used to recognize in herself.

"Rumor has it, you moved a band of Huahuqui and children from Siberia, across Africa, to Antarctica," Melissa said, admiration in her eyes. "Some might say that was impossible."

Freya exhaled slowly, pushing away a fresh involuntary spasm that threatened to ripple through her body. "If I do this, I might be able to find KJ too right?"

Melissa bobbed her head. "It's entirely possible."

"Mrs. Teller! Ma'am!" called someone from the dark. The soldier who had been hauling Allison back to the surface ran up holding a satellite phone.

Freya took it from him. "Jonathan?"

"It's Tony."

"Tony? Where's Jonathan? Did you find the boys?"

"We found them alright. Your boys are something else. They found the Nine Veils."

"What?"

"We're in China. A complex. South West China. The Nine Veils are here. Teller says you might be able to reach the Huahuqui—the crazy ones. Whatever you're gonna do, do it!" Static squealed from the phone. *"Boss... yo... move ... "*

The line cut off.

"Tony? Tony!" Freya screamed. "Shit."

"What is it?" Melissa asked.

Freya wheeled over to the column. "Get me up there, now."

CHAPTER EIGHTEEN

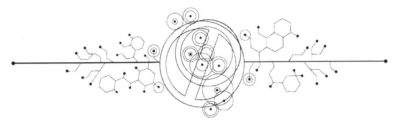

Location: Tocayōtla, Southwest Rice Terraces, China

A blue foot came at KJ, and again he deflected it away. There was something inherently wrong about fighting Svetlana. Naked Svetlana. KJ felt an awkward chivalry and looked away from body parts that became exposed with each strike. That did not help him. Svetlana felt no such shame. Trance like, her onslaught came; elbow, knee, foot, fist. Only KJ's training with the monks saved his face from being bashed in. But she gave him no quarter to strike back. He could only defend.

"Svetlana!" he shouted, parrying away another spin kick. "It's KJ. It's me. You have to remember."

She ignored him and caught him in the stomach with a knee.

KJ toppled backward, clutching is midriff. "Shit. C'mon, Svetlana, try! Don't let this witch win."

Svetlana came again, forcing KJ back toward the edge until there was nowhere for him to go. Over Svetlana's shoulder he could see K'awin equally struggling with a maddened Ribka. His momentary lapse in concentration cost him the battle. Svetlana grabbed him by the throat and pushed such that only her grip prevented him from falling backward down the stone steps to a neck-breaking death. He choked, spittle running down his chin, but fighting too hard would mean his demise.

Below the rattle of gunfire echoed in the courtyard, while far away at the other end of the temple the *pop, pop, pop* of controlled gunfire signalled Nikolaj had met resistance to his climb for the field generator.

Victoria ambled toward him, exuding confidence. The orb shone in one skeletal hand, while in the other she brandished the blade KJ had dropped. "Time to join your father, Kelly Graham Junior," she said, the words sliding from her mouth as if spoken by a snake.

"His father *is* here," came a voice from the other side of the square summit.

KJ squirmed to see past Victoria and Svetlana.

There, holding a Glock trained on Victoria, was Jonathan Teller. His face weary and smeared in grime, but determined and gritty. A stone formed in KJ's already crushed throat, forcing a tear down his cheek. Jonathan had come.

"Ah, Jonathan Teller," Victoria rasped. "The gang's all here. Oh wait? Where's your crippled wife?"

Teller jerked the weapon. "Shut it and back off."

"Or what? You'll shoot me?" She goaded. "It doesn't matter, you're too late."

Teller fired off two shots in rapid succession. The first tore through Svetlana's thigh. She yelped and crumpled to the floor. KJ used her dead weight to ensure he didn't topple backward to his doom. The second stole two of Victoria's fingers. She screamed, dropping the blade which clattered on the stone work.

Though bleeding out, Svetlana struggled against KJ as he pinned her down. He glanced up to see Teller launch forward to tackle Victoria, only to be shoved into the alter by Ribka. K'awin leapt to Jonathan's defense. But, the attack had served its purpose. Victoria had fled.

"Shit, we have to go after her!" Teller yelled.

"I know!" KJ shouted back, still wrestling his friend. "But, I can't leave Svetlana," he said, flicking his panicked stare at the naked woman under him.

The young man who was unconscious before the fracas began to rise. Teller stormed past him and without breaking stride, pistol whipped him back into oblivion.

"Who is she?" Teller demanded, kneeling to KJ.

"It's Svetlana," KJ said through gnashed teeth.

"From Siberia? And that's Ribka?" Teller asked, nodding to the scrapping Huahuqui behind them.

"Yes!" KJ said. "She was the shooter, in Washington. I followed her here. She's not herself. She's been brainwashed or something."

Svetlana snarled and snapped her teeth as if hoping to take a chunk of KJ's face.

Teller scanned the horizon from high up on the temple. The rattling of gunfire called out, the screams of soldiers, Phalanx and Stratum filling the whole complex. He glanced back at Svetlana who was growing weak through loss of blood. "We don't have time for this shit," he said, then delivered a strike with the butt of his Glock to Svetlana's head. She slumped back, out cold.

"K'awin!" Teller called out. "Put him down."

KJ's Huahuqui pushed down on Ribka who seemed dazed from Svetlana's unconscious state. KJ watched in astonishment as K'awin gave a headbutt that rendered Ribka limp. K'awin climbed off her assailant, shaking the pain and dizziness from her skull.

"Shit, girl," KJ said, rubbing at his own head.

"KJ, do you know what's going on here?" Teller pressed.

"Yep." KJ nodded." Crazy British bitch who killed my... killed Kelly Graham... now wants to kill us all. Big asteroid. Blow up nuclear power stations. Generally, world-endingly bad."

Teller nodded and slid a new clip into his Glock. "That sums it up. We need to stop it. She or whoever she's working for must know how. Intel says there's a trigger. They have to manually set it off."

"The Doyen," KJ said. "But, he doesn't seem to be around."

Teller pulled back the slide and locked a round into the chamber. "Then, we follow Victoria."

"Okay, but we can't leave Svetlana like this."

Teller shook his head. "She'll slow us down."

"She'll get killed in a cross fire. I can reach her I know it."

"KJ, you have to listen to me. Leave her up here. We have to move. If we are fast enough, we can end this shit and there won't be anything to get caught in. We have to weigh her life against everyone else's."

KJ's stomach roiled and his limbs felt weak. He'd made it all this way. To save Svetlana. He'd endangered Nikolaj and his friends to save one person. But now the stakes were higher. The end of the world. *Be a leader, KJ,* he thought to himself. "Okay," he said finally.

Teller nodded, then stared out into the distance. "What the hell is Nikolaj doing?"

KJ followed Jonathan's gaze out to his brother. "This whole place has an interference field. It stopped us from finding it for all these years. We think the transmission equipment is at the top of that temple. Nikolaj was going to take it out so we could contact you. I was supposed to take the orb from Victoria and take control of the Phalanx."

"Phalanx?"

"The Nine Veils Huahuqui and human army."

Teller bobbed his head, apparently musing on the information. "Your mom, she's in Antarctica."

"Antarctica? Why?" KJ said, suddenly feeling as if the world might swallow him up.

"She's working with some scientists. They found a knowledge bringer… broadcasting station. She has an orb. A super orb. We wanted to reach out to the Phalanx, as you call them, and perhaps find a way to stop them." He rose to his feet. "If we can get that other orb from Victoria, maybe you can connect with her and together end this fucking madness."

"Then Nikolaj needs to take out the transmitter. She won't be able to reach us otherwise."

Teller keyed up his radio. "Lauder, you copy?"

"Here," came a muffled voice over the handheld, accompanied by the rattling of fire.

"Nikolaj is trying to make it to the top of that temple. Help him take out the transmitter at the top."

"Copy that, boss. Over."

"Let's go," Teller said, then slid a small caliber pistol from his belt and slapped it in KJ's hand.

"Wait," KJ said. "Catherine and the monk brothers are down there somewhere." He peered over the edge of the temple to see a swarm of Phalanx fighting with apparently other Huahuqui and locals with guns and farming tools.

Teller put the radio to his mouth again, while moving to the stairs. "Tony, do you copy?"

"I'm here John boy," came a voice unfamiliar to KJ.

"I need you to get eyes on a reporter and two of the Stratum. She's a red head and they are two big black guys. Hard to miss. Somewhere in the main courtyard. Get them the hell out of there."

"Copy that," said Tony. *"Might be easier said than done."* More shots and screams sang out from the speaker.

"How long do we have?" KJ asked.

Teller shook his head while unclipping his ballistic vest. "No idea. Now take this."

KJ shook his head, pushing the vest away. "You need it."

"Yeah that wasn't a request, KJ. Put in on."

KJ struggled into the protective armor. "Now can we go get this bitch?"

"Now we go get her," Teller said checking his weapon. "And pray to God your mom gets that damn super orb working."

Location: Eldorado, Antarctica

"Is it working?" Melissa asked, pulling on the harness again.

Freya felt the circulation leave her legs as the strap holding her to the makeshift scaffolding cut into her thigh. "I have no idea what the hell I'm doing."

Melissa touched Freya's shoulder. "Just do what you did last time," she said in a soft tone.

"I don't know what I did last time."

Freya stared down from high up at the pinnacle of the column down through the icy darkness to the expectant faces of the men, women, and Huahuqui who all craned their neck up to watch her. The world was about to end and her husband and sons were in a war zone fighting with the Nine Veils. She could potentially stop it all. Her lips and fingers felt numb. It was perhaps the blistering cold, or perhaps the Huntington's attacking her nervous system. Maybe she was just afraid. Because deep down, she knew that saving everyone else, would likely mean she would die. Whatever she did to defeat Koa had been costly. The small amount of blood that trickled from her nose belied the excruciating migraine that now stabbed into her brain. She could literally feel the strain of using the super orb pulling on the last functioning neurons in her head.

"You said you focused on KJ, right? Do that again." Melissa stepped away and carefully climbed down the scaffolding, leaving Freya alone.

High up in the air, vertigo made the stone in the pit of Freya's stomach feel even heavier. Think of KJ, she thought to herself.

There was a light slapping sound. Freya turned to see Dacey awkwardly climbing up the metal framework. She heaved herself over the last bar and plopped her heavy bulk into Freya's bound lap. Freya stared at the little Huahuqui in the eyes. "You don't need to do this," she whispered.

Dacey cocked her head and smacked her tiny lips together.

"If you connect to me, you know what will happen," Freya said.

Again, Dacey's sweet gaze simply told Freya the Huahuqui knew.

Freya gave a sad smile and ran a shaking hand over the symbiote's head and through her soft gills. Then, with one hand on Dacey, Freya closed her eyes and slipped her fingers into the freezing water within the crucible and felt for the orb.

The connection was instantaneous. Immediately every mind in the room was with her own. Without having to fight Koa for control, the Huahuqui gave it freely. But more than that, Freya could feel every human too. The Huahuqui acting like multiple receivers and transmitters to her master signal. Fear and hope overwhelmed every other emotion. The burden of the knowledge everything may end soon occupied each and every consciousness. Their thoughts of home, friends and loved ones, things not said and things that they wished could be unsaid sloshed around inside Freya's mind.

Her own regrets, hopes, dreams, friends past and present rushed in incoherent fragments through her brain. Flashes of Minya's face as she fell to her death. Of Freckles the Huahuqui who had saved her from drowning. Jonathan proposing to her using a handmade ring of steel and meteorite. Nikolaj's proud grin while receiving his first science award for bioengineering at ten years old. Every birthday KJ ever had, where K'awin would bring him a dead fish to eat—yet no one ever knew where she got them from. And of course, Kelly Graham. Their final night in the tent. Their only moment together that resulted in the creation of their son.

A tear streaked down Freya's cheek.

Life was short and cruel, but precious. It took those you loved but gave you others in return. A never-ending cycle of loss and discovery. Some became so burdened by the loss that they were unable to see what they were given in recompense. Kelly had never seen what he had gained following the death of Carmen and Izel. Guilt pressed down on Freya's chest. She herself had mourned Kelly for so long that she had neglected Jonathan. Had not embraced what she had been given.

She sucked in a breath, realizing what she must do; what message she needed to convey to every soul with which she would now bond. The people in the temple, the Huahuqui, the Stratum, the Nine Veils. But most of all to her sons and to Jonathan. They needed to stand together now and fight for the survival of everyone on the planet. So that another generation could laugh and love and cry. Because that was being human and, indeed, Huahuqui.

Freya sank deeper into the orb-powered trance, pushing her mind beyond Eldorado, beyond the ice and the ocean outward into the atmosphere. She felt whales and birds and fish and insects. Past small villages and farms, Freya concentrated on reaching out to China, where Jonathan said they were. Somehow following the path of his consciousness, she shadowed him through Laos and several villages until pressing on into China where the trail abruptly stopped.

Freya's brow knitted in concentration as she forced harder against an invisible barrier. Whatever this was, it was clearly designed to keep anyone with telepathic ability out. She screwed up her face, pushing her mind as hard as she could. A warm stream began to flow freely from her nose and her limbs began to jerk.

Melissa called up in concern from below, but Freya just shook her head.

This was it. This was where they were, her sons and her husband. She had to break the barrier and reach the Nine Veils. Reach her family. Freya clenched her jaw and curled her fingers around one of Dacey's gill stalks. Blood slipped over her lips and seeped into her mouth.

Find them, Freya. You must find them.

Location: Tocayōtla, Southwest Rice Terraces, China

The courtyard was alive with the sounds of war.

Jonathan's arm braced against KJ's chest, pressing him against the wall as he surveyed the battleground and searched for a path through. KJ's wide-eyed gaze moved from face to face. From human to Huahuqui. Stratum to Phalanx. Soldier to Laos tribesman. The distress and rage and confusion coursing its way through the melee was unbearable. Two factions of Huahuqui fighting each other, driven by their bond and sense of loyalty to their individual human. War was not really in their nature; but forced upon them by people. KJ couldn't help but wonder if the Nine Veils had the right idea after all. Humans were inherently violent.

Two Huahuqui rolled past KJ like tumbleweeds, pulling and clawing at each other's gills and limbs. K'awin warbled at them as they bounced off a Laotian man locked in combat with a soldier.

"Where the hell did she go?" Teller asked.

"It's a guess," KJ said, "but she seems to hole up in that temple. A replica of the Pyramid of the Moon. Maybe she hides the trigger in there." He pointed down the dusty road.

"Have to start somewhere," Teller said. "Ready?" He tugged on KJ's shirt then dashed out from the base of the Temple of the Feathered Serpent and into the courtyard, heading straight for the Avenue of the Dead. Soldier after soldier, he effortlessly cleared the path. A roll off one guy's back to deliver a spinning kick to another. A shot to a chest sent one soldier down. He grabbed a Laotian by his jacket, saving him from a bullet to the skull and then thumped two well-placed slugs into the attacker.

KJ watched Teller in awe and for the first time saw the man for what he was: a hero. Jonathan Teller was the real deal. He'd tracked KJ down across the globe and saved his life and now, on KJ's word, was heading to the Pyramid of the Moon to take out a crazy woman all to save the world. For as long as KJ could remember he'd doubted Jonathan. He'd been wrong, so very wrong.

"KJ!" Teller shouted. "Stop day dreaming and move your damn ass!"

KJ jerked to life and chased after Jonathan as fast as he could.

Teller shoulder barged through another soldier and burst out onto the Avenue of the Dead, running full pelt toward the temple. KJ straddled K'awin and together, they galloped along the road toward the Pyramid of the Moon.

The temple's silhouette grew quickly until it was a colossal shadow bearing down on them. Teller quickly dispatched two guards who were posted outside, stole their key card and swiped it through the reader. The metallic door popped open.

"Let's go," Jonathan said, then disappeared inside.

A sharp pain shot into KJ's head. A familiar pain. The same one he'd felt in Washington.

Svetlana.

He scanned behind, gun raised in readiness, yet saw nothing but the billowing cloud of dust from the battle raging far down the road. KJ took one more glance then darted inside himself. The door clanged shut behind.

A shower of ammunition rattled across the telekinetic shield.

Merry and Lex squinted each time, probably terrified their mental power wouldn't hold and the bullets would stream through ripping them all to shreds. They were pinned down, with their assailants taking the higher ground. Nikolaj knew they were screwed.

Another wave of shells.

"I don't know how long," Merry started.

"We can hold this," Lex finished.

Nikolaj scanned the upper levels. The guards were out in the open, but they had the higher ground and to be able to fire out, the girls would have to drop the shields. His mind raced. There was no telepathic control here. No way to manipulate them. *Think Nikolaj, think.*

The protective shield began to flicker, and fizzle—signalling Merry and Lex were all out of power. Time seemed to slow, the screeching of bullets overhead, drawn out. There was only one thing he could do: pull a stunt like KJ. There was no way they were all getting out of this. He had to sacrifice himself. A small smile crested his lips. After all his lecturing, he was about to die doing something stupid.

"Fuck it," he shouted. "Merry, Lex. On my order drop your shield, climb onto Kiska and Kroshka, and get the hell out of here."

"What are you," Merry began.

"Going to do?" Lex finished.

"I'm going to distract these assholes. And Chernoukh is going to take out the equipment at the top."

The black-gilled Huahuqui snorted and shook his head, gills ruffled in annoyance.

Nikolaj grabbed his symbiote firmly around his pear-shaped head. "You're much faster and stronger than me. You can make it. I know you can."

The girls, sweating and exhausted, looked to each other, then to Nikolaj.

He gave a weak smile, acknowledging his fate then, as the barrage of gunfire subsided for the attackers to reload, he sucked in a deep breath and shouted: "Now!"

The shield dropped. Merry and Lex leaped onto the backs of their Huahuqui and bounded down the steep stairs of the temple. Nikolaj let out a war cry as loud and long as his lungs would allow, sprinting toward the guards. Chernoukh darted outward and then up the right flank headed for the summit.

Gunshots rang out, but Nikolaj kept pounding forward, a scream still upon his lips, headed for the nearest soldier who struggled with the action on his machine gun. Every one of Nikolaj's limbs burned and though he knew adrenaline was all that was carrying him through the rain of munitions, he didn't stop. He tilted his shoulder forward and crashed into the soldier, knocking him from his feet and hard into the temple stones. The momentum was too great and Nikolaj toppled over with his target.

Nikolaj gasped for air, his lungs unable to fill properly. He hacked a cough. Warm blood stained his sweat-soaked t-shirt. He glanced up to see Chernoukh. The Huahuqui was already at the top. Nikolaj huffed out a laugh. It had worked.

A shadow cast over Nikolaj, blocking out the searing sun. He shielded his eyes and looked up but could see no features of his assassin. "Just do it already, asshole."

"I thought John boy said this was the sensible one," came an unfamiliar American voice.

Nikolaj frowned.

"He did," came another voice. This one he knew. Tony Franco.

"Tony?" Nikolaj said.

A hand reached out and clasped Nikolaj around the forearm, then hoisted him to his feet.

"Yeah it's me. And this is Matt Lauder."

Nikolaj slumped into Tony's chest. "Am I glad to see you."

He suddenly stood upright and began patting himself down. "I'm not shot?"

"Nope," Tony said. "That's the other guys blood. I have a good aim."

"Shit," Nikolaj said with a sigh. "Wait, Merry and Lex?"

"They're fine. We brought some friends along for them."

Nikolaj peered over Tony's shoulder to see Catherine and Leo hauling a wounded Igor up the side of the pyramid to meet with Merry and Lex. All of their Huahuqui bounded around each other like hamsters in a box. "They all made it."

"Honestly, we don't know what happened," Lauder said with a shrug. "The whole lot of them just suddenly downed sticks and flooded out of the courtyard toward the smaller pyramid. Like they weren't interested in us anymore. Our guys and half the Stratum we came with chased after them. So, we came looking for Tony and you."

In the distance, wavering in the heat haze the Pyramid of the Moon stood tall. A swarm of bodies locked in battle slowly meandered up the avenue. It was impossible to differentiate between Stratum and Phalanx. "KJ," Nikolaj said. "They're going after KJ."

"Did Chernoukh get to the transmission equipment?" Tony asked.

"You knew about that?" Nikolaj asked.

"KJ filled Jonathan in," Tony replied.

"He's here?"

Tony nodded.

A loud crash followed by the fizzle of electrons sounded from above. A mass of steel and wires clanged past them, rolling down the side of the temple. Nikolaj watched it smash into the ground below, kicking up dust and debris.

"We were taking it out to call you, but you're here so that was a giant waste of time," Nikolaj said.

"Not true, we needed that down for our plan to work too," Tony replied.

"Okay great, fine. But, we have to go after KJ now. He was trying to take an orb from Victoria."

"Who?"

"Doesn't matter. KJ's in danger. We need to get to him."

"Yeah, look. Your dad, he'd be pissed if we took you back into that craziness. We gotta—"

A crackle of electricity licked its way over Nikolaj's brain. Once. Twice. It sent a pulse down his spine and into his limbs. He shot a glance at his friends. They were all silent staring up at him. Even the nearby Huahuqui had stopped their antics, their gazes now fixed on his. They must have felt it too. He concentrated harder on it, teasing it out piece by piece, the static sound becoming a voice. A woman's voice. Freya's voice. A single word slipped from Nikolaj's lips. "Mom?"

"What the hell is going on, this place is like a friggin Tardis," KJ said, studying the vast, dark, hollow interior of the temple. Its walls were smooth and black like obsidian, all pointing up in four perfect triangles to the apex. In the center, a column of glass—an elevator shaft.

"Great," KJ said. "You think she's gone to the top, or she has a creepy super villain dungeon under this place?"

Teller stalked further inside, gun raised to track his line of sight, but didn't answer.

A crackle of static echoed off the shiny walls. Jonathan grabbed his radio and keyed it up, all the while creeping toward the midpoint. "Tony? Lauder?"

"Boss... incoming... get... ass... there," came the garbled words.

"Tony? Tony! Did you get Nikolaj? Tony?"

Static squealed from the handset.

"Shit," he said, scanning the space again. "Whatever this stuff is its screwing with my comms. Which means we go up."

"Up?" KJ repeated.

"Up," Teller said. "If she has a trigger, then she'll need a clean signal. So, it's either portable, or fixed up there."

KJ opened his mouth to speak, but there was a banging at the door behind him. Someone had followed them here. Perhaps it was Catherine or the monks? KJ turned to Teller, hope in his eyes.

Teller shook his head, "we keep moving."

K'awin warbled and KJ rubbed the top of her head. "It's okay." He sucked in a deep breath.

Teller reached the elevator and pressed the button and swiftly and silently a car glided down from above and came to a halt at their level. The doors slid open. They stepped in, K'awin squeezing in beside them.

"You know this is a trap, right?" KJ said.

Teller pulled a gun from his side strap and handed it to KJ.

It felt heavy in his palm.

"People always take head or chest shots. I want you to kneel in front of me," Teller said. "If she opens fire, you take her out."

KJ examined Jonathan's gear. "You need your gear back," he said trying to shuffle out of the bullet proof vest.

"Too late," Teller said with a wink and pushed the up key. The elevator car began to ascend at an astounding speed.

KJ cursed and took a kneeling position, pushing K'awin behind him for protection. "If we get through this, we're having words," KJ said without taking his stare from the sight at the end of the gun barrel pointed at the crystal-like doors.

"Uh, huh," Teller said. The *click* of his Glock slide followed.

The elevator reached the top, arriving in a glass box at the very apex of the pyramid. Through the transparent doors KJ could already see Victoria. She was standing, arms held high, facing out toward the Avenue of the Dead. The air inside the glass box grew hot.

The doors slid open.

KJ rolled out and back into a kneeling position, his weapon trained on Victoria who still didn't turn around. K'awin crouched by him, gills erect and face contorted into the best snarl she could muster. He heard Teller step out onto the stone behind him.

"You got some balls, Victoria," Teller started. "I could have shot you in the back."

A shrill laughter filled the air.

"You wouldn't, because you think I have something you need." She turned around, her thin face seemingly gaunter than it was just minutes earlier. In one hand she held the orb and in the other, where her fingers were already beginning to grow back, a small black device no larger than a cellular phone. "But as always you are two steps behind."

"Where's the Doyen," KJ interjected.

"Dead," she said flatly. "Just as everyone on the planet will be soon. God's Earth will finally be restarted. He has the chance to correct all mistakes."

"Not if we don't let you trigger Zeus," Teller snapped back. "Yeah that's right, I know how you're going to send the power stations critical. Rods from God. Fitting since you're some kind of zealot."

KJ's fingers were sweaty, the gun in his hand growing heavy.

Victoria continued to smile. "My dear Jonathan, you might kill me right now. And perhaps you might stop the stations from going critical, but the Earth will still be shaken to its very core."

"The asteroid," KJ said. "Tell us how to stop it."

That sent her into a fit of laughter that made tears run down her face.

KJ looked to Teller who frowned.

"What's so funny, you fucking nut job?" KJ fired, his index finger moving from the gun's side onto the trigger.

Her face hardened. "Nutjob? You can't stop it, you stupid fucking child." Spittle clung to her lips. "Do you think a plan this long in the making could be stopped by two morons like you? The son of Kelly Graham and the man who fucks someone's leftovers—what's her name again?"

"Freya," Jonathan said, through clenched teeth.

"Ah yes," Victoria said, her sarcastic smile returning. "Well Freya and everyone else on Earth will die soon."

"How soon?" KJ spat.

The bony woman turned her wrist to check her watch, glancing at it mockingly. "Oh, about twelve hours."

"What?" Teller shouted.

Victoria cackled. "Your incompetent and very underfunded space agencies had no hope of finding it in time. They were looking in all the wrong places. Like our own back garden." She looked up to the sky. "Yes, it's all quite too late. Of course, irradiating everyone was the icing on the cake."

KJ's heart beat fast in his chest as the information sank in. There was nothing they could do. The Nine Veils had won.

"You're lying," Teller said.

"Oh, I assure you I am not," Victoria said. "Ask Kelly the Second. Here boy, I'll even let you into my mind." She closed her eyes.

KJ's consciousness suddenly became flooded with Victoria's. It was like no mind he had ever joined. A dark mess, a swarm of hatred and rage. A disdain for all life, entwined and sewn into her very being. He concentrated, trying to navigate the labyrinth of hate and filter out if her words were true.

"Well?" Teller pressed.

The pit in KJ's stomach grew and the gun went limp in his hands. "She's telling the truth."

"Of course, I am," she said. "Why lie?"

"Jesus," Teller said, his words but a whisper.

"But she's also stalling. A satellite, she's waiting for it to align overhead."

Victoria scowled.

"Zeus," Teller said.

Two shots rang out from Jonathan's Glock over KJ's, but neither hit Victoria. Jonathan tumbled to the ground, a young man—the same one who'd attacked KJ at the Temple of the Feathered Serpent—thrashing down with a club.

KJ leapt to his feet, clasping his firearm. He pointed it at Teller's attacker, but the tangled mess of limbs meant he couldn't be sure he'd not hit Jonathan. He pivoted, swinging the weapon toward Victoria, only to be met with the naked form of Svetlana. Her shoulders were heaving from effort, presumably because she'd climbed up the outside of the pyramid. The blue paint now streaked across her skin, sweat trails cutting through the pigment. She bore a stare into KJ. Ribka coiled like a spring ready for the attack.

"Svetlana," KJ said, his voice but a whisper. "Don't."

Victoria cackled again. "It all ends here boy." A light on her device began to blink.

KJ's chest cramped. It must have been the satellite, Zeus, in position.

Victoria raised her arm high in triumph, thumb hovering over the device, poised. "Time to die," she said with a snarl.

"Yes, it is," Svetlana said under her breath, then projected into KJ.

His eyes widened in realization.

Svetlana sprang forward and past KJ, colliding with Teller's attacker. KJ squeezed the trigger and his gun barked.

Victoria screamed as her hand and the device disintegrated in a bloody mess. Ribka launched into the woman, forcing her to the ground. The orb escaped her grip and rolled toward the edge of the platform.

KJ pounced, stretching out his arms to catch the orb before it plopped off the edge and burst all over the steps below. His gun clattered away, but his fingers managed to slip around the gelatinous blob. Laid on the ground on his chest, arms hanging over the edge clasping the precious object, KJ's focus shifted from the pulsating sphere to the warring Stratum and Huahuqui at the base of the pyramid. In their midst was Catherine, wielding an axe, swinging at anything that entered her personal circle. Merry and Lex had formed a telekinetic shield but seemed only strong enough to cover themselves. Just south of them, Igor hung, wounded, from his brother's neck. As for their personal Huahuqui, it was difficult to distinguish them from the others without diving into their minds.

Where the hell is Nikolaj? He thought. *Don't be dead, asshole.*

He scrambled to his feet and held the orb high. KJ *had* to contact the Phalanx, calm them. Lead them. He closed his eyes and concentrated. The war filtered into his mind. The clashing of metal on metal. *Pop, pop, popping* of gun fire. Huahuqui clawing at each other. The orb tingled in his hands and he felt warmth rise from within the stonework at his feet. Whatever he was standing on seemed to amplify his ability.

But, the single-minded desire to survive of everyone down below was too great. His pleas to stop went unheard. The Phalanx seemed in zombified state, while his own Stratum merely fended off attack after attack. Soldiers were amid the fray, too. The Russian orphans and from what KJ could tell, Teller's team.

Then, among the noise and the screams of pain, a sense of such strong love it almost stopped his heart. It washed through him, rendering his legs weak. He focused on it, chest heaving. So familiar. So close.

"KJ?" Came a voice. *"KJ is that you?"*

"Mom?" KJ projected.

"Yes!"

"Mom, holy shit!"

"I have an orb, it's a long story. We have to stop the Nine Veils." Freya coughed violently.

KJ's lungs burned. *"Mom, what's wrong? I can feel you."*

She didn't answer for a moment. *"It doesn't matter, help me stop them. There's an asteroid and need to—"*

"We can't," KJ interrupted. It's too late. *"It's already here."*

290

"*What?*"

"*It's already here,*" he repeated. "*We can't stop it. Few will survive. Probably… probably only us. Maybe those at Alpha Base. A few cities. But, that's it.*"

His mom hacked some more. KJ felt pressure build up in his skull. She was dying.

"*KJ …*"

"*Mom, you have to let go. There's nothing to stop. It's not worth dying for, you could survive there. You can be one of the few.*"

"*No, baby. I can feel them. The fight there. If the asteroid is coming anyway, then the Stratum there must survive. You have to survive.*"

"*Mom, no—*"

KJ's thigh exploded open, flesh peeling back as a bullet tore through. He yelped and crumpled to the floor. His connection to the orb lost, now only mortal pain soaked into his brain. He clasped his hand to the wound, blood seeping between his fingers. In the other he managed a grip on the orb.

"You may have stopped Zeus, you little shit," Victoria spat, leveling the gun he'd dropped at his head. Svetlana lay unconscious at her feet, Ribka tending to her. "But Apophis is still coming, and you won't be around to see it." The gun bucked in her hand and the muzzle flashed.

KJ pinched his eyes closed, but no pain came. Only a weight pressing down on him.

He pried his eyelids open. Jonathan's limp body laid across him, blood oozing from a gaping hole in his chest.

"No!" KJ screamed. "Jonathan… oh shit no, please."

Jonathan coughed up a glob of blood, looked up and gave a weak smile. He reached up and touched KJ's face with his fingertips

291

then exhaled loudly. His fingers slipped away. KJ searched Jonathan's lifeless eyes, but his aura was gone.

Tears filled KJ's eyes. No final words. No chance to say *I love you*, as he should have so many times. A piece of KJ's own chi broke away, a hole now in his very being. One that he knew would never be filled again. "Dad …"

"Your turn," Victoria said.

"I don't think so, bitch," came another voice.

KJ looked up to see Nikolaj deliver a roundhouse kick that knocked the gun from Victoria's hand. Chernoukh swished his tail and ruffled his black gills.

"My Phalanx will kill you both," she hissed, lips curled into a snarl.

"The hell they will," screamed KJ, cradling Jonathan's lifeless body in his arms.

Anger rose in him emanating from his core. It reached out and connected with the rage pulsing through Nikolaj. KJ's shoulders heaved with his heavy breaths, locked in sync with his brother's. Their combined loathing of the woman who had killed both of KJ's fathers and Nikolaj's mother melded together in a white-hot ball of energy.

Victoria grabbed at her skull, her face wracked in pain, the veins in her forehead bulging. "What… what is this?" Her scream was shrill, her eyes full with panic. "I am immune!"

"You were, but you let me in. Remember, bitch? Now you're mine," KJ spat back.

"Ours," Nikolaj corrected, his jaw set firm.

The brothers' eyes glowed blue as did their Huahuqui's. A sapphire haze filled the stone platform, lighting up the orange sky. Victoria's screams grew louder. KJ felt her heartbeat, the rapid drumming of her pulse in her chest and head. He focused on the chambers, pushing them to work harder and harder. Nikolaj constricted the vessels in her brain increasing the pressure until, finally, they burst. Victoria's screaming abruptly stopped and her eyes rolled back in her head. Blood flowed from her nostrils and she slumped face first into the stone.

KJ blinked, his trance over, the anger subsiding. He locked his gaze on Nikolaj who stood, his expression a visage of shock. They had killed Victoria. They were both relieved and horrified. They had murdered her with a mere thought.

Svetlana groaned and tried to rise from the floor. Nikolaj broke his gaze from KJ, slid off his jacket, and covered her. She nodded to indicate she wasn't mortally wounded. Seemingly satisfied, Nikolaj stumbled across the small stone platform to KJ and crumpled down next to him. He placed a hand on Teller and closed his eyes.

KJ didn't need to read Nikolaj's mind to know his brother was searching for a sign of life. A small spark. A tiny flicker like a dying candle in the dark. There was nothing. Their adoptive father was gone. "I'm sorry," KJ whispered. "I'm so sorry."

His brother didn't respond.

"The asteroid, the power stations," Svetlana said. "Did we stop it?"

KJ shook his head. "The power stations… they won't explode. But the asteroid is still coming. It always was."

Nikolaj looked up and sniffed away a tear. "Then we're all that's going to be left?"

Clanging and gunfire echoed out from below.

"Yeah," KJ said.

"Then we have to stop them." Nikolaj nodded outward,

toward the war that still raged on the Avenue of the Dead.

"I can't," KJ said. "I tried. Perhaps with mom, she has an orb—"

"I know, I felt her too," Nikolaj said.

"But, it's killing her to use it. Her disease. She's not strong enough. I can't lose her too."

Nikolaj put his hand on KJ's shoulder and held his gaze. "She's my mom too. But, you know she'd want us to save the world. Jonathan, he'd want that too. She would have used the orb knowing what it would do. Because that's Mom. We are the future. They are the future, down there."

KJ couldn't speak. He'd often been told of his father's crushing grief. Pain the likes of which he was unable to let go. It consumed him. KJ had just lost Jonathan. Now he had to take his mother's life to save what was likely the remnants of humanity.

Nikolaj put one hand on the orb, keeping the other on Jonathan, then leaned in and pressed his forehead to KJ's. "Together," he whispered, wet trails cutting through the dirt on his cheeks. "We do it together."

With a painfully deep breath, KJ closed his eyes and allowed the orb and Nikolaj to enter his mind. Together they reached out to the under-ice temple where Freya and the rest of the Stratum waited.

"Mom," KJ projected. *"Mom, are you there? It's us, it's KJ and Nikolaj."*

"I'm here," she answered.

"Mom, we have to tell—"

"Did you stop them, the Nine Veils? Are they still fighting?"

"No not yet, we co—"

"Then we must, you know we must, we're out of time."

"Mom listen to me," KJ pleaded.

"No time, KJ, I know the risk." She convulsed, limbs jerking and pain wracking her body. *"We have to stop it now."*

KJ looked to Nikolaj who simply shook his head. Telling their mother about Jonathan now wasn't going to help. KJ tightened his lips, the stone in his throat growing.

"We're ready, Mom," Nikolaj said.

KJ felt a nudge at his leg, K'awin's snout rubbing at him. Chernoukh and Ribka had joined them too. He looked up to see Svetlana shuffling toward them, Nikolaj's jacket pulled around her. She knelt beside them and put her hands on Ribka.

Together, they focused on Freya, the orb in Antarctica and the Huahuqui there. One inescapable feeling rushed through them all: love. A mother's love. That inexplicable bond of a parent. A closeness known only to those who have children and cannot be known before. The very thing that drives a person's need to be a better human. This was the message Freya wanted them to project to the Stratum and the Phalanx fighting below: the world is worth saving, not for those who live in it now, but for the sake of the children who would inherit it. KJ and his friends must teach the next generation to be better.

The blue haze grew around the three friends and their Huahuqui. KJ squeezed the orb and pushed Freya's message, her love for him and Nikolaj, into the world. He let it flow through him, acting simultaneously as an amplifier and a lens.

The sounds of war below began to subside.

KJ opened his eyes, keeping his concentration, and studied the many faces now staring up at him. Weapons clanged and clattered to the stone work as the topaz miasma grew and began to envelop both the Stratum and the Phalanx. Catherine, Igor, Leo, Merry and

Lex were among soldiers, tribes' people, and Huahuqui on both sides of battle. Bodies lay strewn like dolls between their feet, and blood stained the sand-colored stones. As if suddenly awake, the warriors stared at the carnage in horror, then back up on high to KJ.

KJ climbed to his feet and held the orb high. There was no chorus of happy cheering, only silent understanding at what had happened there that day. Humans and Huahuqui had been set upon one another in hopes of destroying civilization. Somehow, they had come out alive. The war was over. But the fight for survival had only just begun. Those who would survive Apophis now had to rebuild the world.

EPILOGUE

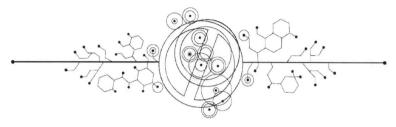

Location: Tocayōtla, Southwest Rice Terraces, China

KJ stood atop the pinnacle of the Moon pyramid. A cold dusk wind blew across the small stone square, making his skin prickle. He scanned the faces in the courtyard far below; his brethren, Huahuqui and Phalanx, soldier and civilian. They stared up at him, their auras wracked with remorse and guilt. It swarmed his mind.

Merry, Lex, Igor, Leo, Nikolaj, and Svetlana were in the front row, their Huahuqui loyal and attentive at their feet. Each held in the arms an infant Huahuqui or new-born baby. The future of planet Earth. His friends kept their minds shielded as if to spare him their feelings, but it was written all over their faces: they pitied him this burden. This role forced upon him. His whole life, he had been told he was a leader. He'd never wanted it. It seemed to him that fate had a sense of humor, sick as it was. And his first job as leader was not a happy one.

His friends gave weak smiles and almost imperceptible nods of encouragement for the task at hand.

KJ closed his eyes, clutching the orb in one hard, fingers trembling, and reached his mind out to his mom and the broadcasting station in Antarctica. Past the rapid beating of birds' hearts and rodents scratching, fishes swimming and trees photosynthesizing. Under the crashing waves of oceans and through the silent air he pressed until he found his consciousness in a dark and cold place.

His breathing began to slow, pulse decelerating to match the rhythm of his dying mother's heart.

"Mom?" he called with his mind into the dark.

KJ felt Freya's consciousness spasm as she woke from her path to death. He could sense how she lay awkwardly slumped in a makeshift harness, high above the ground. The straps seemed to cut into his own legs. His own fingers tingled with the sensations she felt: an orb clasped in one hand, and in the other Dacey's gills. The Huahuqui's life force was weak, tied to his mother's. She would die, too.

"KJ?" his mom projected.

"Mom, I'm sorry. I'm sorry I can't save you."

His mom coughed, and he felt it in his lungs. A warm trickle ran from his nose and onto his lips, though of course only she bled.

"It's okay baby, I know." Even her projected words sounded as if they were wheezed out. *"It's just my time."*

"Mom, I know you're tired. You've worked so hard." A tear slid down KJ's cheek, his lips quivering with each word. *"But, I have to ask you one more favor. I need you to help me, okay?"*

There was a lasting silence, Freya's mind slipping into the next world and back to this one.

"Of… of course. Anything for my… my Mr. Man," she said, finally.

KJ swallowed away the stone in his throat at hearing his childhood name. *"Mom, we couldn't stop it. Apophis, the asteroid, it's coming. I have to tell the world. They need to know. They need to be able to say goodbye ... to loved ones."*

Freya murmured.

"Mom, I need your help to do it. I need you to connect with the orb, one last time okay?" His heart cramped and the tears came in great floods. "Together," he said aloud, the word spat out between sobs.

"Okay... baby."

The familiar power surged into KJ, flowing into his brain and his muscles. His whole being once again on fire. Immediately, he was connected to every Huahuqui both in China but also in Antarctica. And then through them, to their bonded humans. Like biological relays, his connections grew and spread not only among the Stratum and the Phalanx, but to plants and animals, and people.

Like any network, those in closest proximity to the Stratum connected first. At his side, Catherine's admiration, pride and love for him, poured into the collective consciousness. Then, those closest to KJ's heart joined the collective. Svetlana's soul finally free of Victoria, she freely succumbed to the power of the orb. Through Latin America, past New Mexico, KJ's chi found its way to Texas— to Lucy Taylor. There in a room full of high-tech equipment, monitors and a gaggle of government agents, she sat staring into space. He could sense enormous guilt weighing her down, a boulder upon her heart. Utter failure. Lucy's heartbeat raced as she became aware that KJ was inside her head and that she was now part of a global hive mind for the first and the last time.

But, KJ could not linger there to placate her. To tell her she did her best. To tell her it was okay to call her brother one last time, rather than address the American people, as he knew she wanted. That KJ was about to take that awful burden for all humanity. Instead, he pushed further connecting to as many people as he could.

As the net grew so did the strain on his mother, sucking at her last ounce of strength. He had no way of knowing how much of humanity he had now found, but he was out of time. *She* was out of time.

"My fellow humans," KJ began, his voice ringing in every head he could find. *"Who I am, and how I am speaking with you is unimportant. What is important is what I must tell you. And while I want to tell you to not be afraid, I can't."*

Dread washed its way through the consciousness web. Some believed themselves schizophrenic. Others that God himself was talking to them. KJ breathed in deeply and tried to control his own emotions, leading the Stratum and the Phalanx to do the same. It sent a ripple of calm outward all around the world.

"Mankind was given time on this planet. Time as a species, lasting millennia, and time as individuals. Mere decades," KJ continued. *"It has been human nature to squander this time. Play with it as if it were a high-risk poker game, one humans were so sure would be won. But now, God, the universe, fate, call it what you will, has called in our chips."*

Freya hacked a cough, which made KJ's own chest convulse.

Catherine grabbed his arm, but he waved her off.

"If you look to the sky, you will see it darken, not with the coming of night but an asteroid. For most of you, the sun will not rise tomorrow." KJ clenched his jaw, struggling to find the words. *"By way of fate, it will mostly be Huahuqui and those humans who have bonded to them who will be left after the Earth has shaken to its core and the dust has settled. Whether this is fair or not, is not the question you should be asking yourself now. Instead, ask with whom you should be spending these final moments. Find those that you love, grab hold of them. Tell them. Do not let go. Find your …"*

"Huaca," his mother wheezed aloud.

KJ choked out another sob but righted himself. *"Yes. Find your… huaca. Your happy place or person. And may that be the memory you take into whatever awaits you beyond. I'm sorry."*

Though the Huahuqui tried to emanate a blanket of tranquility, the overwhelming terror that exploded from every soul connected to KJ was unbearable. Feeling the grief of more than a billion people. The unnameable gaping hole it tore in his heart. He had to let go. There was no more to say. He had done all he could. He pulled back his consciousness. The light faded away with the receding of his mind, until once again, it was just him and his mom alone in the dark.

Her irregular breathing filled his mind.

"Mom?" KJ said out loud, forgetting to project his words.

"I'm here, Mr. Man," she replied audibly, too.

"Mom, I'm sorry. I failed."

"No baby …" She took in a sharp breath. "You did what you were born to do—lead."

"He died, mom," KJ said, his voice trembling. He could hear gentle sobbing in the crowd before him as they listened to only his side of the conversation. "Jonathan. He died. Saving me."

"I know. I felt it…. but he was your dad, KJ. He would have died a thousand times for you."

KJ sputtered, but no words came.

"Make him proud, baby. I love you and Nikolaj… with all my heart."

And then, she was gone. KJ felt her light go out, a last breath exhaled.

KJ opened his eyes and met Nikolaj's tear-filled gaze. There were no words that could express what needed to be. Not even their bond would suffice here. Freya Nilsson Teller was as much a mother to Nikolaj as she was to KJ. The nucleus of the family. Their guiding star. How were they supposed to lead the world without her?

The crowd shuffled and murmured, their attention drawn upward as a loud boom split the air. Apophis had entered the atmosphere.

KJ broke his lingering stare with his brother and intertwined his fingers with Catherine's. He held on tightly, transfixed on the shadow as it grew larger against the setting orange disk in the sky. Apophis's dark silhouette engulfed the sun, and the sky grew black. A rumbling grew louder as the very air caught alight with the coming of death.

Catherine's grip grew so tight it cut the circulation from KJ's fingers.

As with a solar eclipse, Apophis' shadow slid over the setting sun as it screamed toward its final destination somewhere over the European continent. There it would vaporise hundreds of kilometres of land, cities, men, women, and children before sending a shockwave around the world that would crumple countries and drown coastlines in a super-massive tidal wave, the like of which had never been seen by human eyes.

The age of man was truly over. By tomorrow morning the Sixth Sun would rise, and the Stratum and the Phalanx would inherit the Earth. KJ could only hope they would do better than those who had come before them. But, his kind were young and inexperienced, with the power to inflict death at will, and deep in his heart he knew—those who do not heed the past, are fated to repeat it.

THE BEGINNING.

About the Author

Gareth Worthington holds a degree in marine biology, a PhD in Endocrinology, an executive MBA, is Board Certified in Medical Affairs, and currently works for the Pharmaceutical industry educating the World's doctors on new cancer therapies. Gareth is an authority in ancient history, has hand-tagged sharks in California, and trained in various martial arts, including Jeet Kune Do and Muay Thai at the EVOLVE MMA gym in Singapore and 2FIGHT in Switzerland. His work has won multiple awards, including Dragon Award Finalist and an IPPY award for Science Fiction. He is a member of the International Thriller Writers Association, Science Fiction and Fantasy Writers of America, and the British Science Fiction Association. Born in England, Gareth has lived around the world from Asia, to Europe to the USA. Wherever he goes, he endeavors to continue his philanthropic work with various charities.

www.GarethWorthington.com
www.ItTakesDeathToReachAStar.com